WRAITH

STEVEN E. METZE
Author of
The Zombie Monologues

 DRAGONFIRE PRESS

DRAGONFIRE PRESS

Dragonfire Press is a dba of Scum Crew Pictures LLC

Printed in the United States of America.

www.wraith.com

www.ubergoobergames.com

ISBN 978-0-9846578-2-7

First Paperback Edition

10 9 8 7 6 5 4 3 2 1

For Alwynne

ACKNOWLEDGEMENTS

To Patrick, Cory, and Phaidra for their selflessness.

To Laurie McLean and Harrison Demchick for their insights.

CHAPTER 1

Aditi was her true name, but she was lured into this world with the promise of a body named Alhread. She stood motionless against the building wall, watching Jassim's eyelids lower until the realization he might accidentally set off the bomb startled him back awake.

She saw him check the wires again, one in each hand, the dusty car battery still resting between his feet. The blue glow of the eastern sky had swallowed the last of the night stars, and she knew the first patrols would be by soon. When that happened, she would stop this exhausted man and crush his dream of martyrdom.

Jassim had been up all night burying the artillery shell by the road, with most of the evening's darkness spent running back towards the empty shop against the city wall whenever he heard the thumping of helicopter blades. She'd stepped out of the shadows once and let him see her in hopes her presence would deter him from his task, but his face told her in that one instant that it would not work.

Looking into his eyes Aditi-Alhread saw the soul of a man confident his wife and son would be proud of him after this. A man pleased to be making less than the Americans made in a day, but more than two months pay he'd make any other way.

There, etched on the spirit of the man named Jassim, she could make out black scars like crushed insects reminding him of a shameful day the week before. That day he'd spent ten hours working on the military base stuffing sandbags for five American dollars. The sheik's brother called him an apostate and sent two men over to beat him in front of his children. The men stopped when Jassim swore he hated the U.S. soldiers and would do anything to prove it. Two days later they returned with the artillery shell and the envelope full of money.

Aditi-Alhread shifted her weight, and the crunching gravel under her feet startled the crouching man. Jassim dropped the wires into the dirt and buried them, just like he'd practiced throughout the night. His hands shook as he swept dust to cover the wires.

She felt his nervousness channel quickly to anger when he turned and noticed her standing near the corner of the wall again. Her black abaya billowed in the morning breeze, but even with the veil covering her face she knew her presence upset him. It was rare to see a veil any more, but it was still shameful for a woman to stare the way she was and she knew it.

He shouted questions at her in a language she did not understand, and then made threatening gestures and pointed back towards the city. She did not respond, she did not move. She just watched him with unblinking eyes that absorbed all light even in the golden glow of dawn.

With balled fists he rose towards her, and the distant hum of the American vehicles made him stop. Instead he spun, crouched down, and dug up the wires. The boxes he hid behind would keep him from seeing the vehicles until they actually passed by, which would make the timing difficult.

He put the copper of each wire in his mouth, cleaning the contacts, and then he held them tightly just above the battery. He breathed sharp quick breaths through his mouth, eyes focused on the distant road, but Aditi-Alhread wasn't going to let him make the attempt.

She called upon a prehistoric beast with no name and let it go.

A moment later he flew through the air and hard onto the ground, her weight pinning him to the dirt. He kicked, yelled and tried to spin, but he couldn't get any leverage. The creature inside her tore out chunks of his neck, grabbing and ripping... *biting* and ripping, over and over...

He screamed then, putting all his power into the defiant yell, while he clawed out with both hands to either discover a weapon or get a hold of whoever held him down. He failed on all counts, and then he tired.

She released him enough he could turn and face her, and in his eyes she saw that he understood the dark crimson liquid pooling in the sand was his, but he no longer cared. Before his soul left his body, it glowed with hope and thoughts of the words of praise they would say about him after this night, and then he smiled.

The roar of the convoy on the road rose in the distance, so she ducked down over the body and wiped her face off on his shirt. She would have to rely on the black of her robes to conceal the rest of the blood.

Three American vehicles roared by, hard and tan, spread far enough apart so that no single bomb could get more than one of them. Their gunners held their hands on harsh black weapons, scanning the landscape for any sign of explosives or ambush. Aditi-Alhread's eyes followed the first vehicle, the one she knew held the soldier named Saul Christiansen.

Twelve tires passed the subtle dirt mound at the end of Jassim's wires, none the wiser. When the drone of engines and the dust drifted away she stood and waited. She listened and watched the first signs of life waking and stirring in the city the Americans called Mosul. It was hard to think of it as anything but Ninua, the name it held when she'd fought and died there.

At last the morning call to prayer echoed beyond the walls. A soft melodic wailing took her back to a time with different gods in an older language, but all she wanted now was for it to distract onlookers for a couple of minutes. Aditi-Alhread hauled the body onto her shoulder, and in a few bounds she flopped the shell of Jassim by the road with a loud thump. No one seemed to be around this part of the road as she walked back, which was probably one of the reason's Jassim had picked it in the first place.

She knew he died thinking he would be hailed as a hero, even though his motivations had been anything but altruistic. She reached down for the two wires and the battery. At least this way it would look like he died setting the bomb.

Staff Sergeant Saul Christiansen's 3-year-old daughter looked up and asked him if he wanted to dance.

"Uh, sure" he replied and smiled, a little surprised.

"OK, hold on a minute!" She bounced off back to her room, leaving him standing in the 'would you like to dance' position next to the living-room stereo. Saul held the position for his own amusement.

He glanced up at the woman who was both her mother and his girlfriend standing in the kitchen and she smirked and shrugged. Somehow the baggy khaki pants and the untucked T-shirt suited her. Nicole looked comfortable, relaxed, happy. As she whirled back towards the refrigerator he watched her long dirty blond hair spin in the air like it was magical. For the three thousandth time he wished they were married. Wished he'd asked her.

Clomping footsteps announced the return of the smiling child, now flowing in a bright yellow princess dress and shiny black Mary Jane shoes.

"OK I'm ready!" Rose giggled and held up her hands, her fingers still smeared with too much fingernail polish she'd applied herself. "Daddy would you…"

"Crap." Saul said. That last pile of rocks had flown by and he hadn't said anything to his gunner or the rest of the patrol. Daydreaming got people killed, he now knew very well. He sat up a little straighter in his seat and shook it off.

"Say again Sarge?" Specialist Guerrero's filtered voice in his ears.

"Nothing," Saul replied back in the voice-activated helmet microphone. "I missed a mystery pile, that's all."

The deep bass white noise of the engine resumed its prominence in Saul's ears. He wasn't too angry with himself, but he also couldn't stop thinking about his daughter. She was what the chaplain called his "base," his "link" back home. Mental health relied on those types of connections they told him, and the trick was waiting for the right moment to dwell on them. Patrols were not the right moments.

The pale gray road poured under his humvee in the endless fields of sepia dust. A pair of children bathed in a stagnant puddle off in the distance.

It wasn't his fault he was having trouble concentrating. He'd waited in line for an hour and a half during prime rack time when he was already short on sleep.

When he got to the morale computer station it took him five of his twenty allotted minutes to get her aunt to check her computer and put Rose in front of the webcam. So much had changed in five years from the times she used to call out his name and come running to the door for a hug when he got home, or when she used to hold one of his fingers when crossing the street. Now eight years old, his daughter seemed happy at first, but the conversation had gone stale after another six minutes according to the countdown timer in the upper left corner of the Saul's screen. She didn't want to talk about her school, or what she learned that day, and only casually mentioned that she was doing well. The silence over the line while she doodled on a notepad tied a knot in Saul's chest.

"OK bye," he'd said in a tone he thought she would recognize as irony in hopes she'd laugh and keep talking. She didn't do either.

"OK, bye Dadio." She replied so quickly he hadn't been able to say anything. At least she gave the screen a sort of mock hug and shouted an 'I love you' before she bolted off.

He stared a few seconds at the empty desk chair. His timer still had eight minutes and sixteen seconds left on it. Then Lisa's face popped into view.

"Sorry about that." She said. At least she didn't wear her hair long like her sister Nicole had. That would have been too much. "Do you want me to try and get her back?"

"No," Saul lied. "S'okay." He paused a moment. "I have to get some sleep anyway."

He shook off the memory and focused on the patrol. At least he felt free here. Certainly better than his first tour. Now his free time belonged only to him. No one bothered him, no one talked to him or tried to make him feel better or asked him annoying questions. And when he was on the road, leading his patrol, he was powerful, important. And while he was a good soldier, he occasionally allowed himself to internally gloat that no rules of this country applied to him. None of the people of Iraq, not the citizens, not the police, not the army, could make him do anything. And when he told them to get out of the way, they jumped. He shook that thought off too and felt guilty, again, for thinking it, again.

Someone dressed in black ducked behind a stack of boxes up against an empty merchant shack.

"Hey pivot left" he said to Guerrero. A motion out of the corner of his eye and a bang of metal on metal confirmed Guerrero spinning the turret in the right direction. Sometimes just pointing a big gun was intimidating enough to scare and stop the bad guys. Saul hoped Guerrero glared intently at anyone who moved as well.

"Should I fire a warning round?"

"No." No you don't need to fire a fifty caliber bullet at a single person who hasn't done anything wrong yet.

A voice in his head mentioned that Specialist Watts would have known that, and his chest tightened again. Trying to forget Watts was the reason he'd called home in the first place.

More road. More dust. The outer wall of the city liked cracked skin.

Boom.

Less of a sound and more of a bass thump Saul felt in his chest. It was a familiar macabre feeling, and he knew what it was, including the most probable explosive type used, before anyone said anything.

"Bravo One we have a column of smoke behind us." That was Williams in the trail vehicle.

"Alright everybody stop. We're going back." Saul welcomed the action and then tried not to welcome it too much. "Three-point turns everyone and stay on the asphalt. I don't want to see any tires touch soft dirt and we're keeping the same order of march, check?"

Both the other humvee commanders agreed.

An explosion behind them meant that they had missed something. Again.

They rolled to a stop about a hundred meters from the smoldering crater in the road they'd just passed.

"OK, you know the drill." He said it, but he verified it just to make sure. The gunners stayed on the guns, the other two vehicles moved to form a triangle away from the explosion site, then the drivers and Sergeant Williams got out to investigate.

They walked the area in two teams of two, digging in the dirt in places, examining the ground in others. In the background, any Iraqis who happened near the area kept significantly back, especially if one of the gunners focused on them. A few dogs barked in the distance, along with a singing stray bird or two, but other than that, the only sound Saul really noticed was his boots grinding gravel into the asphalt of the street.

"Sarge we got a leg over here." One team reported.

"And we got wires over here." Said the other.

Not hard to piece together. A bad guy tried to blow them up, it didn't work. Bad guy went out to see what went wrong, and boom. These sorts of incidents were always morale boosters for his team, at least in terms of a bad guy losing, and this was the third instance in as many weeks. He wondered how the Iraqis seemed to be screwing up more than succeeding lately, but he shoved that thought back where it came from and concentrated on the fact another bad guy was dead, and another good guy wasn't. Unfortunately, Saul thought, it made the Iraqis out to be so incompetent he was afraid it might make his team overconfident. Then again, he doubted anyone would forget that a month ago one of the Iraqis got it right.

"Sarge, female hadji heading this way." Guerrero spoke loud enough Saul could hear him but the odds were against any of the locals overhearing it. Not that Guerrero cared.

"Guerrero," Saul said, moving closer to the humvee, "you gotta knock that crap off. Got it?" He consoled himself knowing that Specialist Watts had been just as bad with that particular racial slur.

Guerrero seemed puzzled for an instant and then his eyebrows raised with understanding. "OK, some Iraqi chick heading this way. Better?"

Saul kept his back to the city and glanced over at Abrahim, their interpreter, who was already heading towards the woman. Abrahim hadn't worked with Saul before, but seemed more competent than other terps Saul had worked with. Wearing local tan armor over a blue T-shirt and a bare helmet, and armed only with a pistol on his thigh, he easily stuck out as the person any Iraqis should approach if they wanted the least chance of being shot for doing it.

Nobody in Saul's company had ever had to shoot a random civilian, at least not yet. There were stories, of course, cautionary tales passed around the mess hall and the barracks. Supposedly one of the bases down south had to shoot a little boy once. He came walking up to the checkpoint in front of their gate and wouldn't stop when they yelled at him. The story goes that by the time he was twenty meters out in front of the gate there were at least ten soldiers yelling at him to stop and go through the searching area he'd passed by. The Sergeant of the Guard popped him right there, in the stomach, in front of everyone.

The rule was simple. The odds were good either someone sent the boy, or if not, for sure someone was watching the boy. Maybe he was wired with explosives, maybe he wasn't. But if the soldiers let him walk through the gate without stopping him just because he was a little boy, then the next day there would be ten or fifteen more kids running through gates all over Iraq, all smiling and laughing, and this time all really wired with explosives because somebody figured out an American soft spot.

Saul had heard the story several different ways, sometimes at different bases, sometimes with a little girl or a teenager. He was sure someone had to fire a warning shot at some innocent youth getting too close to a gate somewhere, but with this many variations he held that no one had ever really been shot. If they had he didn't want to know.

"Sir," Abrahim always called Saul sir no matter how many times he pointed out that he wasn't an officer. It always came out sounding like 'seer' with his thick but tolerable accent. "She wants to talk to you."

"Really?" Saul finally pulled down his dark protective sunglasses and turned to look at the woman. Pale skin, a tuft of black hair showing, from what he could tell she seemed in her twenties, maybe thirties, although women aged faster here than in the U.S., so she could have been younger. It was hard to tell through those ninja dresses anyway. "What does she want?"

"She said she wanted to talk to you, specifically pointing at you."

"Did she say why?" Saul began to feel a little un-comfortable as he realized she was staring directly into his eyes. That wasn't something he saw very often in this country. She didn't blink much either, and her eyes seemed so dark Saul got stuck on them and almost didn't hear Abrahim's response.

"No sir, she didn't."

"Well go ask her…"

"I think you should talk to her sir."

Saul turned to glare at the short man next to him. He was annoying sometimes, but seemed sincere.

"OK, c'mon, let's go."

"No sir, she asked me in English." Abrahim said, "I don't even think she speaks Arabic."

CHAPTER 2

Brian Moore sat fidgeting on the edge of the bed wearing nothing but red striped boxers and the motel white terrycloth robe. Through the room's sliding glass door he watched a light snow coating the motel parking lot and the leafless woods beyond it. A great deal of this part of the highway was built that way, with a motel just off an exit, flanked by gas stations, and nothing much beyond it but local wilderness. Three inches of pristine snow just made the handful of buildings seem that much more out of place.

The ornate crystal vial felt cool in his hands as he passed it back and forth and rubbed it lightly with his fingertips. This was the expensive one, the lesser vial in his robe pocket contained the leftovers.

"You paid for the good stuff." The man in the midnight blue suit and tie had said to him after thumbing through the bulk of Brian's life savings and casually tossing it in a briefcase. "This vial is all you really want, but since you bought the whole package, you get the whole package. I'm including a second vial with the ending in it."

Brian's hands shook earlier that morning when he took the vials in the lobby of a much nicer hotel than his. He'd waited there over an hour for the man to show up, all the while with no more company than a strange white marble statue of a half-naked woman carved with a rope tying her to the pedestal.

"I'm giving you this second vial because I've got no other use for it," the man continued. "but I wouldn't bother with it, really. Endings are never very pleasant." Brian missed the knowing smirk that crossed the man's face. The vials and the potential inside them were all he noticed.

The cap of the decorative phial dropped to the motel floor, although Brian didn't remember consciously uncapping it. Something like liquid obsidian sloshed gently inside, thicker than water, but just barely. It had taken three weeks and eight hundred miles to get this far, and now, in a mostly empty run-down motel in the middle of nowhere, he would experience something truly unique that no one else would ever understand.

There was no chance that the man in the midnight blue suit had cheated him. Brian's research had shown time and time again that the man always followed through with his promises and then some. And the way everyone talked had convinced him the outrageous fee was worth it. Even if it wasn't worth it, Brian hadn't been able to learn of anyone else on the planet who sold this particular product, so it was that price or nothing.

Brian licked his lips, cocked his head to one side to crack his neck, and poured the dark contents of the vial onto his bare chest.

Trees with wet green fuzz dripping from every surface flew past him. The cold air in his mouth spurred him on, his hunger spurred him on, the movement up ahead spurred him on, but most of all, the baying of his pack gave him boundless energy. On four legs he flew over moss covered rocks, tore through fern-like bushes, shifting his movements to match the fleeing creature up ahead.

He could do anything, he knew, in the rush of that moment.

Most of the pack was behind him now. They turned after the horned beast darted quickly in a new direction that led it practically in front of him.

With another burst he reached the creature and snapped at its legs. The animal dashed back to one side, saw the bulk of the pack in front of him, and turned back right into the open jaws Brian now recognized as his own. Another snap missed the neck, but one more finally took hold of the beast's hindquarters and it fell hard to the ground, exhausted.

Brian relished the hot copper taste of the wet fur in his mouth. He could feel the heartbeat of his prey against his tongue, and only the fear of a vicious beating kept him from devouring the animal right there. A few seconds later and two more sets of mouths clamped the massive creature by the neck and back. The baying stopped, and they waited for the stronger, taller members of the pack who walked on two legs to arrive. They would be pleased with this kill, and would reward the rest of the pack with generous portions of meat for several days, and let them sleep near their fires.

As Brian directed all his strength to his jaws, daring the beast to try and escape, he became vaguely aware of a pain in his feet and hands.

Hands?

The green of the forest faded to a monochromatic mix of snow and bare bark. For an instant Brian laughed. The experience had been far more than he'd expected, and he retained every second of it, every bound, with absolute clarity. Yes, he thought of the man in the midnight blue suit, it was worth the price you bastard.

Gradually it dawned on him he must have gotten confused and run out into the woods beyond the parking lot, where he was now sitting up against a dead tree. Quite high on the moment, he thought that it had just added to the realism of it all. The taste of bloody fur in his mouth did not lessen, however, and as his head cleared he realized there was something dangling from his teeth.

He spit it out violently and shuffled back away. Before he noticed his hands and feet stinging in the biting cold, he realized that he'd somehow caught, killed, and partially eaten a half-starved feral cat.

He forced down a small amount of vomit and struggled not to lose all control in a fit of brutal retching. After shoving a handful of snow into his mouth to try to kill the taste, he looked around and realized he didn't know where the motel was. He couldn't see anything but skeletal forest in all directions. His first thought was to follow his footprints back in the snow, but his hands and feet were bright red now, and trying to use either of them to right himself or to stand up brought waves of pain that forced him back to the ground.

Tears streamed down Brian's face as he called out to the empty woods for help. His weak voice cracked as the air bit his throat. No one would hear him, he knew, and if they did, he was sure he was going to lose the bulk of his extremities to frostbite as a minimum. He shivered wildly, and then fumbled for the second vial in his robe pocket.

His hands trembled, and he couldn't bend any of his swollen fingers, but managed to pull out the vial by pressing it between his two flat palms. His furious fumbling spun the vial out of his hands and into the snow.

"No." He cried, sounding like a small child denied some cherished treat.

Bending over and resting his elbows into the unbearably cold wetness, he was able to push both palms against the vial again and lift it to his mouth. He bit down on the cap and with an aching in his teeth, turned it enough that if finally fell loose.

He rolled over onto his back to make sure if he spilled any of the liquid that it would drop on him somewhere. He felt, somehow, that if the man in the midnight blue suit were there, he'd watch, quietly, with that smug look on his face, and wouldn't help.

He tilted the open vial and the contents poured down onto his face.

The cold followed him this time, as he huddled against several of the pack against the wooden fence of their pen. Wherever his fur touched theirs, he felt soothing warmth, but not enough to allow him to sleep.

The last few hunts had brought back little more than a pair of rabbits, and the two-legged pack members hadn't fed them or let them out in several days. Finally one of them walked up to the pen gate, with several others behind. Brian felt his body jump up, excited for the hunt to come. The two-legger opened the gate and grabbed him by the scruff of his neck, leading him out.

They walk passed a few small fires and to a circle where more of the two-leggers waited.

"Why didn't they bring the rest of the pack?" Brian thought quietly to himself.

It didn't matter though. His heart raced, ready for the hunt, grateful for the attention of the smaller two-leggers hugging him and brushing him as he passed, and he was eager to please his pack.

The leader walked up to him, slowly, and rubbed his hand behind Brian's ears. Brian tried to lick his face as the leader leaned forward and whispered something Brian didn't understand, although he recognized that one of the sounds was the one that meant his name to the two-leggers.

The leader stood then, turned, and walked away. Brian glanced around, happily waiting for whatever happened next. In the back of his mind, Brian recognized that all the rest of the pack surrounding him each held a stone tipped club in their hands, but in the moment, he felt nothing but excitement.

Then without warning, they brought up their clubs, one of them made a sound and they all moved in unison. Brian instinctively flinched, and then everything went dark.

Two days later they found Brian frozen solid in the woods, a white fluffy form covered on every surface with an inch of snow. The terrycloth robe crackled when they moved it, and his arms were rigid crossed in front of his face, shielding him from something truly unique that no one else would ever understand.

Around that same instant, Haqdar-Brian nodded to the lackluster crowd of investigating police officers and left his body behind. This being his third life, he had little trouble crossing over to the Netherworld. As soon as he arrived, however, he understood that this time was different. The unliving nearby stopped and faced him without speaking, staring with twisted expressions and eyes open wide. He glanced down at his own appearance, and realized what that simple container of black liquid had really held, and what he'd done.

The wraiths circling him stepped back in unison, looking up at something above and behind his tiny form. He tensed, too horrified to turn, and waited. An instant later, loud enough to send shivers through the Dead, a scream echoed across the Valley of Souls.

CHAPTER 3

The comforting roar of his vehicle sealed off the rest of the world, and Saul left that existence behind without resisting. He'd assigned Williams as the front vehicle under the guise of letting him practice leading the patrol instead of admitting he just wasn't going to be able to focus. Not after her. Not after the woman who called herself Aditi-Alhread.

Part of it was her voice, rimmed with one accent that morphed into another while retaining a quiet tone that remained clear and crisp so he didn't miss a word. Part of it was the trace of what Saul believed to be drying blood between her fingers. Both those paled next to her eyes.

Peering through the gap in the black niqab covering the rest of her face, she'd kept her gaze down as she spoke, a strangely Iraqi, or traditionally conservative Muslim habit for someone who spoke in fluent English. After they'd walked a few steps away from the road and away from the others, she pulled down her veil and turned to face him.

Her first few sentences flew by unnoticed. Her eyes were deep black, with a hint of Asian at the corners and a feeling of liner without any actual make-up. Her porcelain face was pale and smooth, and when she smiled at Saul it affected him so much he wondered exactly how long it had been since a woman had done that.

"I hope you don't mind." Those were the first words Saul remembered hearing.

"I'm sorry say again?" He blinked hard and turned his ear towards her so he wouldn't be looking directly at her.

"I said I've been watching you go by in this area. I hope you don't mind."

"Well it depends," Saul sobered a bit. "Why you were watching us."

She paused until Saul looked up, and then she smiled again, trapping him there.

"Not the whole group, just you." The moment of small talk dangerously near flirting made Saul glance around to make sure insurgent gunmen weren't collecting on the walls nearby. No, and his team maintained a perfect vigilant perimeter. Only Abrahim seemed ill at ease, clearly unaccustomed to having nothing to do in these sorts of situations. Looking back at the woman in the dirty black burka, Saul wondered for a moment if he should get her to pull it tight so he could see if she had any weapons hidden under there. A pat down of a woman by a male soldier in Iraq was out of the question.

"I've worked with the military for years," she continued, her smile fading just a bit. "I met some people who knew you."

"Like who?" Saul relaxed a bit. She might be someone from one of those three-letter agencies working in the area, or some flavor of special ops, or even one of the contract mercenaries like Aegis or Triple Canopy or Blackwater. He hoped not, because generally speaking he hated those guys.

"I thought if I helped you, you might be able to do me a little favor."

Saul started to repeat his question out of reflex, but he went with the topic change instead.

"Help me how?" He laughed when he said it, and then wished he wasn't such a cocky jerk sometimes.

"Helped." She glanced towards the road. "Past tense."

Saul could be notoriously dense at times, and knowing this about himself made him pause whenever he got confused to review the facts of the conversation. Was she talking about the guy who just blew himself up…?

His brow furled while he tried to work through anything else she could mean.

"I only need a little information about this area," She continued. "But I don't have a computer."

The words 'information' and 'area' triggered all the anti-espionage training they ran every soldier through six times each on the way into Iraq at about ten times too fast to remember any of it. She seemed to anticipate where his thoughts were going and interjected quickly.

"Actual ancient history. Nothing about your base or anything military. Promise."

The distant sound of a cackling radio drew Saul's attention away from the thin dark-eyed woman. Patrolling he understood, it was his comfort zone. This conversation bordered on surreal.

She told him her name, and being a good sergeant he wrote it down in his tattered brown notebook with the waterproof pages that still managed to get stained with sweat-soaked dust. Then she gave him the details of what she wanted researched and said she'd meet up with him again in one week.

He tried to remain non-committal, the one thing he remembered from the anti-spy classes that he was supposed to do, but somehow when she covered her face back up and walked away, Saul was absolutely sure she expected to see him again in seven days.

"Delta Six this is Delta Three, coming up on the turn now." The voice in his ears made Saul look around the present for an instant. They were two intersections and a marketplace away from end of mission.

They were paralleling the Tigris now, a foul brown river with dark black torrents swirling in something that smelled so soiled Saul couldn't understand how it nourished anything. In ancient times this area supposedly flourished. According to Aditi-Alhread, in ancient times the city on this river also held a great library.

In his head, he kept playing that look she cast back towards the road with the dead bomber. Either that guy just accidentally blew himself up and she was implying credit for it, or she actually blew that guy up. In both cases, all for a few quick Google searches?

Saul couldn't make any sense out of it, and every time he thought too hard about her he settled on her eyes, and that smile. Now he regretted not telling her to pull her burka tight, although not because he wanted to know if she had a weapon.

The rest of his day was split between a nap, a few chapters of an old science fiction novel, some potato chips from the mess hall, and getting ready for the afternoon patrol. He passed the base's internet café several times and intentionally didn't go in. It wasn't the right day of the week for Rose or her aunt to be looking for him, and he wasn't about to do any research yet, if at all. In fact, the more he thought about it, the less he felt it necessary to turn in Aditi-Alhread as a potential spy, or to pay any attention to her request. At this time in his life he just didn't have the mental bandwidth to deal with either option.

The next three days went by uneventfully. Six patrols, the last half of the novel, and five ineffective mortar attacks on various patches of empty sand near the base.

On the fourth day, he saw her again.

It started with a trail of black smoke rising up in the distance. Saul noted it was darker smoke than the kind from explosives, this one had fuel or oil mixed in it.

A half-mile later a pastel blue pickup truck burned on the side of the road. Saul halted the convoy as soon as they could make out what it was and then he called it in to headquarters.

WHOMP!

The whole back of the truck shot up in an orange ball of fire, triggering the soldiers of all three humvees to duck down long after it would have been too late. Saul looked up to check on Guerrero. His body was not limp and hanging at a ridiculous angle. There was not a piece of shrapnel sticking in his neck and jaw. He was not dead. He was not Specialist Watts.

A few black cylinders fell in random spots in the dirt close enough Saul could identify them.

"OK," he spoke over the headset, "we got a truck full of mortars on fire so we're going to back up another hundred meters and let this thing burn itself out." He paused to study the truck more carefully. He hadn't noticed before, but it looked like the charred husk of the driver was still at the wheel. Saul's stomach turned a little and he looked away. "Delta Two, call our explosives disposal buddies and call this route up as closed until they clear it. Everybody else, standard three hundred meter circle, nobody army or civilian goes past us unless I say so."

Saul settled down and adjusted the thick ceramic SAPI plates in his body armor. Just as he reached into the thigh cargo pocket on his pants for a package of crackers, he noticed her sitting on a nearby dusty hill. Her niqab veil was down, and the expression on her face remained stoic. She sat with her knees pulled up to her chest, and watched the burning fire, not Saul.

A guy blowing himself up setting a roadside bomb made sense, at least every now and then. Someone blowing themselves up while firing mortars from the back of a truck was practically a physical impossibility. He knew sometimes the Iraqis fired while their truck was moving as a method to avoid detection, even when it meant they would have almost no chance of hitting anything, but that didn't explain this either. Hell turning the tube upside down and aiming for the gas tank probably wouldn't do it.

"Hey Sarge," Guerrero spoke from the gunner's hatch, "Is that the same woman from the other day?"

"I have no idea Guerrero," Saul lied. He wasn't sure why.

"I think it is. Check it out I think we have a guardian angel."

Saul shook his head. Whether they did or didn't, everyone would think they did by the next morning. Soldiers loved superstitious stuff like that. Or at least he assumed his did since they'd sent up multiple requests for the division chaplain to come down and perform an exorcism on their barracks until Chaplain Daniels finally dropped by. Maybe a guardian or mascot was just what the team needed.

When Saul glanced back her way she was staring at him, her expression unchanged.

Saul clicked off the voice activation button on his headset so he didn't transmit.

"OK, OK, I'll look up your damn library." He muttered.

Seeming to hear him, she smiled, stood up, and walked down the backside of the hill.

Six hours later, Saul had his turn at a computer terminal. It took him longer than expected because while she knew exactly what she was looking for, she hadn't a clue how to spell it.

"Oh mighty Google," Saul said to himself, "is there anything you can't do?" His botched attempt to match letters to sounds had failed several times, but when he added "Iraq" at the end of the search it had suggested a new spelling and got the city name right. Once he had that, finding the rest was easy.

He jotted down all the notes he could find on the ancient library that used to be in the area, created by some king named Ashurbanipal. It had been filled with tens of thousands of ancient tablets that had been found in the late 1800's and early 1900's and taken to the British Museum. He figured this Aditi-Alhread person had either stumbled across a few more tablets or some other significant ruin and wanted to see how she could profit off of it. Saul even went so far as to download a cartoon map of the museum's location in London. Somehow this felt like a good deed, or a paid debt, one or the other. Either way, he wanted it done and over with so he could move on.

On day seven, just after dawn, she stood motionless by the side of the road on the opposite bank of the Tigris from the main part of Mosul. Saul ordered his lead humvee to stop beside her, realizing it was a terrible breach of security to stop for a civilian. With anyone else, he would have assumed they were standing on a bomb, or they were there to distract him from an attack on the other side of the street.

Neither of them said anything as Saul opened his door and handed her several pieces of folded paper he'd kept in one of the few pockets he could easily reach while sitting in armor. She held the paper without pulling it or looking at it, and kept eye contact. With her veil up, Saul could still feel her smile underneath.

Saul lost track of her almost as soon as his humvee started to pull away. Through the rearview mirror he watched the sand where she'd been standing until it vanished under a spiraling ochre cloud.

CHAPTER 4

Saul enjoyed a love-hate relationship with international plane flights, primarily stemming from what he called the "veal treatment." The airlines forced passengers into tiny confined spaces, unable to exercise or move, and then fed them almost non-stop. He was always a fan of free food, even airline food since it was different than army food, but he was afraid of gaining weight as soon as he got back to the States. No one else on the flight seemed to mind, all charged with visions of hamburgers, beer and sex after over a year of mental, emotional and physical desert.

Since it was a chartered all-military flight, someone found the highest ranking person, in this case a Major up at the front, and nominated him as the flight commander. His primary duties were to make sure soldiers didn't drink on the flight home and to decide who got to sit in First Class. He picked the few other officers, one sergeant major, and all the privates who had helped load the luggage in the hot sun. Unfortunately, none of those included Saul.

Saul had a book for the plane, but after about the third hour of his knees rubbing against the seat in front of him it became too annoying a distraction to do much reading. That and the cramped position made the small of his back hurt.

The plane suddenly dropped, inspiring a quiet collective gasp from most of the people on board. Instead of bothering Saul, however, it reminded him of Rose's first plane flight. Nicole sat near the window with Saul in the aisle and Rose in between them. The plane hit a bunch of turbulence and Rose remained entranced with the new toy they bought her for the trip. She kept opening and closing the little plastic doors on the little plastic barn, oblivious to the violent shaking of the plane that had her mom white-knuckling the armrests. In one very harsh dip Rose even yelled "Wha-ho!" That was when Saul first understood innocence, the glow of it, and the need to protect it for as long as was possible.

A few hours later soldiers sprawled over every scrap of furniture in the USO room of the German airport. Saul didn't get off the plane early enough to claim a spot, so he spent the bulk of the five hour layover wandering the massive terminal. Walking around was allowed so long as he didn't do any drinking in the process. It didn't help that even the McDonalds sold beer.

Not that the drinking rule mattered much. Saul was fighting sensory overload as it was. A sea of people swarmed around him, and none in brown camouflage. A pair of black shorts lined with yellow, a blue low cut dress revealing a slim female form, a charcoal sweatshirt with bright red Greek letters.

Before long he was napping in one of the pay-per-view television terminal seats. His carry-on bag strap stayed looped around his leg, a leftover security measure from the days when the drill sergeants used to try and steal soldiers' rifles while they were sleeping during basic training. He woke up and noticed an old couple resting in the chairs next to him. American, clearly, the man wore a hat with "82nd Airborne" stenciled on it. World War II, had to be, back when airborne had an entirely different meaning. That made two since he left Iraq, adding to the male flight attendant with the Vietnam service pin on his jacket. He never said anything, but he made it a point to notice other vets wherever he could, just in case. Maybe if they needed money, or help carrying something, or someone to argue on their behalf, he'd step in and help. He wished he was strong enough to think thoughts like that for everyone, but he needed an excuse to go out of his way, just like everybody else. He settled back down into the chair and drifted off again.

"OK, here's the deal." The sergeant in the freshly pressed desert uniform spoke to the haggard group just off the bus. The last twelve hours were a blur to Saul, although he recognized the Douglas firs and cool wet air of Fort Lewis Washington right away. "You're going to go into the gym in single file and form up in four ranks. Try and keep the rows even but no one is really going to be paying that much attention."

Someone in the back shouted for him to speak up, but the sergeant couldn't be bothered to raise his voice for more than the next three words.

"Anyway," he started, "the general will say something, and then the Major will dismiss everyone at once. Your leave starts immediately, and you're all due back in two months."

Whoever the general was, to his credit he kept it short. An instant later all the pent up energy in the stands and on the gymnasium floor released at once, and two crowds of people, one all in desert camouflage, the other in variations of red, white, and blue, both spilled out and flowed into each other.

Saul scanned the throng, fighting back the urge to expect Nicole. He weaved through a mass of people; mostly soldiers' wives, young and gorgeous, most in dresses, and either pregnant or with a newborn on their hip.

The grinning face of Lisa, Nicole's sister, finally caught his eye, and he rushed to her. In all the noise and movement, he couldn't see Rose. When he got to Lisa he stopped, confused, and she closed the gap to hug him. He hugged her back without the least interest in doing so.

"Where's Rose?" He asked.

Lisa's grin became very forced. "Up in the stands, still."

Saul scanned the bleachers behind her. "Where…?"

"Saul, wait." He hadn't even noticed he was already walking.

"What?"

"We had a big fight on the way over here." She looked down each time she stopped to think. "She wanted to see you, she really did, and she missed you…"

"And?" He had no patience for her pauses. "And what?"

"She's… she's a little worried you're going to take her away from me and Richard right away."

"Well I'm her dad." His tone lashed out sharper than he meant it to.

"Look, I know, I know. I'm just telling you what she said."

Saul paused a moment to shake it off. Spouses might not want to sleep with you right away, small children might not remember you, middle school children might be angry at you, blah blah fuckin blah. Saul thought he'd be an exception to all those "how to reintegrate with your family" briefings he'd sat through for now two deployments.

"We'll talk about it later." Saul strained to speak in a civil voice. "Let's," he managed a smile, "Let's just hang out for a little while, OK?"

"Yeah, sure Saul." Her face did a poor job hiding how many emotions she suppressed right along with him. Saul knew Lisa and her husband Richard loved their niece Rose, but Saul felt at that moment Lisa was feeling more pity for him than anything else. That hurt him almost as much as it helped.

A few steps later and they stood in front of Rose and Richard, sitting side by side. Rose wasn't going to run up and hug Saul like she did the first time he came back. She might not speak to him at…

Rose stood up, took a step, and slowly wrapped her arms around him. Saul squeezed her in a tight grip, but she didn't reciprocate. Five minutes sooner than he wanted, he let her go and backed away. Her eyes were red.

"Hey there." He said, unaware of the water gathering in his eyes.

"Hi dad." She'd gone through many nicknames for him throughout their lives. She hadn't called him just 'dad' in as long as he could remember.

"You wanna get something to eat?" As Saul spoke Richard stepped up slowly and put his arm around Lisa in the background. Both stood back, remaining quiet, unsure what to say.

"They have pizza in Iraq?" She didn't bother to look happy as she asked it. Saul resisted mentioning that the army had, in fact, figured out a way to get pizza contracted in to some of the larger bases.

"Pizza would be great."

They all moved towards the gym's exits.

"So I was thinking maybe you could stay with your Aunt Lisa and Uncle Richard a little while longer while I got used to being back home." His voice cracked when he said it, but there was no mistaking Rose's shift in mood when she heard him.

"Really? Why?"

"Well," Saul searched for a convincing lie, "I've got to get all my stuff out of storage, find a new apartment, and unpack all those boxes, for starters." He'd stumbled across the truth instead. "As much as I KNOW you'd like to help with all that, your teachers might not appreciate it." The attempt at humor seemed almost genuine.

"Are you sure?" Rose seemed ready to be happy about it, but something in that earlier argument with Lisa had her hesitating, at least to show it.

"Oh yeah, absolutely. I'll still see you every day, no getting out of that, but staying where you are right now seems to make the most sense, don't you think?" She nodded. "At least until I'm settled in again."

The rest of the day lagged, alternating between Saul attempting to seem cheery and lost in his own thoughts. He yelled at Richard once for not changing lanes when he drove beneath an underpass. They all conceded that was probably not as necessary in the United States as Iraq, since few Americans threw explosives down at cars from the walkways above. Most of the time though, Saul simply felt lost. Not getting the running jokes, not recognizing the names in the stories they told, feeling awkward every time he had to ask for background information. By nightfall he considered himself completely outside his own family, what little there was left of it.

CHAPTER 5

The next week Saul did not get his stuff out of storage, he did not find a new apartment, and he did not unpack any boxes. He stayed in a cheap no-tell motel at the edge of town, spending most of the days sleeping, sitting in darkness, or watching pay-per-view soft core porn. A pattern formed quickly. The bulk of each afternoon was spent gathering the strength to pull himself out of bed, shower, shave, get dressed, and go over to Lisa and Richard's house so he'd be there to help pick Rose up from school.

Rose would seem happy to see him, although, no more so than she seemed happy to see Lisa. Saul would ask her how her day went, and she'd mumble something about not remembering much about it, or how nothing special really went on, and then Lisa would ask a more pointed question about a particular teacher or girl friend or one of the boys that taunted or teased her, and Lisa would open up and babble about it the rest of the way home. At least, Saul consoled himself, he was getting to hear about her day.

Rose spent the few hours before dinner mostly alone in her room, or on the phone or the internet (Richard bought her a computer a few months back), and Saul would sit alone on the couch in the living room, replying eagerly to any chance comment thrown his way from any of the three of them. Normally he hated small talk, but part of the energy he gathered earlier in the day was to focus on being as social as possible for these few hours before he'd slink back to his crappy little twin bed motel room. Dinner usually went well, although Saul had to fight not to say anything about all the things that had changed. Rose drank soda for dinner now, and ate whatever she wanted, whether vegetables were included or not. Talking with her mouth full was generally looked on as amusing, and if she brought a toy or doll to the table to "help her eat" that was fine too. Lisa and Richard were still treating her as a "visiting niece" instead of a child they were responsible for, and probably would continue until they had a kid of their own. Saul didn't want to be all military-dad authoritarian, but she was his daughter, and it seemed like he ought to have some say in how she was raised.

Or maybe he should just give it up. Rose seemed happy, Lisa and Richard seemed happy, and Saul could always go back on another deployment if he needed to. If he re-enlisted in the fall when he was scheduled, then that would happen anyway in another year and a half. A staff sergeant's salary wasn't great, but tax free, plus danger pay, and with no rent or food bills to pay, it added up.

On the drive back to the motel he referred to as home, in an attempt to stay awake, Saul pictured how easy it would be to veer to one side and smash into a concrete overpass beam, or a good thick tree. Fast, yes, painless, probably not, and with all the built in safety features in cars nowadays the damn thing would probably figure out a way to leave him a vegetable instead of what he was going for. Besides, even with how strained things were between him and Rose, no eight-year-old girl did deserved to have two parents who killed themselves.

Still, the big concrete pillars seemed very solid, with nothing around them to stop him…

"Hey Sarge, you OK?" Watt's voice. Saul's heart jumped when he realized he was dreaming. Dreaming and driving.

"Watts, yeah I'm fine. What are you doing here?" Saul pictured himself sound asleep in a car that seemed to be driving itself just fine, while he spoke to the empty gunner's hatch that had suddenly formed behind him. His emotions seemed numb. In dream world this didn't seem that odd.

"Just checkin' up on ya." Watt's voice called back. "You worried about your daughter?"

Saul felt an invisible crowd of parents, no, just fathers, all crying out "hell yeah!" in angry unison. He echoed their cry and continued. "I don't know what else to do. I've tried everything I can think of. I can't even tell them how messed up all this is because that will just be more awkward and make them think I'm even more messed up and make things worse."

In the silent immobile car, it was the world that moved by outside. Finally the Watt's voice chimed back.

"The juice ain't worth the squeeze man."

Saul lifted his head, but didn't open his eyes.

"You're saying my daughter isn't worth it?"

"Not if you want to kill yourself over it."

Saul swatted at his face like he was being swarmed with flies. "Shut the hell up Watts"

Silence.

Saul woke up in the parking lot in front of his hotel room. The car seemed undamaged, and parked relatively straight in the yellow-lined concrete plot. In retrospect, he obviously just spaced out the last part of the drive and fell asleep after he parked the car.

His eighth morning back in the States, in the biggest show of willpower since resisting Julie Johnson his sophomore year in high school, Saul went for a run. He never understood people who ran with headphones, or with fancy running outfits, or for the love of God on a treadmill. He did exactly one stretch, bending over to loosen his calves a little, and then sprinted off down the street wherever it took him. It rained, of course, because Washington State hadn't changed since he left, but that just made the run better. He'd forgotten the smell of the wet pine needles and the trees that towered above and watched over his morning activities. For a moment he called the rain on his face a baptism, but then couldn't think of what internal change it would be inspiring, and so dropped the idea entirely after another half mile. He did feel better after running, he always did, and he didn't bother keeping track of how far he'd run other than it was roughly ten or eleven minutes out and the same amount back. He'd measure out two miles with his car in the next couple of days, and until then this worked just fine.

He stopped at the motel parking lot to walk a few loops for his cool down. He hadn't bothered with cool downs until that rumor about the 2nd Lieutenant who went straight from a three-mile-run to a cold shower and died of a heart attack at age 22.

The five minutes of walking included one bold squirrel, one guy in a gray suit and a ridiculous green tie, and a discarded box that Saul avoided in case it happened to be filled with explosives. While any apparently discarded trash was probably a bomb in Iraq, it only took a few steps to realize how improbable that was in Washington. He steered clear of that corner of the parking lot for the next two loops anyway, just to be sure. Saul felt the man in the green tie watching him, probably wondering exactly what he was trying to accomplish in this parking lot, and so he quickly ducked into his room and headed for the shower.

Picking up Rose with Lisa went smoothly. Saul didn't bother to say much and just let Lisa ask the questions. Rose's friend Anne got ketchup on her dress at lunch and cried about it. They learned all about Italy that morning, and Ms. Gwendolyn complimented Rose twice on her penmanship that afternoon. She might have said some other things, but Saul just wasn't into listening.

Saul half-heartedly offered to play with Rose as she headed to her room, but when she hesitated he said, "Yeah, yeah, I know, don't worry about it" and waved her off. To another adult, Saul would have been embarrassed by something that seemed so overtly passive aggressive, but with Rose, he didn't think she'd pick up on it, and the truth was he was just too tired for his normal speech filters.

He had no desire to eat dinner, but some military-enhanced survival instinct kicked in and he cleaned his plate as soon as he smelled the food, even though he re-membered the taste of none of it. Lisa helped Rose with Book Time while Saul sat on the couch and tried to occa-sionally interject something intelligent. They both politely smiled and thanked him when he did.

More rain escorted him home, swallowing the light from the full moon overhead. He cranked up one of those "we play literally anything" stations to make sure there would be no possibility of repeating any sleep-dream-driving.

He pulled up to the motel banging the drum solo of Rush's *Tom Sawyer* as best he could on the steering wheel. For a moment he almost felt OK. That feeling faded quickly when he saw the woman with the deep black eyes waiting in the rain outside his door.

At first he thought she might be a lost prostitute. For one, instead of a burka, she wore some costume that looked like a foreign military uniform. She kept eye contact with him from the moment his car turned her way. After he parked, engine still purring, wipers sloshing back and forth, he sat there a moment, just watching her in the headlights. Her gaze stayed with him until it registered that she was the woman from the desert seven months earlier.

Finally he turned the key and stepped out of the car.

Walking up to her, he reevaluated her outfit. She wore a black top, with a high stiff collar and long black sleeves. Large brass buttons held it together at the front, and tattered red corporal's stripes stood out on her shoulders. Her pants, also black and trimmed with red, tucked neatly into a pair of black leather boots that were tightened with straps instead of laces. It may have been a foreign uniform, but Saul now guessed more likely it was a historical replica.

Neither said anything as he walked up to her. He stopped just shy of intimate range, but slightly closer than western personal space norms. A few seconds of looking into his eyes though, and she grinned.

"Let's go." She turned and headed for his car.

Saul tried his best to pretend he might hesitate, but she opened the door and plopped in with no regard for his reaction. His heart jumped for a minute, just to be near someone from the deployment, someone from what his mind and body considered more 'normal' than things had been since he'd been back. Even better it also was someone not from his unit. And a woman.

"Out of idle curiosity," Saul spoke as he closed his door. "Where are we going?"

"Someplace where this outfit won't stick out." She offered him only a quick sideways glance. "Drive and I'll let you know when to turn."

They took the highway for a bit, and exited in a part of town Saul didn't know very well, if at all. A few turns down streets that grew seedier each mile, and she finally stopped them in a pay parking lot. Saul wondered for an instant if she was going to offer to chip in, but as she walked off without looking back he took that as a no.

The place merged dance club with bar with warehouse, and she was right, her outfit blended perfectly with the wild assortment of near costumes that a few of the men and most of the women displayed. Saul recognized the generic name for the brand of music – alternative mixed with techno – but didn't recognize any of the songs. He also wondered how the doorman let him in the place without eye liner.

"So," Saul shouted over the music as Aditi-Alhread cut through the crowd to the bar. "I take it you're back. Do you normally live around here?"

She shot a smile over her shoulder and didn't speak until she'd ordered two mugs of "some sort of dark European beer." When the drinks came, she displayed no intent to pay for them. Saul quickly fished out a ten and passed it to the bartender, then stuffed the two dollars change into the tip jar.

He sipped his, wincing a little at the stoutness of it, and noticed she made no move towards hers.

"Saul," She didn't seem to have to yell for him to hear her over the music. "I was thinking we should work together."

"Say again?" He'd heard her fine the first time, and the second time her volume did not increase.

"Work together, you and I."

"Work together doing what?"

"What have you done since you've been back?" She scanned the crowd, not looking his direction.

"Not much of anything really."

"And what do you plan to do?"

"More of the same." The taste of the beer got better around the third sip.

"No no, I mean a few months from now. A year from now."

Saul hesitated. "Probably go back."

"Why?"

The speed with which she fired off her follow up questions made him feel she already knew the answers to the previous ones.

"Basic reasons. Sense of duty. Desire to beat the bad guys. Be a part of something big."

She turned to him, again with the piercing stare and hint of a smile. "Well a half-truth is marginally better than a whole lie I guess."

That stopped Saul, who cursed his normally quick wit for failing him.

"Let's pretend all those reasons are true." Her smile faded a little as she spoke. "What if I said you could hang out with me and get all those same things?"

Saul nodded and took another sip to give him time to think. She had to be some sort of agent with one those secret squirrel organizations floating around. Or a member of one of those mercenary groups the government kept contracting out to help in Iraq. The later seemed more likely, and Saul didn't have a lot of faith in their retirement programs.

"Who are you with, exactly?" Saul didn't yell as much as he had been, but she seemed to have no trouble hearing him.

"Larry." She said in a louder voice than normal.

"Who the hell is Larry?"

She lazily pointed at an attenuated man facing her. As he moved closer, she reached back for the second beer and handed it to this new person. Larry was a little shorter than Saul, but had probably only three-fourths the body mass. He had virtually no chin, but big ears, and he regularly cleared his voice with a strange and improbable cough-wheeze combination. Creases on his face and perpetual bags under his eyes made him look old beyond his years.

"Is this your boyfriend?" Saul meant to craft the wording of that one a little more subtly.

Aditi-Alhread neither laughed nor grew angry, the only two responses Saul expected.

"He's my poster child." She said, and then headed off away from the bar. Larry followed without speaking, and Saul eased up to tag along.

She led them through a curtain to another part of the building with a pool table, a couple of booths, and less music. The smoke there hovered as a smooth blanket just about neck level. She pointed at a booth and grabbed a passing waitress to order two more beers, even though Saul was still only halfway through his first.

"Do you ever drink?" Saul asked as she slid next to Larry into the booth that smelled like sweaty shoes.

"Not in this lifetime." She paused while the waitress dropped down the two fresh dark drinks. This time Larry paid. "Look, I think you could help us, and I think it would do you some good."

"I don't even know what you're talking about. But just so you know, I'm not big on jobs people normally interview for in techno-beat dance clubs."

"Would it help if I said I was a vet?" She said that with a little too much confidence.

"Really?" Saul wasn't convinced.

"Yes, two wars."

"Where and when?"

"You're too young." She cut him off quickly, "But back to my original point, I think this could be exactly what you need."

"I don't NEED anything." Saul realized no one who ever said that really meant it.

Aditi-Alhread paused as both men took a few more sips of their beers. Then she turned to Larry and watched him until he seemed to realize he should speak. He cleared his throat first.

"So, long story short, I used to be an addict," he said.

"You two are cops?" Saul spoke while his mind went a totally different direction. Cop was impossible, unless cops operated in Iraq. "DEA?" He wanted to correct himself before either of them called him on it, although he didn't think the DEA worked that way either.

"Not that sort of drug. Not a drug." Larry added. "Not exactly."

Aditi-Alhread's head whirled towards the room, and for an instant she sat there, watching nothing. She snapped out of it just as abruptly.

"Larry will get you caught up." She still faced the same direction. "I have to go." Without waiting for any replies she zipped out the door.

"Great," Saul still hadn't finished his first beer. Condensation from the second one pooled in the many sets of initials carved in the old wooden table. "OK Larry, go ahead, catch me up."

Larry cough-wheezed several times in a row. Saul hoped it wasn't for effect, because the effect was near nauseating.

"So, again, not a drug, but let's stick with that analogy to keep it simple." Larry stared down at the table, concentrating on transforming thoughts and memories to words. "First, let me say that we're talking about something extremely rare. You can't make it in a bathroom chem lab, and you can't grow it. In fact, I'd say there are less than a handful of suppliers on the entire planet."

Saul nodded without really listening.

Larry continued. "With most drugs, well, really all drugs, it alters your mood, gives you a burst of energy, cuts off your inhibitions, gives you hallucinations, you get the idea."

Saul had never actually experimented with any drugs – army piss tests made both a good deterrent and an excuse not to – but he had at least dated people who he'd seen stoned, or on 'X'. "Yes," he replied, focusing more on his beer. "That is how I understand it works."

"But in all those cases, when it's over, it's over." Larry cleared his throat again. It made Saul's stomach turn enough that he put the beer down. "I mean, the high fades, and then you crave more, or some way to get it back."

"I'll take your word for it."

"This though, this doesn't fade. At all. It becomes an integral part of who you are." Larry's speech quickened. "It's like a quick trip to an exotic country or instantly learning a new language or suddenly having sex of any variation with someone you never would have had a chance with before." Larry looked up from the table and leaned in a little bit. "And you never, ever forget it."

Saul lost interest in the second beer. He was quickly losing interest in this whole thing, especially without Aditi-Alhread or her deep dark eyes.

"Right, so, in this scenario, if you are her addict poster child, what is she?"

Larry considered how to respond. "Well, technically, she's the drug."

CHAPTER 6

Saul tuned out after the part about her actually being the drug. There just didn't seem any point in listening,
and the rest of Larry's words were lost in the second beer,
the second very tall beer, which Saul didn't remember
drinking. A year without alcohol seemed to have lowered
his tolerance. Or possibly Larry was just so boring and
incoherent that it just made someone feel like they were
drunk, or should be drunk.

Two quick knocks at the door stirred Saul awake
enough that he at least rolled over.

"Housekeeping." A muffled voice spoke through
the door.

"Come back later." Saul muttered while looking
for some pants to put on in case the door opened anyway.
He'd forgotten both to put out the do not disturb sign and
to lock the door in a way that an outside key couldn't get
in. He heard an electronic key zip through and pulled on a
pair of jeans just before the door knob turned.

"Come back later please," he said walking closer.
"I'm good for today…"

The first person through the door wore a charcoal
gray suit and a ridiculous green tie. The next man wore a
collared striped shirt and slacks, and the very large man in
the back wore gray slacks, a black shirt, a black jacket, and

a black undershirt sticking up around his neck. Clearly not housekeeping.

In a brutal fight-for-your life smack down, Saul figured he could scrap well enough to possibly beat the first two, or at least shove his way past them. The third guy inspired nothing but jumping through a window and sprinting for the nearest well-lit well-traveled highway. Saul played through several urban fighting methods that all involved which target he would pick if he had any sort of gun. He'd had training and real world experience on clearing small rooms filled with dangerous people, but all those techniques involved his M4 carbine and possibly a 9mm pistol. If that failed, he had experience calling in very large rockets from very far away. Despite Hollywood's depiction and the opinion of everyone he ever met in a Denny's during breakfast, the army rarely actually imparted any special ninja hand-to-hand fighting techniques to the average soldiers.

Without a gun in his hand, simple survival won out over any other thoughts. He figured if these three guys tried to grab him or pulled out any weapons, he'd leap in the bathroom, lock the door, and either crawl through the window or stick his head out and scream like a little girl until someone called the police. Maybe not the screaming option, but thinking that bit of humor helped calm his breathing.

The first man, Green-Tie-Guy, seemed to be the scout, with the last man as the enforcer of the group, so Saul wasn't surprised when the middle guy did the talking.

"Hello there," He said holding out his hand. "I'm Dennis. I was just kidding about the housekeeping thing."

Dennis did not impress Saul at all. Thin brown, tan, and maroon vertical stripes decorated his off-white baggy shirt. He wore a gold chain bracelet on one wrist and a ridiculously large steel watch on the other. White and brown speckled his almost military haircut, and his face wore the perpetual frown of a grumpy old man. In short, he looked like an asshole.

When Saul didn't move, Dennis stepped forward. "Anyway, didn't want to take up your whole morning, just wanted to leave you this." He pulled a metallic thin vial out of his coat pocket and set it on the coffee table. "Larry said you wanted to try a sample."

"Larry sent you?" Saul struggled to remember everything from the night before. Two very large European beers may have hit him harder than he'd expected, but it was going to take a lot more than that to make him blackout drunk.

"Honestly," Saul started. "I can't recall anything remotely like me saying, 'Hey, Larry, how about you get me a hit of that stuff you've been talking about and have three Sopranos extras bring it over and break into my room at the crack of…' he glanced at the coffee table clock. 'Uh… eleven thirty.'" He paused. "OK, the eleven thirty part I could believe."

"Believe whatever you want, I'm just the messenger." Dennis slapped Green-Tie-Guy on the shoulder a little harder than was necessary and they all headed out the door and closed it behind them.

That afternoon Larry felt even more pathetic than most mornings. His alarm had stopped repeating itself after the fourth snooze, and the coffee that brewed several hours earlier now sent the smell of burnt grounds wafting through the musty one-room motor home.

Even though his bladder ached, he still took the time to fumble around for a cigarette and lighter. The first hit of hot gravel on the back of his throat carried the rush of nicotine he knew would make everything better. He kicked open the door and stumbled to reach the wood line of the park before he pissed himself and just barely made it. He didn't notice the large dark blue SUV parked in the shadows until the trip back. Realization came slowly, like a migraine.

"Larry, how ya doin'?" Dennis sat just inside the metallic egg-shaped shelter, thumbing through a greasy copy of *Outdoor Life* he found on the floor.

"Hey Dennis." Larry took a long hit off his cigarette and wished he'd put the whole pack in his pocket. Dennis was the type of person who wouldn't let him get another one.

"We dropped by your buddy Saul today, gave him a free sample." Dennis didn't look up from the magazine. At least two faceless figures watched him through the glass shroud of the SUV. "He really liked it."

"He took it? Really? But why did you…" Larry's voice sounded weak in his ears. He struggled not to clear his throat, which only made it worse and resulted in a fit of phlegm clearing which disgusted even him.

"If you want a shot we've got a spare for you." Dennis pulled a metallic vial out of his pocket and rested it on the step beside him.

"No thanks" Larry rehearsed moments like this nightly, and again every Saturday at his AA meetings.

"It's on me." Dennis looked up from the magazine and tossed the vial to Larry. He barely caught it.

Larry looked at the vial, his mouth suddenly dry, and licked his lips. Another throat clearing, smaller this time, and he clinched his eyes as tight as he could. When he opened them again, he seemed calmer.

"No, really." He knelt down and put the vial in the grass. "I'm good."

Dennis put the magazine down and walked towards Larry, who backed away from the vial. Two men Larry didn't recognize got out of the SUV and moved in behind Dennis. Dennis picked up the vial and popped off the wax sealed cork.

"Last chance Larry…"

Larry's eyes widened, but he didn't move.

"OK then." Dennis turned the vial to spill the contents onto the dirt. Larry winced like a beaten child, but managed not to say anything. When the liquid poured out, it was clear, not black.

"What the hell is…" Larry started.

"Just water Buddy." Dennis smiled and the other two men laughed. At some point the bigger one had moved right next to Larry's side. "I was screwin' with you. But I did give Saul the real deal."

Larry tried to force a laugh.

"Larry, you've lived a crappy life. Really crappy." As Dennis spoke, the bigger man grabbed Larry's arm, hard. "And the good news is, today all that ends."

"Hey now, is there something you want…?" His attempts to break free caused the big man to use both hands to restrain him, but otherwise had little chance of success.

"Don't worry, you won't be gone long." Dennis smiled and stretched. "And then some of my buddies will throw together a little ritual and you can give a little bit of that troubled soul of yours back to the community."

"That's not… that's not fu… fu… funny." Tears streaked down Larry's shirt.

"OK," Dennis spoke to the Green-Tie-Guy. "Give him way too much heroin laced with… I don't know. Something that kills you." He put the vial back in his pocket. "I'll be in the car."

CHAPTER 7

Twenty-six centuries before Aditi would be summoned to a hollow shell called Alhread, Aditi's third life took shape as a boy named Iyar.

From his place on the tower near Adad Gate of Ninua, Aditi-Iyar could barely make out the half-naked form of Kigal-Asu in the distance. Dancing with the rest of Ishtar's cult, she joined the other women preparing for one last sacred orgy with the nobles before the Babylonians and Medians renewed their assault on the walls of Assyria's capital city.

Aditi-Iyar ached to be a part of something so holy, so powerful. He heard his heart beat in his ears every time he saw her at the temple. Kigal-Asu usually wore clothes within those guarded walls, but never covered the lion symbol, the icon of her goddess, tattooed between her light brown breasts. As a courtesan to the gods, she took it upon herself to combine love with war, just as Ishtar had.

As much as Aditi-Iyar longed to be able to stare at Kigal-Asu without being chased off, or to someday be the one to slide her blue tunic off her shoulder to the beat of the sacred drums, Aditi-Iyar knew she'd never soil herself with a mere foot soldier.

Technically the son and apprentice of a scribe, he'd been conscripted by the local governor when the scouts first returned with reports of the armies of the curs-ed alliance crossing the Assyrian border.

Conscripted foot soldiers like Aditi-lyar made up the bulk of the military. The cavalry and charioteers had armor. Regular archers worked in pairs, one with a bow and one protecting the bowman with a reed shield. Aditi-Iyar didn't even get a helmet.

He'd just turned fourteen, his year to work beside his father, and instead he'd been taken from his home and handed a bow and a quiver full of arrows with little in-struction beyond what direction to aim the pointed end.

He knew the walls would hold though, just as he was told they had two years earlier. Then he would return to his work. He would rise through the ranks to work in the royal court. Then he would have access to the great library filled with cuneiform tablets, papyrus sheets, wax boards, and leather scrolls. There every story ever written rested gently in a precise shelf in a particular row or cor-ner. All the tales his father told him resided there, and some day he'd run his hands along the original texts to read aloud to his wife and his children…

Shouts behind him rose up from the city.

He and the other archers strained to see what caused the outburst.

"They've turned the Khosr!" One of the regulars down below shouted.

Aditi-Iyar could see it now, torrents of water rush-ing against the wall while the normal river bed sat sudden-ly dry. If they couldn't knock the walls down with hammer or stone, water would do it for them, and faster.

An Assyrian noble on horseback ordered the re-serves to reinforce the wall where the river was smashing, while the Median army appeared upstream, their archers and spearmen ready to charge the first sign of a break in the stone.

A light thunder grew back outside the walls, and clouds of dust rose up from the north. Babylonian chariots, pulled by four horses each, roared down through the rows of dried crops towards the gate. Rows and rows of archers followed behind, running to keep up as much as they could. Each army attacking from a different direction, and chaos building in the streets below.

Someone gave the order to block the gates, and Aditi-Iyar rushed down to help throw more sand and rock into the entry way. Arrows flew overhead, but he ignored them, confident the Babylonian archers were too far away to have any chance of hitting him yet.

The Assyrians returned arrow fire back, while Aditi-Iyar dug through dirt for any rocks he could use. His fingernails bled but he didn't notice.

As he struggled to carry a rock as big as his chest into the gate, one of the Babylonian chariots attempted to smash through it. One of the horses crashed into him, knocking him to the ground and trampling him in its fury to go forward. The chariot bounced against one of the walls and tipped sideways, dragging it over Aditi-Iyar and into the city where spearman fell upon it and slaughtered the horses and the three riders.

Aditi-Iyar rolled over and vomited crimson bile into the dirt. He looked down and saw a very white bone sticking out of his leg, surrounded by wet red caked sand.

Men yelled nearby. Horses galloped past the gate, their rage muted by a dark edge forming at the edge of Aditi-Iyar's vision. He let out a weak chuckle looking at a few of his arrows and the bow lying in the dust nearby. Never fired once, he thought, so he'd gotten enough training on it after all.

"Kigal-Asu." He called quietly. He closed his eyes and imagined her coming to him. Imagined her taking his head gently into her arms and resting it against the lion tattoo between her breasts.

CHAPTER 8

The wipers squealed back and forth in front of Saul's vision, smudging the highway into black and white electric droplets. Spending the day with Lisa, Saul watched awkward slowly morph into uncomfortable, and then to painful on its way to ridiculous. For eight hours he told himself it had to be better than having guys in suits kicking open his motel room door. It took him four hours to figure out he should have changed motels instead of leaving all his stuff there. All his stuff except the clothes on his back and the shiny metal vial in his jacket pocket.

He checked the vial every twenty minutes or so to make sure it hadn't leapt out or emptied itself in his clothing. He left it sealed, unsure if he should turn it in to the police as evidence, destroy it, or use it to confront Aditi-Alhread if and when he ever saw her again.

Saul cursed his life for attacking him in several directions at once, instead of one at a time in a field of honor. His almost-sister-in-law's patience wore thin with his presence now. He remained a jobless depressed lump sitting around watching TV and asking for food while she worked on chores in the background. She reminded him of his dead girlfriend when she laughed, which was something he realized might have subconsciously influenced his surly attitude around her. His daughter treated him like a distant uncle, tolerated especially if there was a chance for a free gift or some money out of it. And now there was the woman with the jet black eyes who found him from the other side of the world, and there were freaks like Larry and the three dudes in suits that Saul recognized as problems but had no idea to what extent. All four men and the woman smelled like drug dealers to him, although his perception grew entirely from what he'd seen in movies or cable TV.

"OK I guess." Rose regarded him exactly like the taxi driver he was when she agreed to let Saul take her to a party downtown. The parents of one of her friends rented one of those pizza and play places where kids could eat the worst food for them imaginable and run around dancing or shooting at arcade games until they threw up or were ready for more. Naturally, since it was a closed party and supervised by several of the parents, Rose requested that Saul's role be strictly of the drop off and pick up later variety. He watched her run laughing into the crowd of friends without so much as a look over her shoulder to say goodbye. All he knew was that the party ended at ten, exactly at ten, and he was to be waiting outside.

For two hours he drove in concentric circles around Tacoma, alternatively floating through the downtown area and along various roads parallel to Highway Five. The green block numbers on the dashboard said nine thirty-seven, snapping him out of his hedonistic moment when he realized he had lost track of the part of town with the party. He sped up and strained to recognize a landmark.

Dennis wanted a rum and coke. Waiting for Guy and Jack to kill Larry and sanitize the crime scene took hours, and the last forty-five minutes on the phone with the boss drained all of Dennis' spirit. He'd asked Dennis to explain every detail, every thought process, and how every minutia went until he felt like he was in an interrogation room. Although, he had developed a tolerance for that sort of thing.

Looking out at the lights of the darkened city he reemphasized his importance to the world. He had a window office on the twenty-third floor, just five from the top, and he had lackeys to do his bidding, even kill for him if he asked. True, Jack seemed a little too quick to anger, and true, Guy wore stupid ties and incessantly babbled about his fantasy football picks, but still.

Along with a rum and coke Dennis craved a day when he could stop dealing with all these people he detested. He detested most people, now that he thought about it, but would be a lot more tolerable if he could sleep as late as he wanted and drink as much as he wanted and have his pick of the best of the stuff he passed on to desperate senior citizens and no-life losers. Not the random moments, but the premium stuff right out of *Penthouse* or fantasy novels.

His desk phone rang again, which at this hour meant only one possible caller.

"No I totally screwed that game up," Guy continued to Jack, who glanced around the room with no interest what-so-ever. "If I'd left him on the bench, I'd have easily shot up two slots."

Dennis frowned and picked up the phone, wondering how he'd managed to get someone even less interesting and less intelligent than the hired muscle working for him. A few seconds into the conversation with his boss and he swallowed hard. Hands shaking a little, he hung up the receiver and scanned the streets lit with dots of streetlights for any sign of movement in the shadows, but knew he wouldn't see any until it was too late. The service elevator would buy him enough time to get out, but he needed insurance.

"Who would have imagined that many yards rushing against a defense like that?" Guy said. Dennis looked at Guy and his ridiculous green tie and made the obvious choice.

Saul actively cursed every street, light, car, and pedestrian that passed by, damning them for their lack of insight to his location or destination. Other drivers taunted him ruthlessly, coming to complete stops at stop signs and not pulling out into intersections to make their left turn when the light turned yellow. Some even drove the speed limit, or less.

He struggled between a desire for calming music and a need for complete silence. His hand repeatedly reached out for the power button on the dashboard before he caught himself and pulled it back again. He couldn't imagine a sound that might help him find his way back, but there was always a chance the music would distract him too much. He learned that lesson the first time one of their gunners didn't swerve to cover oncoming traffic for two intersections in a row south of Mosul. Jamming to Guns and Roses attracted three AK-47 rounds into the side of his humvee before anyone noticed. Saul banned headphones on all patrols after that, which was supposed to have been the rule all along, had Saul been a stronger leader and enforced it.

Now in the lackluster streets of Tacoma, he would be late to pick up Rose, he knew. He would screw up his first task alone with his daughter in over a year, driving up to a cold, wet, eight-year-old and some other kid's angry parent waiting for the delinquent father to arrive.

He flashed back four years before to the thump in his chest when he couldn't find her pink nightgown with the butterfly on the front for Pajama Day. They dug through piles of clothes just lying on the floor, in the hamper, under stuffed animals, and as his failure became clearer, so did the bawling and the look of complete disappointment on her little face, red and streaked with tears…

This would be worse. This would seal the deal. He might as well just pick a direction and keep driving. The juice wasn't worth the squeeze.

Saul's energy faded for a moment, his eyes grew heavy, the landscape shifted a bit in a way Saul couldn't quite identify. He felt then, that even though these buildings seemed wholly unfamiliar to him, that he knew the way to go. His grip on the steering wheel relaxed, and he turned towards the tallest clump of skyscrapers nearby.

Aditi-Alhread didn't understand the mechanics behind elevators, or elevator shafts, but parts of her knew tunnels and how to move through them. Floor by floor she paused in the dimly lit duct, straining the senses of a thousand different creatures for her prey. On the twenty-third floor, she finally caught a scent she recognized.

Moving down the hallway she realized that the other two were already gone, although she wondered if it was coincidence or if they had somehow figured out she was coming. The door made no sound as she pushed it open.

Guy stared directly at her, but the tiny half-vial on the table told her he couldn't see her at that moment. He was somewhere else. Sometime else. Someplace that had once belonged to someone else.

Aditi-Alhread roared in anger, mixing all the predatory growls, hisses, and calls she could at once. Guy stood up, dazed, and shook his head to focus on her.

"Shit." He said, slapping himself in the cheeks. Maybe this was part of the trip. Maybe he was still sitting at the desk, waiting for the boss to call back while Dennis and Jack went for drinks. The boss wanted to speak to him personally, Dennis told him, about all his hard work. Dennis tossed in the free half-vial for all the hassle with Larry this morning. He'd even called to check on him to see if he wanted them to order cheese sticks while they waited.

The woman barring her teeth right in front of him didn't seem to care.

"I want you to know," she said in a smooth voice that frightened him. "What I do next, I don't do because you took a life, but because you took a soul."

Guy glanced down at the half-vial. "Hey, C'mon, this was my first time." He remembered that Dennis kept a gun in the upper drawer of the desk. She took a step closer. "OK, my second time, but give me a break, huh?" Another step closer. "I've got a wife to support."

He ripped open the drawer and grabbed the pistol.

She called up something from the Pleistocene era.

Saul continued through the streets, confident that his destination sat just ahead. An odd feeling of calm, to be sure, since cognitively his senses produced no evidence to support the claim that he had any idea where he was going.

They fell together, entwined almost like lovers, in a slow moment, a surreal calm moment surrounded by glittering spinning stars in a time where there was nothing to do but relax, the need for violence having passed once they flew through the window.

Saul pulled up alongside the concrete yard of a silver-blue skyscraper that went up well above his field of vision. The warmth of the heater reassured him. He felt safe, snuggled down in his jacket and the heated seat, lulled by the rhythmic thumping of the windshield wipers. Then it started raining diamonds.

Two sickening thumps landed over next to the building, bathed in a shower of sparkling glass. Saul jumped out of his seat, leaving the car door open, and rushed to confirm what he thought he saw.

A twisted artist impression of a man with a ridiculous green tie lay next to a motionless woman in a black antique military outfit. He was lined with a pool of rubies, while she was surrounded by shiny flakes of obsidian. In between them, the jet black and bright red pooled together, tendrils of each exploring the other. Then, suddenly, the fingers of midnight mercury pulled back from their crimson partners, like the hand of a frightened child, and took refuge back inside the motionless woman.

And then she was standing.

"We need to go." Aditi-Alhread said quietly.

Saul's eyes registered the motion of her rising but never left the misshapen form of the man who seemed like someone Saul would recognize if he were still upright.

"Saul." She spoke again with the same velvet voice.

He looked up at her, eyes wild and darting back and forth. His lips formed words that didn't come.

"Shhhhh, Saul, it's OK. It will all be OK. We just need to get in the car now and drive away, OK?"

He nodded and followed her to the street.

"I need to call my daughter." He said calmly after he plopped down behind the wheel.

"OK Saul, but start the car first."

Saul's hand shook and three tries later managed to put the keys into the ignition. Without looking he pulled out into the street and drove straight ahead. "She's going to be mad at me."

"Go ahead." She stared at his face, studying his reactions. "Just keep driving."

He dialed and spoke to his daughter in the same calm voice. He told her she needed to call a taxi, and that there'd been an accident, and he might not be home for a while. He didn't register her emotions, or perhaps he did and dismissed them as irrelevant to his world at that moment.

They drove in silence for ten more minutes before a stoplight gave Saul a chance to look over and study her. She stared back at him, unharmed, not bleeding. Her hair wasn't even ruffled.

"Before you slam on the breaks and demand to know what's going on or what just happened." Saul scowled at her words because he'd been pondering that very thing. "Take me back to your motel room."

He'd had worse offers. He could hold his questions that far at least.

CHAPTER 9

After his laptop signaled that the bank transfer went through, the man in the midnight blue suit escorted the fragile woman to the door, handed her a two hundred dollar bottle of wine, and wished her good night. Then Seamus stood quietly in his entry way like a kid with a new toy. In effect, he did hold a new plaything inside the small pine chest he'd purchased for what most people would make in a year.

An evening with this new specimen promised to expunge the unsavory business from earlier this morning. Larry was an oxygen thief as far as Seamus was concerned, and had been for the better part of the last decade, but that had only made Seamus' first kill order marginally easier.

"We took care of everything. We took care of everything." Seamus mimicked an exaggerated version of Dennis' voice as he pulled open the kitchen pantry and clicked the switch that revealed the hidden stairway. He stepped carefully down into the darkness, cradling his latest prize like a newborn while worrying just as much about dropping it.

To his credit, Dennis answered every question Seamus threw at him with what sounded like a well thought out answer. Still, the call ended with an air of uncertainty, as if Seamus missed the critical question that would mean the difference between a harmless drug overdose and a police investigation. Seamus looked at Dennis as someone who always got the job ninety percent done, sometimes ninety five, but never completely. There was always some detail, some tiny minutia that Dennis missed, and knowing that cut into Seamus' sleeping habits and resulted in his demanding three layers of invisible barriers, wards, and watchers around him almost anywhere he went.

If he'd been paranoid before, it was nothing compared to how it would be after tonight. He'd been able to warn Dennis she was coming for him, but it had been close. Lucky break by one of his passing street watchers, just barely got the message to him in time. See, that was exactly the sort of thing that fell in the five percent category that Dennis always missed.

Seamus sighed. That probably wasn't fair, even for him, but he liked blaming others for his inconveniences. Instead he decided to revel in his ability to protect his people through foresight and planning… and luck. Seamus assumed Dennis and his lackey made it out in time. He still hadn't gotten an update.

At the bottom of the stairs Seamus reached around and fondled the wall until his fingers tripped the light switch and lit up his primary sanctuary. He'd kept it as modern as possible with the medieval trappings it required to function. For example, the primary circle and all of its arcane symbols were burgundy glass melted into grooves precisely machine cut into the smooth polished concrete floor.

"Daddy's home." He mumbled as he forced his vision to shift through the Curtain. He noted several of his opaque servants in their occult manacles attempted strained laughter.

"By now you have to know that obsequious sucking up from Beyond doesn't impress me at all," he said. "And yet you try it anyway." Seamus shook his head. Dennis was like that sometimes too.

Dennis had been the replacement for who Seamus thought of as the Eighty Percent Solution, who had in turn replaced the Fifty Percent Solution. Fortunately, neither one of them had been given any tasks related to anything officially illegal, so their screw ups and half completed jobs hadn't set him back too much. And when it came time to let them go, Seamus had arranged for their disposals through supernatural channels.

He smiled for a moment when he remembered bringing them both back for their afterlife resale value. That was a few years ago, when he still did all his summoning himself. He'd had so much free time since he gave that up.

The bounty system had worked really well. It took a few years to set up, but now, for what seemed like astronomical fees, local necromancers and mediums and shamans and clairvoyants happily gathered the souls for him. Then after a fake rebirth ritual brought the spirits through the Barrier, he would sift through their raw souls and package them into tiny portions that sold for so much he easily made back his investment thirty times over.

And he had grown used to a life where restaurant tables had brass plates with his name on them, where waiters took away the silverware and brought all new sets with every course, and where they poured table water from bottles imported from Italian springs. He enjoyed carrying a roll of twenties for tips that he gave out like business cards, and hopping on first class flights at the last minute without even asking the price, if he traveled commercial at all.

He gently set the box down on an alter covered in red cloth, then turned and leapt back up the stairs. Gutting a fresh lamb and then sewing it's hollow torso back up again was his least favorite part, but if it wasn't still warm it wouldn't fool the soul into believing that it was entering a newborn baby.

Something reached out as he walked by and the hint of a cold hand passed through his arm. He stopped, startled and annoyed.

"What the hell do you want?" Seamus responded before checking to see who he was yelling at. After he allowed his vision to shift, he recognized this as one of his scouts, and forced a more pleasant tone. "Forgive that moment of unwarranted grumpiness. Report."

Final tally in. Dennis and Jack had escaped, Guy was dead. So, not a total loss.

Seamus sat down at the kitchen table and leaned over it on his elbows. Still, she shouldn't have been able to get any of them.

"Go on." He waved without looking at the scout and sat there without speaking, soaking in the rest of the information.

"Good info. I am impressed. You've gone a long way to earning your freedom." It saddened Seamus that he would actually have to make good on promises to release some of his better scouts, but the grapevine in the Netherworld could sometimes move faster than the internet, and the last thing he needed on his hands was a rebellion. "That's enough for now."

And with that Seamus was suddenly alone again, and his mood dropped. He had ordered murder, which, while it didn't bother him morally, it only added to his fear that someone would link it to him. Or more likely that someone would squeeze it out of Dennis. That troubled him more than some angry soul cutting down his minions. He'd long ago mastered any fear of the Netherworld and its occupants as long as he lived. But now, something glittered in the back of his mind. It was a disturbing new theory that needed testing before he'd be able to sleep again.

The soul downstairs could wait another night or two. As soon as Dennis and Jack got back they were all going on a hunt.

CHAPTER 10

Saul stood staring down at the dirty carpet of his hotel room with Aditi-Alhread behind him. Saul's breathing mixed with the hum from the heater and the light patter of rain outside. He didn't want to sit. He didn't want to relax. He didn't want to speak.

Saul lost track of how long he stood there. He did shift his weight when the muscles of one leg eventually tightened and pleaded for relief. He fought to let no thought enter his mind at all, to feel no emotion, to simply let time wash around him and pass without notice.

"I expected it there." His mouth betrayed him. "But it was supposed to be a place in my past. Different. Expected it there, not here." The hotel room became a plywood building filled with soldiers listening to a military counselor. "That's what they said. That was the deal. All that is behind you. You can count on that much. Rely on that. You saw some terrible shit, but it will never be that bad again. You'll have more basic, mundane things that will demand your attention now. They will more than occupy your time. Focus on those things. That's what helps your world become normal again." He allowed his body to ease into a slightly different position. "But then it isn't."

"Saul," Aditi-Alhread brushed her fingertips lightly across his back. When he didn't respond she said his name again. He attempted to grunt an acknowledgement but no sound came out. She sensed it anyway. "That man killed Larry."

It hadn't even occurred to Saul to ask why, or even how. All he acknowledged was that random death could follow you back from a place he thought he left it. Each time leaving behind a body that was missing a piece you wouldn't expect, or twisted in some way that the brain couldn't untangle.

He forced himself to come back. He made his eyes focus on the carpet, listened to the ambience of the room, tilted his neck enough for a small pop.

Now he felt foolish. This was no big deal. He deliberately replayed the two people smashing to the ground; one getting up and one not. Then he did it again. No big deal.

Finally he realized his hand was rubbing the thin metallic vial in his coat pocket.

He pulled it out and held it up without turning towards her.

"What's in this?" He said in a quiet voice.

"Where did you get that?" She asked.

"Just answer the question." He responded a little sharper.

She walked around him and stood in his field of view, although he didn't register the movement.

"It's a rare mix, no doubt designed to tease you into wanting more."

Saul tilted his head up to meet her gaze.

"Please," he said.

Her mouth forced a sad smile. "You hold in your hand the entire being of a Chinese girl who died of pneumonia when she was 10, the first and last three quick breaths of an Ethiopian infant, and a particularly perverse sexual experience of a French shoemaker from the 12th century."

"And this came from you?"

"No." As she spoke, she gently gripped his shoulders and eased him down into the room's only stuffed chair. She sat on the edge of the bed across from him.

"OK, so?"

"Those are parts of someone's soul."

Saul looked at the vial. "Can I open it?"

"Let me do it." She held out her hand and he passed it to her like he might pass a pinless grenade that should have exploded five minutes ago.

She twisted the top, breaking the wax seal, and moved it to where Saul could see in. It seemed thicker than water, but dark, like jet-black quicksilver. He stared at it a moment, watching it swirl as Aditi-Alhread gave the vial little twists of motion. His hand rose up on its own, and she jerked away from him.

"Sorry," Saul said, again forcing himself to focus. "I wasn't going to…" He didn't even know what it was he wasn't supposed to do.

She walked over to the dingy sink with the hard-water stains and pushed down the drain stopper. Right before she poured the liquid out Saul moved over to watch. It seemed to fill more of the sink than he thought would have fit in the vial.

The liquid shifted from a slice of oblivion to a shadowy mercury that swirled long after it should have calmed. Saul felt like he had eight years ago, looking down into Rose's crib for the first time. It didn't seem like a pool of liquid. It seemed alive, and he wanted to comfort it, to talk to it, hold it.

"Don't touch." She warned. She rested her hand on his chest and pushed him back a little. Then she leaned over and blew a long steady breath into the surface of the black fluid. Wherever her breath touched, the liquid turned to tendrils of black mist, and then drifted up and vanished.

"What did you do?" Saul asked.

"I freed them. That part of them, anyway."

Saul leaned against the wall. Standing seemed harder than usual. "You bleed this same liquid."

She smiled and guided him back down into the chair. After a moment of silence, he tried another question.

"So, what would have happened if I touched it? I'm assuming that was the point of them giving it to me."

She sat back on the edge of the bed, elbows on her knees, leaning forward. "You would have absorbed those memories. You would have experienced them like you experience every other event of your life, but stronger, and never able to forget."

"And that's what addicted Larry." Saul didn't need to see her response to know he'd gotten that one right. "And he said you were the drug."

"I'm a soul Saul, nothing more. A ghost in corporeal form, I suppose is another way to think about it."

"A ghost?"

"Wraith. Let's go with a solid soul, how's that?"

"So if I touched you…"

"No. Not while I maintain this form." She sat up straight. "But right after I hit the ground for example. If you'd touched that liquid, yes."

Saul grinned, started to speak, and thought better of it.

"Let me skip a few steps for you." Aditi-Alhread lowered her head as she spoke to catch his eyes again. "These people summon… souls, spirits, whichever works for you. They summon them, then they trap them, then they distil them into little containers and they sell them."

"I don't understand what that makes you."

"I'm the one who got away." She paused and searched Saul's expression. "Summoned, then escaped." She stopped there. There was no point in describing the party of retirees gathered to watch the ritual, waiting for their shares of younger, more interesting lives they spent their savings on. No point in mentioning what pulled her out of the sacrificial lambskin just before they would have split her entire being into individual containers.

Saul let out a long sigh and his shoulders sunk. A few moments more of silence passed.

"Why don't you lay down?" She stood and gently lifted Saul out of his chair. He let her lead him to the bed and then shrugged her hand off his shoulder.

"What about you?" He asked as he slipped off his shoes.

"I'll just rest in this chair for a little bit until you drift off." She said.

"I'd rather just hang out here alone, I think."

"OK," she smiled. "I'll be nearby."

Saul barely registered her exit until the gentle click of the door lock catching. He stripped down to his boxers and curled up on top of the bed. He resisted moving until the chill of the room forced him to pull over the main bed cover, and then stared up at the ceiling, daydreaming but not falling asleep until almost dawn.

Asleep, he pictured himself lying in the bed of the hotel room from a position slightly above and behind. The room shifted to his old room in his old house, and though his view didn't turn to check, somehow he felt that Nicole was alive again, lying next to him in the bed. He felt warmth rising from that side, and imagined her cold feet slowly wiggling between his calves to warm up.

His body stayed sprawled in the same position, and then the room shifted again, this time to a sleeping bag on a cot on the plywood floor of a dusty tan tent.

He tried to roll over, and realize he couldn't. Then he understood none of his limbs worked. He suddenly sat in a wheelchair in a hospital with his arms and legs dangling lifeless, while he steered himself around with a bar pressed against his chin. Then his arms and legs vanished entirely, and he realized he couldn't speak either.

"You know what this is, right?" Watt's voice. Just behind him.

Saul tried to respond but nothing worked. He believed he managed to part his lips in some pathetic half wheeze.

"This is your fear of helplessness. Your fear of having absolutely no control over your environment." Saul heard who he presumed to be Watts rise up out of some leather or vinyl chair, again, just out of his field of view. "Fear that your life could be changed in an instant and no matter how much you train, how much you prepare, how much you practice or plan, you couldn't do a thing about it."

Saul forced his head to move, forced his head to turn slightly, even though he continued to watch himself and not what his head should logically be seeing. Then he forced his voice.

"You'd kill me, wouldn't you Watts, if I were really like this?"

"No can do Sarge." Saul's point of view moved forward, like he was looking through Watts' eyes. "Maybe you should ask that new lady friend of yours."

"You're a huge help Watts."

"Hey I got you to talkin' didn't I?"

"Yeah, thanks."

"Whatever I can do."

Saul suddenly saw himself again on the hotel bed, and then popped back down and into his body. He opened his eyes and waited for the blurriness around the digital clock to clear. It revealed he'd slept until dinner time, a new personal record, even though he didn't feel the least bit rested.

After a few basic personal hygiene and bodily functions, Saul stood looking at the room and rubbed his eyes. He replayed most of the night before, mostly in reverse, stopping abruptly on the misshapen form of the man looking up at him, tiny shards of glass glittering on his blank face. At that moment Saul finally recognized the green tie, and understood who the woman who calls herself Aditi-Alhread pushed through a window ten or twenty stories above the street.

Then he glanced at the door, somehow knowing she was standing just on the other side. As long as the door stayed closed, everything stayed normal.

He opened it anyway.

CHAPTER 11

He was only off by a few feet, as he looked up to find her sitting on the hood of his car.

"C'mon let's go." She moved to the passenger door without losing eye contact with him.

He unconsciously stepped forward and then stopped to inventory his condition. No shoes, yesterday's clothes, unwashed. No car keys. Without a word he slipped back inside and closed the door.

He indulged in possibly the longest shower of his life, laid down and tried for another forty-five minutes to fall back asleep, flipped through some pay-per-view options, and then went back and opened the door again, this time physically ready for leaving the room, although mentally clearer on why he shouldn't bother. She still stood next to the passenger door, only now she cradled four large blueberry muffins in her arms, presumably from the motel's lobby.

"I'm assuming I'm driving." Saul said moving towards the car.

"I left my license in my other lifetime." She replied and plopped in the passenger seat.

Saul sat down and started the engine. He stared out the windshield without moving.

"Go downtown, head north." She handed him a muffin and then more specific instructions on where to drive, completely on the other side of town.

He took the food and paused. He hadn't checked on Rose. Since no one called, he assumed she made it home, but that didn't mean she made it home happy.

"You can call her on the way." Aditi-Alhread said. "Eat some muffin, put it in gear, and let's go."

Saul's hand moved to the gearshift, but stopped short. She started to speak again and he interrupted her.

"Wait!" Too sharp, he lowered his tone. "Just wait, OK?"

Everything supernatural aside, the woman next to him killed a man last night. And not just any man, a man who had scouted him out and barged into his room, and who she claimed killed an ex-addict named Larry. She'd also been to Iraq and back, by herself, and survived. She may have even helped him there. Possibly saved him or members of his team. He'd forgotten that little piece of trivia. That alone seemed enough to go along with her for a little while. That and her eyes.

Eight minutes and two muffins later Saul dialed Lisa's house phone.

"Saul? Are you OK?" Her tone confused him a bit.

"What? Yeah, yeah." He strained to figure out how she might have learned about last night. Maybe Green-Tie-Guy's death was on the news.

"Rose said you were in an accident."

"What?" Crap. That had been his excuse to tell Rose to get a cab. "No no, I said there had been an accident. I wasn't in it, but I was a witness." He paused to flush out the story.

"And you couldn't leave?" Lisa's voice picked up an edge.

"There were three or four cars," Saul added, "but it was really bad. Lots of ambulances, one guy died." That last sliver at least was true. "The police said everyone had to stay for questioning whenever someone gets killed." Technically, taken literally and out of context, that sentence wasn't a lie either. He shifted tactics. "Did Rose get home OK?"

"Yeah." Lisa's tone drifted down to normal. "Yeah one of the other mothers got in the cab with her and rode with her to here.

"Rose was a little upset though."

Some small talk followed that Saul didn't hear much of until they eventually hung up. All he'd managed to do was widen the gap that much further. Suddenly driving to some random section of town with a women who claimed to be a walking soul didn't seem to be an issue. What else was he going to do with his time?

Saul appealed to the small portion of his brain capable of keeping the car in his lane without smashing into anyone in front of him while he concentrated on calling up, and then fighting down images and emotions and memories to go with his latest family failure. A sweet, low, even voice had the nerve to cut through his moment of self-destructiveness.

"Want another muffin?" She held one up, shiny spots on its fluffy surface revealing butter, grease or some other manifestation of the sixteen grams of lard common to such fat pills.

"You can have those two." Saul replied. "I'm full."

"I don't actually eat."

Of course you don't. Saul tried to focus on the road, to ignore the endless questions or the many ways to test her sanity or honesty. Eventually he likened his "just ignore her" strategy to telling a severely depressed person to "just be happy."

"So, earlier, you said that thing about your license and another lifetime." He formed his sentence carefully. "Does that mean you've had more than one?"

She watched him out of the corner of her eyes and grinned before answering. "Yes, I've had several." She crossed her arms and turned to face him. "Do you really want to know?"

"Yes." Another pet peeve of Saul's included people who asked questions they didn't actually want the answer to. "Otherwise I wouldn't have asked."

"Do you want to know about the existences too, or just the lives?"

"What's the difference?"

"Existences are animal bodies, some as low as insects. Lives are human."

Saul paused and decided what the hell. "Sure then, both."

"Thousands of existences first, then many lives. Let's say more than ten."

"Oh lets." Saul welcomed a brief feeling of levity.

"And before you ask, I was never a pharaoh or a princess or a general."

"Really?" Damn. She passed one of the whack-job test questions. Whack-jobs always claimed that they had been someone like Elvis or Napoleon or Helen of Troy.

"I spent most of my time in agriculture."

Saul nodded his head, uncertain what facial expression or commentary went with a discussion like this. He noticed a pair of headlights behind him and realized he had been hogging the left lane. Another thing that he hated in others. After pulling ahead of a log truck and shifting to the right, he decided to just let the questions flow through him without a filter.

"So you were, what? A woman soldier in your last life?"

"No. Turn here."

How far they had traveled Saul had no idea. He didn't know this part of town at all, and they passed the sign identifying their destination before it dawned on him to read it.

"I was a woman in my last life though. Nearly forty years ago. Divorced, had one child, then died in a garden variety car crash."

Saul never imagined anyone claiming a previous life would claim one so recent. Or so banal. He felt vaguely disappointed.

"So, how do you explain the outfit?" He asked.

"Just what ensemble from a Seventies single mom wardrobe do you think is going to strike fear in my enemies?"

Saul laughed a moment, his head flashing with images of women in orange bell bottoms with names like Cleopatra Dynamite.

"Turn at this light."

Saul's unconscious identified buildings, neither houses nor skyscrapers, passing by his window. A closer look and he recognized a part of town with bars, clubs and restaurants. A few seconds later and he tacked on the unique identifier, "the type I'd never actually go to."

"Pull into that parking lot." Aditi-Alhread's voice lost the traces of humor when she gave orders, something Saul recognized all too well from years of military hierarchy. He didn't mind it too much, but he certainly noticed it.

"We're going in there." She said, pointing at a one story building that someone decorated with rusted sheet metal and car parts.

"Why?" Saul asked, sliding into a parking space.

"Because I need to talk to a medium."

"What?" Saul struggled over what a medium was. "How do you know there's one in there?"

"Because it's surrounded by ghosts." She said it matter-of-factly and then got out of the car.

CHAPTER 12

Ishaan-Larry sprinted down the midnight streets without thought of direction or surroundings. Buildings and road signs had little bearing on the dead, and all he wanted was to put some distance between himself and those howling behind him. He hated the city and its endless expansion of concrete and trash. And the smells. The smells of standing next to someone with sour halitosis or stale sweat, or freeing himself from the throngs only to catch the rotting garbage wafting up from each alleyway. He felt it a cruel joke that scents carried over to the afterlife.

His hatred for cities was why he lived – had lived – in a one-room motor home in the country, away from all the gray and steel and noise. Which is not to say he was a granola nut. He smoked and drank like the best of them, but he just really hated crowds of people who huddled together in bars filled with animated flat screens and repeatedly laughed loudly enough to drown out all his attempts to join in.

Another absurdly human wail ripped through the night, followed by the echo of motorcycle engines revving somewhere far behind. If they caught him, it meant enslavement. And eventually, when they grew tired of him, they would sell him to a younger generation eager to test their new binding spells, or worse, simply leave him shackled in a basement somewhere for eternity. That still appealed to him more than the alternative if he crossed over to the Netherworld. After six lifetimes Ishaan-Larry finally understood what it meant to be damned.

He barreled ahead past a couple of kids making out in a recessed doorway, past four homeless guys laughing beneath the graffiti of a random building, and through an intersection without any regard for potential traffic. No one saw his form racing through the shadows, just as he made no sounds to them. His chest didn't burn with the fire it would have if he'd run a fraction of this distance while he lived. Nor did anything pound in his chest or scream in his ears. Being free of all that gave him nothing to focus on but the horror of how he imagined the night would end.

As he flew through a dormant clothing outlet he wondered if there was a way to contact Aditi-Alhread. Week's earlier she'd found him in a chapel begging some poor confused Methodist pastor for forgiveness for his sins. Had she seen anything but true self-loathing in Larry's eyes, horror at what he realized he had done, she would have gutted him right there on the second pew. Instead she led him away from the speechless religious man and granted him her own personal absolution. That hadn't saved him when that jerk Dennis and his lackeys decided he needed to die, and it wouldn't save him if they caught him tonight.

The lights of an alleyway startled him for an instant when he burst out of the building and another scream from his left caused him to change directions slightly and head directly between the buildings instead of through them. How many dead playthings did they have out running around pretending to be dogs?

Ishaan-Larry slammed into a wall and bounced back in pain, which he thought was totally impossible. Brick and steel meant nothing to him now, and on top of that he stood near the end of a cul-de-sac, surrounded by open air. Then he noticed the line of white dust on the ground. Flour? Salt? Some arcane mixture, unblemished except for the dark metal "X"s spaced every yard or so along its length. He reached out his hand and felt the air above the line and found it solid and invisible. It blocked his path completely and turned behind him to form a massive open "U" shape. They had herded him in here like some damn animal… yes, exactly like a damned animal.

He spun and waited. Two naked people – dead ones – barked at him on all fours from the opening where he had come from. A third joined in from the side, also on all fours, stopping on the opposite bank of the white powder barrier and growling like a person with delusions of lycanthropy.

Ishaan-Larry wanted to scream, yell, flex his pathetic skinny arms and bare his teeth in some primal show of force in hopes that his sheer anger, his total resolve would somehow cower these wannabe hounds and drive them back. They did not face Larry the wheezing recovering addict who died shot up with three times the normal hit of heroin. Ishaan-Jugurtha fought under Hannibal as a Numidian horseman, and two lives before that Ishaan-Tien had... The first hints of motorcycle headlights quelled those thoughts. Even if he fought off the other spirits, the necromancers had arrived.

Then all that annoying howling and barking stopped. At first Ishaan-Larry assumed Dennis or one of the others had yelled some command while getting off their slick blue Japanese crotch rockets. Then he felt something change. The ground nearby cracked with an impossible black which he knew wasn't visible to the living. The three spirit hounds flattened against the concrete, cowering without really understanding what caused their fear. Ishaan-Larry looked up then and smiled and flipped his middle finger at the three breathing men walking in his direction. At least he could deny them the pleasure of casting some spell at him.

The ground opened all around his feet, followed with a smell of dust and old blood. The sudden sound of beating wings hurt his ears and an ice-cold wind cut through his torso. Teeth and claws, dirty white like marble, and the after image of dark feathers surrounded him, and then Ishaan-Larry was gone.

"What the hell was that?" Seamus asked as he pulled off his motorcycle helmet. The sleekness of it contrasted with his conservative midnight blue suit and matching tie.

"I missed it Boss, whatever it was." Dennis replied, struggling to catch up. "But something sure has the hounds spooked… if you'll pardon the pun."

Jack stayed back, embracing the role of bodyguard, and scanned the pockets of darkness in every direction for threats he could fight. He resisted the temptation to pull out the gun he kept in the pouch behind his motorcycle seat.

"I had no idea anything like that really existed." Seamus said, bending down and touching the cool asphalt where Ishaan-Larry stood a few moments earlier. He cursed first in English, then Latin, and then turned and threw his helmet. "Send the hounds to their cages. I'll meet you in my office."

Twenty minutes later, as they passed the first of the viewing rooms, Dennis tapped Jack on the shoulder with a grunt of mild indignation.

"Fix your tie." Dennis said.

Clearly not accustomed to anything more formal than a T-shirt and jacket, Jack looked down and fumbled with the knot he couldn't see. Dennis wore a suit now too, and while it cost twice what Jack's did, Dennis' tacky gold bracelet and oversized watch made Jack feel the better dressed of the duo.

They continued down the hall, both trying not to glance into the open rooms on either side. In most the caskets were closed. Some were open with hints of occupants just barely visible over the lip, and mercifully, only one had mourners milling about examining who left which set of flowers.

Passing through a door marked "Private, do not enter" they then eased up an oak staircase and came to a halt in front of the first door so far that didn't smell like disinfectant.

Dennis gave the frame two sharp knocks, even though he knew his presence had been announced through supernatural channels several minutes earlier, and then led Jack in to a room of dark auburn wood. The ceiling and its massive crossbeams, the floor, even the bookshelves built into the wall, all of the same color and grain of wood from a time when logging knew no bounds.

"All the hounds locked up?" The man behind the mahogany desk – a slightly darker lumber than the rest of the room – poured grape juice into a crude silver cup. His midnight blue coat hung on the wooden hook in the wall behind him, although the white shirt and dark tie still looked professional without it.

"You bet sir." Dennis hated small talk, which is probably why his boss insisted on it so much.

"Want any?" Seamus gestured at the decanter of purple liquid. Dennis knew black tasteless crackers would be next. Supposedly unfermented grape juice along with unleavened unsalted bread – 'lifeless food' – helped maintain the link to the dead. The drink was always poured into the same silver mug carved with the ancient Etruscan symbols for "from a tomb" on it, indicating it had been stolen from someone's grave. His boss really loved that stuff, and Dennis tried not to wonder if Seamus had ever taken to 'borrowing' an occasional coat, shirt, or tie from any of the 'tenants' downstairs.

Dennis shook his head. "Sir are we going to be meeting here… regularly?"

"Portland is practically right next door Dennis." He took a cracker from a small pine box and dipped it in the grape juice.

"No sir, I meant, here, instead of your office." Dennis noted that Jack stood perfectly still beside him. They hired that guy from the right stock, completely obedient.

"My great great grandfather built this home and started this business." He sipped from the cup. "My great grandfather added onto the house and onto the business. My grandmother spent half the family fortune expanding it even further." A drop of grape juice lingered on his lip. "I'm comfortable here. The office is for trades and sales."

Dennis nodded, unsure how to respond.

"Sir," he finally added. "I have no idea what happened tonight. I don't see the dead as well as you do and…"

"Seriously?" The sharp but quiet cut of the tone stopped Dennis short. "Really? Are you that completely uninformed of the basics of our craft and what is going on? Why the hell do you think I called a meeting right after a hunt?"

Dennis' mouth opened. No sound came out. Seamus sighed and took another bite of cracker before continuing in a more even tone.

"Larry is a criminal in the Netherworld, get it? Being held somewhere, somehow. Guy probably is too, the useless bastard, and it will take a lot more than a casual Sunday summoning to bring them back from that." He wiped his mouth with a monogrammed purple napkin and put the crackers away. The cup he kept out though, and stared at Dennis while rolling the smooth silver between his hands.

"Which," he continued, "is probably where we're going to end up if we don't figure out some way to protect ourselves whenever we kick it."

Out of the corner of his eye, Dennis detected the slightest twitch in Jack's cheek. Not a man who liked to be reminded of his own mortality.

"On a related topic," his boss continued, "what else do we know about the little free spirit? Anything we can use from her?"

At last, Dennis thought, something he knew something about. He pulled out a notebook and read from the smooth white pages. "The original four idiots who summoned her and let her escape are long dead. She hunted all of them down a couple of years ago."

"Any contact with them on the other side?"

"No sir. I presume they're prisoners somewhere too."

"Great. Awesome. Next."

"We're still not sure how she got free after the summoning, but based on her instant ability for violence,

I'm guessing she came back wrong. Like, *Pet Sematary* wrong, that kind of wrong."

"I think we sort of suspected that already. Next."

Dennis quietly sighed. "We've had a lot of intel that she recently traveled to England, not sure how exactly, and broke into the British Museum. Specifically the Austen Layard exhibit."

"Don't know him."

Dennis had used an obscure name on purpose in hopes it would make him seem that much better prepared. "He's the guy who discovered all those old Assyrian tablets in Iraq in the mid Nineteenth Century. From the Royal Library of Ashurbanipal." Dennis loved appearing like he knew everything there was to know on a subject. It dawned on him in his moment of glory that he hadn't researched who Ashurbanipal had been, so hurried on before his boss could think to ask. "Anyway, no one living actually saw her in person, but they had security camera footage of her sneaking around, and almost all of the thousands of clay tablets were removed from their display cases or storage areas."

"Stolen?"

"Nope, just spread out all over the floors, like she was reading a very old, boring newspaper."

"The fact that you've slowed down tells me you haven't had a chance to figure out what was on those tablets."

Dennis' cursed to himself.

His boss continued. "I expect updates tomorrow."

"Hey sir, we do know her true name," Dennis threw out the topic to distract himself from the distinct lack of praise. "Why don't we just summon her again?"

"Because she's already on this side of the Barrier." Seamus answered like he might answer a small child. Dennis felt his success slowly slipping away, his incompetence growing in the eyes of his employer. "She's a being of this world now, and the other. A hybrid of sorts."

"Well then can't we just send someone after her?" Dennis added. "Like someone we've got chained up in the basement?"

"Since all of our captured spirits exist on the other side, I doubt they would have much power over her." His boss thought for a moment and then added. "Although, I suppose one of them might be able to hurt her if she were able to cross back over again. No idea what rules apply to her anymore." He looked off at nothing for a moment. "Hurm. Worth investigating."

Dennis relaxed a moment, having regained a small toe-hold above banishment or sudden termination – any form of termination.

His boss continued, "But this recent discovery about Larry and our inability to affect him in any way in the Netherworld distresses me greatly.

"To be clear," Seamus said, "we're screwed. And not just from the very angry ghost woman in the Victorian uniform. Assuming we can ward her off – and we will – then in ten, twenty, thirty years tops, when something as simple as high blood pressure or a brain clot takes us out, we're going to be looking at literally an angry mob from hell. We're going to be standing face to face with people who will have all of eternity to fuck with us for what we did to their friends and families."

He stood up for emphasis. "That means until then, no soul – be it attached to a breathing body or hovering above our heads – is worth anything at all to us if it doesn't help us get some protection on the other side." His eyes danced around in thought. "Or alternatively immortality on this side."

"Yes sir." Dennis said, feeling completely out of his league.

"I'll do some research on what we can do to Aditi and what she might be able to do for us." the man sat down again behind the desk. "You find out everything on those tablets."

Dennis tensed up again. He knew the answer he would get if he asked whether that order included every single tablet. He motioned to Jack and left disturbed when he realized that he felt more upset about his boss's opinion of him than this new revelation on what the afterlife held in store.

CHAPTER 13

The deep throbbing of the bass depths of music hit Saul first. His heart raced until he sent out the memo to each body part that the booms were rhythmic and they didn't come with a rush of air overpressure. These were not explosions. All clear.

Aditi-Alhread darted across the parking lot and vanished before Saul even shut his door.

As the details of the building came into view, Saul couldn't make out anything that hinted at any sort of haunting or otherworldly activity. He squinted at shadows, stared at open spaces, and even just let his vision relax and focus on nothing in particular, and still saw no sign of ghosts.

He did, however, notice that the car parts on the walls were actually metal sculptures, probably from some nearby graduate art student. Mostly humanoid, mostly rusted – no doubt on purpose – generally thin and twisted impressions of dancers as they might appear exiting the other end of a black hole.

Saul moved to the back of the short line of people showing IDs to the doorman and wondered how his traveling companion had move past so fast.

While he waited, he eavesdropped on a nearby conversation and studied some of the locals. The woman in line in front of him wore an ill-fitting short sun dress nearly as pale as she was, and sported random tattoos peeking out of every edge of fabric. Egyptian hieroglyphs ran up the back of her leg and disappeared up under her skirt on their way to destinations unknown, a Frankenstein -like scar jutted out from her sleeve, and when she turned toward the parking lot for an instant Saul noticed a tattooed mustache over her lip, all in that grey no color of old or cheap ink long since faded from the original brilliant artwork. For an instant he pondered touching her or asking her if she was a ghost, but figured the dead had better things to talk about than which bands qualified as "emo" and which ones didn't.

He turned to a wall covered in flyers advertising bands in a way that seemed designed to drive potential fans away rather than attract them. Names like Twisted Dwarf, The American Dental Association or Two Headed Cat concealed themselves within crude hand-drawn figures or designs. It seemed to Saul that every night a new generation of poorly copied paper violently settled on top of the old with staples, nails or glue, and sometimes the ones beneath took it with dignity, and sometimes they tore at the backs of the new champions or clawed frantically to reach around their edges.

The chunky doorman with the scraggly graying beard let Saul pass with the same grunt he gave everyone who approached who wasn't young and female. Inside the door was a mostly open space that looked like the original builders had stopped a few weeks shy of finishing and someone else had come in and spray-painted black over all the exposed rafters, pipes, and wires in hopes that no one would notice. One side of the room held a bar and several tables – mostly the kind you stand next to so no one had to bother with chairs – and a crowd of people milled around next to the stage on the other side. On the slightly raised floor, instruments sat ready in quiet darkness, waiting along with the audience for someone to come and bring them to life.

The women of the crowd wore mostly black or white dresses of a random variety and length, with a few in dark pants and tank tops, while the men sported similarly monochromatic jeans with T-shirts, or untucked short-sleeve collared shirts. College aged, Saul realized, with a few graduate or post-graduates trying to pass as younger. No sign of Aditi-Alhread.

Saul found a good empty spot against the wall and waited. An hour passed. A woman came up to the mic and spouted purple turgid prose to a mostly indifferent audience and Saul decided he needed a beer. He took his time, almost thirty minutes, and by the time he returned a thin man with long blonde hair had taken the woman's place and played solo acoustic guitar before an only slightly more interested crowd. He went on for what seemed like forever to Saul, followed by a trio of college boys who screamed unintelligible songs accompanied by a guitar, a bass, and an electronic drum they carried up on stage with them, leaving the original instruments untouched.

Saul continued to nurse beers, dragging them out well beyond the point where they warmed and lost all flavor, and had just resolved to leave Aditi-Alhread behind when someone new got on the stage and announced the main band for the night.

When the lead singer stepped out though, Saul felt the energy of the place change a little, intensifying and converging on a single point. She had jet-black vintage Bettie Page straight hair with flat bangs across her forehead. On the near paper-white canvas of her face, bright red lipstick contrasted overdone eye-liner. A red and black swirled guitar pick hung from a leather strap around her neck, and she wore a worn black leather jacket over a Fifties poodle skirt that stopped just above a pair of old combat boots. Airborne variety, Saul noted.

"Oh yes, I am HOT!" She spoke into the microphone with a Cockney accent and a tone of utter contempt for the universe. Saul could barely make out any of the words after the first ones, but the profanity and anger were unmistakable. All that vanished with the first song. Brimming with a sudden American accent, energetic and happy, it told of off-norm sexual acts in an almost pop-like tone, and she sang the lyrics like a giddy schoolgirl, dancing subtle junior high moves and smiling and wrinkling her nose in cute flirtatious gestures to the audience.

"Her name's Aimee." Saul recognized Aditi-Alhread's voice by the way it seemed to move directly into his brain without regard to the roar of the crowd or the blare of the music.

"I'm guessing she's why we're here?" Saul didn't bother to yell. The strange communication seemed to work both ways.

"We need allies Saul."

Saul mulled over that one a bit. Allies implied a fight, and more to the point, a big fight. Who the hell was she… were *they* supposed to fight against?

"She is the ally or she's going to help us get allies?" Saul said.

"Both."

Up on stage Aimee's gaze settled on Aditi-Alhread and her expression changed. The songs continued, but the flirty smiles faded until clearly forced. The set went on for almost two hours, and when it ended, the room cheered appropriately for a few minutes, and then everything, including the lights on stage, dimmed to a dull neutral grey energy.

Instead of storming offstage in a dramatic finish, the band immediately started tearing down their equipment, and Aimee sat down on the edge of the platform to talk to a small group of fans who gathered around her. The bass guitarist – a heavy set man with long black curly hair – sat down beside her with a bag of homegrown CDs and a small cash box. Individuals passed over wadded bills, and in exchange Aimee would add a hug, kiss on the cheek, or autograph to the musical purchase. Her followers seemed evenly split among the gender options – including some in the 'mystery' category – and Aimee greeted them all with equal affection.

Saul and Aditi-Alhread waited right in front of the end of the line, watching, but making no move to get close to her until the line had completely diminished. The bassist went back to help the others roll away the amps. Aimee started to rise, seeming not to notice the last two fans at first, and then turned back at the last minute to address Saul.

"Did you need something Love?" Away from the microphone the accent faded, but what little remained caused Saul a small smile. He realized he had no idea what to say and fumbled over his words, pointing to the woman Aimee clearly didn't want to notice.

Surprise crossed Aimee's face and her eyes double checked where Saul was pointing.

"I confuse you, don't I?" Aditi-Alhread took a half step forward, but kept her arms crossed in front of her. Aimee stared into her eyes and nodded slowly. No one spoke for a few moments, both women locked in each other's eyes.

"Maybe we should go somewhere," Saul started. "like, backstage, or something."

Aimee snapped out of it. "Are you daft? There is no backstage." She smiled. "Follow me."

Aimee led them through the crowd which now treated her with the indifference due any other peon not up on a raised platform. They broke through a back door and into a small barren yard decorated with worn garden furniture, beer bottles, and red coffee cans filled with cigarette butts.

"Crap, I didn't get a beer." Aimee spoke as soon as they hit the cool stale air.

"Uh, yeah, I could go…" Saul started.

"In a minute." Aditi-Alhread stopped him, eyes still on Aimee. Saul's brow furled, annoyed at himself for obeying so easily. Too late to change now.

"Do I know you?" Aimee asked as she took a cigarette out of her pocket and held it between her fingers. She made no attempt to light it.

"What's different about me?" Aditi-Alhread asked. "To you, I mean."

Aimee sighed and sat down on a black wrought iron chair.

"I have synesthesia." She said and then looked up for any sign of recognition. Seeing none, she continued. "It means I see sounds as colors. Not all sounds, mostly music. In fact, only music."

"Yes, that's what they told you." Aditi-Alhread eased down into a chair beside her.

"Anyway, when I sing, you glow. Not like a little glow, like, you could be your own light show."

"Ever seen that before?" Saul threw in the first question to come to mind just to be in the conversation.

"No." Aimee fiddled with her unlit cigarette, drawing comfort from the thought of it as much as the potential chemical release it held for her.

"But you've seen glows before," Aditi-Alhread said, almost maternal in her calmness.

"Never on a person."

"No, but you saw them, back to the very first lullaby. And you grew up thinking they were alive. Childhood friends. Spirits watching over you. Angels…"

"Yeah yeah that's ace." Aimee's gaze fell to her hands. "I need to go check on my stuff." She looked up, but didn't stand.

Aditi-Alhread turned to Saul. "Saul, why don't you get Aimee that beer now?" This time it felt like a request, not an order, so he went with it. By the time he returned, both women were quiet. Aimee focused on grinding the last bit of her cigarette between her fingertips to push out the final bit of burning tobacco. Saul passed over the brown bottle and she took it without speaking.

"I think we're about done here." Aditi-Alhread stood slowly but kept her eyes on Aimee.

"She going to help?" Saul had no idea what 'help' consisted of in this case, but figured they'd already communicated the details. Aimee seemed cocky, defiant. She hadn't agreed to anything and was fiercely proud of it.

"So, who are you in this scenario?" Aimee asked Saul.

"Saul," he held out his hand for a second then drew it back. He felt like Aditi-Alhread had an agenda for the rest of the conversation, but if she was going to give him orders or send him away, he could toss in a little sabotage to make her think twice about cutting him off in the future. "What's your deal?"

"What do you mean?" Aimee seemed to welcome talking to Saul instead of her other option.

"You do this to pay for a one bedroom apartment you share with two other guys? Working your way through a radio-television-film degree?"

Aimee smiled, "Yeah, that's it. You got it spot on. For sure I'm not a registered nurse working to support her disabled father while also just happening to have a hobby on the weekends."

Saul let the grimace come without fighting it. She'd earned the satisfaction she drew from it.

"A nurse? Really?" Saul asked.

"I thought you'd determined for sure that's what I wasn't."

"Well are you?" Saul spoke but Aimee only grinned in return. Saul sighed and grinned back. "OK, think it's so easy, you tell me what I am in this scenario."

"Think I can't?" A mischievous tone now.

"Bet you can't."

"Really?" Aimee's grin widened. "Stakes?"

"I dunno," Saul lied. "Whatever she wanted from you if you get it wrong."

"And if I get it right?"

"Name it." Saul meant to add "within reason" at the end, but some part of his Y chromosome was too caught up in the moment to show any weakness. Aditi-Alhread shuffled back a step, watching quietly but not making any move to interfere. Vaguely like a spectator at *Thunderdome*.

Aimee studied Saul for a moment, then made a little "turn around" swirling gesture with her finger. Saul reluctantly turned, unsure what information she might gain from his backside.

"Do I get any questions?" Aimee asked, still looking him up and down.

"First, that was a question. Second, no. I didn't get any, so you don't."

"Right." Aimee swigged her beer without taking her eyes off of him. "OK, short haircut with no gel or sideburns or stylized alterations, so I'm going with military. I'd go with cop, but you seem completely out of place in a club and nowhere near arrogant enough. Totally boring clothes, so I'm saying you're on holiday, probably from Iraq or Afghanistan, and had to grab a tiny piece of an old wardrobe at the last minute. Plus, you're bumming around with this person, who I'm not sure you know very well. You're unshaven and your clothes are ridiculously wrinkled, so I'm adding 'single' to my final answer. Although you're pretty cute in a vanilla sort of way, so I'm taking a risk on that last one." Another swig. "Good enough?"

Saul stood a moment, weighing his options. All his bravado sloughed off his back and slithered down a nearby sewer opening. That left humility as his only chance. Throw himself on her mercy. "Yeah, certainly closer than I got with you."

Aimee stood up, triumphant.

"This is going to be bad, isn't it?" More humility. Perhaps she'd go easy on him.

"We didn't agree to *when* I had to cash in the bet." She finished off the beer as she moved past him. "I'm going to help the band finish tearing down. If I were you, I'd keep your distance…"

"You're just going to leave me hanging?" Saul hoped she would, given the odds of them ever seeing each other again. She stopped and turned.

"Good point, give me your phone number."

"What?" Not what he'd expected.

"I'll need to be able to ring you whenever the muse strikes me."

Saul couldn't decide if he liked the way this was heading. "I don't have a pen."

"Here, ring my cell and I'll save your number." She told him her number and a few seconds later Saul imagined the signal traveling from his hand, half a mile away to a nearby tower, up into an orbiting satellite, and then back down to another phone within arm's reach.

"Got it." The last words she spoke before ducking back into the club.

"That went well." Until she spoke those words, Saul's senses had completely lost track of Aditi-Alhread.

"If by 'well' you mean you got nothing and I owe something – who knows what – then yes."

"I was able to set things up for later. It wasn't a total loss." Aditi-Alhread moved over to a hinged piece of the back fence Saul wouldn't have found if he'd been searching for it.

"I still don't get your interest in her."

"She can see the dead, obviously." She pulled the fence open, revealing the parking lot.

"And you can't?"

"Look, see that group of women over there?" She pointed to a gaggle of college freshman that some compact car just belched out next to the main entrance.

Saul sensed a trick question but went with it. "What's your point?"

"Why don't you go ask them to join us?"

"Really?"

"No, not really." She headed back into the rows of small cheap cars. "Just because I can talk to someone doesn't mean I can get them to do what I want. Mediums tend to have a following. Some bigger than others, but still. And any following is more than we had before."

"She didn't seem very interested in helping."

"We'll see her again."

"What makes you say that?" Saul asked.

"Besides her flirting with you?" She led them quickly to Saul's car.

"She wasn't flirting, so no, don't count that." Saul plopped down in his seat. He hadn't thought of Aimee in any sort of romantic way before that. Probably because he was out of practice, more possibly because nothing in her stare could compete with Aditi-Alhread's bottomless black eyes.

"Took your phone number." She said.

"So she could collect on a bet."

"Oh completely innocent." She turned to stare at the car keys in Saul's hand.

"Could be."

"If you say so." She looked up at his face and back down at the car keys, as if trying to start the car with her mind.

"Drop the flirting. Not flirting."

"You know I was an actual live breathing woman once… well, more than once."

Saul paused and skipped right over her claim she wasn't still living. Instead he registered that this woman noticed flirting, flirting that wasn't even there. And women who see flirting that isn't really there are usually jealous, even if they don't know it. And jealousy means she cared about him on some level… He looked at her lips then and wondered what they would taste like.

Saul shook it off. Wrong place wrong time.

"Regardless," Saul continued. "I think we can safely say she wasn't interested in me."

"You can say it."

"OK OK, putting that aside, what else makes you think we'll see her again?" Saul finally turned the key and put the car in reverse.

"Well I left Watts with her."

Saul put the car back into park.

CHAPTER 14

As a child, nothing made Aditi-Chic'Ya happier than to see the thin white mist resting over the crop mounds at dawn. Each morning she jumped over the network of warm canals and crouched down in the soft cool kinwa leaves and just sat there, listening to the gentle sounds of the lake surrounding her island and the occasional bray of one of the village llamas. When the sun rose high enough to start burning off the fog, she tended to the plants, plucking off the bugs and tearing off the dying edges. Some of the thick green leaves she would pick for dinner, some she would ignore and allow to sprout weeks later with the crimson flowers she harvested for their seed grains.

This described the greater part of her youth, broken up every year by the pilgrims who came to see the Father and Mother mountains. The lake itself nourished scores of villages, more than she could count, and they all welcomed the annual pilgrimages from those from lands less blessed. Aditi-Chic'Ya had only traveled to a handful of nearby lake islands, and never even as far as the actual mainland, so she looked forward to those with tales of realms beyond the light blue waters of her home.

At age ten her family gave shelter to one of the questing families, including their son, Kigal-Huallpa. Over evening meals they spoke of their lives in the thick forests to the west, and the rains that fell for months in a row. One visit turned into two, and before long the coming of the summer winds marked a regular annual stay.

Initially Aditi-Chic'Ya referred to the scrawny child as 'stick boy,' and stayed late in the fields to avoid his endless questions. When he found her in the mounds, she swam to the reeds. But no matter how far she ran or swam, or how long she hid, Kigal-Huallpa kept searching until he caught her eye.

When she turned fifteen, her father took her to a fishing family on the other side of the island and introduced her to her future husband. Aditi-Chic'Ya said nothing. Later that night she said nothing. Two weeks before the wedding date, the first warm night of the year, she ran to the edge of the island and looked for the slow moving rafts of the pilgrims. Kigal-Huallpa had grown enough that 'stick boy' no longer seemed to apply, and this time she did not run from him. She led him away from his parents and took him to the reed meadows, and they stayed there until the next morning.

She didn't see him again until her own children were in their teens. His family had long ago stopped coming, and now his visits were about gathering pottery and bringing back rocks with metals in them. He presented himself politely to her husband and children and left them small bags of spices from the rainforest. "A friend of the family" he called himself, which was true enough Aditi-Chic'Ya never felt the need to talk about it, and her husband never felt the need to ask.

For eight more years Kigal-Huallpa brought them treats, stories, and company. They fed him, gave him a warm place to sleep, and invited him back. In all that time he never touched Aditi-Chic'Ya nor made any move to do so, but each trip he made sure her eyes met his at least once when no one else was around.

On his final visit he found her washing the grain seeds in the lake. One look and the small jar of peppers slipped from his fingers and smashed to the ground. Pronounced wrinkles from the sides of her mouth cut into her once soft cheeks, now sunken and pale. Swollen eyelids crowded orbs he'd never seen so dull. The Withering, he knew, had no cure, and could last for weeks or years before claiming its prize.

From then on Kigal-Huallpa stayed quietly by her side. As her children and her husband found more and more excuses to stay out at the mounds or fishing the lake, Kigal-Huallpa brought her seed meal and drink. As she grew weaker, he bathed her, combed her hair, and changed her clothes. When her lips cracked and bled and her mouth could no longer take food, he held her head and gave her water from a wet cloth. One night, when her breathing slowed, he looked into her graying eyes one last time before they closed. When she didn't wake up, Kigal-Huallpa waited until the first hint of blue edged into the black of night, and carried her out to the mounds. He laid her down there, setting her in a bed of red kinwa flowers under a blanket of early morning mist.

CHAPTER 15

The sharp hiss as he twisted open another Coke bottle brought a wry smile to Dennis' weary face. More Coke meant more rum, and after four hours chanting and deciphering his notes and mixing all sorts of arcane crap into big bowls, Dennis deserved more rum.

Dennis hated dealing with what he called the busybodies of the Netherworld. At least his reputation kept them from pretending to pass off mundane information as clairvoyance.

The first ghost seer had given him hope, listening and searching and asking for all the right details, but ultimately unable to help him. The second was in it only for the sacrifice, and Dennis nearly bound him out of spite. Three and four had the courtesy not to even fake it, and now, number five finally gave Dennis something he needed.

This one hadn't been in the museum itself, of course, but did spend most of her time in one of the bigger evidence rooms of Scotland Yard. Mixed with just the right incense and meditation techniques, if she did her part right it would play in Dennis' head almost as good as seeing the security tapes on an actual monitor. The rum wouldn't hurt either.

"Oh spirit." Blah blah. Dennis really hated some of the language this business forced him to use, but protocol was protocol. Given that he was lucky to have gotten this ritual right in the first place, he had nowhere near the talent to deviate from the official formula. "Please grant me the vision I request and require." He took a modicum of joy releasing a small belch after the last sentence.

The hints of afterimages on his eyelids wandered aimlessly for a moment, and then suddenly jerked, twisted, and started to take shape. Without dwelling on the mechanics, Dennis found himself floating above a black and white image of a large room of the British Museum. The vision curved around the edges, a result of the original camera's fish-eye lens.

He sat there a moment, uncertain how to proceed. Much as Dennis would have liked it, the seer didn't have a mouse or any knobs he could turn, and she almost certainly wouldn't want him touching them if she did. After a few trial and error mental exercises, he found that if he imagined a tape rolling fast forwarding, the image followed. Unfortunately he had no ability to make it turn or zoom in beyond what had actually been visible months earlier.

Several hours of video flew by with no change to the frame. Rows of tablets stayed in cases, scrolls remained pressed between thick sheets of UV resistant glass. Finally a dark image zipped by and Dennis had to invent a mental command for rewinding.

At first, Aditi seemed like a tourist who'd just been locked in after hours. She didn't move like a cat-burglar, and she certainly didn't dress like one. Watching her wander around studying the displays, Dennis made a mental note to research later why she wore an old uniform.

In the first few moments, he took some small sadistic glee in the fact he wasn't immediately attracted to her. It gave him strength to know she'd have no seduction powers, realized or subconscious, over him. All that faded when she glanced up at an exhibit near enough to the camera so Dennis could see her eyes. Wow, now those were compelling.

Motion blurred. He blinked and drew back. Since the image contained no audio, his Hollywood-conditioned brain didn't understand for a moment how someone could shove their hand through a wall of glass without any sound. It looked like she broke it with no thought at all. No fear for the thick shards that sliced near her shins. No concern about anything in the display case.

She pulled out tablet after tablet, touching each one and staring, like a teenager struggling in a high school language class. Very soon she had three categories – tablets she didn't bother to take out of their cases, tablets she took out, glanced at, and neatly set aside, and tablets she laid out in a series of rows on the floor.

Well crap. Now that Dennis knew what she was reading, he had no way of actually knowing what she was reading. He had hoped he'd be able to see the labels or a pamphlet or something. Instead he got scribbles and barely visible lines cut in rock. That wasn't going to look good in a report.

The seer sensed his frustration, and communicated that for an additional offering of milk and blood, she'd see if Scotland Yard had already done the translating somewhere. She of course already knew that they had.

"You're killing me here." He said, pulling out of the trance and reaching for the knife he'd used to cut himself all night. Dennis felt bled dry already, but knew better than to fight the order of things, particularly dead things. That was for people like his boss.

A few hours later, Dennis smiled again at the receptionist to confirm she couldn't have been any less interested in him. To remove all doubt, she went beyond casual indifference and on to an actual scowl. Boredom appealed to her more than talking to him. That left Dennis to choose between a *People*, *Sports Illustrated*, or *Science Digest* on the table nearby.

Instead he took in the waiting room again, contrasting its white, cold, almost antiseptic feel to Seamus' brown, cold, almost antiseptic feeling timber-frame bungalow slash funeral parlor. Most people wouldn't have seen the link, but then, most people didn't work for a necromancer.

Technically, Dennis counted as a necromancer too, just not a very good one. In addition to contacting seers, he could do a basic random summoning on his own if someone handed him a true name, and when he concentrated he could sense spirits nearby, but sometimes Seamus did things to or with the dead that Dennis couldn't even fathom. Jack, on the other hand, Jack was just a big ex-doorman with a sense of honor far outreaching his sense of morality, and absolutely no interest in anything "occult" or anything related to the memories of others. Keep with the basic cash exchanges on a regular basis and he'd throw himself on a grenade for you – or in this case, stay downstairs with the car scanning for any sign of Aditi, which, if she found him, was about the same thing.

The door finally opened. Dennis resisted the urge to stand, knowing that a good five minutes more would pass before all the small talk, handshakes and back slaps ended and Seamus would acknowledge his existence. Seamus was all about the customer, particularly if they were the type who could afford becoming a regular. Those who couldn't afford repeat purchases, well, sometimes Seamus gave them something good in hopes word of mouth would spread, and sometimes he gave them something from his 'special' one-way-trip collection so he wouldn't have to worry about them again.

The particular couple that came out that afternoon – old money, Dennis knew – were on their third big purchase, and Seamus, in return, gave them his undivided attention until they passed completely out of sight and sound range. Seamus turned back into his office without saying a word, leaving his door open as the only sign Dennis should follow.

"Hey boss I…" Dennis stopped when Seamus raised his hand to 'shush' him. The gold, silver, platinum, and jewel-encrusted vials still sat in their display case on the glass-topped desk. Seamus came up with the transparent desk idea himself so he could watch new clients and make sure they didn't try to pull any weapons under the table. Brilliant.

Seamus carefully slid the trays into the sleek metal vault in the corner and then stood and smoothed out his suit. "What?" He said flatly.

"More on that Royal Library of Ashurbanipal thing boss." Dennis hesitated, unsure if he should continue or wait for the command.

"And?" Seamus snapped, answering Dennis' question. In a way the idea of Seamus eternally tortured for this business venture made Dennis happy enough to not care that the same fate probably waited for him.

"So," Dennis continued. "lots of things in that museum and in the library, but bottom line, all the stuff she focused on was all stuff related to the same story. The original tablets of the *Epic of Gilgamesh*."

Seamus scratched his whiskers. "Anything else?"

"Uh," Dennis checked his notes. "Only that she'd also pulled out any tablets related to the story, or commenting on the story, expanding on the story, related to the original Sumerian myths, etc."

Seamus walked over to the window and leaned against the wall. "I wished you'd told me that the first time."

"Sir the cops hadn't even figured that much out…"

"Yes yes." Seamus cut him off again. "So, just so you know, since you will be intimately involved with this situation soon, she's after a man called Nappy. Oh, so nick-named because he sleeps a lot, not because of the derogatory hair reference."

"Do we know his real name?" Dennis asked the question to stall for time while his fingers frantically searched his pockets for something to write with. He found the business end of a broken pencil in his jacket just in time.

"Yes I do." Seamus rolled his eyes. He looked forward to the day he could test if Dennis would make a better employee from the other side of the Barrier. "It's Ut-Napishtim." He spelled it, twice, and then suffered through Dennis reading it back to him.

Seamus spoke again, no longer caring if Dennis got it all down. "She wants him for the same reason I did when I went looking for him last year in the islands of Bahrain." Seamus seemed proud of himself and eager to show how much more he knew than Dennis. Dennis nearly broke the pencil with frustration as he scribbled hasty notes. "The most common texts say he was taken to the island of Dilmun, but if she's looking for him on the Western coast of the US, then the truth is far further to the original interpretation of "the place where the sun rises," since we're far east, across the sea, in relation to where they were."

"If you don't mind me asking sir," and really, thought Dennis, screw you if you do mind, "How is this Nappy guy going to help her?"

"He has something she wants. The holy grail of necromancy, so to speak, which is something I... something we need much much more than she does."

"So, find him first, kill him and ransack his house then?" Dennis expected Seamus to counter with some sort of way to use the slave spirits to do it, but he thought he'd offer up the chance to take the credit for pointing Jack at some unsuspecting man's house.

"No, focus on keeping Aditi subdued instead."

"You sure boss? Killing this guy seems a lot easier, and quicker." Especially because Jack would be doing the work.

"Oh you can't kill him." Seamus said, clearly baiting Dennis.

"Already dead?" Dennis figured it was as good a guess as any.

"No." Seamus shook his head. "Immortal."

CHAPTER 16

"When you say you left Watts with her, what do you mean exactly?" Saul stared out into the parking lot as he spoke.

"Just what I said." Aditi-Alhread reached over and put her hand on his shoulder. "Could we drive while we have this conversation?"

Saul felt like shouting 'hell no!' until she followed it up with a gentle, "Please?"

He put the car back into gear and headed back to the highway that led through town. The light mist streaked across the windshield and he let it form tiny streams that somehow flowed up and against gravity. Again in the car. Again her ordering him to drive when he didn't want to. A vision of the green-tie man twisted and motionless in a glittering pool of dark red flashed by for an instant. He forced it away and it came back twice more until his will won out and he finally saw only the road in front of him.

"Maybe," Saul hesitated, unsure how to continue. "Maybe you could expand on that, a little bit. How do you know Watts? How do you even know about Watts?"

"He was new." She replied. "Whenever you hear about anyone sticking around – hauntings, ghosts – those are people who've just recently come up from animals. They are the First Lifers, confused, frightened, uncertain what the Netherworld is or its purpose. They cling to their history, shallow though it may be, holding to the place or the event that affected them most in life. Often times it is the scene of their death, but could also be the death of another, or a birth, or a rape or the discovery of a long sought treasure.

"In all cases an event that touched them deep enough to etch itself on their soul, guiding the rest of their life as the first seed of their morality or their psychosis. None of these souls can cross back over to your side, like I have, but many can beat against or push the Barrier, causing waves in the world of the Living. Like, someone trying to reach through a big sheet of stretched clear rubber or something."

"OK, good, but not answering the question."

"You and that patrol were easily the most significant part of Watts' life, such as it was. So he was, and is, linked to you." She sighed. "He panicked after he died. Ran around screaming, yelling for help. Honestly I just wanted to shut him up at first…"

Saul felt unable to sit still. His skin burned hot, itchy, and the air in the car seemed suddenly stale.

"When I finally calmed him down," she continued, "he asked me to help you."

"What? Why? Why did he think I needed help?"

"Well, think about it, there were a lot of Iraqi First Lifers hanging around too."

"And?"

"And some of them had gathered to watch the ambush that went along with that bomb." She turned to face him. He glanced over as often as he could while remaining in his lane.

"What are you talking about? What ambush?"

"Exactly." She smirked a little when she said it, and with just enough feminine charm that Saul involuntarily smiled back with her, but only for an instant.

A second later her meaning got through to him. Saul struggled to remember the scene of Watts' death – the surroundings, the people, any hints of a planned ambush – but his memory brought up nothing but images of Watts' and the medic who tried for a few token minutes to help him.

"So what if an Iraqi First Lifer had asked for your help? Would you have helped one of them?"

Aditi-Alhread cocked her head to one side, genuinely taken aback.

"You know," she finally said in a voice quieter than usual. "I might have, at first, if they'd promised me a way to find the library. And if they spoke one of the languages I knew."

"Why do you say 'at first'?" A car behind them flashed its bright lights, informing Saul that he was driving slower than the speed limit. Saul moved to the right lane, where erratic speeds and swerving drew less attention. His hands shuffled back and forth on the steering wheel.

"If you've ever heard the phrase that eyes are the gateways to the soul, it's true. Literally. I can see your soul and everything in it when I look into your eyes or anyone else's." She chuckled. "It makes it a lot easier figuring out who to help and who to toss through a window." She reached out and rested her hand on his arm. He tensed a bit and she withdrew it. "Anyway, Watts said you were the smartest person he knew and could help me if I helped you."

Saul felt the urge to yell, or hit something, or yell while hitting something. But he didn't feel anger. Instead he felt energy, wild and struggling to do something outside the damn car. They drove in silence, and he grew more and more visibly restless.

"Hey you know what?" Saul's tone bordered on yelling. "I think maybe right now…"

"Pull over." She interrupted him while watching the tree line, or the roads beyond it, Saul couldn't tell.

"Hey! I was talking."

"I know you were Saul," her voice remained calm, which both frustrated and soothed Saul at the same time, dispersing the hindered energy into something more mental than physical. "You're overwhelmed, I get it. So you're going to drop me off here and then go back and get some rest."

At that moment Saul noticed that the sky above the treetops had brightened with a growing blue edge. They'd been out all night.

"What are you going to do?" Saul's anxiety moved into temporary remission, overcome by curiosity.

"Well I'm going to wait, mostly. You clearly need time to process this, you seem annoyed with me, and I don't think you believe me." She gripped the doorknob and glanced back. "But Saul, like I said, I need allies. I need your help, and now we're linked whether you believe it or not. So, I'll wait for you to see things the way I do."

"I don't know what makes you think I'm going to see anything any…"

"Sweet dreams." She pushed open the door and the sudden blast of noise and air made Saul jerk the wheel. The door slammed shut just as quickly, followed by instant quiet. He scanned his rearview mirror and saw no trace of her. If she was lying or delusional… if she was living or mortal, then she just hit the ground at speeds that probably ended all that.

Something in the deliberateness of the act compelled Saul to keep driving. If she had just killed herself, it wasn't his fault. He had one suicide to blame himself for already, and one was enough.

Skepticism nestled up against Saul's neck on the drive back. There were too many coincidences in Iraq, true, but nothing about it had to have been supernatural. He saw two bodies lying at the base of a very tall building, also true, but had he actually seen them hit the ground? Could Aditi-Alhread's part been staged? And the black goo wasn't anything a street magician couldn't do, or a good chemistry teacher probably. In the brightness of the morning Saul found it a lot harder to believe anything she'd told him. How many of these things were specters of some sort of mental trauma he'd brought back from the desert?

He remembered Watt's body bent backwards from the turret and over the roof of the Humvee, face perfectly white, neck perfectly red with a swath of black where the shrapnel stuck out. Barely bigger than a silver dollar, wedged in his jawbone, it would have been nothing but a fun story to tell if it hadn't sliced the jugular on the way to the jaw. Just one inch higher is all it would have taken.

Then there was the chaplain speaking words Saul didn't remember over the small shrine made up of Watt's helmet resting on the butt of his rifle stuck down between his boots. Saul had stayed up until midnight the night before polishing those boots until they shone as smooth as glass.

All those things were real. Saul repeated it to himself a few times. Watts was gone. He was not hanging out with some rock girl with a 1950's fashion fetish in a bar.

Although, Saul thought, if Watts had been alive that did make a certain amount of sense.

But Watts wasn't alive. Watts wasn't with anyone. No one was talking to Watts. If someone could talk to Watts then they could talk to Nicole…

Just thinking her name stung Saul somewhere deep in his stomach. Those were thoughts best left boarded up or buried somewhere. He was not going to allow them to return.

Somewhere between the morning rush hour and lunch Saul pulled into the familiar area around the hotel. The road shifted from a trench cut through hills and forest to one bordered by gas stations and fast food franchises. The light inside a nearby Chevron sign blinked off as he passed, having somehow sensed the suns first rays peeking over the hills.

He realized he'd missed his window to call Rose before school. He wanted to hear her say she loved him and missed him. Or maybe to hear her laugh. Her giggling laugh wasn't quite as pure as her pre-K days, but the playful light tones still forced a warm smile whenever it happened. He struggled to remember the last time he'd heard it and came up with nothing. His cell phone felt heavy suddenly, holding the knot of dark potential that a call would end unfavorably, or worse yet be ignored entirely.

When he parked in his usual spot, his back ached from sitting in the same position for so long, even without ceramic body armor plates or a Kevlar helmet weighing down his spine. He got out, looped around and passed through the main lobby hoping to scrounge free continental breakfast leftovers on the way to his room. Once he glanced at the clock above the check-in counter he wasn't surprised to find the cereal dispensers, fruit bowls, and heater lamps all clean and free of anything edible. On his way out he passed one of those tourist brochure stands. Nestled alongside all the pamphlets on the Point Defiance area and museums like the Museum of Glass, Saul noticed two "Ghost Hunt" options and a "Haunted Adventure." One promised the founder of a paranormal network as a tour guide, one provided thermal cameras and EMF detectors – whatever that meant – and the last offered nothing more than millions of dollars of live actors and animatronics. Before heading back Saul wondered briefly if any of the tours included someone surviving a twenty story free fall onto hard flat concrete.

When he reached his room, he pondered if he should cautiously open the door or search for uninvited men in suits who called themselves Housekeeping, but fatigue drove his body inside without asking for his brain's opinion on the matter.

He sat down on the edge of the bed, far too wound up to even pretend to rest. He figured it best to go for another run, which he hoped would push his body so far he would crash right afterwards. Instead, after twenty minutes out along random roads and twenty minutes back, after resting and stretching and a few sets of push-ups and sit-ups, and after a quick shower, Saul reached a stage others called "too tired to sleep."

Nicole used that expression around Rose one night and the little shite repeated it any time they caught her talking to herself in her bed instead of sleeping. Rose hated going to bed at night, afraid of what amazing thing she would miss out on if she closed her eyes for one single instant. Saul knew with a hidden amount of pride that this trend came from his side of the gene pool. He'd always secretly believed that sleep-deprived people were the ones getting the most out of life, and resented anyone who had the foresight or ability to go to bed early. Whenever he talked about Rose's nocturnal habits, he used to tell people that watching her fight sleep was like watching Captain Kirk resist if he were held prisoner on the planet Ambien.

Saul felt an urge to call Aditi-Alhread and talk to her, but if she had any sort of phone she'd never told him about it. Instead he read a few chapters in another old half-price science fiction novel. Unable to focus on the words enough to retain what he was reading, he eventually gave in and settled on a few hours racking up more pay-per-view charges. After a very late lunch purchased entirely from vending machines, he picked up his cell phone and hit the "dial" button twice.

He immediately cursed himself and the automatic caller-ID built into cell phones. Hanging up now would just make him look stupid.

"Hello?" A female voice near what he expected, but different enough that he lost his opportunity to think of something clever while he mentally confirmed the right person answered.

"Hi, uh, this is Saul. The guy you won the bet from last night."

"Oh, right," Aimee's accent significantly less pronounced, but still there. "I haven't actually decided your sentence yet, plus I'm a little busy right now."

"Yeah actually I wanted to ask you a few questions." It was a good thing Saul wasn't trying to hit on her, because this felt like a disaster. "Are you busy?"

"I'll give you a hint, I'm wearing matching industrial lime green and I only answered the phone as an excuse to put another two minutes between me and Mr. Kowalski's bedpan." Come to think of it, the white noise of a busy place with an intercom did hover back behind her voice.

"Still hanging on to that nurse story are you?"

"Two minutes, then I gotta go. What's up?"

Saul hated time pressure on telephones, and web cameras, and emails. Someday he'd be able to sit as his own desk with his own stuff and talk and surf and anything else he wanted until he passed out from exhaustion.

"That woman, the one who was with me…"

"Aditi-Alhread, yeah, go on."

"She told me last night that she left something with you." Saul hesitated, feeling like a complete idiot.

"I'm not sure I know what you mean."

"OK so really she said she left someone with you. An old friend of mine. She said she introduced you two."

"You understand the words coming out of your mouth don't you?" Her voice didn't sound annoyed, which Saul thought a good sign, but it had lost some of the upbeat energy.

"Yeah I know." He hesitated. "And that thing about seeing colors. She told you they weren't just colors didn't she?"

Her turn to delay responding.

"OK look," she said at last. "This isn't a conversation we can have in two minutes. But my shift ends at twelve thirty. In the morning. Since you're currently unfettered by family I trust that won't be a problem?"

He hesitated, wondering if Aimee was right.

"Oh God you don't live with your mother do you?" She asked.

"No." Saul thought for a moment of little frilly princess dresses and buying stuffed animals in international airports and the smell of baby powder as part of a hug goodnight. "No you're right. I'm all alone. Shouldn't be a problem."

She told him the name of the hospital and they agreed to meet in the main lobby. Saul felt tired now, really tired, physically as well as mentally. He set an alarm, stripped down and slid under the covers.

Saul took a moment to soak in the softness around him. He wondered how many people took beds for granted – simple mattresses instead of moldy sagging cots, fresh cotton sheets instead of dusty Nylon sleeping bags, and a warm rug or carpet to step on first thing in the morning instead of cold concrete littered with fresh rat turds.

It took him less than five minutes from the time his head sunk into the pillow to fall into a deep sleep.

Then Saul went to Hell.

CHAPTER 17

It wasn't a dream. Too many details for a dream. All the inputs that the brain just gets to "know" in a dream were coming in as regularly firing nerve impulses. Body aches from his run, grogginess, several layers of sounds, all far more than the normally streamlined dreamscape. And none of it made any sense.

He stood high up on the edge of a sheer cliff looking down on a massive valley. The scene was mostly dark and lit only by a faint reddish-purple glow from a cloudless, starless sky. Hard stone spread out in all directions, with spires and pillars twisting horribly up towards something best described as the absence of the heavens.

Saul noticed that shadowy figures moved down below with sounds muted by a light wind echoing across the vale. Several miles away, breaking up the grayness of the earth, a massive jet-black structure jutted up with a wicked array of thin towers that ended in spikes or otherwise sharp edges. Looking at it longer, it appeared to Saul to be some sort of large city, abandoned by the looks of it, with no lights or obvious movement inside its walls.

Saul turned his attentions to more immediate surroundings. The cliff would be easy for an experienced climber, but challenging and easily fatal to someone with no practice or equipment, which included Saul. It didn't help that he wore only a T-shirt and some flannel pajama pants. On another spur of the cliff, he thought he saw the top half of a figure silhouetted for an instant before it eased its way down another trail and disappeared down the far side where Saul couldn't see it. Saul turned back to the cliff, slipped his bare foot over the edge and tested the nearest ledge.

"No Saul," He recognized Aditi-Alhread's voice, although he didn't see her nearby. "We can't go down into the Valley of Souls. You didn't bring an offering, and I'm not welcome there."

He pulled his foot back and looked around. There, in the shadows up against the stone to his left, only the red of her corporal stripes and the white of her face giving away her position.

"You're going to say this is the real Hell, aren't you?" Saul said it without emotion.

"Do I believe in actual Hell? One's own mind is actual enough." She spoke in a strange lilt, and Saul realized she was imitating someone's voice. "C.S. Lewis said that."

She walked into the light and continued. "This is technically just the Netherworld, or rather, the far far edge of the Netherworld, neither good nor bad, except for what its people make of it. I'm paraphrasing, but Lewis also said that the living don't realize their own lives because they can escape from themselves. They can look out a window, smoke a cigarette, take a nap... but when there is nothing left, no body, no books, no landscape, no sounds and no drugs, when it is just your soul, well, then it is as actual a Hell as a coffin is to a man buried alive."

Saul wanted to tell her this was all obviously a dream, but since it obviously wasn't, he found himself incapable of such a bold faced lie. She walked up beside him and looked at the gloomy countryside below.

"What do people do here?" Saul finally asked.

"Primarily, they examine their most recent lives, and how those lives mix with the ones before it. It is a time of contemplation, not socialization, or vengeance, or interaction with the living."

"So no damnation, no reward?" As Saul spoke he caught more movement out of the corner of his eye. There were others up here, lurking in other shadows. The nearest one appeared to be a man focused on something he carried in his hands. Beyond him and to his left, walked a couple, teenagers Saul guessed, both wearing thin black veils over their faces.

"The Netherworld is a place to bask in the warmth of accomplishments and hardships overcome, or to wallow in the cold and harsh methods used to get there." Aditi-Alhread didn't look up from the valley, and something in her face indicated concern at whatever she saw. "It is rare to see the quiet soul who will meet your gaze, smiling with inner calm at where they just came from. The air of the Netherworld fills instead with soft sobs and echoing wails of those hiding their faces behind rocks and stones. All in the hopes that it shapes them for the better the next time… their next chance."

Saul realized that the man carrying the object in his hands was facing toward him now instead of his prize. Saul took a half step closer and stared back, unable to stop, his mind struggling to match what he saw with what he could possibly be seeing. The man's face was a bare skull, void of flesh and eyes, but still topped with hair and retaining both ears. In his hands he stretched out what looked like a flap of leather, but which turned out to be his actual face, complete with moving eyes, that he held out in front of himself so he could see.

"Oh my God!" Saul toppled backwards and Aditi-Alhread stopped him hard, barely keeping him from flying off into the darkness below.

"No worries. He's no different from the others." She whispered in his ear. "Another trait of First Lifers is that when they finally do find their way here, they tend to take on the most extravagant forms – how they died, faceless zombie, flaming shadow, tortured corpse, winged martyr…"

"OK OK, but damn." Saul righted himself, but kept his eyes on the face held out at arm's length.

"Not exactly damned."

"Right, Right." Saul pointed at the veiled couple, who seemed closer, although he hadn't seen them move. "Same with them?"

"It's about time to go Saul." She pulled lightly on his arm.

"Yeah, OK." He turned to follow her, and then stopped. "Wait. Did you not want to tell me about those two?"

She turned, less enthusiastic than before. "No, I don't."

"Can I ask why?"

Her voice turned cold. "They're suicides Saul."

"So?" He glanced at them again, fixated on the veils so think he wondered if it blinded them as well. He noticed the couple was definitely closer this time. That didn't matter just yet. "Oh shit. Something bad happens to suicides doesn't it?"

She pulled on him again, and by silent agreement he walked with her in exchange for information. She kept her voice lower than normal.

"The rumor is that they spend more time in the Netherworld waiting for a new life, punished to think about those loved ones they left behind, and to remember that moment of perfect despair with perfect clarity." A few steps seemed to be all she needed. She stopped and looked into Saul's eyes, resting a hand on his cheek. "And worse, others believe them to be cursed, or damned, or both, and avoid them until their next death, or longer. Most won't speak to them until their next unlife, if ever.

"And yes, she's here, but you aren't going to see her."

Saul opened his mouth and forgot how to talk. He simply couldn't process any more information. Some part of him understood that the veiled couple had continued to move closer, and that same part of him understood that three more people had stepped up the hillside in front of him, and later, when he thought back on it, he would remember the comment about him not bringing an offering and her not being welcome here.

Seeming to sense Saul's pain, Aditi-Alhread gently moved her hand to his chest, and gave him a slight push. She stayed facing him, exactly as she had been, but the drone of a hotel air conditioner replaced the eerie distant howling he'd mistaken for wind.

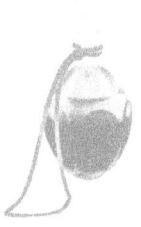

CHAPTER 18

They stood there in the hotel room, Aditi-Alhread staring at Saul, Saul staring at nothing, until, still half dazed, Saul moved to gather some clothes and get dressed.

"So, now I've seen things the way you do." He said while pulling on one of his two pairs of jeans. "Thanks for that. I guess."

"Do you want to talk about it?" Her voice seemed soft again, young, almost naïve. Saul knew better. This was just one aspect of one life she could pull forward when she needed it.

As he tossed a sweatshirt over his head he wanted to pop off a quick "I gotta see a girl" before storming out the door without looking back. That's how he saw it in his head. That's how it would have worked on TV for sure. It just sounded so cool for some reason. But he knew he wasn't the type to pull that sort of line off. Instead he stopped just shy of leaving and turned to face her.

"It's eleven thirty, and I told Aimee I'd meet her at twelve thirty." He said. "But I don't know where I'm going exactly, so I thought I'd go early."

"Would you like me to go with you?"

Saul shook his head and meant to say "no" very quietly, but he ended up just mouthing the word. He marveled for a moment how much his life had changed in so short a time. High school punk-ass chump didn't seem too long ago, nor did either of his last two deployments. Now he could tell people he'd been to Hell and back because he'd agreed to help a woman he barely knew. Then would come the barrage of questions about what made her so special.

"Look," he started. "I'll help you, OK, but, tonight I'm just going to be away from you for a little while. You can stay here if you want." He knew she wouldn't. "I shouldn't be gone that long." He knew he would. He planned on staying away as long as he could.

She stood, perfect posture, hands crossed in front of her lap, head tilted slightly down, combining the looks of innocence, guilt, and patient understanding. Saul wanted to kiss her and throw something heavy at her, but he was unclear in what order.

"Right." Saul took a breath. "I'll be back." He pulled out his car keys, opened the door and stepped outside.

"Saul wait!" Her voice bit like the orders of a First Sergeant. Saul stopped in his tracks, just outside, and about a foot past the line of white powder crossing the doorway. He looked for whatever upset her, and met Jack's gaze just as a massive hand clamped around his forearm.

Aditi-Alhread threw herself at the door like an enraged tiger, and smashed flat like she'd barreled into a wall of bullet-proof glass. She crouched down, fingers curled into claws, growling like something far worse than an enraged tiger.

"If you could move him a little further from the doorway please Jack." Saul recognized the sleazy guy with too much jewelry and allowed the bigger man to move him a few steps further towards the parking lot. Saul actually reached for the 9mm he'd worn on his thigh throughout the second deployment, and then remembered he'd turned that in the instant he got off the plane.

Dennis stepped forward and put himself between Saul and his room. Dennis pointed to the white line and Saul noticed that the man had added another large gold ring to each hand. "Kosher salt crossed with cold iron nails." He said. "A simple spice to us, absolutely impervious to spirits. Don't even need an incantation. Sprinkle it down and you're done. Easy stuff."

Saul noted that they hadn't replaced their third member, and the more he studied Dennis the less it seemed like he'd ever been in a real fight. So that meant just one person to worry about, the one who gripped his shoulder tightly with his left hand, and kept his right hand out of sight. That probably meant there could be a knife or a stick involved if things got stupid, maybe even a gun. Saul figured he hadn't been stupid in a while and he was probably overdue.

"Right," Dennis said, "Let's go." He pointed at a dark (of course) SUV in the parking lot. Aditi-Alhread stood just inside the doorway now, again perfectly straight, again head tilted slightly down, but now she seethed with something feral, and it looked terrifying.

"So that little line is all that keeps her from crossing?" Saul asked, resisting Jack's arm enough to make him pause.

"I just said that didn't I?" Dennis' voice stayed bitter as he struggled not to look at her over his shoulder. Truth be told his hands were shaking and he was horrified that he'd forgotten something and at any moment would be gutted from behind.

"Did you line the whole building with it or just the doorway?" Saul said, pretending to be genuinely curious.

Dennis whipped around. He *had* forgotten something. Aditi-Alhread threw herself at the wall adjoining the next room. The first hit crushed the drywall and cracked one of the studs.

"Oh crap." Dennis said. Saul had actually expected her to just make a run for the bathroom window, but either way, as soon as she moved he had backed away from Jack and threw his arm up in the air. The combination was just enough to loosen Jack's grip and Saul flew back and away and in between two parked cars, smashing his head against a bumper in the process. Jack quickly closed the gap.

Ignoring the stinging in the back of his head, Saul scrambled out of reach and sprinted through the parking lot. He let survival instinct run on auto pilot since he figured they couldn't hurt Aditi-Alhread if he left her behind.

Behind him, she charged again, and another loud crack signaled the one stud breaking in half and a second one splintering. Even though the adjacent room appeared vacant, lights were coming on all across that wing of the hotel.

"Jack!" Dennis was halfway to the SUV. Jack heard Dennis and ignored him. Maybe he didn't realize that one word was all the help or opportunity he was going to get from Dennis. Maybe he was such a poor judge of character that he thought his supervisor might try to help or possibly look for him later. Instead, Dennis pulled out of the parking lot with the SUV lights off, hoping no one got his license as he left.

Probably in a normal sprint, Saul's assessment that he could outrun someone as big as Jack would have been right. But that assessment came without knowing how many hours Jack put in the gym every morning. At night, without running shoes and still dizzy from hitting his head, Saul barely kept his lead, and if he stumbled once, it was over.

Shortly past the parking lot Saul had the option of turning left onto a well-lit street or turning right into a small patch of woods behind the strip malls. The street meant the safety of more witnesses, the woods gave him every other option but safety. The few seconds of running gave Saul enough time to clear his mind and override his body's flight reflex. With a curse and a vow, he cut sharply into the tree line and started looking for ways to hurt his pursuer.

Nearby street lights cut through the spaces in the limbs above, casting shadows and pools of light in a confusing pattern that left Saul guessing where the ground was. Jack dropped back a little, but not enough. Saul heard an even pace and steady breathing just behind him, waiting for the slightest misstep. This chase wasn't going to last. Saul's chest already burned and the ache in his head throbbed with every heartbeat.

Having already passed the Event Horizon of Stupidity, Saul resolved to try one of those moves he learned during a combatives class and never thought he'd use again. Without warning – that was the point – he turned, dropped to his knees and stuck his arm out towards Jack. Jack naturally stumbled forward until Saul's arm was between his legs. Using Jack's momentum, Saul lifted his arm into Jack's crotch and grabbed the back of his neck with his other hand as Jack flew overhead. The end result flipped the goliath and threw him to land hard on his back several feet away. As Saul watched for a reaction, Jack spun quickly and rose to all fours, now genuinely angry.

"I should beat your ass!" He roared and then stood. Jack took a deep breath, adjusted his pants, and took a step towards Saul. "But then I'd have to carry you."

Saul let his lungs suck in all the air they could while he smirked the tiniest smirk. Even if he got pounded to death, that flip… seeing that look on Jack's face as he flew overhead…

Back to reality. Saul glanced to the side, picking the path for another dash. When he turned back to confirm Jack's location, he saw the gun. Saul resigned himself at that moment to at least temporary captivity. Gun beat no gun fifteen times out of ten.

Then something whipped by him. It sounded like a dog running through a patch of leaves, but the first image of it Saul saw was a dark blur flying towards Jack's face. The flash of the gunshot in such complete darkness combined with the deafening crack knocked Saul back, all senses turned off for a moment to reset themselves.

Hearing returned first, filled with screamed cursing and the growls of a very large, angry animal. Before his vision cleared he knew he'd find Aditi-Alhread bent over Jack's still warm body, but even obscured by a white-blue blind spot in the shape of a gunshot flash, what he first saw shocked him. She looked up from her kill, face caked in blood and dirt, disheveled hair, eyes wide like she didn't recognize him – like he was another threat.

"Whoa whoa! It's me! It's just me!" Saul raised his hands and tried not to move.

And then it ended. She rose from the crouch and as she did somehow humanity returned to her features. The blood stayed, but even her hair straightened itself out.

She walked over to him, not flushed, not breathing hard. Not breathing. "You have your wallet, yes?"

"Yeah, why?" Saul, on the other hand, shook with adrenalin.

"The police are likely already at the hotel and may come looking for whatever ran this way. You can't go back there, and you can't go home. They probably won't arrest you, but wherever you go now you have to suspect either the police or one of these thugs will be looking for you, or me with you."

Saul nodded, unclear of all the implications but agreeing to it in theory.

"Several people saw me at the hotel," Aditi-Alhread said. "So the cops won't be looking for you until they figure out that was your room, and then only as a witness."

Between deep breaths of air, Saul managed to reply. "So… how many people have you killed since… well, since all this?" He tried to calm himself with deeper breaths, with little effect. "I mean, should I expect this sort of thing every day?"

"Until people stop threatening the lives of my allies and until all the soul eaters are dead, probably yes."

"We…" He took in some more air. "In Iraq we used to send people who talked like that to the shrinks." He lightly touched the bump on the back of his head. A little blood, but not much. "Sometimes we even sent them home."

"Killing someone should be a life wracking event – something terrible and guilt stricken. I agree," she helped him to his feet. "But for me it isn't a new experience. Nothing is. Only reflections of things much older, things of the past."

"Are you hit?" He half expected her to laugh at him after he asked the question.

"Nope. Clean miss."

She let him rest a few minutes, and as the rush drained from his body, a mild euphoria rose to take its place. They used to call that the "combat high," and while he would never say it out loud, sometimes he did miss it.

Some soldiers got hard-ons during their first gunfight. Saul never had, but he did generally feel more amorous afterwards, something that caused only frustration in a platoon of all males.

"You know," he said, without really hearing himself say it. "If you weren't covered in blood right now I could kiss you."

"There would be no point Saul. None at all."

Saul hadn't read surprise, or anger, or sadness, or pity, any of the emotions he might have expected when rejected by a member of the opposite gender.

"I think there could be a very big point to it." He replied, feeling a little desperate. "I'm not saying we'd work in the long run but…"

"Saul." Again emotionless. "There's something you need to understand that I just don't think you're getting." She picked up a stick and slowly jammed it through her hand and out the other side the same as if she was stabbing a pile of modeling clay. No blood trickled out at all, although Saul thought he saw a few drops of black before she absorbed them back into herself. "I feel no pain, no warmth from the touch of another. The pleasures of the flesh are reserved for those with flesh. I am only walking memories."

Saul nodded without saying a word. Something clicked off inside him the way it did any time a woman discarded him for any reason. It came with pain every time he'd ever done it, but also with a modicum of freedom. One less question to ask, one less thing to worry about, one less relationship that needed tending. He ignored that the situation also included one more step towards a long, lonely life.

"Besides, don't you have a date tonight?"

That was unexpected. He'd forgotten about Aimee, and twice over forgotten that he had mentioned the meeting to Aditi-Alhread.

"I just want to ask her a few questions." He said. If she seemed a little more jovial with this new turn, he'd fallen at least as far the other direction. It felt like pity. Unsolicited pity.

She moved over and tore off a sizeable piece of Jack's already torn shirt. When she found a dry patch, she used it to wipe some of the blood from her face. "Well, if you can, try and think of it as a date at some point during all that business."

"Why?" Saul scoffed. "I'm telling you, I don't think of her that way."

"OK," she turned her head, but Saul thought he glimpsed a smile before she did so. "But you did hum one of her songs the entire car ride back."

"Well that probably means I like her songs."

"Maybe."

He quickly changed the subject, and from there they devised a fairly simple plan involving Aditi-Alhread hiding Jack's body and then going back to distract any police officers in the area so Saul could get to his car and drive off. In the meantime, he made it a point not to get close enough to see what Jack's face looked like dead. He knew images like that stayed with him, and he already had plenty dancing behind his eyes struggling to get attention.

He did stay nearby a few minutes to rest, and watching her drag the body around and dig a shallow grave with her bare hands, Saul realized she'd quite clearly never seen an episode of *CSI*. Then again, the local police had probably never dealt with a killer who had no blood, no DNA, and wore the fingerprints of a dead woman, if any.

"How will you find me again?" Saul asked when his breathing finally stabilized.

"Same way I found you before, in your dreams."

Obviously.

The red and blue flashing lights cut through the forest long before Saul could make out the actual police cars surrounding his old room. He waited, as ordered, just on the edge of the parking lot while Aditi-Alhread circled around to a spot perpendicular to him.

From his vantage point he could see that the door to the room next to his lay off its hinges in two separate pieces on the concrete. Hotel guests continued to watch from the parking lot, and their numbers grew as more people spilled out of their rooms in various stages of sleepwear or hastily thrown on outfits. Saul eased up to one of the groups and placed one hand over his mouth. He figured he'd blend in more if he seemed concerned, and covering his mouth helped him not be recognized.

He waited, unsure exactly what his partner in crime would do for a distraction, but whatever he expected, it certainly wasn't what happened.

"Down! Down!"

"Halt!"

"Freeze dammit freeze! Freeze freeze!"

The shouts got closer accompanied by the sounds of startled civilians and someone hitting metal. The police shouted and drew weapons as Aditi-Alhread ran overhead, leaping from one police cruiser to the next. While she gave only an afterimage of black with red stripes, the pandemonium she left behind grew almost instantly. True to plan, almost every officer ran off after her, unknowing that they could chase her until dawn and she would never tire. The few that didn't give chase at least darted a few steps and watched towards her general direction.

Saul took a moment to look around. His home since he'd been in the states was now a crime scene, along with everything he owned but his car and the clothes on his back. He couldn't go visit his family, his daughter, couldn't go back to his military unit, at least not yet, and earlier the woman he'd risked his life for turned him down without hesitation. "Unfettered" Aimee had called it. Yes, that was a good way to put it. Saul felt absolutely without ties at that moment. A light evening mist fell on his face, and this time he understood the baptism.

"Excuse me. Pardon me." Saul pushed his way through the chaos and to his car. He gently moved one truly startled truck driver out of the way, who then in turn looked at him as if to say, "How can you possibly leave this?"

Saul smiled before ducking down into his seat. "I gotta see a girl."

CHAPTER 19

Turns out that for Saul, finding a hospital, even at midnight, wasn't actually that hard to do. Going inside that hospital and finding a specific nurse when he wasn't a patient or family member of a patient, proved a little harder. Saul spent around twenty minutes trying to decide which doors he could go through and which ones would get him in trouble as part of his search. Asking the ER group if they knew her didn't help either because a) they didn't and b) if you weren't a stab victim or suffering a heart attack, they really weren't interested.

Finally Aimee called his cell phone and guided him to the wing so she could meet him. Neither approached as they stood and recalibrated how the other person really looked and contrasted it with how images had been stored in their memories. Aimee wore her hair up in a tight bun, which by itself was enough to make Saul question if he was looking at the right person, plus a Mickey Mouse T-shirt, and she'd added a tiny diamond nose stud he hadn't noticed before either. Same pale face and red lipstick though, same guitar pick necklace, and as soon as the accent came out, the voice removed all doubt.

"You can follow my car. Call me if you get separated." Just like that. Then she moved out to the parking lot and he pulled in behind her maroon 10-year-old pickup truck with a covered back. In his mind he assumed she kept that thing around so she could carry instruments in the back. Any other options frightened him.

They went back to the same bar where she'd performed the night Saul met her, and she waited for him with hands in her jacket pockets until he caught up. She took him in the back way, past a doorman who greeted her by name, and then to a couple of stools in the corner opposite the bar. A waitress carrying a tray loaded with empty glasses rushed by immediately, greeted Aimee with "Hey Love" and a kiss on the cheek, and then rushed off again to bring them both a beer and a shot of tequila.

"So where's your friend tonight?" She asked. It startled Saul for a moment, having someone speak to him in a voice that didn't bypass background noise and somehow embed itself directly into his head.

"She's out. Well, actually, I left her running from the police."

"You just left her?"

"Actually she was distracting them so I could get away."

Aimee nodded her head slowly for a few seconds. "Right. Bank robbery?"

"Destroying a hotel room." He nodded back. "And a little murder."

"Really?" Her tone didn't indicate she thought this anything more than a joke, which was what he hoped for. "You killed someone then?"

"Oh no no. Just an accessory." The waitress brought them their drinks and Aimee pulled a five dollar bill out of her pocket.

"Five each." Aimee said without hesitating. "But you should tip Liz here too cause she's bloody awesome."

The waitress named Liz smiled, took Aimee's five, and then looked only at Saul until he handed her a five and three ones. She thanked him, calling him "Sweetie," and then told Aimee to wave whenever they were ready for refills.

"So, I wanted to ask you about a few things." Saul said, leaning forward to speak over the din of the crowd.

"Oh are you one of those guys who likes to ask a girl a bunch of sex questions before asking her out?" Aimee sipped her beer and left the shot temporarily untouched. "I mean that's OK as long as I get to ask them back. I never got much sex education from my mum, so, this isn't entirely uncommon for me."

Aimee sipped half the shot and continued. "Really the only thing she ever said to me was one day over breakfast she looked at me and said, 'Aimee, just remember your vagina is not a playground.'"

Saul choked a little on his beer, but managed to resist a coughing fit.

Aimee didn't slow down. "Which was ironic given that hers was practically a theme park."

Saul let a few small coughs come now, just to distract her for a second.

"Well," Saul replied after a bit. "As pleasant a distraction as that would probably be, no, sorry. I wanted to ask you about stuff far less interesting." He did wonder for a moment if Aimee had listened to her mother or not on the playground advice, but then forced himself back on topic.

"So, my friend…" Saul started.

"Aditi-Alhread, yes, do go on."

Saul paused. Talking to a new young female had never been his strong point even when the goal was something simple and biological. "Let me start over. Why don't you tell me about that seeing sounds as lights thing."

Aimee grinned and finished her shot. "I'm assuming you aren't looking for the simple definition are you? Which means you're asking an awful lot for a first date."

Saul wanted to argue the date point but realized she wasn't serious. He shivered, which he knew he always did whenever he got nervous. He body even went to all the trouble to disguise it as a chill for him, although an unfortunate side effect usually included a sudden need to pee. He decided to ignore it for now.

"Well, OK" Saul said. "I go first a little, how's that?"

"Right. Go on."

"I have a friend, who is dead. He died in Iraq. With me. And she said that she left him with you. As a spirit. Because she said you, I dunno, were a medium. Or could speak with him. Or something." He had hoped with each of those sentences that she would have heard enough and stopped him. Not so. She let him finish to the end and remained stoic to his comments.

"I think you might have mentioned that a bit on the phone." She took a small sip of beer.

"Not the dead part." He replied.

"No. I'd think that would have stood out."

"Probably."

She regarded him a moment, using her sips of beer to add dramatic pause. "Are you sure you wouldn't rather talk about vaginas?"

Saul grinned despite himself. "Well, I mean who wouldn't?" He laughed. "Tell you what, you sit here and think about it, while I go to the little soldiers' room."

She nodded and he left.

When he came back, for an instant he thought she might have left him. That would have made a lot of sense. In front of where Saul had been sitting now stood a larger man, slightly taller than Saul, wider at the shoulders to indicate a little natural muscle mass, but also showing the first signs of a gut that would bloom into something truly spectacular once he got married. He wore dirty blue jeans, an oversized sweatshirt, and a white baseball cap on backwards. His slight drunken swaying only added to the cliché.

"C'mon, tell me your name." The man slurred it to Aimee without noticing Saul behind him. Aimee caught Saul's eyes, winked, and subtly held up a hand to keep Saul near enough to listen but not close enough to interfere.

"I told you, it's Delores." Aimee told him.

"That's not your real name." Everything the man did took Herculean effort for him when combined with the concentration required not to pass out.

"Oh yes it is you silly!"

"Do you go to school here?" As the man spoke, Saul cringed. At least someone was doing worse than he was.

"Yes! I'm working my way through a radio-television-film degree, and I play in a band to pay for a one bedroom flat I share with two other guys." She aimed that last one right at Saul.

"Right on." The man said, and then his gaze fixed on Aimee's chest. She let it go on a second to see if it would come with more fun dialogue opportunities, but realized he was more than content to keep on just doing that.

"Maybe, you could not look so directly at my knockers." She said at last.

"Why not?" Still staring.

"Well it is a little distracting."

He looked up. "Well how do you think I feel!?!"

"Valid point." She said and gave Saul a nod conceding that round to the drunk man.

"Is your name really Delores?" the man asked.

"I told you it was didn't I?" She motioned Saul to step back a few steps. "If you don't believe me, you can ask my brother Chris."

Chris?

"Hey Chris!" She shouted past the drunk in Saul's direction.

Saul walked up debating if he should attempt some sort of accent to go with hers. He went with some horrible mish-mash of all the Monty Python he could remember from high school.

"Oh 'ello Delores, who's your new friend?" The drunk turned and struggled to focus on Saul.

Aimee winced at Saul's accent and then rolled with it. "You know, I'm not actually sure."

The man watched Saul a moment. "So you're her brother?"

"That's right." Saul replied.

"And her name's really Delores?"

"As sure as my name is Chris." Saul replied.

The man turned back to Aimee.

"Hey, would you like to have sex with me?" The man asked.

Aimee didn't respond. Something that blatant defied a clever retort.

"Cause if you did," he pointed to her crotch. "I would get so stuck in that that the only person who could pull me out of you would be the next king of England." Aimee grimaced through a grin.

The man turned back to Saul and said, "No offense bro."

"Wow. None taken." Saul lied between a fake smile. The sad thing, he realized, was that this was probably one of the drunk's standard lines, and not even cleverly tailored to her British accent. "But hey, it's almost curfew, and we've got an early cricket game tomorrow."

"Oh, right!" Aimee hopped off the stool and took Saul by the arm and spoke quickly to the man as she pulled Saul away. "Look, you rock, don't let anyone tell you otherwise. Ciao!"

She led Saul through the crowd, passed the bar, out the door and into the parking lot perhaps holding onto his arm a few seconds longer than she needed to. Saul felt both amused and cheated. He resolved to be less easily distracted for the rest of the night.

"Am I following you again?" Saul asked, stopping at his car. Aimee looked back and smiled as she nodded.

She led him closer to the Puget Sound campus and finally pulled in front of an indie all night coffee shop. Saul followed her in and realized what a different breed of people this was than the average soldier. Or drunken person. She caught his eye studying the people spread out in the stalls and tables and she leaned over and whispered to him.

"I like to come here at night. All the artsy types remind me why I have a real job."

Saul smirked, and then wondered how Aimee separated this crowd from someone who spent her weekends singing to an audience only slightly darker in clothing and paler in skin tone.

This time they grabbed an actual table, in as secluded an area as they were able to find. Saul waited at the table while Aimee grabbed a Latte for herself and, at his request, a hot chocolate for Saul. He found it pleasantly surprising that she didn't mention money this time.

"So to answer your question, yes." Aimee spoke as she sat. "He's a very pleasant fellow, and he speaks very highly of you. What else?"

It came so quickly that Saul stopped to review everything he'd said in order to verify she wasn't answering some other question he might have asked earlier and forgotten about. He realized for the first time she had turned her gaze away from his, and realized she had to have been talking about Watts.

"Can you see him now? Hear him now? Is he here?"

Her expression didn't change. "No, no, and I don't know." She sighed. "Back up. To me most sounds are just sounds like they are to everyone else. Every now and then a car horn might have a glint of yellow, or a bell might glow blue for a second, but otherwise, it is just like everyone else. Except for music. If I get into the music, if I let myself go with it, then what I see changes…"

She smiled then, a different kind of smile than Saul had seen on her before. Not teasing, not flirty, not sexy, but something more innocent. Her eyes lit up with child-like excitement, like she was getting to tell something she'd wanted to talk about for years.

"She was right about how I grew up, and how I saw them. But then in high school, one of my classmates mixed a little over two dozen Luminal with a bottle of wine. A few days after the funeral, one of my little special glowing mates had a disturbingly familiar voice." She leaned back, studying Saul's reaction. "So to skip a bit, the more I get into the music, the more clearly I can see them, hear them, interact with them. That's why I started writing my own."

They sat silently a few moments, neither touching their drinks.

Three quarters of a hot chocolate later, Saul spoke without looking up. "You know how it's always some little old lady who wants to contact her dead husband and gets swindled out of her life savings by someone who claims they can speak with 'those who have passed beyond'?"

A few seconds clicked by before Aimee replied. "You and two therapists are the only ones I've ever talked to about this." She rolled her eyes. "Sober anyway. I don't think dorm room Jaeger parties count."

"Probably not, no."

"Anyway, if you don't get stupid with it, I could probably let you off for only half your life savings. Special one-time offer."

"You mean talk to Watts? Through you?"

"Well nothing *Exorcist* or anything. You'd ask him questions, he'd tell me the answers, I tell you. Again though, nothing creepy or I quit."

Saul considered it. He wanted this, he really did, but feared something he would say or do next would screw everything up. Or worse yet, she'd break out laughing for him being such an idiot. "Well, do you need anything, you know, special?"

"You mean like a room full of candles, a lock of his hair and a circle of people holding hands?"

"Yes."

"No." She finished off her Latte. "Mediums use rooms filled with candles about as often as real people really lose their virginity in rooms filled with candles."

Saul wondered if she could tie any topic back to sex, but decided not to comment on it. "Right, well where should we…"

"Right here, if you can keep it from drawing attention."

"How?"

"I put on headphones, you make it look like you're talking to me, I talk back. As long as no one hears the actual words, we should be fine."

Saul took a moment to register her sincerity and run through in his mind what this conversation would look like. Finally he managed a single "OK" and then waited. Aimee pulled out an iPhone, plugged in some ear buds and flipped through a song list for what seemed to Saul to be an inordinate amount of time. Finally she leaned back with a small grin and closed her eyes.

Saul looked around wondering what to do and then tapped her on the arm. She held up one finger and mumbled, "Wait for it." A minute later her eyes opened and Saul noticed they seemed a little glazed over. She looked around to the empty spaces around Saul and nodded her head.

"Hey Kami-ko." She said to no one Saul could see. "Yeah right back at you mate." She turned to another open space. "No Love, not tonight, got a special gig going." She paused as if listening. "I'm glad you liked that one. I didn't think it would go over as well as it did but you were right, the crowd really seemed to like it."

Saul wondered how long this would continue, and whether or not if it was part of some act, or worse yet some delusion, how far she would take it. After a few more one way conversations with pockets of air, she finally seemed to remember Saul and locked on his eyes.

"OK, he's ready, what do you want to know?" She said. "And keep in mind that I'm listening to music, so I can't hear you, I'll only be able to hear his answers to whatever you say out loud."

"Right." The awkwardness of the situation rose a little. "Well, so, right. OK, so dude, just so I don't feel like a complete moron, say something to her that I'll know came from you."

After a short pause Aimee, focused on a space to Saul's left, said, "OK, so I can do this one of two ways, I can repeat what he says word for word, or I can give it to you in third person. So, if he says he's awesome, I can either say 'he says he's awesome," or I can say "he says, 'I'm awesome,'" in which case he'd be referring to himself."

This suddenly felt to Saul like working with a terp again, where the official rule was translate word for word. Most terps didn't take to that naturally, and it usually took some training. He told Aimee to go that way and after another pause she said, "then he says, 'now she's worth the squeeze.'" She turned to Saul, "and he's looking at me, whatever that means – although I think I have some idea."

Saul struggled not to grin and nodded. That seemed a pretty specific quote, specific enough it wouldn't be something she'd guess if this turned out to be some sort of scam or psychosis.

"So, Watts man, you've been hanging out near me this whole time?" Saul felt like he should be looking at the same space Aimee was, but imagined himself looking in the wrong spot entirely or not noticing if Watts moved and then having all the other ghosts laugh at him.

"He says, 'yeah man, until I met *this* hottie.'" She rolled her eyes but didn't make too big a deal out of it.

"And you've been watching me?"

Aimee let out a quick loud laugh and then forced it back down. "He says, 'yeah, and oh by the way I could have done without all those hotel pay-per-view moments.'" She turned back to Saul. "Would you like me to show you the hand gesture that went along with it?"

"Ah, no, thanks. I got it." Saul felt himself blushing, or what he felt blushing must feel like if he'd ever done it before. He glanced around the coffee shop. No one seemed to think Saul's conversation with Aimee the least bit extraordinary, although he did catch a quick glance from a woman reading Nietzsche two tables over.

"Maybe we should continue this later." Saul said. He wasn't so much worried what others nearby might think, as he was completely at a loss for what to say to Watts, assuming this really was Watts. "How's the dead life treating you?" and quotes from the movie *Poltergeist* were all that came to mind, and he didn't want Aimee to feel she was wasting her time. It dawned on him then that he also had no idea how to hang up on a supernatural phone call, particularly when the other side would still be able to see and hear him after the connection ended.

"Wait, what?" Aimee seemed caught in translation. "He asks 'Are you done already?'"

Saul felt an opportunity slipping away, then his eyes lit up. "OK, no, one more."

Aimee looked from Saul to the air, nodded and then waited.

"So when she found you, Aditi-Alhread, what did she say to you?"

The pause lasted longer than the others.

"He says, 'Well, after she told me to shut up, she asked me a bunch of questions about some old guy and then some library…'" She absorbed some more. "'…and then when I didn't know what she was talking about I told her you were a smart guy and certainly knew computers better than I did.'"

Aimee held up a finger, indicating more was coming.

"OK, then he says, 'Dude, I think she thought Google was something sexual when I said it.' And now he's laughing maniacally."

Saul let out a small little snicker. "What was the name of the old guy?"

"He says, 'It sounded like Ootnapesh Tim. Something like that. When I didn't know the name she described him as the a guy who survived the Great Flood – not Moses, or Noah, whichever one it was – and he got cursed to never die or some shit.'"

Saul rushed over to the condiments table and grabbed a napkin and one of the tiny pencils people used to write on their cups. He asked Aimee a few times if Watts had any idea how to spell it and he didn't, so Saul sounded it out the best he could on the napkin. When done, Saul's gaze stayed down a bit.

"Hey Watts man, I appreciate you helping me and all." He wanted to add, "especially after I got you killed" at the end but resisted.

Aimee grinned a little and turned to Saul. "He says he's not hugging you and you're on your own from now on. Apparently I'm much more aesthetically pleasing to watch at night than you alone in a hotel room." The switch from first person confused Saul for an instant, but then he got it. They were done.

Aimee's voice rose a bit in mood. "OK everyone, Bob's your uncle. That's it for tonight." Aimee looked around to several spots near Saul. "Don't have time for any singing, but I'll try and do some tomorrow, OK?" She smiled at an area off to her other side, then popped the ear buds out and pushed a button on her iPhone.

Saul's skepticism returned quickly as he realized how quickly he'd accepted that he'd actually been conversing with Watts. Reviewing the last few minutes he couldn't think of any clues he might have given Aimee for her to deduce even one of those answers.

"Well?" Aimee met his eyes and held there.

"I wasn't expecting that. I admit it."

"Am I leaning more now towards con artist or mental patient?"

"Con artist for sure, although, one obviously with no sense of how to pick a mark if you're in it for the money."

"Nyah, just something I do to screw with dates to ensure I stay single forever."

"There are always one night stands." He offered, wondering why he did so.

"Also known as auditions." She said without missing a beat.

Saul smiled, and then shifted mental gears, reviewing Watt's words in his head, wondering if he sat in a nearby chair or floated above Aimee's head.

"Thanks for that." He spoke to Aimee without looking at her. "I guess that's all I needed for tonight."

"Oh I'm free to go?"

"I didn't mean it like that. It's just, I've got to figure out what I'm doing now, and where, and you've already done a lot…"

"What do you mean what you're doing now?" Aimee's voice drew Saul's eyes back up. "You mean tonight or with this new information?"

"Both, really. The cops are probably looking for me – not as a criminal, but still – and, well, I told you what happened to my hotel room."

"You were serious about that?"

"Yeah." Saul's lowered his voice, and with his expression he answered the next question before she asked it – whether he was serious about the murder part too. Aimee studied him, searching for a trace of humor or a hint this might be a joke. Finding none, her shoulders sank.

"Why don't you stay with me?" She asked, all indications of flirting or humor drained out of her.

"No that's OK. I'm fine." Saul lied. His next best option was the back seat of his car.

"Look, I listen to music before I go to bed, and I don't want to have to hear Watts all night long telling me to check on you or rescue you or bail you out of jail."

Saul hated accepting help from others sometimes, but he did need it and she did seem sincere. "I can sleep on the floor."

"You can sleep on the couch."

"Better than a cot in the desert."

With that they finished off their drinks in silence and headed out to the parking lot.

"It's mostly easy driving, you should have no problem keeping up." Aimee said over the hood of her truck. "After we pass the park, the turn is a little hard to see. If you get lost, turn left at the creepy dude puking on the side of the road. He's usually there this time of night on the weekends and doesn't move much, so he makes a good road marker."

True to her point, Saul was able to keep her maroon truck in sight with no issues. She led him just past another strip mall that did indeed have a drunk man on all fours on the corner sidewalk, although Saul stared and strained and didn't see any signs of vomit.

Finally they arrived at an old apartment complex tucked back in a clump of trees and ivy-covered rocks. Saul parked next to her truck and surveyed the area. Two stories of dirty white wood and green-stained shingles struggled to fight off moss with a strange paintjob that seemed unconcerned about matching any of the previous shades beneath it.

Aimee's apartment sat crammed on the edge of the row on the bottom floor right up against a Queen Anne style house that no doubt belonged to the owner of the complex. The asymmetrical structure bristled with bay windows and turrets, all with a dry outer crust of pink painted scales. Saul's eyes lingered on the white lace curtains framing the windows filled with near-perfect darkness.

Inside Aimee's apartment Saul almost took back his comment about a couch being better than a cot in the desert. The scent got him first, some sort of vanilla air freshener over dust over the hints of past parties gone wrong. One bedroom, but with a very big living room area connected to the kitchen, and decorated in late neo-graduate student. A divan sat against the wall glaring at a stuffed chair from an opposing decorator, all under lighting provided entirely by strings of white Christmas lights or hanging paper Japanese lanterns. The carpet seemed to be the original tan splotched with faded stains Saul preferred not to think about.

Before he realized she was gone Aimee returned with a pillow and blanket and tossed both onto the couch. She plopped down in the chair and gestured for him to sit as well.

"I'm going to guess you're not a nightshift person and are probably about ready to crash." She said. Saul pushed the blanket to one side and eased himself down on the couch. As he did so he noticed that all the frames on the walls contained band flyers like the type he'd seen outside her odd dance club.

"I do feel tired." Saul had almost said he felt like he'd been to hell and back that day, but kept it to himself.

Then just as abruptly, Aimee stood up. She walked to the entrance to the hallway that led to the apartment's solitary bedroom and then stopped. She turned to regard him in a moment that made Saul's heart jump. For an instant he thought she might invite him for a romp on her special playground, and he tensed at the thought. He had neither the emotional or physical strength for any sort of sexual encounter just then, and ran through a few ways he might gently say no if she asked.

"Are you sure you don't want to stay up a bit?" Aimee pointed to a large but old tube-style TV. "We could watch *Hoarders* and play 'I spy.'"

The tension broken, Saul laughed a short laugh but not enough to convey actual interest.

"I guess that is better as a drinking game." She said and sighed. "Well, I'm going to go read for a while, check my email, that sort of thing. We'll figure the rest out tomorrow."

Then she smiled, and with the single word, "Night" disappeared out of view.

CHAPTER 20

An hour after he stretched out on the couch Saul still stared at the ceiling. There seemed something about resisting sleep, knowing that until he drifted off he was free, that neither Aditi-Alhread or Dennis or the police or anyone who actually walked and left footprints could find him.

Then he imagined Watts standing in the corner, waiting for his eyes to close so he could write embarrassing messages on Saul's chest or face with shaving cream or permanent markers. The smell of the room – of every house party he'd ever been to – probably had no small part in creating that image.

He wondered then if ghosts needed to sleep, and regardless, if Watts had chosen to curl up on the bed with Aimee. Saul entertained himself for a while listening to her footsteps and trips to the bathroom and all the puttering about someone does while trying to be quiet in a house with sleeping people. At last he gave in and let his heavy lids fall, welcoming whatever horrors this stretch would bring to him.

An instant later, he struggled to figure out where he was. Cool sheets, scratchy couch, muted daylight outside, ah, still in Aimee's apartment, although now the party smell was smothered under a thick air of bacon.

"Hey." Vaguely happy voice, but clearly not too happy. Through fuzzy vision Saul made out her form standing in the kitchen.

"Morning." He mumbled back, sitting up and immediately realizing he needed to keep the sheets bundled over his lap for the time being.

"Yeah I have that effect on a lot of people." She said smiling, and then immediately changed topics. "So I got up early. Early for a night shift person. You slept over eleven hours."

Saul decided the math was too hard and reached for his watch on the coffee table. He confirmed her accuracy and then rubbed his eyes until everything cleared up. Aimee's hair hung in a disheveled dark mess, and she stood wearing what looked like a T-shirt over another T-shirt, plus standard issue black sweat bottoms, prodding a sizzling pan with a long fork.

"No offense, but I got bored last night after you went to sleep." She said. The toaster behind her popped up two pieces of bread, although from Saul's point of view they seemed barely warmed. "So I looked up that name Watts gave you."

Saul still couldn't stand without holding a pillow or something in front of himself, so sat there and listened patiently, focusing on her words as much as in he could in hopes that would help.

"Cool." He said, still too groggy to come up with anything more inspired.

"I found out how to spell it, and found out the original legend, but that's it. Basically a story about a guy who can't die trying to convince another guy he doesn't want immortality." She speared some of the bacon and flopped it on a large plate covered with a paper towel. Each time she did, she dabbed another paper towel on top to soak up the grease. "Everybody loves bacon."

"Yes, sorry, I was about to thank you for that." Saul flinched. She hadn't actually offered him any, and it was possible she'd just been making her own breakfast.

She set the platter of bacon on a large round folding table in the kitchen and Saul noticed two plates. All good.

"Grub's up! I'm not bringing it to you in there," She said calling from the kitchen, "But I'm willing to avert my vision if you need to throw on some trousers or something." Or something. Saul threw on his sweatshirt and then, when her back was turned for the instant it took her to get the butter out of the fridge, jumped in his jeans.

As he stumbled in and sat at the table, she stared back into the fridge and spoke. "I have water, and, water." She turned. "Well and gin. And scotch. A little Crown Royal I think." Saul suspected at that instant that she wouldn't have hesitated if he'd picked one of the later.

Saul dug into the buttered toast and bacon a little more ravenous than he would have preferred, but only tempered himself marginally. He had no reason to impress this Aimee person, and in fact the opposite might not be a bad idea. She ate too, pausing to hold her greasy fingers up in the air after each strip before wiping them on another paper towel.

"Anyway," she said between bites. "My uncle is a computer networking guy." Another mouthful of toast put an unnatural pause in the conversation, and Saul marveled at the apparent non-sequitur whiplash. "But before that he was a legal assistant, and a computer programmer, all sorts of crap." Her eating/talking style told Saul she wasn't too worried about impressing him either, but he also didn't like that the food dulled her accent a little.

"My point," she continued, "and I did have one, is that he's good at finding stuff. He was a private investigator for about five years in there too until someone caught him taking pictures of their torrid affair and beat him bloody. He lives down in Eugene. Oregon."

"Finding stuff? You mean finding stuff like the guy Watts was talking about?" Saul heard his own words less than he tasted the bacon. He couldn't remember the last time he'd had bacon, and a whole meal of it with just some bread to help absorb the grease seemed heavenly at the moment. He snapped out of it for a second. "Wait, do you mean like for reals like find a walking around immortal guy, or just like in theory or let's find stories about him or his ancient tomb?"

"I don't know. I'd say a tomb or something and laugh at you for suggesting the real option if, you know, I didn't see dead people."

"So you think he was talking about a ghost?"

"Look I don't know." She shoved the last piece of bread and bacon into her mouth and stood up with her plate. "But after tonight's shift I've got three days off. I'll call my uncle and ask him about it, if he seems up to it, maybe we could take a road trip." She set her plate in the sink and reached back for Saul's. Not wanting to hold her up he picked up his last corner of toast and quickly wolfed down his two last overdone but somehow still succulent strips.

"We can call your friend if you want." She said, then quickly rinsed the plates and washed her hands. "Unless you guys already had plans."

"I'm a little confused she's not here this morning, to be honest." Saul replied. "But no, we don't have any plans that I know of. Besides, sounds like she was looking for this guy anyway."

She grabbed the skillet off the stove and held it in the sink, waiting for the water to heat up.

Saul finished off his water. "How far a drive is Eugene from here?"

"I can usually make it in five hours, but that's during traffic."

"Would it be easier to just call?"

With the water finally hot enough, Aimee scrubbed the skillet with a soapy blue sponge. "I was going to ring him anyway, prep him a bit, but that's all we did then we wouldn't get an answer for a month. We can do that if you want."

"No no." Saul felt awkward watching her do the dishes and gathered up the paper towels in a token attempt to help. "No no. You're right, a month is too long."

"He's a tower of iron will alone in his house," she said. "but he's powerless to resist anyone face-to-face. I mean a guy in a $2,000 suit could show up on his doorstep and say he needed money for food and my uncle would empty his pockets right there for the guy."

"Would we stay with him?"

"He won't mind. He's got space." She dried the skillet on a hanging rag and hung it from a hook on the wall.

"Well if he's good with it, like I said I'm free."

"Well whatever. You've got some time to decide. I'm going to the gym. Then I'm going to shower and run a few errands before my shift starts." With the last word she disappeared into the hallway that led to her bedroom, leaving Saul still sitting at the table.

He got up, refilled his glass of water from the tap, and meandered through the living room. Eventually his eyes caught sight of the green outdoors, so he moved to the corner of the apartment with windows at right angles to each other, one looking forward, one to the side.

Cloudy, of course, but with enough sun behind it to give the sky an electric fog glow. Nothing captured his attention until he turned towards the Victorian house next door. A middle-aged woman – no doubt the landlady – stood on the porch holding a glass of wine in her hand studying the parking lot. She looked thin enough to either be a chronic runner or someone with an eating disorder, although after a few seconds Saul decided that judgment unfair and added potential depression or genetic trait to his mental list.

"Watching Ms. Crabtree?" Aimee again, now in workout clothes with a big bag under her arm filled with towels and Saul couldn't tell what all else.

"She's drinking wine before lunch."

"What you haven't?" Aimee smiled and then moved to fill a bottle with cold water from the fridge. "Crabtree obviously isn't really her name. I forgot her real name, even though she tells me every time I see her. Anyway, she likes me, she doesn't mind any noise I make, which is good since my wall butts up against hers. She's good people as far as I'm concerned."

"The landlady likes you?" Saul studied Ms. Crabtree as he spoke. She took another sip while maintaining her casual surveillance.

"She gave me a discount because she likes musicians." Aimee ducked her head between the couch and the coffee table and brought up a pair of worn tennis shoes. "In fact, my first week in town I met her at the club watching my show and she offered me a month's free rent to move in right then. Thought she was a lesbian at first, but she's never made a move towards me. Anyway, she's creepy, and mean to some of the other tenants, but not me. Maybe I fulfill some long lost daughter role. Not sure."

"When do you think you'll be back?" Saul turned to watch Aimee, who struggled not to spill her bag while tying her shoes.

"In about fourteen hours, give or take. But if it makes you feel better, Watts hates hospitals, so he'll be hanging with you today." Successful in her shoe tying, she stood and walked to the door. "I've got no secrets here, so do whatever you want. Eat what you want, drink what you want, buy us food if you want, stay, go, no redecorating though, please. And if you go porn surfing all I ask is nothing illegal, and don't leave anything open that might offend my delicate sensibilities the next time I sit down at my desk. Just bookmark it for me later."

Again she left Saul speechless for just long enough she could pass by without reply. She tossed a farewell his direction and closed the door behind her.

"Alone again, naturally." Saul barely whispered the old song and turned back towards Ms. Crabtree. Still standing in the same spot, wine glass now nearly empty. He debated going out to chat with her. Old, lonely, probably could use a conversation, even a lame one about weather or how times have changed. Fate solved the issue for him and she took the last sip and headed back inside.

Saul surveyed the apartment and summed up options for his day. The idea that Watts stayed behind hampered him somewhat. Was he hovering nearby, sitting on the couch, taking notes to report everything to Aimee?

That settled it. Whatever he was going to do, it wasn't going to be here.

Thirty minutes of aimless driving and two fast food ham sandwiches later Saul found himself taking the exit that led to Lisa and Richard's house. It dawned on him then that he didn't have any idea what day of the week it was. He was that out of touch. It bothered him even more that he couldn't come up with any easy way to figure out the day without asking someone.

As he pulled into the neighborhood, he reasoned he could either wait until school normally let out, or take a two in seven chance it was the weekend and go in right then. The suburbs continued on with their lives as he stayed undecided in his car seat. A pair of older black ladies waddled arm-in-arm on the side of the street. A tall one in a pale long dress that emphasized the years she carried with her, the shorter one in tan slacks and a bowling shirt composed of black, red, and white checkered squares. The women alternated, one supporting the other until loose footing reversed their roles. Each step threatening to topple them both, everything about them casual except for the tight grip of their hands. Saul marveled at the pair. Such a simple act morphed by necessity into a desperate symbiotic relationship. Then a young boy, no older than thirteen, hair cut in a short Mohawk, passed them from the other direction, walking his cross-eyed red hound using an old length of rope as a leash.

There you go, Saul thought. Kid on the street, must be the weekend.

Just as he reached for the car handle some movement in the kitchen window caught his eye. He paused, and then Rose bounded out the side door, leaving it open behind her.

Saul's heart leapt for an instant, hoping she'd seen him in the street and was running out to greet him. Just as quickly he forced that unlikely option down when she instead threw open a large box and pulled out a pink and red bicycle helmet.

Lisa came out next, followed by Richard, both in biking shorts. Matching, biking shorts.

Trapped, Saul could either wait for the awkward moment they noticed him sitting a pathetic lump in his car, or drive off obviously fleeing the scene.

"Watts man, you're supposed to be helping with crap like this." In a moment of focused anger he threw open the car door and put every ounce of mental energy into an air of happiness.

"Hey guys!" He waved as he crossed the street. All three stared for that suspicious instant before recognition. Their unfamiliarity, however small, still stung.

"Hey Saul," Lisa responded first. Rose kept her eyes on him, but threw her arm around her bike while she did so.

"We were about to go bike riding." Rose said, straight to the point.

"Well hello to you too." Saul oozed all the charm he could muster. "How about a hug there kid?"

"Sure dad." Rose said and waited for Saul to approach before opening her arms. A short hug, but strong. Saul wondered if that was out of habit or actual enthusiasm.

"I didn't even know you had a bike." Saul told her. He wondered what he actually did know about her any more as he tried to keep an upbeat energy.

"Hey Saul," Richard said. "Why don't you take my bike?"

Lisa glanced at her husband with a look that said both good idea and bad idea.

"No it's OK. I'll just wait for you guys to finish." Saul replied.

"Saul, we normally ride for an hour." Richard said.

"We could go a shorter route today." Lisa suggested. Rose glanced at her when she said that, clearly disappointed with the idea but old enough to understand this was a grown-up conversation for now.

Saul could almost hear it in his head. Please don't make me talk to him. Let's go already. Leave here him. Just like he left me.

"Stop stop stop." Saul crossed his arms. "I can wait, it's no big deal. I have to go run some errands anyway. I'll go out and should be back right about the time you return, maybe even a little after."

Lisa and Richard conceded, Rose remained quiet.

"You guys need anything while I'm out?" Saul asked.

"No, no." Lisa said quickly.

"Milk?" Saul asked. "You always run out of milk."

"OK, well, we are out of milk. And I was going to get some cereal later."

"Look, see? Everybody wins. You ride, I'll shop, we'll meet back in an hour."

They each studied the faces of the other, searching for clues so subtle that only they would understand the messages. Everyone seemed to silently agree this was the best plan.

Minutes later their three forms disappeared down the far end of the block with Saul standing watching in the middle of the street. He knew he would, of course, go get the milk and cereal. He also knew he would leave the grocery bag on their porch with some sort of lame excuse note to go with it. Saul turned and noticed the two old ladies still in visual range, and for a moment, he envied them.

CHAPTER 21

Aditi-Ioannes understood more about politics than he did medicine. The tax collector got paid on the 4th, Demos the Bey took bribes on the morning after the full moon, and any time Aditi-Ioannes found information on any of the nobility that could be used for extortion, that went to the Agha Thanos or his battalion's executive officer immediately. Every government official, every Tourkos aristocrat, and every high ranking member of the local military, Aditi-Ioannes knew them all and most of their families.

In medicine, he could sum up what he knew in three rules: the humours diagnostic system was discredited around the time he was born, so demean anyone who still brought it up; sweet tasting urine led to gradual emaciation followed by sudden death; and that he should add wintergreen liberally to every medicine he mixed. All that combined to make him one of the more respected doctors in Athens.

True, he owed at least part of his success to the brutality of the Tourkos. Brutal to others. The people too stupid to pay who they were supposed to pay when they were supposed to pay them. The Tourkos enforced simple rules with easy to understand rewards and punishments, yet Aditi-Ioannes had seen whole neighborhoods vacated by the weak in the name of oppression.

Most of the more knowledgeable doctors, for example, moved to the Ionian islands or one of the less civilized corners of the empire thirty years ago. Aditi-Ioannes had rushed to fill the vacant niche before anyone else came up with the same idea, and he'd held and defended it for the last two decades.

On days like today he harvested the sweet rewards for his diligence. A few hours earlier that morning replenishing his supply of "powered unicorn horn" would earn a night of pleasure from his delectable, if simple, mountain girl.

Once every moon Kigal-Cliantha came down to the city as she had for the better part of the last year. Their first meeting he turned her away. She cried unnoticed in the alley outside his door while wealthy patients dropped by for bags of herbs or special dusts to pour in their wine. By dusk, in the custardy glow of the setting sun, she jumped out of the shadows and threw herself as his feet. A long babble followed – in the common tongue that hurt Aditi-Ioannes ears – going through a long history of the plight of her kin and their endless illnesses. Again he told her to go back to her bandit family and threatened to have her imprisoned.

Then he caught a good look at her dirt-stained face between the thick dark strands of hair, and her hand moved up his leg just far enough to communicate how desperate she was. When he hesitated, she smiled a smile he found almost pleasant, and he ordered her to the back door of his shop to wait.

From that day forward a bottle of ground up deer antlers sprinkled with salt and of course, wintergreen, bought him whatever carnal desires he could dream up within the span of a moon cycle. What began as shy but enthusiastic rutting evolved over the months into a chance to experiment with every perversity he heard about from his patients or from passing soldiers or from someone a few seats over in the local pub. And those three crowds together provided an apparently inexhaustible supply of depravity for actions he justified in the name of medicine.

Tonight the routine would begin again, starting with a light rapping on his alley door just after the curfew bell rang. He'd draw the curtains and let her in, smiling and greeting her with all the formality of any of his regulars. Then he'd listen patiently as she went on about her father's latest ailments and how great a hunter he was and how much the family needed him and so forth and so on. Aditi-Ioannes rarely absorbed anything more than that, lack of interest combined with a dialect he never bothered to master, although through no effort of his own he had inadvertently retained that Kigal-Cliantha's mother and husband were recently dead. She thought the world of her father, and she and her three children relied entirely on his health for their survival.

And each time when she finished discussing her family maladies, Aditi-Ioannes would make a show of considering a new herbal mixture. After puttering around with jars and bags full of ingredients for a few minutes, he'd hand her the 'special' concoction sitting in a specific drawer on his workbench. With eager eyes she'd watch and listen as he'd go over how this remedy differed from the previous batch – oil of roses to help with breathing, spider webs to help minor wounds mend faster, whatever other nonsense struck him that evening – and then, her mind at ease, he'd scribble some meaningless numbers on a strip of cloth and tell her how much she owed for his services. Each time her father's unique needs drove the price a little higher, and each time Aditi-Ioannes waited patiently for her to admit she couldn't afford it so he could act moderately surprised.

At some point in the last few months he must have noticed that she no longer flirted nor smiled in the haggling that followed, but his lust numbed him to all that. No matter what he suggested she eventually agreed, her face as blank as her eyes were distant, again unnoticed by Aditi-Ioannes. He always drew a bath for her next, sometimes leaping around and even giggling in anticipation while she quietly scrubbed herself in the next room.

Aditi-Ioannes stepped outside. He looked up and past the narrow streets and small houses with their walled yards, and focused on the church clock tower up on the hill. He stared until his eyes adjusted and he could see the hands on its face at the top. Six more hours to go.

He paused then, as he always did to admire the mansions of the nearby elders. Two stories of multicolored stones, rows of chimneys, and the dark wooden doors near the top. How he longed for a balcony like that. To look down on the busy streets as late as mid-morning, above the stench of all the people. In two years, maybe less, he could double the size of his house, perhaps even buy his own villa someplace fertile and wealthy like Kifissia.

"Hello." A tiny voice, a simple word, yet the sound of it slammed a lump just above his stomach. He turned to see her standing beside his door in the middle of the afternoon. Information flew at him, muting his voice while he processed it all.

Pink moisture filled the whites of her eyes, and she seemed even more dirty than normal. Behind her a brown mule with highlights of white stood patiently bearing the weight of blankets, furs, tools, cooking utensils, over-stuffed bags and the long prominent musket of a hunter. A hunter who no longer needed it. The time had come sooner than expected, and Aditi-Ioannes cursed himself for his lack of preparation for it.

A movement to her side caught his eye next, revealing a toddler leaning against an older girl who cradled an infant. The girl - the daughter - glared more than stared at him, her eyes a stark contradiction to the gentleness her embrace offered the baby.

Kigal-Cliantha followed his gaze to her children.

"Oh you've seen them before." She said. "Or at least they've seen you. You probably overlooked them crouching in the alley corners, ducking behind walls, crying outside your window in the middle of the night while you... while you..." Her voice cracked and she turned away. She muffled a few light sobs with her hands and hair, but the gaze of the two older children never wavered.

A nearby merchant swept the same stretch of street over and over, feigning no interest in the doctor's new visitors. Others too, Aditi-Ioannes felt more than saw, watched from doorways and windows for what could become dinner conversation for days.

His mind bounced between what to tell her, how he would justify this scene to the local community, and that damned musket. Grieving or not, a gun would attract attention in this city. By now the Azabs had to have heard of her – a mountain Klepht who foolishly wandered into the wrong part of town. Soon a pair of armored men would round the street corner, muskets in hand or sabers drawn. They would find her standing on his doorstep, talking to him, perhaps yelling at him, and then they would demand his explanation, and for him to explain his relationship to this woman...

CHAPTER 22

In retrospect, Saul figured that the average intelligence of the average criminal being what it was, the police probably rarely if ever had to resort to things like credit card monitoring or psychic consultants or complicated cell-phone triangulation to find suspects or missing people like they did on TV and the movies. In any case, all it took to find Saul was an enterprising sergeant sending a patrol car out to the home address on Rose's school records.

On his way to the station Saul thought the whole thing a minor blessing, since at least it gave him something interesting to write on the note he left with the cereal and milk. Officer Daniels – the sergeant who picked Saul up – didn't bother to handcuff him once Saul agreed to get in the back. No frisking either, which Saul took as another bonus and hoped that meant that whatever happened next wouldn't be that bad.

At the station, a police cadet with "Gagnon" on her nametag took his fingerprints, but only after making it clear she had to ask his permission and that it was standard procedure so they could rule his prints out from the real bad guys. She used a fancy machine that copied his hand like a computer scanner, although Saul noted they did have ink pads nearby presumably in case of a malfunction.

Along with three plastic chairs with wooden armrests, he spent the next half hour sitting in a small waiting room that seemed more like an abandoned bit of hallway. He amused himself by searching for signs Watts might be in there with him, and what he could say or do to amuse his dead partner without looking too much like a crazy person.

"Hey there, have a seat." The stocky Asian detective in a short sleeved white shirt and tie watched a computer screen behind the small desk and gestured at the small office's only other chair. The detective punched a few keys, read a bit more, and turned to Saul. "Well, so how are things going with you today?"

"You mean besides being in a police department?" Saul's tone remained friendly.

"Yeah, not the way any of us like to start our day." He took out a pad of paper and a pen. "And that includes the people who work here."

"No one's told me why I was brought in, by the way. Just so you know." Saul didn't want to come off as nervous, arrogant or overly cooperative, three things he thought cops must zero in on.

"Well," the detective checked the screen. "Officially you're just a person of interest in a rather violent outbreak at a local hotel."

"Is that the same thing as an interesting person?" Saul chuckled to himself. It just came out. Honest.

"Believe it or not I've never actually heard that one before." He cracked a small smile and wrote something down. "My name's Nguyen, by the way." He reached across the desk and shook Saul's hand.

"I thought you all had one of those big rooms with the small table and the one way glass mirror." Saul said, looking around the rather plain office.

"Oh we do." Nguyen replied. "That's for interrogating criminals. I'm just doing an interview with you Mr. Christian. Unless you're a criminal." He said that last part almost like a question.

"Not as far as you know." Saul regretted saying it the instant the words left his mouth.

"Really?" Something about Nguyen's tone seemed a little less friendly, but for the most part his voice remained even and emotionless.

"No, that was a… that was a joke."

Nguyen studied Saul a moment, then flipped through a pile of papers and brought out a picture of Dennis and held it up. It looked like a bad blown up driver's license photo.

"Do you know this man?"

"Vaguely, yes."

He switched to a second picture, this one of Jack, also not unlike a driver's license photo.

"How about him?"

"Even less so, but technically yes."

"Names?"

"Dennis and… actually I don't know the other guy's name."

Nguyen wrote, but kept his eyes on Saul. "Dennis says that the three of you met at a hotel room to go out for drinks and then you attacked his partner Jack. Is that true?"

"We were in the same location for about 15 seconds, that part is true."

"But you didn't attack Jack?" Nguyen studied Saul intently. If it was supposed to be intimidating, it was.

"No. Look I've never willingly committed any crimes that I know of."

Nguyen put his pen down and interlaced his fingers on his desk. "Have you unwillingly committed any crimes Saul?"

An image of driving Aditi-Alhread away from Guy's body popped up in his mind, followed by another image of her wiping the blood off her face with Jack's shirt. Saul sucked at lying to authority figures and he knew it.

"Are you sure this isn't an interrogation?" Good save, Saul thought as he spoke.

"We're just talking here Saul. No handcuffs, no bars, I'm just trying to make sense out of what happened."

Saul paused before replying, "OK."

Nguyen continued staring, and didn't seem to have any need to check his notes now.

"Several officers claimed a woman ran across the tops of their patrol cars that night, know anything about her?"

Saul looked down at the desk, which right afterwards he knew was a sign of guilt. He focused on what truth he could work to his advantage. "I don't mean to be confrontational or anything, or even problematic, but I've never been in a police station before, for any reason, and I'm a little over my head."

"We're just talking."

"I know, but I'm a bit overwhelmed right now."

"Really?" Nguyen sounded deliberately skeptical.

"Yes really."

"You need time to think?"

"Yes."

"Get your story straight?"

"Clever, but no." Saul smiled as he evaded the verbal trap, and then wished he had Nguyen's near perfect stoicism.

"You need to take a break?" Nguyen leaned back in his chair. Saul noticed that he didn't ask if Saul wanted a lawyer, which is good because Saul probably would have taken one, and then he would really look guilty.

"That'd be good." Saul said.

"Yeah, sure." Nguyen turned back to his screen and put his hands on the keyboard. Without looking he continued. "OK, why don't you take five minutes, get a drink, go to the bathroom, then come back and we'll finish up."

Saul stood up and hesitated. "Do I need an escort or anything?"

"No no, I trust you."

I bet you do, Saul thought. When he stepped out of the doorway he felt Nguyen deliberately looking away, while a nearby police sergeant tried a little too hard not to be watching what Saul did next.

On his way from the bathroom, back through an open bay filled with desks, laptops, and people talking or typing, a completely new uniformed officer stopped Saul and gestured toward a door off to the side.

"Mr. Christian, I need you to step into this waiting room for a minute." The officer said.

"Why is that?"

"Someone here to see you." The officer opened the door and revealed a tiny room with two chairs and a small table.

"Who?"

"Don't know 'em."

Saul moved to the furthest chair, turned it towards the door, sat and waited. Not thirty seconds after the officer disappeared, the door flew open again.

"Hey there. Louis C. Ford, friends call me Lou." Silk suit, starched over-white shirt, dark hair with styling gel, everything about this man screamed the type of high paid lawyer Saul hoped to never have to be in the same little police room with. After the initial shock, Saul realized Lou's hand outstretched in the "waiting to shake" position. Saul reflexively shook it.

Lou grabbed the other chair and wheeled it around the table so he could face Saul. "And you're Saul? Did I get that right?" Lou said.

"Yeah, that's right."

"Good, here's my card." Lou slid a thick embossed card with raised letters across the table. Saul pocketed it without looking. "Now, let's see what we can do to get you out of here today. I don't need you to tell me names or anything, but I need to know enough about what happened, and what you've told the police happened, in order to make this work, OK?"

"I'm not sure I have anything to talk about." Saul replied.

Lou crossed his legs and unbuttoned the bottom button of his coat. "There's no way anyone can argue you out of this if they don't know what to argue. So if you want my help, you can either tell me the safe, abridged version, which might work, or you can expand on that a little bit and tell me what the police might dig up so I can have a defense ready for it when they ask. It's really your call, but I'm telling you, the more you tell me the better. You do understand attorney client privilege, right?"

Lou pulled a tiny leather-bound book out of his inside jacket pocket along with one of those thick designer pens worth two months of Army combat pay. Saul spoke to him very slowly, thinking out what he should reveal and what he shouldn't, and Lou watched him and scribbled notes the entire time, nodding as he went.

Saul skipped the part about Guy's death entirely and focused on the night at the hotel. He referred to Aditi -Alhread as a military advisor he met in Iraq, although he didn't know what agency she worked for. The story Saul told went that she'd invited him out to drinks, they went back to his place, and then Dennis and Jack showed up and started harassing her. Saul claimed he didn't know what their issue was, but that he and Aditi-Alhread ran into the nearby woods and Jack followed after them. Saul said he knew that she got in a fight with Jack, but Saul couldn't really see it. After that they separated, and since then he hadn't seen her, Jack, or Dennis. Saul figured that depending on how the questions were asked, he might even be able to pass a lie detector test if he got to use that exact wording.

"So, this woman," Lou checked his notes, "Aditi-Alhread, you said. She hasn't called you or said anything at all since that night?"

"No. I don't think she even has a cell phone."

"Really? That's odd. So, she was more of a one night stand thing then?"

In his head Saul heard Aimee's voice correct "one night stand" to "audition," but didn't have time to let his mood lighten. Instead he squirmed in his chair. "Not exactly, I mean, I knew her in Iraq a little bit."

"Well she's not much of a friend if she leaves you sitting as a possible murder suspect is she?"

"So the cops are saying murder?" Saul knew that Nguyen guy knew more than he was saying.

"They're saying they found a shallow grave, lots of blood, signs of a struggle, no body. Evidence suggests someone came back and dug the body back up a few days later." Lou smiled. "But in a way that's good news. No body, no murder."

"Yeah I guess."

"So, and again, remember, I'm just making sure we don't have any surprises if you ever end up testifying, are you saying your relationship with Aditi was a romantic one?"

It annoyed Saul a little that he shorted her name. For some reason it had never occurred to him to do so, as a show of respect that Lou didn't seem to share. "No no, not at all. I mean, I might have been a little attracted to her, but she clearly wasn't interested at all."

"Ouch. OK, so you're saying your relationship was professional then?"

"Yes."

"Professional how? I mean, were you two in business together?"

"Not exactly."

Lou sat back. "Well Saul, if this goes to a full interrogation, they are going to want to know how exactly. Can you define your relationship?"

Saul didn't speak for a few seconds. "Well, I think whatever she had going on with Dennis, it has her scared. I think maybe she was looking for friends, maybe even protection, although she certainly seemed like she could take care of herself to me."

"She came to you for protection?"

"Sort of."

"Just you?"

"No, others too."

"How many others are we talking about? Anybody we need to talk to?"

"No, not really." Saul thought of Larry, pathetic as he was, being dead, and made it a point under no circumstances to mention Aimee to anyone.

Lou paused a moment and scanned his notes before continuing. "So you don't have any way to contact her. Do you think she's gone for good, or will she be coming back?"

"She said she would," Saul wondered if he should have admitted that before continuing. "But I don't know when or how. She finds me. I have no idea where she is."

Lou added a few more questions focusing on what happened to the hotel room wall and if Aditi was the person who ran across the police cars. Saul provided a neutral response to all of them. Finally Lou's cell phone rang and he answered.

"Yeah, are you standing there with them now? OK, they've got nothing and they know it." Lou's voice took on a serious authoritarian tone. "The accuser is a repeat offender and Saul is a decorated war veteran."

Well, Saul thought, decorated with the same ribbons everyone who went to Iraq got.

"OK, OK, thanks. Sure." Lou continued on the phone and then hung up. He turned back down to Saul, smiling again. "You're free to go. They aren't pressing any charges."

"Really? That's it?"

"Yep, not bad eh?"

"Cool. Well, do I owe you anything?"

"Oh don't worry about that now. Get back home to your family. I'll get your contact information from the officer outside and I'll have someone get in touch with you later."

And then after another quick handshake, Lou rushed out the door as fast as he had entered.

Three hours after dropping off the milk and cereal, Saul got out of a cab and quietly drove his car out of Lisa's neighborhood. He ignored the two voice messages from her and deleted her text message without reading it.

Just before nightfall, he pulled into the parking lot of Aimee's apartment complex, turned off the engine, and just sat there. The green mossy tint to the buildings looked better in daylight, he decided. He'd never dealt with the police before, in any capacity, or with a lawyer in any way other than to help him figure out how things were going to work with Rose after Nicole's death. He didn't know if he should ignore the police or worry about them. Should he try to remain hidden, or not give a crap if the cops were watching him. His history with Aditi-Alhread and two dead lackeys suggested the hiding approach.

As he got out and headed for the apartment, he noticed Ms. Crabtree, or whatever her real name was, sitting on the grass pulling weeds around a small flower bed out by the street. Given how much of her grass had died in long thin patches, he thought the flowers must either be newly planted or very lucky.

Seeing no way to walk by without passing within greeting range, Saul accepted it and tossed out a hearty "Hey there!" as he approached.

Ms. Crabtree looked up. "Why hello." She stuck her attenuated arm down to push herself up and then decided that was too much work and just turned her head towards him. "You're with Aimee, right?" Her voice held a sweet tone, although she didn't smile with it.

"Yes ma'am, but we're just friends."

"Uh-huh." She sounded unconvinced. "You gonna be here long?"

"No ma'am, leaving tomorrow. I think. Maybe tomorrow."

"You out of Fort Lewis?" She asked.

"Yeah. How'd you know?"

"Haircut."

"Of course." Saul didn't have the energy to continue. "OK, well I gotta go get ready for dinner."

The older woman nodded but kept watching as he walked away and into the apartment.

After a quick run to a gas station for some toiletries Saul spent the next four hours snacking and flipping through a handful of select cable TV channels. There were many things he felt he should be doing, but he didn't feel like doing much of anything at all. Maybe if he relaxed his brain, he reasoned, he would think clearly later.

Aimee entered wearing a purple set of scrubs with her gym bag slung over her shoulder and white wires leading from it up to the buds in each ear. She nodded at him and waved.

"Listening to ghosts?" Saul asked.

"What?" She popped out one of the earbuds.

"You listening to ghosts?" Saul said louder.

"Violent Femmes." She smiled and headed towards her bedroom. "Gotta shower."

She came out a half hour later in jeans and a sweatshirt, her black hair still glistening, but now in two curly pigtails. "So," she said, leaning against the hallway opening. "Why don't you tell me about your day."

Saul summed it up for her as best he could, sticking to the facts and leaving out any emotions he felt along the way. She watched him the whole time, without moving. When he finished she tilted her head as she spoke.

"So that's it then?"

"Yes, pretty much." Saul wondered what he was missing.

"Can I see the card that lawyer gave you?"

"Sure, here." Saul studied her as she took it. "What's up?"

"Well, it's funny, because Watts had a little bit different take on it."

Saul sighed. Having an invisible friend spy on your life was just unfair. "OK, well what did he say?"

"He said," Aimee started and then walked to the kitchen. Deliberately drawing it out she pulled a bottle of water from the refrigerator and took a sip before continuing.

"He said that this guy," she held up the card, "wasn't a lawyer at all."

"Was he a cop?" Saul stood now, annoyed.

"Better." Aimee took another sip. "He's a necromancer. And not just any necromancer, he's Dennis' boss on top of that."

"Bullshit." Saul replayed the scene in his head, looking for evidence one way or the other.

"According to Watts, your 'lawyer' friend's real name is Seamus. He walked in flanked by two spirit bodyguards. Big dead guys, and they even told Watts to sod off or else. He claimed he didn't know you and was just hanging out there because he died in the jail. Odd that they bought it given that Watts walks around in a blood-stained military uniform all the time."

Saul plopped back down, his body weakening. A tiny flash of Watts' body on the Humvee rooftop flashed by and Saul ignored it. "Is that it?"

"No. Watts also described your new mate as a patchwork of souls, more than he could count, bits and pieces -- mostly the good bits and pieces -- all clearly stuck together like some crappy teenaged collage."

Saul struggled for something to say.

Aimee held out the business card and laughed. "I mean the man's card says Lou Cee Ford? How could you possibly take that as a real name?"

"I just suck I guess."

Aimee sensed Saul nearing some sort of emotional line and eased her tone to something more friendly than accusatory. "Didn't you wonder how you got an attorney without calling one?"

"I've never been arrested before."

"Really?" She waited for a response. He just nodded. "Right, either you call a lawyer, or you ask for a court appointed one. They never just show up, unless I guess you're a bazillionaire or a TV star."

"That's good to know and the next time I'm in a police station I'll use that."

She walked in and sat down on the chair across from him and put her hand on his shoulder. "Hey, I would have been fooled too probably. Except for the card. And the not-calling-him-first part. OK I wouldn't have been fooled. Sorry." Aimee pulled her hand back.

"Tell Watts thanks for me." Saul leaned back and rubbed his eyes. He felt too shamed to make eye contact with anyone. "Wait, I can do it. Thanks Watts."

"There's more but he couldn't tell me what it was."

"What do you mean?"

"I mean Watts says there's more to the story, but he needs permission from Aditi-Alhread to tell you."

"What? Why?"

"How do I know? Sometimes the dead can be a bit dodgy."

Saul felt a sudden need to regain control of his life. "Watts is keeping secrets now? You mind if I, you know, had another word with him for a moment?"

"What? You mean like you talk and I translate again?" She watched Saul for a moment. "No, not now. I don't do domestic arguments. I say we hit the road tonight instead."

"Seriously?"

"Look," she said, "this thing hasn't gone all Pete Tong yet. You didn't tell them my name, or anything about me, and I'm just getting my second wind for the night. We'll drop your car off at some random hotel, the authorities and possibly the necromancers will busy themselves watching the parking lot or searching rooms for you, and we'll be off in my truck headed to my uncle's."

Saul didn't want to give up the topic of whatever Watts was keeping to himself, but suspected she wasn't going to help him anymore that night for sure.

"Do we even know your uncle would help us?"

"I'm going out tonight one way or another. You can either come with me, or go back to... wherever it is you would go if you weren't here." Aimee's voice didn't put any conviction into the threat, and then it softened even more. "You wanted me to help you, so let me help."

Saul weighed his options, and realized he didn't really have any. No, screw that, he had plenty.

"OK we'll go, but if anything goes wrong... if we bump into any cops or thugs or ghosts or whatever, even if I mess it up royally, I get the final word. Deal?"

"Oh yes sir." Aimee made a mock salute.

"You don't sound serious. Are you serious?"

"Maybe." Aimee smiled and then left to pack.

CHAPTER 23

The first hour of the trip coughed and sputtered with last minute preparations, purchases, and discussions on exactly what precautions they would need to take. They left Saul's cell phone in his car, and he made a single but notable withdrawal from the ATM nearest the hotel where they parked it.

The next hour filled with uneventful small talk. Here Saul found himself pondering what made this trip different... no, what made Aimee different from Aditi-Alhread.

For one, Aimee didn't have the endless deep eyes, but something about an honest bright smile instead of one that seemed practiced (or, more likely, remembered from some other life), helped to make up for it. Along with that came actual emotions, good and bad, plus Aimee got tired, she got hungry, and as she'd already demonstrated more times than Saul cared to admit, she had to stop for bathroom breaks. And no orders. Not once. Everything was a question, or a request. For the first time in a long time Saul felt relaxed around another person. Although she did talk about sex a lot, and since Saul just couldn't see a relationship between the two of them going very far, that made him a little uncomfortable. Fortunately, she brought up other topics too.

"So, you Army guys are in pretty good shape yeah?" Aimee asked from the driver's seat, having just taken over for Saul.

"I suppose. Not like in the movies, but, better than average."

"You run a lot? Lift weights? Break boards with your bare hands?"

Saul smiled. "I run, mostly. Push-ups and sit ups. That's about it. In the old days we did grass drills and stuff, but not so much anymore."

"Grass drills?" Aimee laughed. "Is that like when you crawl under razor wire with things exploding nearby?"

"No no, just a bunch of exercises out in the grass. What about you?"

"Do I crawl under razor wire with things exploding nearby?"

"Exercise. Work out."

"Right. Well I do the elliptical at least three hours a week, sometimes four or five."

"The elliptic-what?"

"It's a machine at the gym. Your legs move, like you're running, but you've got these hand-holds that you pull back and forth with it so they get a work out too."

Saul couldn't quite picture the machine, but he imagined something covered in wires and fancy read-outs. Possibly an espresso machine. "Oh God that sounds worse than a treadmill."

"No not at all."

"Just please tell me you don't listen to music while you do it." Saul repeated the request in his head while waiting for an answer.

"Of course *I* don't listen to music while I work out. Workouts are a time for myself. Last thing I want is… well, you know."

"Right, of course." Saul said, a little embarrassed for asking.

"They do have these giant TVs playing everywhere if you want, although I usually fancy a crossword puzzle…"

"You do a crossword puzzle?! While you work out?!" Saul sat up to confront her.

"Oh piss off!" She laughed. "Why not? Work out my mind and body at the same time."

"That is so lame! Running, that's exercise. If you can read or watch TV, you aren't doing it hard enough. Exercise is supposed to happen outdoors, not some sweaty humid building with sports stars' faces plastered all over the walls."

"Really?" She cast him a quick sideways glance.

"Yes, really."

"So you volunteering to take me running then? Show me a real workout?"

"Sure. I can do that." Saul sat back and watched the twin circles of light on the dark road up ahead. He meant it when he said it, but suspected it would never happen.

"Wait," Saul continued, "aren't you a smoker too?"

Another glance, this one more tolerant than flirtatious. Saul realized his tone had probably sounded a bit judgmental.

"Just asking." He held up his hands and smiled to relieve the tension.

"Only when I drink." Her tone perked up again.

"And how often do you drink?" Saul asked, and then quickly amended, "I mean, if it's OK to ask and you feel like telling me."

"New rules." She said without looking his way. "I realize you're in charge, but I'm taking this one liberty. For the rest of this trip, any question goes, but the answers have to be truthful. No lying."

"We still have a long way to go." Saul replied.

"Right, which will be awfully boring if we limit ourselves. Besides, you already know one of my biggest secrets, and I know sod all about yours."

Much like the idle invitation to go running together, plus a bet he'd lost and hoped she'd totally forgotten about by now, he thought that since their relationship probably had a shelf life of two of three more days at the most, it couldn't do much harm.

"Deal." Somehow he felt tricked again right after he said it, but shrugged it off.

"OK then, what was the last question?"

"How often do you drink?"

"Not as much as I used to. A few here and there after a gig."

"And how much did you used to?"

"Hey! We alternate questions. Otherwise it's not fair."

"Fine, go ahead."

"How much do you drink?"

"I've never been much of a drinker. In fact, except for a few nights out during basic training, I'm not sure I've been really drunk but two or three times in my life."

"To answer your next one, I used to get pissed every weekend."

"Pissed about what?"

"No no, not pissed like pissed off, pissed like drunk."

"British thing?"

"Anyway, at one point I held a record of eighteen consecutive months without missing getting drunk on the weekend."

"Wow, that sounds healthy. What changed?"

"You really want to know?"

"Oh, probably not after you asked it that way." Saul flinched and waited.

"There were a few parties I went to that helped support my drinking habit, regulars. And so one morning after I wake up at one of them, in this apartment, no idea what had happened the night before, naked on a bed with two other guys."

"Yeah that would do it."

"No it wouldn't. That happened before."

Of course it had, Saul thought.

"No this time," she continued, "this time I woke up with one of those big red easy buttons superglued to the small of my back."

"What?" Saul burst out louder than he'd intended.

"Yes! Superglued to my bloody skin! Anyway I felt like such a mug I ripped it off – another ace move – and a week later, after those wounds healed, I paid to have a tramp stamp added over it to cover up the scars."

"Nice." Saul was at a complete loss how to respond. She'd just broken his internal meter for atypical behavior, and yet somehow he still felt empathy towards her. "I think I'm going to have a hard time giving you any answers that top that one."

"Oh I'll find something." She said. Then after a pause, "anything else on that topic before we move on and I get a shot?"

Saul thought a second. "So, why did you drink so much in the first place? I mean, was it just because that's what you do in college?"

"Bastard! I knew I should have stopped it there."

"We can stop there." Saul felt actual anxiety in her voice.

"No, can't go against my own rules now can I?"

"You can change the rules." Saul honestly didn't want to upset her, but also wondered if she hadn't given him that opening on purpose.

"Things changed when I got to university, and I didn't deal with it very well I guess."

Yes, the more Saul thought about the more he suspected they were heading down a path he'd seen before. Soldiers, when they needed to talk about something, rarely just came out and started chatting about it. They tossed out teasers and waited for you to pull it out of them. That way they didn't seem like wimps who couldn't keep things to themselves.

"Things changed how?" Saul knew his role. Ask questions until the dam broke and then just sit and listen.

"OK, my dad was American and met my mom in London on a business trip. They got married, I was born in the States, then went to school in England until I was twelve. Dad's job changed, we moved back to the States, mum hated it, divorce, back to England with her, dad had a minor heart attack, so back to university in the States where I could look after him. Anyway, it didn't take me long into grade school to learn that most of my mates had grown out of their invisible friends while I kept mine." As she spoke, Saul noticed her hands subtly wringing the steering wheel. "So fine, I learned to keep them a secret. No problem. But they were always there, you know. They were my real mates. They understood me, and never judged me or made fun of me."

"And that changed?"

Aimee noticed her hands and forced them to stop moving.

"When I was a kid, when a new soul latched onto me, they stayed with me. Like, bodyguards or protectors or nannies or advisors, for like, ever. No matter what I did, they were there to support me."

She paused. Saul waited quietly for her to continue.

"So after I got here and got my own place and started taking classes… I guess I got less interesting or something. Or maybe less innocent, or maybe they thought I just didn't need looking after anymore, I don't know."

"They don't stay anymore?"

"If someone sticks around a whole month now I'm surprised." She said, and Saul thought her eyes might be more glossy then they were a few seconds before. "In fact, Ginger Tim – a red-headed fan who came to every show before and after he died of alcohol poisoning – he just left me the other day, right before you called me."

Left me, Saul noted, like breakups.

"Down to three again, including Watts." she continued, "And soon they'll all move on too." A tear broke loose and she let it fall without acknowledging it.

"Not as long as Watts can keep seeing you shower." Saul added. It worked, and she laughed a little laugh and quickly wiped her cheek.

"I'm a mug aren't I? I shouldn't have told you all that."

"I'm not actually sure what a mug is, but it was my fault," Saul lied. "I did ask you the questions."

"Like I said, I'll get you back."

Saul forced a laugh but didn't comment. Rules or no rules, he didn't feel quite ready to bare his soul just yet.

It hadn't mattered before, but now, even if he never did see Aimee again, he felt he wasn't ever going to forget her.

"But first," Aimee said, brighter in spirit, "chocolate break."

"You mean pee break."

"Right, that too."

She took an exit and pulled into what looked like the single cube of light surrounded by its own little void. The radiance gave form to gum-covered concrete, over-flowing trash cans, and the shells of dead bugs blown up against the dirty walls, while everything just beyond fell off into total oblivion.

A chunky man in a thick jacket adorned with the golden Shell symbol waddled out to their car and leaned in the window. Tufts of gray hair poked out from beneath his black ski cap like little antennae trying to sense the car's interior.

"Regular?" He grinned and nodded when he got a good look at Aimee's face. Saul hadn't noticed they'd crossed into Oregon where it was illegal to pump your own gas. Every time he drove south and needed to fill up he felt like he hit the State That Time Forgot and half expected to find a Mel's Diner just across the street.

Every stop, their routine consisted of Aimee going inside while Saul waited and paid – he'd agreed they'd split the food, but he insisted he covered the gas and she reluctantly agreed. Afterwards he'd go in and they'd both usually grab a crappy-for-you snack and something with caffeine in it. Again Saul marveled at the lack of stress involved. Neither pressured the other to hurry, any healthy eating critiques were met with responses in kind, and usually at least one or both of them got distracted at some point by 'shiny pretties' for sale near the register. Aimee tended towards the metal stylized cigarette lighter covers, while Saul drifted more to the glass display cases filled with fantasy figurines or plastic trolls. They determined early on that they both had a weakness for the stands of comedy bumper stickers and mutually agreed to avoid them the rest of the trip.

The next leg Aimee kept driving, and they ate their fat pills in guilty silence for twenty miles. It didn't take long for her to start the questions game back up again, and Saul did his best to stay honest.

As he could have predicted, once she learned he'd been in Iraq twice she immediately asked if he'd killed anyone. Civilians always ask that.

No, he started, but then went on to explain the number of times he'd ordered people, including Watts, to shoot at the bad guys, which usually ended up killing them. They talked about his first patrol, and his worst patrol, and the worst (read goriest) bodies he'd seen, and what it was like living in a place where sex was against the rules. In return she compared life in London to life in Tacoma, spilled the details about her crazy oversexed mother, and imparted Saul with knowledge of as many college sex standards and drinking games as she could think of.

The topic Saul feared most, Nicole's death, passed by only briefly, and for some reason Aimee didn't press him for a whole lot of details. Perhaps when she sensed she had indeed found Saul's weak spot that she felt no need to exploit it. Maybe finding it was enough, maybe she didn't want any more drama in a single car ride, maybe she was saving it for later. Fearing the later, Saul ended the topic by simply saying, "She thought I picked the Army over her. That was it." He hoped that would keep her from bringing it up again anytime soon. He wasn't sure what else there was to add anyway.

With all the talking, Eugene Oregon arrived almost as a surprise, quietly springing up around the highway and waiting to see if they would pass through without noticing. Not fooled, Aimee whipped through the side streets and small hills straight to a suburban home surrounded by a tall wooden fence. Just inside the gate Saul noticed a long carport shelter filled with plastic storage containers and dilapidated cardboard boxes. Beneath the remnants of a blue plastic tarp, he also made out two half-finished Harleys sitting in the grass surrounded by motorcycle parts.

"My uncle's a bit of a collector." Aimee muttered as they walked to the door.

The man who greeted her with a jolly bear hug looked nothing at all like Aimee. Uncle Brad, as he introduced himself, possessed short unkempt hair, a thick mustache that dove down almost past his chin, and wore a tan utility vest over a blue short sleeved dress shirt. Absent an accent of any sort, Saul figured him clearly from the American father's side of the family. Brad seemed in relatively good shape, but also didn't seem to have showered in anticipation of their arrival. Then again, Saul doubted anyone would look their freshest given the early hour.

Brad ushered them into a living room that wore the title in name only, as it seemed very little could fit in it to live. A desk in the back held two computer screens plus a laptop, all, Saul noticed, facing so none of the windows or the door could see whatever they displayed. The couch held white file boxes, as did the coffee table, both chairs, and most of the area in between, including the space beneath the Kiss pinball machine Saul suspected hadn't worked in decades.

"Don't worry," Brad said, "I keep the beds and bathrooms clear and clean. Promise."

"It's true," Aimee said to Saul, "he does. But stay away from the kitchen."

Since the kitchen had long ago been converted into what looked like a darkroom, Saul suspected that wouldn't be a problem.

"OK, you two can stay in here," Brad opened the door to a side bedroom, "and Aimee I'm sure you can show him where the facilities are."

Saul glanced in and saw only a queen sized bed and a few more stacks of boxes pressed up against the walls.

"Um," he started, hoping that word alone would convey what he thought.

Aimee smirked and turned back to her uncle. "What my eloquent friend so completely failed to communicate was that we actually are only friends."

Brad's eyebrows shot up in confusion, and then after glancing back into the room laughed, "Oh! I get it. Well then, OK, there's another couch in there, which has a much better chance of being comfortable than this one does. It is OK to be in the same room?"

Aimee turned back to Saul and gave him another one of the flirtatious glances she must know by now made him uneasy. "You're in charge."

Not wanting to sound prude, Saul agreed that would be fine and they both tossed their bags onto the bed. This room's couch held a few music stands that Brad whisked away somewhere and came back with another set of sheets and a pillow. A filing cabinet and a stereo system that had been state of the art ten years ago completed the room's inventory.

"Well," Brad started, clapping his hands together, "did you want me to put on some coffee and start on this little project of yours or shall we get some sleep first? I'm easy either way."

"I don't know," Aimee replied. "I mean, I don't really know how long this is going to take."

All three of them stood in the hallway between rooms, which would have annoyed Saul if he hadn't spent the better part of the night on his butt.

"Why don't you tell me what it is and I'll give you an idea." Brad said.

Aimee looked down at the floor, thinking. "So, if you were trying to find someone who was immortal, how would you do it?"

"You mean like 'there can be only one' immortal?"

"I have no idea what you're yakking about but sure, why not, how would you do it?"

Brad drew back. "Are you high? If you're high I promised your mom… "

"I'm not high. Look at my eyes." She leaned over and pointed. "See, not high."

Brad studied her, and as he did so, Saul noticed she clinched both her fists.

"Actually I am a bit tired." Saul chimed in. "Why don't we sleep on it?"

Aimee seemed frustrated but conceded. "OK boss."

After brushing his teeth, Saul stretched out and waited for Aimee to come in and turn off the light. The couch gave off a dusty smell with a hint of some sort of cleaner with lemon in it masking something that could have once been mildew. It reminded him of the smell of the couch in Aimee's place, although he was fairly confident that sofa scents weren't passed along hereditary lines. Looking around, he made a mental note not to reach his hand out above his head like he normally did for fear of getting it caught up in some of the stereo wires.

Aimee came out of the bathroom and, to Saul's relief, nothing weird happened. She didn't stroll out buck naked, she didn't invite him over, and she seemed just as tired as he was. He wondered what sorts of dreams that night – what very little was left of it – would hold for him, but before he could even anticipate the worst, he drifted off.

For the living, the slightest amount of pressure, a few ounces of force at most, is enough to push the power button on a home stereo receiver. For the dead, it requires a moment of pure rage, or utter fear, intense enough for them to push back against the Curtain, slam against it with all that they are worth, and move that tiny piece of plastic just so…

The room erupted with the automated sounds of a nearby pop radio station, ripping Saul and Aimee both forcibly back into consciousness.

"Aw bloody hell!" She screamed over the din of some over-processed female singer. "Saul what are you doing?!"

Saul struggled to remember if he'd bumped against anything. Aimee flipped on the lamp, still dazed but growing angrier by the second.

"OW!" Aimee held her hands over her ears. "Watts! Calm down! What are you saying?!?"

Saul jumped up. "What? What's going on?"

"Watts! Watts! He's screaming!" her eyes flashed about unfocused and wide. "Watts!"

Saul flexed and crouched with adrenalin, looking for anywhere to focus it. Aimee flew back and flailed madly on the bed, crying out in anguish.

"WHAT!?!" Saul yelled at her. "What can I do?!?"

"They took Watts!" She didn't open her eyes as she spoke, tears flowing freely and her fists balled and white-knuckled against her head.

"Who did?"

"I don't know!" She sobbed.

"What's going on?" Brad burst in wearing nothing but boxers and holding a nine millimeter pistol pointed up in the air.

"They took Watts…" Aimee kept crying without getting up. Saul waved at Brad to lower the gun, and then stroked Aimee's hair. He knew there was nothing to be said, and so he didn't try.

After a half hour Aimee calmed to simple sniveling, and despite Saul's protests she decided to take Brad up on his coffee offer. She cupped the mug in both hands and sat on the edge of the bed with Saul sitting beside her. With the words "I'm OK" she stopped all physical contact, and now he waited.

"It was like listening to a kid being dragged away by a stranger." She said in a quiet voice, staring out at some point in front of her. "He said it was hurting him."

Brad stood in the hallway without speaking. A knock on the front door pulled him away and at that point Saul realized that it was just starting to get light outside and the rest of the world was probably getting ready for their normal day. A few seconds later Brad returned.

"Visitor." He said.

He moved to the side and a familiar figure stepped into the doorway of the bedroom. Saul and Aimee both looked up, haggard and red-eyed, and when she saw them there Aditi-Alhread raised her eyebrows.

"What I'd miss?"

CHAPTER 24

Saul and Aimee stumbled through an explanation of the last hour while Aditi-Alhread listened impassively. They included the details from Saul's trip to the police station and how he met Seamus, plus everything Watts had told them about the encounter.

When they finished she stood silent for what seemed like a very long time. No one around her could gather the strength for idle banter, so they all remained quiet. Finally she asked, "Why are we in Oregon now?"

"Actually," Saul grumbled, "that pause was the part where you were supposed to reassure us that we wouldn't stop until we got Watts back. Or help him. Or care. You know, something."

"Saul, you know better than to make promises like that," Aditi-Alhread said, "and so do I."

She walked over and put her hand on his shoulder. "But moving forward is what we need to do right now. That OK?"

Saul nodded. Yeah what-the-fuck-ever.

"We thought my uncle could help us find Ut-Napishtim." Aimee said.

"Where did you hear that name?" Aditi-Alhread asked and pulled her hand off Saul's shoulder.

"Watts told us you were looking for him."

"Did anyone mention that name to Seamus?" She watched Saul as she asked.

"No," Saul said, "but if they took Watts…"

"OK." Aditi-Alhread said with a hint of sharpness, cutting him off and keeping the conversation from going down that path again. Then she moved closer to Aimee and spoke in a gentle tone. "And can your uncle help us find Ut-Napishtim?"

"Is that the 'immortal' you were talking about?" Brad almost grinned as he spoke, but thought better of it.

"I don't think he believes us just yet." Saul replied.

"I'm in the room." Brad added with a jovial tone edged with fatigue.

Aditi-Alhread turned towards him. "Do you believe Aimee can see and hear spirits?"

"I don't know I believe she can, but I've also never said she couldn't."

She studied his face a moment then glanced back at Aimee and Saul. "Don't worry, I'll convince him. You two get cleaned up."

"We've barely slept and…" Saul started.

"And you'll probably have a chance for a nap later on today after we get Brad started on his part." She smiled in a way that erased the rudeness of the interruption, and then guided Aimee's uncle out to the living room.

With Aditi-Alhread back, Saul immediately felt both relief and resentment. They had been doing fine without her, and she wasn't back ten minutes and it already felt like... like if someone didn't give him orders people like Watts would end up the worse for it.

Aimee leapt off the bed and into the bathroom, and Saul stumbled over and back onto the couch. He did not feel like a leader any more, he only felt like a soldier, and sometimes soldiers just didn't listen. Without even caring that the lamp light filled whatever corners of the room the rising sun missed, he draped his arm over his eyes and was sound asleep out before Aimee returned.

Around ten he woke to the sound of Aimee's light snoring, which by itself seemed worth noting. Forcing open one eye he could see her sprawled diagonal to the normal length of bed, her head nearest him and her feet draping off the opposite side. He didn't see any indication of how much time had passed other than that the room remained brightly lit.

He threw on the same layers of clothing from the day before and tried not to wake her as he slipped on his shoes. Then he stretched and went out to find Aditi-Alhread standing behind Brad at the computer desk. Brad seemed pale, but focused.

"I guess she convinced you then?" Saul asked, rubbing his eyes.

"I don't want to talk about it." Brad's eyes stayed on the middle of the screens, three total now with the laptop humming quietly beside the bigger computer. He jotted something down on an index card and put it on top of one of several large piles sitting wherever wires, mouse pads and keyboards didn't already occupy. Saul wondered if Aditi-Alhread had used the pencil-through-the-hand-trick or something even more disturbing.

"Sure thing." Saul said. "Got it figured out yet?"

"The good thing about necromancers," Brad replied, "and probably the dead, is most of them don't know jack about computers." If Aditi-Alhread took offense, she didn't show it.

"I'll mark that off as a firm 'not quite but almost' then." Saul rubbed his unwashed hair – longer than it had been in years – and sauntered over to the door. "I'm going for a walk."

Saul never really liked walks. Drive if you need to get somewhere, or better yet run if you can, but walking just took up extra time. His desire to get out of the house coerced his feet to move despite all that, and he just let them take him into the cold air and down the street.

As he walked he recognized his mind's method for dealing with the aftermath of tragedy or failure – it simply shut off his memory and concentrated on drawing energy from his surroundings. He could fight it if he wanted, force himself to anguish over the past, but some part of him knew he needed a mental palette cleansing, as it were. Sleep did that for normal people, with normal problems, he supposed. But they never woke up to a mortar attack, or in the Netherworld, or while someone ripped the last wisps of a dead friend away. No, for him, he needed to control his surroundings, soak in the simple things, notice the details, convince himself there were things in life other than problems and peril.

He stopped at the edge of a park without any idea how he'd gotten there. Oregon, he remembered from childhood visits, liked to landscape the areas beneath underpasses. Saul never understood why, but he also never bothered to ask the question. He glanced around the rich thick grass in an area cut out of a wall of Douglas Fir. Flower bushes dotted the edges of the field, spheres of multi-colored blooms like organic fireworks frozen in mid burst. A single couple bundled up in dark clothing walked a pair of Irish Setters around the perimeter.

He stood and watched a few moments, and then continued on until he came to a bridge over the Willamette river. He took in a deep smell hoping for the salt water scent of the Puget Sound north of Tacoma, and instead caught a moldy odor he didn't recognize. Odd that he sometimes still missed things like the "Tacoma Aroma." Whenever he thought of it for some reason it always brought up images of the day he and some friends went jumping across a line of logs floating in the water, followed by the hour of lectures on how dangerous and stupid he'd been.

Somehow he'd reached another neighborhood, and now stood in front of the local coffee shop. He knew this because, in a fit of originality, the sign out front proclaimed the building to be the "Local Coffee Shop."

Saul noted that the owner left the inside mostly unfinished dark crimson brick covered in message boards heavy with fliers for local plays, bands, and miscellaneous hippy events. Saul's body moved to stand in line while his brain focused on the woman ringing people up.

Short stringy dark hair, prominent pointed nose, small horn-rimmed glasses, she greeted everyone with well-rehearsed sincerity. If the person in line wore any sort of professional attire, then every time without fail she said, "All business all day or is there some time in there scheduled for fun?" It didn't matter that the target of this sentence heard that exact same question asked of the three people before them. And just like every day since that enterprising young fellow drew a cup of coffee on a napkin, crossed out "$0.10" and wrote "$4" above it, almost everyone in the coffee line paid with some sort of plastic. The register girl worked this into her routine by holding up each card, lifting her off hand up like a maestro, and then straining to say the name on each card like a French teacher emphasizing pronunciation to freshmen. It didn't matter if the name was "Smith" or "Galifianakis," she wanted each customer to know she cared enough to get it exactly right. Saul, paying in cash while wearing jeans and several layers of long sleeve shirts, received only the phrase, "Righteous my friend" before she passed him his change and frappuccino.

It took him a moment to notice Aditi-Alhread waiting for him at the front door. He didn't know what she expected, and he didn't care. He sat at a table covered in the local arts chronicle, and a few seconds later she sat down in front of him.

"Where were you?" Saul asked without looking up. Instead of glanced over an article about some local film student who showed some type of promise in the eyes of the Eugene community.

"You mean when Watts was taken?" Again that unnerving ability to speak softly and still cut through all background noise.

"Yes, what else would I be talking about?"

"That's not impor…"

"I got arrested, and you didn't show up then either." He sipped his drink. "Good thing I guess, since I ended up speaking with the head necromancer. Might have been awkward."

Saul still hadn't pulled his gaze from the chronicle. "Actually," he continued, "Seamus was the one who asked what sort of friend leaves another to be blamed potentially for murder."

"Saul." The way she said the word and stopped clearly implied she would say nothing else until she had his undivided attention. He looked up.

"Remember what happened to that soul?" she said, "The one I poured in the bathroom sink? The way it misted up and floated away?"

Saul nodded.

"This world recognizes I don't belong, and the longer I stay the harder I have to concentrate not to have that same thing happen to me."

"Well then, why don't you just go back?"

"I'm an abomination in the Netherworld." She said. "Here I'm immortal, fast, lethal, virtually invulnerable. On the other side of the Curtain my only ability that separates me from the masses is the singular power to run away. I can come here any time I want, they can't. So when I can no longer hold my form, I go there and hide in the shadows of the City of Shadows until I gain enough strength back."

"OK," Saul said, "then why don't I just go back?"

Aditi-Alhread leaned back, watching him as she did so. Her voice in his head seemed calmer somehow. "What do you mean?"

"You and these necromancers hate each other, got it. You don't like them stealing souls, they I guess are afraid you'll throw them out of windows." Or maybe there is more to it than that, Saul thought, since it seemed they knew about her before she shoved a guy through a window. "But you're asking a lot from me and I'm not sure this makes a ton of sense anymore."

A few seconds of silence before he continued. "You have to admit it is asking a lot for me to take these sorts of risks for…" Saul's words trailed off and his hand waved as if to search for the rest of that sentence. He hadn't thought this conversation through and wasn't sure how to end it.

Her voice stayed the same, but her expression went rigid and more stern than normal. "If I lose. If they stop me or capture me, they will know all that I know, including how you have helped so far."

Saul weighed in his mind whether he cared if necromancers came after him or not. At the moment, it didn't seem real or significant.

"Saul," she spoke as if she knew his thoughts, "they go after easy targets. After me comes you, after you comes anyone dead you knew well."

Nicole.

"And after that they start scouting out the living."

A chilled wave washed over Saul, something he recognized as helplessness.

Aditi-Alhread watched him, waiting. He felt like putting his face in his hands, or running his fingers through his hair, or hitting the table, or any other stereotypical shows of emotion he'd seen on TV to make sure everyone knew he was upset. Because he wasn't. He was blank, and that worried him.

Then, he noticed the faint tightening in his stomach, the tingling anxiety in his fingertips, the warmth on the back of his neck. Those were things he'd spent his life learning to suppress and ignore, things he normally buried, but they were still there. Disappointed that they weren't stronger, that they weren't crippling or overwhelming, he welcomed them anyway.

Saul let out a long slow breath. "What about Watts? Do we know where Watts…"

"Saul stop talking." Very quick, sharp. Her glance targeted something behind the coffee counter.

"You are REALLY starting to piss me off!" Saul felt a rush of blood moving to his face, all the other emotions combining and feeding off each other.

"Saul," quiet voice, calm, as she looked at him eye-to-eye. "We should talk about this outside."

"Fine." Saul intended to storm out the door before she could react, but she stayed right beside him.

Saul stopped just outside the door and spun on her. "OK, what?!?" He yelled. She gripped his arm with a strength that reminded him of Jack.

"Can we walk as we talk… please?"

Saul weighed the outcomes of a potential struggle and gave in, just like he always did. As they walked Aditi-Alhread led with a pace just shy of running, exactly the speed Saul hated. She looked back over her shoulder once and her expression changed Saul's mood.

"OK what?" He said.

"Long version or short?" She asked.

"If we're walking back, we've got some time. I say long version." Already his breathing made it difficult to speak. Aditi-Alhread, of course, had no such problem.

"OK, over the years, we've done the math. Nearly seven out of ten people go straight to the Netherworld when they die. They've had past lives, they know the routine. If you get really bored sometime I'll tell you about your previous four, but I'm sorry to say you probably won't be inspired by them."

"Good, good. Thanks."

"Anyway, only one out of ten is a First Lifer. The ones who tend to hang around and sometimes show up as ghosts."

"What happens…" he double checked his math, "…to the other twenty percent?"

"We don't know." She continued to drag him along, scanning their surroundings as they went. "There are theories, of course. Some say they go to an actual heaven, or hell, or receive some sort of salvation or oblivion, or possibly find some secret place in the Netherworld to live. We're counting the ones taken by necromancers in the numbers by the way. Regardless - and it's most obvious when it happens with the famous people - we can't account for that last two out of ten."

"OK." Saul slowed. The only thing worse than walking was speed walking. He wondered how far he could run in his current shoes.

"Back to First Lifers. One out of ten means 15,000 new ghosts every day in the world, 650 to 700 in the United States in particular." She stopped pulling so hard on Saul and slowed to a normal pace. "And most of those find their way to the Netherworld in a few days or so. All that adds up to mean the average number of ghost s in a given location isn't that many. Enough to be constant, but not enough to be too crowded."

"Maybe I should have gone with the short version."

"That coffee shop started with one ghost. In the few minutes after I walked in, two more showed up, and all three were watching us."

Saul mapped out the nearby terrain for possible ambushes, places to take cover. "And now they're behind us." He said.

She didn't turn. "Yes. We can't let them follow us Saul. Right now I'm solid. I can't affect them any more than they could affect you normally." She paused, thinking. "But they're new. They probably haven't figured out to call up their animal experiences yet. If I shifted over, I could probably take two, maybe three."

"So all of them then?"

"No. Five now."

"Crap."

"Run Saul. Take winding turns, duck in small places, treat it like you were trying to lose a living person. It should work the same way. Except they won't tire, so you can't either."

"Wait! I…." Saul stopped, alone in what seemed a peaceful quiet stretch of road between the highway and the park.

He gathered up his fear and frustration, let them come naturally, took two deep breaths and released it all in a mad sprint. A few hundred yards later he veered sideways into a neighborhood. Straight for a while, sticking close to houses and walls, cutting sharp turns through any small openings he spotted between fences, bushes or parked cars.

Saul cursed under his breath over and over, welcoming the anger that numbed him to the pain from the shoes, the furnace in his chest, and the first hint of stabbing needles just below his ribcage. When his body rebelled, he screamed at it, demanding it go further until at last the throbbing in his side spiked and nearly pulled him to the ground.

He darted into a gas station parking lot and nearly knocked down a gaggle of teenagers. He turned into the tiny alley between the building and a barber shop and slowed his pace to a mere jog. If anyone still followed him, they'd won. Besides, continuing to flee like a madman would eventually attract the police, if those kids weren't dialing 9-1-1 already.

Maintaining a very slow but steady shuffle, he circled around until he recognized a landmark. A few minutes later he collapsed, covered in sweat and feet burning, on Brad's front porch steps. Rolling over to his back, he pulled off a shoe and threw it at the front door. After the second shoe, Brad answered.

After one look he called back for Aimee and they both ran out and knelt down beside Saul, asking if he was OK, checking for wounds and pestering him about what had happened. He explained it as best he could, which calmed the immediate situation, and Brad went back in to get Saul a towel and a glass of ice water.

"What do we do?" Aimee asked.

"I have no idea." Saul said. He took two sips of the water and poured the rest on his face.

Sudden motion startled them all as a dark figure leapt over the fence like a panther. The form landed on one knee and stayed there, a total absence of light, with wisps of black tendrils floating behind and off into the air. Two clear white eyes formed first, and as the tendrils drew back into the shape, first the outline and then the familiar colors of Aditi-Alhread and her uniform shifted into focus. She rose, stumbled, and then stood, deliberately straight and defiant, the way a wounded general might in front of his troops.

"Brad?" She said in a clear low voice.

He stared, mesmerized for a moment, then spoke with a start. "Yes! Sorry! I have something! Everyone inside!"

Brad opened the door wide and Aimee took a step his way. Saul pulled himself up and waited for Aditi-Alhread to walk slowly past him and up the steps.

"How much time do we have?" Brad turned all the screens on his desk facing the group.

"Say what you need." Aditi-Alhread said.

Brad looked down at the middle screen and took a moment to collect his thoughts. "OK, first I sat down and made a list of job opportunities I would imagine for an immortal. Then I collected a list of everyone on the west coast famous for antique collecting and historical writings and teachings etc. That got me nothing but a list of names."

He hit a button on the keyboard and a document opened on the computer. "Then," he continued, "I focused on those names – particularly anyone interested in Ancient Babylon, Sumerian culture, etc. etc. – and looked for repeat hits. That's when I noticed Ahmad al-Yani."

Brad smiled and looked for reactions.

"Go on," Aimee humored him.

"He wrote a book of ancient history essays in 1834, focusing on the Middle East. That's fine, but then in 1947 that same name, Ahmad al-Yani shows up as one of the main characters in a piece of historical fiction written by a guy named Charles Barthold. I thought it might just have been that Charles Barthold liked Ahmad al-Yani and put him in as an homage, except that Charles Barthold's story was about an Arabic couple who moved to Northern California and lived with a tribe of Miwok Indians, and I thought the Arabic couple thing was awfully coincidental."

"He's just going to keep going on like this." Aimee crossed her arms and leaned against the boxes on the couch.

"I don't mind." Aditi-Alhread said.

"Maybe we could hit the highlights?" Saul added.

"These are the highlights." Brad said. "Right, so here's a picture of Charles Barthold taken in 1943." Brad hit another button and a black and white image of a man in a suit popped up on the middle screen.

Brad gave them a second to view the image before talking. "Now, flash forward to today. I find a professor by the name of Leopold Kondakov who is most famous for his research in Miwok Indian anthropological studies, but also holds a doctorate in Ancient Babylonian history. Which is weird. He does the guest lecture circuit around the Northern California circle of colleges and… here's his picture."

Another button click and a modern image of a man's face filled the first screen. Side-by-side, there could be no doubt they were pictures of the same person, but taken sixty years apart.

"Holy crap." Saul said.

"Ace work uncle." Aimee said.

"Do we have an address?" Aditi-Alhread asked. She walked forward and put her face right in front of the two screens.

"In fact I do." Brad smiled. "And I've already Map Quested it for you." He held up a printout to Aditi-Alhread who took it and handed it straight to Saul.

"Brad," Aditi-Alhread approached and put her hand on his cheek. "Thank you."

"Hey no problem. Friends of Aimee are always welcome."

Aditi-Alhread turned back towards Saul. "As soon as you two are ready. I'll be in the car."

CHAPTER 25

Seamus marveled at the teeth of the steel comb popping down into the grooves of the large copper plate of the mahogany Porter music box. The tinny sound of *The Impossible Dream* on endless repeat gave the gift shop the surreal air that the manager no doubt thought appropriate for the Winchester Mystery House. A mood heightened, Seamus reasoned, by the arcade palm reader, love rater, personality tester, and the dispenser of Zelda's personalized fortunes. More fodder for the same idiots who would buy one of the disposable cameras for sale directly beneath the "no photography allowed on the tours" sign.

Five hours earlier the lucky sighting of Aditi-Alhread in Oregon spun things into action. With her on the move, she had to have learned something about Ut-Napishtim. The only thing Seamus had paused for on his way out the door was the rosewood case with his special vials of liquid souls. Stolen sexual experiences may have built his fortune, but what he brought to San Jose was going to change his place in the mortal world. That assumed the three mercenaries who Dennis hired to replace Jack merged with these souls the way Seamus anticipated.

He glanced at his watch and let out a small cough to catch Dennis' attention. The last tour would end soon, and then the two men would get to conduct the "overnight private paranormal research" Seamus paid two thousand dollars for. Still, no need to rush. The evening's pinnacle was several hours away.

He knew Ut-Napishtim lived in the mountains – all the texts agreed on that – and with Aditi-Alhread heading south, that meant one of California's eight significant mountain ranges. Seamus couldn't cover that much territory with the handful of spirits chained up in basements across Portland. He needed to recruit a legion, all at once, to put up a net across the mountain passes and highways. And that is what brought him to the greatest necromantic edifice in the Western Hemisphere.

Mrs. Winchester, so the common legend went, worked on the construction of her home non-stop for thirty-eight years in order to create something to appease – or confuse – the ghosts of all those killed by the Winchester rifle. Seamus smiled every time he thought of it. What passed as simple idiosyncrasies to the guides and their tours stuck out so clearly to someone of his craft.

Best of all was the "logic" behind why she sealed off the front thirty rooms after the San Francisco earthquake of 1906. The books said she thought the earthquake might have been punishment for her spending too much time on that part of the house's construction.

Bullshit.

Not a coincidence that the Grand Ballroom was one of the ones sealed off. A ceiling with nine sections of thirteen tiles? A room of six hardwoods painstakingly put together with almost no iron or nails, lit by an imported gas chandelier which Mrs. Winchester personally added a thirteenth light to? So many symbols of power for a simple room where a simple little old lady used to play a pump organ alone in the middle of the night. Seamus couldn't even walk near that chamber now without getting a headache. Packed full of restless dead, wall to wall and spilling down into the basement, at least he would offer them… not freedom, certainly, but perhaps a taste of the great outdoors.

And those were the ones ensnared in the *flawed* room. The real collection, the tunnels where the lures and traps for the undead still worked to this day, those branched out from the lost wine cellars. Still unknown to the general public, Seamus found them not through Mrs. Winchester herself – he never could locate her soul – but from the long dead John Hanson, the foreman who helped her build the place.

"Sir," Dennis slapped shut his cell phone. "Just so you know, the three new employees took the… ingested the… " Dennis looked around the gift shop.

"Yes I know what they took."

"Right, well, as you predicted, the initial reaction went violently, but all three survived and seem to be in line with what we wanted."

"Collateral Damage?" Seamus asked.

"Nothing we couldn't handle sir." Dennis didn't want to go into details. Since their private jet ride landed, he'd spent most of the time on the phone having bodies removed and either hidden or cremated.

"OK," Seamus said. The grounds seemed empty now but for the few staff members checking the doors and alarms. "I'm going to where I need to be. What are you going to do?"

Seamus asked the question without looking at Dennis, like one might ask a child to repeat a line they memorized for the school play. The day's events had Dennis so distracted he didn't even take offense at Seamus' manner.

"I wait here, and ring the bell tower three times at precisely midnight, and again at two in the morning."

"Good." Seamus sighed with relief when someone shut off the music box. He finally felt like he was getting to flex his new-found muscle, to take his power out for a test drive and see what he could really do to this world… these worlds. "We may not burn in hell for eternity after all Dennis."

CHAPTER 26

"Think she's up for it?" Aimee glanced between the front seats at Aditi-Alhread in the back. Saul glanced up from the road to Aditi-Alhread's reflection in the rear-view mirror. He recognized Aimee's jovial tone, but to be honest, it didn't look like Aditi-Alhread could handle much of anything at the moment.

"What are you talking about?" She asked.

"On the way down here Saul and I played this questions game. You know, all honesty, that sort of thing." Aimee smiled. "You in?"

"It might be an interesting change for someone to have to ask rather than to simply glance and see the history of your essence." Aditi-Alhread didn't smile back, but also didn't frown. She seemed distant, and more pale than usual.

"Wait," Aimee said, "do you already know everything about us?"

"Not everything." She replied. "I can't read your thoughts, for example, but I can see everything you've experienced, in any lifetime."

"I was young, I needed the money!" Aimee yelled out and laughed.

Saul recognized the movie quote and laughed with her. Their companion in the back, of course, did not.

"Yes," Aditi-Alhread said after they quieted down. "But you went on from there to marry a very respected and successful silk merchant, so it all worked out in the end."

Aimee's eyes widened as she let that sink in. "That's not funny."

"Maybe." Aditi-Alhread maintained eye contact and then, although Aimee wasn't sure, she thought she saw her wink.

"Sod! Off!" Aimee turned to Saul. "I think she just totally burned me."

"She might have." Saul replied.

Aimee opened a fresh bottle of water and sipped it, glaring sideways towards the back seat as she did so. "So where's the uniform from?"

"95th Rifles." She answered.

Aimee leaned over again and studied it. "It's Ace." She said. "And torn." She pointed at a small two-inch rip on the right side of the stomach.

"Bayonet wound."

"That how you died?" Aimee hesitated before she asked, uncertain whether she touched upon a taboo topic.

"More or less." Something about Aditi-Alhread's voice hinted that the story held a lot more than that, but Aimee decided to leave that for another day. Something else troubled her more.

"One of the last things Watts said was that he'd learned a bunch of stuff about Seamus when he saw him face to face." The energy drained out of Aimee's voice. "But that he needed your permission to tell us about it."

Aditi-Alhread didn't say anything for a moment, studying Aimee's expression.

"He probably glanced a few seconds into Seamus' eyes." Aditi-Alhread said. "He had no experience with that, with seeing the souls of others, so he didn't know how to process everything he saw. Maybe he wanted to verify what it meant with me. I'm not Watts though, obviously."

"That's it?" Aimee asked, a little edge to her voice.

"That's it." Aditi-Alhread said in her flat even tone. Aimee seemed to want to say something else, but didn't. Instead she watched Aditi-Alhread for a little longer than awkward, then spun in her seat and stared out the window.

They drove a little longer, but Saul felt Aimee had opened a door, and as long as Aditi-Alhread was answering questions, he'd keep asking.

"So I know roughly where we're going, and who we're going to see, but I'm still unclear on exactly why we want to find this immortal guy."

"I know why I want to find him." Aditi-Alhread said. "Are you a bible person Saul?"

Saul felt like she already knew the answer to the question. Maybe she asked more to see how he'd answer, not only in front of her but in front of Aimee as well.

"I know Acts of the Apostles. Well, part of it anyway." Saul looked up at the mirror for a moment. He also watched Aimee out of the sides of his eyes, trying not to make it obvious. "I liked it as a kid because it had my name in it. You know, Saul falls to the ground, God talks to him and blinds him for like three days. In the end he got his sight back."

Aditi-Alhread smiled.

"Do you know the Book of Samuel?" She said.

Saul thought to himself for a moment. It seemed familiar, but the details escaped him. Given that his entire biblical experiences included Genesis, Revelations and the verses he'd just mentioned, that hardly seemed surprising.

"In it," Aditi-Alhread continued, "it speaks of the Witch of Endor summoning the spirit of the dead prophet Samuel, ironically at the request of the king you were probably named after, in order to ask Samuel questions. In the modern Old Testaments it stops there, but in the older versions, the much older versions, it mentions that she used an amulet to do it."

"But you can already speak to the dead," Aimee chimed in, still staring out the window. "And so can I."

Aditi-Alhread laughed. "Right. Well, any verses mentioning that amulet were dropped from almost all translations because of all the problems it caused, almost always in the form of crimes related to people trying to find it, steal it, or kill for it."

She leaned forward between the two chairs before resuming. "Most of the older legends of zombies, ghosts, spirits, hauntings, all come from that amulet passing hands for a few days, sometimes as little as a few hours. Some even say the only reason any necromancy works at all is because this amulet exists. It is the first and only physical link between the living and the dead."

After a second Saul said, "OK, wow, important safety tip. And Ut-Napishtim has it?"

"He knows where it is." Aditi-Alhread leaned back. "He knows where everything is."

They drove in silence for a while longer and into the darkening moments before sunset, when a passing Chrysler with tinted glass and booming bass inspired Aimee to lighten the mood by arguing with Saul about his musical tastes. Saul's ignorance of any of the bands Aimee mentioned combined with his complete unfamiliarity with the lingo left him trampled and wounded in the blood-soaked sand of the musical arena while Aimee laughed at his expense. After the other two quieted down, Aditi-

Alhread chimed in at the end with her favorite bands from the Sixties and Seventies. Even though each one she named rose to fame and often times disappeared into obscurity before Saul's birth, he still identified more with them than any of Aimee's. The topic died in a moment of almost surreal synchronization when all three acknowledged that *Led Zeppelin* had profoundly affected them at some point in their lives.

As Saul drove, he wondered if Aimee's uncle could have picked a more secluded route. For the first two hours they traveled through a cavern cut into a wall of endless fir trees. No street lights, gas stations, or strip malls to break up the horizon, and only about one other pair of opposing headlights every ten minutes. They rose up and over the Cascade mountains and continued down their east side aimed at Reno. They didn't find any place to eat until nearly nine, and even then the only place open was a little 24-hour place named the Kla-Mo-Ya Casino. Aimee and Saul grabbed a couple of sandwiches from the deli and steered clear of any gambling. Saul suspected that the two women could do a lot of damage in a poker game with their invisible friends. He also pointed out that they didn't really need the money and they needed the attention of winning big even less.

Aimee drove the next shift, and it didn't take long for the dark corridor of trees to lull Saul to sleep. Time passed, a sightless void filled with the hum of the engine, the indistinct voices of two women, and the light motion of his head moving against the cool window glass.

A sudden silence pulled him out of sleep, and he hovered for a moment with his eyes closed until he recognized the sounds of keys turning in the ignition. Another pee break.

"I just don't think it's fair that Saul got to go and I don't get to." Aimee continued a conversation with Aditi-Alhread without regarding Saul. "I mean I should get something out of all this."

"You can ask, but I won't take you there." Aditi-Alhread's voice. Saul squinted his eyes and tried to will them open. He winced with a muscle ache in his neck.

"OK fine." Aimee started, her voice and manner energetic and animated. It seemed to Saul a topic that must have consumed a lot of her mental bandwidth over the years. "For example, in Buddhism the dead are born into a hell for bad past lives. The Muslims go to sort of a cold storage hibernation zone and wait for their version of the Rapture, the Japanese think the Netherworld is a place where souls rot and the dead carry on as shadows forever regardless of how they behaved in life … Hell the Samoans even believe it's just a jumping off place before heaven or hell."

"OK."

"OK? OK?" Aimee asked. "OK so which bloody one is it?"

"All of those." Aditi-Alhread's replied.

Images came into focus for Saul. Another gas station, probably somewhere in California. He turned to see Aimee almost fuming, but doing some sort of deep breathing exercise to calm herself.

"Hey." He managed. His mouth tasted foul and dry, and a dim ache grew behind his right eye.

"Pee break." Aimee replied, then threw open the door and rushed inside.

"OK," Saul said to no one in particular. "I guess I'll pump the gas then."

When Aimee came back out, she didn't carry the usual bag of sugary or caffeinated goodies. As Saul finished at the pump, Aimee suggested they find a rest stop or just pull over in the woods somewhere and nap in the car. Aditi-Alhread argued against this, but given that it was two in the morning and they still had a good three, maybe four hours to go, Saul sided with Aimee. Aditi-Alhread protested again until Saul cut her off.

"I still don't get why you can't drive." He asked. "You lived in the Seventies, right? You had a driver's license at one point."

Her body moved in a way similar to a sigh, and her shoulders dipped a little. "OK, you two can nap. I'll stand guard."

"You didn't answer the question." Aimee chimed in before Saul could. "Why can't you drive?"

Aditi-Alhread's eyes darted from Aimee to Saul and then she replied. "I know to you it looks like I'm always in this one lifetime, my last one, but I've got essentially thirteen people and over a thousand animals inside me all the time. When things remind me of moments from other lives, I go to those lives, if sometimes only for a split second, and relive entire portions of my past."

She paused, apparently anticipating she'd provided enough of an explanation.

"I still don't get it." Saul dispelled that thought right away.

"Imagine, even for one instant, what would happen if, say, a Byzantine monk suddenly found himself behind the wheel of truck barreling down the highway in the middle of the night with the headlights of an eighteen-wheeler shining right in his eyes."

Saul nodded slowly as the right connections fired in his head.

"Right." Aimee said. "You made your point. Let's go."

It didn't take them long to find a place to pull over. Aimee and Saul both leaned their seats back and stretched out as best they could, using jackets as blankets and some extra sweatshirts for pillows. Aditi-Alhread got out and vanished into the shadows of the wood line and stayed there for the next three hours. Before Aimee and Saul drifted off, she leaned towards him and whispered.

"Saul, do you trust her?"

"What do you mean?" Saul cleared his mind, not sure what to expect.

"I just, the whole Watts thing, and needing her permission to talk to us. It really bothers me."

He didn't want any challenges to the order of things as they stood now. He'd invested too much into it. "It was probably some code of the dead issue. They have weird rules."

"She didn't care though, when I told her about Watts, she didn't react at all."

"She doesn't react much to anything." Saul said, which he believed to be at least partially true. Something in his tone stopped Aimee's questions, and they both sunk into a deep sleep.

Aditi-Alhread woke them both just before dawn, saying that for some reason it was important they all be moving before it got light out. No one argued, and Saul took the wheel. The next leg went by in relative silence, passing through the outskirts of Reno and then turning back west, steadily rising back up into the mountains. And while the traffic remained light, Saul studied his two passengers.

Aimee hung on to consciousness for a few minutes, then went right back to sleep, drool on the window and all, head bobbing with the rhythm of the road. She seemed very young to him then, and he noticed for the first time the smoothness of her complexion, and how her cheeks took on a rosy tint as she slept.

Through his view in the mirror, Aditi-Alhread seemed different to him in the hours that passed. She never closed her eyes, but he could see her gaze drift periodically, and now each time she did it he imagined her off to another time, another life…

"Saul stop!" She yelled without warning, eyes wide and frantic. "Stop! Stop! Stop!"

Her scream sent him into immediate fight or flight mode, heavy on the fight, and in the instants between each word he scanned his surroundings for any sign of a threat. They had reached a narrow cut through the mountains, but the walls were too high for an effective ambush. Not seeing anything, his first instinct told him to speed up instead, and the adrenalin rushed up to warm his ears.

"What!?! What?!?" Rage drove his voice. He compromised and hit the brakes hard, but only to slow them, not to the screeching halt she'd wanted. "Dammit! You can't just scream at me like that!"

Aimee flew forward and her seatbelt locked. Jarred and confused, she said nothing and waited for an explanation. Aditi-Alhread held up her arms to shield her face and then as they passed a certain point, she spun around and looked out the back window.

"Oh God." Aditi-Alhread spoke in a near whisper. "There are so many of them."

Saul relaxed with the understanding. They probably passed a spot where a bus had turned over, or rolled down the mountainside, or something else that killed a crowd of people recently. No big deal.

"Where did he get so m…" Aditi-Alhread stopped, startled. "Go Saul. Keep going! Keep going!"

More in control of his body's trained impulses, he recognized her tone as one which contained a belief of sincere threat, and this time hit the gas first, asked questions afterwards.

"Clear?" He said, and got no response.

"OK, so?" Aimee's hands twitched with a slight tremble.

Aditi-Alhread kept watching through the window. "They stretched across the entire road, four rows deep, holding hands like a giant game of ghostly Red Rover."

"I'm guessing not from a recent accident?" Saul spoke, searching for any signs of otherworldly activity.

"No. Aimee, what are your friends' names?" Aditi-Alhread asked. Aimee seemed puzzled, so Aditi-Alhread continued. "I mean, I can see their true names, and even their last family names, but I get the sense they don't go by those."

Aimee expression widened with understanding. "Oh, you mean my mates? Right, the cute female with the purple hair goes by Kami-ko, and the tall gangly fellow just goes by Sidney."

"They got Kami-ko." She said. "I'm sorry."

"What!?" Aimee's eyes darted back and forth.

"They were waiting for us. Looking for us." Aditi-Alhread said, finally turning around. "They stretched out like a giant net, and they just pulled her right through."

"Is she going to be OK?" Aimee's voice cracked. Saul felt a pang in his stomach, imagining what this meant to her, losing two of her friends in less than two days.

"Not if those souls work for Seamus. No."

"Aw bloody hell…" Aimee spoke, holding back tears. Not as many as for Watts, but enough.

"So that was a trap?" Saul said. The complete innocence of the empty highway mocked him. Enemies he couldn't shoot, hit, run over, even see.

"More of a scouting party, or an alarm." Aditi-Alhread said. "Seamus somehow knew where we'd be and posted all of those spirits in the mountain pass."

"Can we do anything?" Aimee spoke between sniffs.

"We are doing it." Saul said and turned to Aditi-Alhread. "Right? That's why we're going where we're going?"

"Yes. But we should hurry. Three or four of those ghosts held onto Kami-ko, but the rest are chasing us."

Saul spoke with unfocused anger. "Well they're going to have to chase us a really freakin' long time."

"Not too long Saul." Aimee said as she looked down at the notes her uncle printed out for them. "We're nearly there."

CHAPTER 27

Thirteen hours after their journey began, the trio turned passed a large green mailbox and down a long narrow driveway cut into the woods. They coasted up a steep hill with subtle curves, and the whole thing gave Saul a sense a pathway to a castle intentionally constricted and twisted to keep the enemy from rushing up en masse.

"Whoa." Saul said when the sculptures came into view. Flanking the road sat two massive scorpions hewn from solid rock, pincers open and facing oncoming traffic. The stingers on both tails were stained black, and seemed impossibly sharp even from a distance.

"Slow down." Aditi-Alhread's voice seemed firm, but not urgent.

"More dead people?"

"No." She replied, "But you have to admit those are really creepy statues."

Saul let gravity pull back their pace until they drifted to a stop. In his imagination Saul felt the gaze of both stone creatures following him, aware not only of his presence but his purpose.

"When I read the part about giant scorpion guardians," Aditi-Alhread added, "I assumed it was a metaphor."

"I'm not sure I want to keep going." Aimee said. "Maybe we should honk."

Saul paused to see if Aditi-Alhread disagreed, and when she said nothing he went ahead and hit the horn in three long blasts. They sat long enough that Saul mapped out in his mind the best way through the woods on foot to possibly avoid the scorpions, and was just about to honk again when a small man with dark skin and salt and pepper hair walked into view up ahead. He wore a long blue bathrobe, sweatpants, and sandals.

"Saul," Aditi-Alhread said, "I forgot to mention you're probably going to need to do the talking."

"Really? Why?" He replied.

"In the thousands of years he's been alive," she replied, "woman have only been recognized as equals or near equals for a portion of the last century."

"Perfect." He said and then everyone stepped out of the car. They gathered on the driver's side, although no one stepped any closer to the statues.

"Leopold Kondakov?" Saul held out his hand and took a step forward. He thought for an instant he heard a pebble drop from the scorpion to his left, and froze in place.

"Yes!" the man spoke in a jolly tone laced with an indistinguishable accent. He stopped between the two statues, leaving Saul five feet shy of a handshake. "Which university are you from?"

Saul lowered his hand. "Actually, we're really looking for someone who knows about ancient floods."

"Oh," not quite as jolly. "Well then for sure you've got the wrong place."

"Ut-Napishtim?" Saul added.

"Never heard of him."

Saul chuckled. "Someone with a PhD in Ancient Babylon who's never read the Epic of Gilgamesh?"

"It was my polite way of telling you to go away."

"We can't just leave." Saul liked conversations like this better through an interpreter, which gave him twice as much time to think up his arguments. Also, he liked it better with a gunner manning a fifty cal behind him.

"I'm calling the cops." The man said, and reached into his pocket.

"You going to call them as Leopold Kondakov or Charles Barthold?" Saul asked.

The man hesitated.

"Possibly Ahmad al-Yani?"

In a calm motion the man pulled a Walter PPK from his robe pocket but said nothing.

"Hey, hey, I'd really like to not get shot here today." Saul said quickly.

"That's what I thought," the man replied.

"You can shoot her though." Saul pointed towards Aditi-Alhread.

"What?" the man's brow furled in confusion.

"Yeah, it's OK." Saul hoped he sounded casual while he struggled to hide the tremors in his voice.

"You're on my land, it's legal."

"Really, I don't mind." Saul smiled.

The man turned to regard her and Aditi-Alhread raised her eyebrows with a hint of a grin. He cocked his head to one side.

Blam!

Aimee jumped with surprise, but otherwise, nothing. Aditi-Alhread shrugged as if he'd missed her.

"Hurm," he said, then held up the pistol and took careful aim.

Blam! Blam! Blam!

No doubt that time, at least part of her uniform rippled with one of the shots. He put all three of those rounds in the center of her chest.

Saul, Aimee, and Aditi-Alhread maintained their grins. The man squinted one eye and turned the gun on Aimee. She stopped smiling and took a step back. Then the man moved his aim back to Saul, whose smile faded just a hair.

"So, her, but not you two." The man said. "Interesting." Movement caught his eye, and Saul followed his gaze to a spot behind Aditi-Alhread. There two tiny pools of obsidian quicksilver snaked along the road and back to her heel. They crawled up her calf and then sunk down into the black leather of her boots.

"OK, you got me." The man said, holding up his arms. "What the hell is going on?"

Aditi-Alhread spoke to him for a moment in a language that sounded vaguely Arabic to Saul, but rougher. He smiled and spoke back to her in the same tongue. After a few more exchanges with her, the man turned and said something to both scorpions. They didn't respond, but Saul felt a distinct sense of relief.

The man put the gun away and turned up his driveway. "Well come on then!"

Aditi-Alhread went after him first, and Aimee only followed after Saul did.

"Ut-Napishtim," Aditi-Alhread started as they walked.

"Nappy is fine." He replied with a resigned sigh. Clearly a man not used to giving up his secrets.

Aimee let out a sharp involuntary giggle and then swallowed it, clearing her throat.

"Sorry," she whispered to Saul. "We would say Nappy in England where you would say, uh, diapers I believe."

Saul grinned politely and gave her a "shush" signal.

"Get a lot of visitors?" Aditi-Alhread asked Nappy, ignoring Aimee's outburst.

"None without invitations." He replied. "But I guess that's my fault."

"I read you had a wife. Will we get to meet her?" Aditi-Alhread continued.

"She's in Southwest Asia, last I heard. We're on a break." Saul and Aimee caught up but didn't interrupt.

"Really?" Aditi-Alhread matched Nappy's pace. "How long?"

"Two hundred years, give or take." He glanced back at Saul. "She's waiting for the White Man phase to pass."

They rounded a corner and entered a clearing dominated by a large house of mixed design. The first floor and some of the second seemed almost medieval, lined with stone with only narrow slits for viewing portals. The upper floor, on the other hand, glistened with tinted glass windows that reached floor to ceiling in most places. Bottom floor for defense, Saul figured, top floor for comfort, very little fire or flood risk; this was a house built by a man who lived a long time through a lot of dangers.

Nappy took them to a wooden porch covered with open beams overhead and gestured for everyone to grab a chair around a table ornately carved from one solid tree trunk. As they sat Nappy rushed inside, leaving the back door open.

Saul decided he would pretend to offer to help as a way to get a look into this man's home. He stopped to the doorway and tilted his head towards it.

"Hello," he called out, "need help with anything?"

As he spoke, his mind struggled to catalog the room just inside the door. Every wall held shelves, floor to ceiling, and every shelf filled every inch with VHS tapes,

DVD cases, old books, or cans of film, all with home-made labels. Model airplanes, wooden, hand painted, and covered with dust, hovered by strings from almost every foot of the higher-than-average ceiling. An old brown cor-duroy couch dominated the center of the room, and where a TV would have normally gone in front of it, stood a white marble statue of a couple engaging in impossibly acrobatic mutual oral sex.

"You probably don't want to cross the doorway threshold," Nappy's voice rang out from somewhere. "That could be very bad for you until I disarm it."

"OK," Saul shouted up, "I won't." The temptation to just reach his hand across moved his arm a few inches before he could stop it, but he yanked it back just before where he assumed the trigger would be.

A few seconds later Nappy rounded the corner with a tray holding three cups of steaming hot tea.

"I got it," Nappy said, smiling.

As Saul stepped aside he pointed, "I um, like your statue."

"Huh? Which one?" Nappy stopped to look back. "OH, yes, that's from my Roman Empire porn collection. Twisted stuff." He closed the door behind him as he exit-ed, moved to the table, kept one cup of tea, and offered the other two to Aimee and Saul.

"So," Nappy said, sitting. He pulled out what ap-peared to be a hand bound journal and a pen and wrote down a quick line before continuing. "How much time do we have?"

Aditi-Alhread answered. "Ten minutes, give or take. Depends on if they follow the road or run through the forests. Once they find us they'll report back every-thing they see or hear."

"How many are we talking about?" Nappy asked.

"Fifty, maybe sixty," she replied, "they crossed the whole highway several layers deep."

"And they might be covering several highways," he said. "Hurm, how did one Necromancer get so many?"

"More than one Necromancer." Aditi-Alhread replied. "He pays lesser summoners to bring him fresh stuff, or special souls by request."

"Any physical threat from them?"

"Very little, if any." Aditi-Alhread instinctively scanned their surroundings, as if to confirm what she said. She turned to Aimee, "Although, you might want to tell Sidney to stay hidden. I'd tell him, but I don't think he likes me."

"No, he doesn't," she replied, and then spoke out at nothing in particular. "Sidney, do as she says please. Stay hidden until we tell you to come out, and if we don't tell you, stay hidden, OK?"

Aditi-Alhread watched a very specific spot of open air and then turned to Aimee and nodded. Relieved, Aimee held her tea up and inhaled its aroma.

"Well then," Nappy wrote another line. "Let's get it out in the open. What do you fine travelers need?"

Saul saw Aditi-Alhread about to speak and cut her off.

"Why are you writing this down?"

"I write down everything," he replied. "My flesh is immortal. My memory, I'm afraid, is not."

Saul couldn't resist the irony. "Like her," he pointed to Aditi-Alhread, "But in reverse."

Nappy put down his pen and lifted his cup of tea. "I suppose it is. Never would have imagined it myself." He thought a moment, and then smiled a sad sort of smile. "I'm living, never able to die, and she's dead, never able to be born. Both fettered to worlds we grew tired of long ago."

After a pause, Aimee asked, "Look that's ace and all, but to get back on point, we do actually need something."

"What? You need money?" He reached into his pants under the robe and pulled out a pair of wrinkled bills. "Here, I've got two hundreds on me, will that do you?"

Saul jumped in, "No no, we're not looking for money."

"My God what a crappy picture of Franklin." Nappy said, smoothing out the bills. "Ah, Ben. Met him on my first trip east. Good guy, discovered electricity. Well, I mean, I had to push him along a little."

"What?" Saul asked. "How?"

"I flew the kite." Nappy stuffed the money back into his pants.

"The kite with the key?"

"The very one."

"And?"

"And I was electrocuted – shocked the crap out of me – and he took credit for it."

"Really?"

"Yes, but I liked going out with him and the ladies. Boy he was a playboy. What he really discovered showed up later in the Kama Sutra."

Aimee's eyebrows rose a moment, temporarily distracted by an unspoken challenge to see who could be the most sexually inappropriate in a casual conversation. Something stronger crossed her face though, and she signaled Saul to change topics.

Saul shifted in his seat, cleared his throat and said, "Aditi-Alhread here says you know where things are." He paused. "And we're looking for a thing."

"Oh yeah." Nappy took a sip of tea. "The Ark of the Covenant, pieces of the one True Cross, the Japanese Ame-No-Murakumo, the lost pages of the *Libri recedentia loginquitas*, Excalibur, on and on it goes ad infinitum. Seeing as I'm half of all the immortals in the world, it seemed my duty to keep up with those sorts of things."

Saul reflexively looked up at the house behind Nappy.

Nappy caught his gaze. "I don't keep them here, of course. Most don't even exist. The ones that do exist which have significance but no power, I track and make sure they get locked up somewhere safe, like the Vatican or a sacred shrine, etc."

Aditi-Alhread let out a polite cough and Nappy avoided her gaze before continuing. "You must be after the Amulet of Endor then?"

When all three of them nodded, Nappy chuckled. "Oh is that all? Sure, I put it in the center of the City of Shadows you dumb bastards, the end."

"That was easy." Saul said. He sipped his tea for the first time. Just the right amount of honey and brown sugar to cut the bitterness, it inspired a second slower sip so he could relish the details.

"No it wasn't." Aditi-Alhread's voice held less power than usual.

"Why, where is it?" The tea took some of the stress from Saul's shoulders.

"Wait," Aimee interrupted, "if I may. Did you just say the 'Amulet of Endor' and 'City of Shadows?' in the same sentence? I mean really, did you two spend a lot of time playing *Dungeons and Dragons* as kids or what?"

"Why?" Saul smiled, "would that turn you on?" He hoped a little witty banter, particularly sexual witty banter, would cheer her up now that the main question was answered.

"Oh I'm way more into the jock lot." Aimee replied, although Saul noted her heart wasn't in it.

"Really?"

"No not really."

"Enough!" Aditi-Alhread balled her fists but didn't hit anything. The mood dropped and for a moment Saul wanted to put his hand on Aditi-Alhread's arm. He didn't.

"I get it. You said you'd been in that city before, so this part of the city he's talking about," Saul said, watching Nappy, "either no one knows where it is, or it is someplace impossible to get to, isn't it? I'm guessing impossible to get to."

Nappy's grin and Aditi-Alhread's blank stare answered the question without words. Saul recalled her mentioning that her time in the city had been spent hiding. Then he pictured a city filled with people capable of everything she was capable of.

Nappy closed the book and stood up.

"Well then," he said, "now that the primary business is over, how would you two like a snack before you go?"

"You don't want us to leave?" Aditi-Alhread asked. Saul glanced at his watch. If she'd estimated correctly when she spoke earlier, then he reasoned that spirits should come pouring out of the forest in a couple of minutes.

"Oh let 'em come. We'll make a party out of it." He turned and headed for the house. "I'll be back in a bit." He went around the corner of the structure and Saul noticed that he distinctly avoided the nearest door this time.

The three of them sat around the table without speaking. Saul finished his tea about the same time Aimee did.

Saul leaned back and let the sun burn off some of the cool mountain air tickling around his face. For some reason he felt like his time with these two women would end soon. Aditi-Alhread knew the location of what she wanted, even if it turned out to be impossible to reach. She'd have to give up her fight, and the necromancers would lose interest in chasing her down. If they weren't chasing her, they weren't chasing him.

Aimee would need to get back soon and probably would have to call in sick at least one day of work as it was. His report date back to the Army loomed just over the horizon as well. He didn't know Rose's plans, or Lisa's plans for Rose over the summer, but he assumed neither involved him. By now his cell phone no doubt overflowed with messages that spanned the spectrum from annoyed to worried, or possibly those five stages of grief he could never quite remember. It didn't matter.

Nothing mattered.

In time he'd be back someplace where he served a purpose other than family figurehead or driver for a misplaced ghost. He'd be alone, but that wouldn't matter either.

"Aces." Aimee said, pulling Saul out of his private pity party. Nappy walked towards them carrying a big bronze serving tray covered in steaming yellow rice with half a rack of lamb on top. He set it on the table and rushed back off.

"Don't touch it yet!" His voice trailed behind him.

He returned with a silver tray filled with tomato and cucumber slices in one hand, and a large clay pot in the other, and set them down beside the other.

He hovered over them and rubbed his hands together. "Ah, there you go. I usually keep this stuff warm and eat the same thing for a week at a time. Saves on cooking."

Saul and Aimee glanced down at the food, but neither moved.

"Oh, right, this is a meal from the old country." Nappy said. "You eat it with your hands, like this." He poured some of the contents of the bowl – a red thick soup – into a small portion of the rice.

"See, the rice gets wet, and then you can scoop it up and it clumps together." He demonstrated and shoved a handful in his mouth. He spoke again through the food. "Follow it up with some meat or cucumbers. Repeat as necessary."

Saul dug in first, while Aimee started with the tomatoes. After a few bites, Saul found himself practically scooping the soup covered rice into his mouth. In the meantime, Nappy left again and returned with napkins and a metal teapot. Saul didn't even notice him missing until he refilled his mug of tea. Saul slowed to a stop when his gut finally protested with actual pain. He hadn't eaten that much in a long, long time. He glanced at his watch, surprised to see thirty minutes snuck by without him noticing.

"I forged the silverware myself," Nappy added. Saul noticed for the first time that no two pieces of the set matched, and they weren't particularly ornate or well done. "One of my many skills."

"It's very good," Aimee lied, popping the last of the cucumbers. She didn't sound convincing.

"Down about something?" Nappy said to her.

She chewed a few bites before responding. "A little maybe."

"Well knock it off or I'll bite your nose." Nappy delivered it so straight-faced that the corners of Aimee's mouth curved up for an instant.

"Aimee," leave it to Aditi-Alhread to break the mood. "You might want to call Sidney back."

"Eh," Nappy grabbed a pinch of lamb. "The party finally show up?"

"No," Aditi-Alhread replied. "I haven't seen a single new spirit since we've been here. I just think we should be going."

"Well, all the better." Nappy said after popping the cucumber into his mouth.

Saul didn't move. He didn't feel like taking orders, implied or expressed, at just that moment. Instead he closed his eyes. The scent of lamb overpowered most others, but if he concentrated, he caught the whiff of the trees as well, mixed in with the cool wet air. No identifiable animal sounds, but the white noise of a distant highway gave a comforting sense of the real world outside of Nappy's. Another sound gradually rose to his consciousness, a familiar bass pulse he'd heard almost every night in his sleep in Iraq.

"Is there an airport nearby Nappy?" Saul asked, opening his eyes. The sound grew, rapid chopping approaching from the south.

"Yes, about twenty miles past the town." He followed Saul's gaze upwards.

A dark green helicopter rose over the treetops. Civilian make and model, the words "Sky Mountain Tours" stuck out in bright yellow lettering on its side.

"Is that normal?" Saul asked.

"Not particularly." Nappy rose.

The helicopter hovered overhead just high enough that the rotor wash only disturbed the treetops. Saul caught sight of the face of a bearded man in the co-pilot seat watching them. The man's eyes fixed on Aditi-Alhread and held there, the type of stare down that any mammal would instantly recognize as confrontational.

Without warning, the helicopter banked and followed the driveway back down towards the mailbox. Saul stood up and watched it go. A few seconds later the pitch of the engines changed.

"Hear that? It's landing." He said.

"I'll be right..." Aditi-Alhread started.

"No!" Saul cut her off. "Real people, real weapons, real tactics. They know you're here and they're probably ready for you. No point in you running down there by yourself, especially if one of them is Seamus."

"OK, then what now?" Aditi-Alhread asked.

"Got any other guns?" Saul asked Nappy.

"No need," he smiled. "They won't get past the twins."

"So you say." Whatever defenses Nappy had set up, Saul still wanted a backup plan. "Is there any other way out of here?"

"No, not by car." Nappy answered. "Plenty of paths to run down, but nothing a vehicle will fit through."

A few seconds later the sharp cracks of distant gunfire cut through the air.

"Speaking of the twins." Nappy stretched to see any sign of what occurred down the driveway.

"Aimee." Saul said it stern enough to make her turn. He moved behind a small stone wall and motioned for her to do the same. "For us mere mortals."

They sat with their backs up against the wall and listened. Along with the gunfire, Saul thought he heard a man scream. Aditi-Alhread and Nappy strolled over to them once the violence fell silent.

"OK with you if I go scout them out now?" Aditi-Alhread crossed her arms and looked down at Saul. Nappy stood beside her with a tea mug in his hand and took a sip.

Saul relaxed and started to answer, but stopped when he heard a loud Brak! A dark circle spread across Nappy's shirt and he looked down, surprised.

Brak! Nappy stumbled back and fell to the ground with an ungraceful thud.

Brak! Brak!

Two jet-black splatters flew onto the wall behind Aditi-Alhread. She staggered a step, disoriented.

"Shooter! Get down!" Saul yelled, specifically to Aditi-Alhread. She crouched down beside him, and after her vision focused again, her missing memories slid down the wall and across the concrete towards her. Nappy moaned but stayed flat on his back.

"That stung a bit." He said.

"Nappy!" Saul whispered loudly. "Nappy, move over here."

The old man rolled over and crawled up beside the others. The last of the black goo traveled up Aditi-Alhread's foot and vanished.

"Nappy, are you really immortal?" Saul said, expecting at any moment someone to poke their head over the wall and spray them all with automatic gunfire.

"I'm only 4,223 years old!" he said, "Everyone knows life doesn't really kick into until the mid 4300s."

"I mean you can't die?"

"Are you kidding?" Nappy glanced quickly down to the three blood-soaked bullet holes in his shirt and robe. "Yes, I would think so."

"Then I need you to run that way. Draw fire." Saul pointed towards the woods.

"You're mad!" Nappy said.

"Look, they can't kill you." Saul argued.

"It still hurts!"

"Then hurt a little," Saul said, softening his voice so it sounded like more of a request. "OK? Not that big a deal."

Nappy stared, mouth open slightly for a second, and then laughed out loud. "I like you!" He patted Saul on the shoulder. "I'm in."

"Aimee," Saul continued, "you and I will run for the truck right after Nappy takes off. Run to the back first, we'll all climb in the passenger side because I think that's the side away from the shooter. Don't be afraid to use the truck as a shield."

"I'm going last?" Aditi-Alhread said.

"Yes, if he tires of Nappy as a target and goes for our line of movement, he'll most likely only have time to hit the last person." Saul shrugged. "In theory."

They agreed, and on Saul's count Nappy ran screaming towards the trees.

Brak! Brak! Brak!

Hit to the arm, one miss, hit to the body. Nappy fell in mid stride. Saul and Aimee watched one second too long before bolting for the car. That one second cost them one shot, and as Saul dove behind the car, Aimee fell behind it.

He pulled her more behind the protection of the truck.

"Oh I'm such a bloody mug!" She yelled, grabbing her leg. Saul examined it. Light wound across the back, missed the femoral artery.

Brak! Brak! Brak! Brak!

Aditi-Alhread ran through a barrage of gunfire. Every step another spray of midnight mercury flew out from her body and onto the ground. By the end she fell down behind Saul with her eyes glazed over like she was going into shock.

He cursed his plan. Pinned down behind a car with two wounded and nothing to shoot back with. Brilliant.

"Yaaaaaaa! Ha! Ha! Ha!" Nappy ran like a maniac from the spot where he fell to another section of woods. This time, he didn't run for cover, he ran with his pistol pointed out in front of him firing with every step.

Blam!
Brak! Brak!
Blam! Blam!
Brak! Brak! Brak!

Saul didn't wait for the outcome, and rushed to open the passenger door. He reached back for Aimee's wrist and pulled her to him and helped her inside. He held his hand out for Aditi-Alhread and she stumbled forward and into the back seat. Saul dove in and crawled over Aimee's lap to the driver's seat.

"Duck down!" He needn't have said it, both women were way ahead of him.

"Wait!" Aditi-Alhread yelled and reached down out the back door.

"We have to go!" Anger laced Aimee's voice.

"Not yet!" Aditi-Alhread kept her hand on the concrete until the dark liquid slid over and merged with her fingertips. "OK now."

"Sidney!" Aimee yelled. "SIDNEY!!"

Saul lowered himself down in the seat and slammed his foot on the gas. The truck lurched forward and the last image from the scene that burned like a snapshot on Saul's brain, was that of the bearded man – much bigger than Saul would have guessed – standing in a pristine green setting, holding Nappy up off the ground by the neck and firing some sort of assault rifle into his stomach.

That paled compared to the carnage just past the two scorpions. Without slowing, Saul counted four bodies, or more accurately, three full bodies plus two halves, scattered around the clearing. He dodged them as best he could but wouldn't have cared if he ran over anything. He also thought he might have caught a glint of red dripping off the stinger of one of the stone statues, both of which otherwise appeared exactly as they had when Saul first arrived.

A second later the helicopter came into view, resting in a small patch of grass across the street from Nappy's mailbox. The doors remained shut, but with hints of movement in the darkness behind the windows. At the last moment, Saul ran the truck up and over the road and right into the rear propeller of the helicopter. It made a horrid sound of metal grinding metal, but in the end the collision only left a long gash in the truck's hood, and bent back one of the rear rotors at a ninety degree angle to the rest. Enough to keep it from flying, Saul thought, and slammed the truck into reverse. A few seconds later they broke out onto the highway and for lack of any other direction, turned and headed west.

CHAPTER 28

They drove without talking with Saul clenching the steering wheel and scanning for potential threats while Aimee grabbed whatever fast food napkins and old T-shirts she could find under the seats and pushed hard against the slice in her leg.

"You OK?" Saul asked.

"Light laceration across the back, missed the femoral artery," she replied. Nurse. Right. Also explains knowing to apply pressure to the wound. "Still feel like a mug though."

Saul glanced up in the rearview mirror so Aditi-Alhread would know he aimed his next question at her. "How about you?"

"Still holding it together." She replied.

"Is, uh…" Aimee began, "I mean I could just turn on some music and see for myself, but is Sid…" Aimee stopped when she saw Aditi-Alhread shaking her head. "So, Sidney's gone too." The tiniest crack in Aimee's voice hinted at the emotion behind it.

"What's going to happen to Ut?" Saul asked.

"They will torture him," Aditi-Alhread said. "He'll probably resist just to see how long he can do it, so it makes a good story, then tell them whatever they want to know. But it won't matter."

"Oh no, it won't matter." Aimee said under her breath.

"Seamus won't be able to get to the amulet either?" Saul asked.

"Necromancy is mostly to use against the dead. Not to visit them," Aditi-Alhread replied. "Seamus doesn't know any spells to carry him to the Netherworld."

Aimee spun around. "How do you know what he knows? Have you seen him before?"

Saul's head twitched and he twisted to focus more on the conversation while he drove.

"I've asked about him. Seen him through the eyes of others. I know enough."

"What else do you know about him, eh?" Aimee asked. "Something you didn't want Watts to tell us?"

"Aimee, I'm not…" Aditi-Alhread started.

"Look just answer the bloody question!" Aimee cut her off.

Aditi-Alhread stared for a moment, the spoke in a softer tone than normal. "It's odd. In this form, I find I actually have the freedom to lie. I mean, neither one of you can see anything about me. Yet I feel compelled, obligated at least, to tell you anyway."

"Tell… us… WHAT!?!" Aimee gritted her teeth and pushed even harder against her leg wound.

"Saul, pull over please. Someplace secluded." Aditi-Alhread said.

A half mile further down Interstate Eighty Saul found a scenic outlook. A family of German tourists occupied most of the space at first, but stopped their picture taking a little early and vacated for who they perceived as the next round of nature lovers. Saul looked out over some absolutely breathtaking brilliant blue lake and truly didn't give a shit about it.

He put the truck in park and he turned towards the back. He could almost see Aimee's pulse racing in her temples, the stinging pain in her leg, the frustration focused in her clinched fist. But there Aditi-Alhread sat, unmarred, emotionless, simulating a few life signs for their convenience. Deliberately avoiding direct eye contact, he couldn't find anything besides her eyes that might have once attracted him to her. For some reason that made him feel better at that moment.

"Right." Aimee said, propping herself on her knees so she could face the back seat easier.

"You aren't the first person to have this gift Aimee," Aditi-Alhread said, leaning closer to the two of them. "And people have wanted those abilities and the secrets that go with them for eons. When someone figures out a way to share them… well, word gets around."

"I actually don't know what you're talking about right now." Saul added.

Aditi-Alhread smiled at him and closed her eyes. Without opening them, she reached out and pulled Aimee's hand away from the blood-soaked T-Shirt and held it up, still dripping crimson. Then she took Saul's hand and pressed her thumbnail into the palm. Gently at first, then hard enough to hurt, and then in a quick flick she ripped open a cut that let out just a slow ooze. She pulled Saul's hand to Aimee's and interwove their fingers together, then rested her own right hand over Aimee's heart.

"This will only work if you both want it to," Aditi-Alhread said. "So don't resist any part of it."

A quiet string of languages Saul didn't recognize eased out between Aditi-Alhread's lips, floating up to hover between them like a spoken summit of continents and cultures. It ended in English.

"The bond of blood is the bond of life." She said, loud and alone at first. The next time she said it Aimee whispered it with her. She repeated it five more times until in the end Aimee spoke it clearly and Aditi-Alhread barely mouthed the words.

Saul looked over and watched Aimee's pupils grow dark, until they reached the same endlessly deep obsidian as Aditi-Alhread. Now Aimee spoke alone.

"My eyes are your eyes, your eyes are my eyes, so mote it be." Again, it began just as Aimee. The next time Saul felt his lips forming the words without saying anything. He wanted to try to stop it but didn't for fear of what either woman would do to him if he messed this up. Five more times he and Aimee repeated the mantra, and it ended with them both saying it out loud.

Saul let his eyelids fall and gave in to the total fatigue that came on so fast he hadn't noticed it. He was sure they would yell at him for napping like this, but when his eyes opened, he only saw himself, half-asleep, looking back at himself, from Aimee's point of view.

"You both see the same now." Aditi-Alhread said. "So let me give you something to look at." She reached over and tapped the button on the dashboard and the radio clicked on, filling the car with music from some alternative band Saul didn't recognize.

Saul's field of view turned to Aditi-Alhread as she had always been, now staring back from a few inches away. After the first verse of the song, Saul's focus faded – no, Aditi-Alhread faded. Her form diminished in the center, but stayed opaque around the edges. She became a window, with her outline the frame, and past her, through her, stood a scrawny dark-haired boy, barely in his teens, holding a crude bow and arrow atop some ancient sand-dusted battlement.

Saul moved in behind the boy, looking over his shoulder at the half-naked woman with the lion tattoo as she danced in the distance. Saul understood with absolute clarity how the boy felt about the woman, and in this moment of sharing, he felt the same lightness in his temples and warmth growing between his legs.

With a jolt, Saul pulled back, a mere observer again, as the boy turned to face the roar of chariots gushing down towards the city. Then the boy too became translucent in the center, a new window that shifted Saul's attention.

Saul drifted through the boy and out to a field of green-topped mounds, each nestled in a soft bed of thick fog. There a young girl plucked cherry-colored flowers into a woven bucket, careful not to spill the seeds. When the girl turned to walk, she blossomed as well, growing a little further into adulthood with each step through the high reeds. By the time her body had swollen into that of a young woman, a boy followed behind, always within sight but just out of reach. He aged too, a little with every stride, gaining first muscles, then facial hair, and then somehow carrying an urn filled with metallic rocks. The couple passed by a pair of children playing in the knee-deep canals, while another man behind the two teens pulled a net full of fish up from the deeper waters.

At last the couple reached their destination, the same mound where they had started. The girl now a woman near 40, attenuated and weak, and the boy a man with hints of gray in his beard. The man knelt down, lowering the woman's head onto the flowers, where he gently kissed her forehead and stroked her hair.

The thin woman faded in the center then, just as the two previous forms before her, and Saul moved to look down into that gateway. He saw a city beneath him, a historic city of some sort, at the foot of a mountain range, and he descended towards one specific building.

"That's enough."

The music ended. Saul jerked awake, ripped from a dream. As Aditi-Alhread's hand pulled back from the radio switch, he struggled to regain his equilibrium. His senses vaguely remembered the limits of his body, but could only control his extremities in the most general sense. His head swayed, his arms and hands hovered and moved in awkward patterns, burdened with some inexplicable imperative not to accidentally touch anything.

As the images flew from his mind, he strained to grab as many as he could, repeat them, concentrate on them, remember the boy and girl that bore the true name Aditi, and the woman and man who would someday become Kigal-Seamus.

"Ah bugger." Aimee said, shaking her head with muddy vision and her eyes back to their normal green color. Aditi-Alhread waited patiently for them to recover.

"You knew him!" Aimee rubbed her temples as she spoke. "You pined over Seamus when he… she was some sort of slag priestess and you loved him… LOVED HIM for practically an entire lifetime?"

"Those lives are gone," Aditi-Alhread replied. "They do not affect today."

"How do we know that?" Saul spoke through his own haze. He realized the answer without her saying anything. In those small instances of her soul literally open and peeled back for him to view, he absorbed more about those lives than just what he saw. They felt resolved, over, complete. He looked up at Aimee and saw she believed the same thing, or at least part of it. "Never mind."

He rubbed his hands together and the dried blood brushed off like dirt.

"We good?" he asked Aimee.

"Yeah, we're good."

Saul opened the door and walked to the front of the car. He considered sitting on the hood, and decided on a nearby large rock instead, and a few seconds later he felt Aimee move up behind him.

"I'll guess I'll be heading home now." She said. "I'm pretty sure any first year nurse would recognize this as a gunshot wound, which means police report. But there's a new guy in our ER I bet I could get to sew it up for…" she paused, gauging Saul's reaction. "…for a smile. Maybe a wink. I don't think I'll have to go as far as a song."

Saul counted himself a small victory. If he'd looked up or winced, who knows what sort of sexual term she might have ended that last sentence with. No reaction, no fun. Plus he could tell flirting, or whatever she thought she was doing, just took too much energy at this point.

"I'm sorry we lost all your friends." It seemed awkward as he said it, but he couldn't think of any other way to phrase his thoughts.

"It's not like it was the first time," she replied. "Probably only a fortnights each before they took off on their own anyway."

"You don't know that."

"Yes, I do." No joy in her voice, no energy, not even anger. "I meet a new mate, they leave. Get another one, gone. I mean, how many times does it have to be Nobby No-Mates before I get to call it a fact?"

Saul wanted to add something witty about how if she waited a few hours someone else would die and be along shortly but couldn't think of any way to make it work. Just like her, too tired to be witty.

Instead he relished the silence that came next, like his despair muffled the hum of the highway and all the nature audio around the lake. He closed his eyes and imagined all the sounds of the world sucked into his torso and smothered. The sound of Aimee's foot shuffling away on the dirty asphalt crushed the illusion and he opened his eyes.

Aimee stood leaning over a historical marker of some sort, her one pant leg soaked brown below the mid-thigh where a red and auburn drenched T-shirt clung tenuously through the power of clotting. From where he sat Saul could just barely make out the hint of the tattoo in the small of her back. Dark blue and black colors were all he could identify, but they stuck out, bright and vibrant against her ashen skin.

He turned, half expecting Aditi-Alhread to be meditating, or performing some stylized physically impossible version of Tai Chi during this downtime. Instead he found her sitting, just as before, in the backseat. He leaned to the window and put his face near the surface. His mood raced as he anticipated something clever he could do to the glass, but nothing came to him then either. He just looked.

She held her hand in the air, scrutinizing it like someone on hallucinogens might study their own appendages, and Saul saw she had a good reason. Tiny black wisps curled off her fingertips and hung in the air like ink in water. Ebony tendrils that held single moments or entire memoirs sloughed off her skin and then, after exploring the air like newborn seedlings, darted back, afraid, to the bosom of their original owner.

"I'll have to go back soon," She didn't turn towards Saul. "In an hour, maybe two."

We three are pathetic, Saul thought as he backed away from the car. Alone, alone, and alone, clean sweep, and no excuse to keep even the lonely together anymore.

Soldiers weren't supposed to stand around scenic overlooks watching their hands or reading historic markers. They were supposed to do things that mattered. That's what Rose thought anyway. Or, had thought, once.

He remembered her once wearing his camouflage soft cap and marching around the room doing her best to imitate the elephant brigade from *Jungle Book*. "Hup two three four hup two three four gentlemen! Halt!" she would yell as she marched around the living room exaggerating her arm movements and lifting her knees as high as she could with every step. "Gentlemen! Begin!" Whatever she couldn't remember she improvised, including a personalized version of a salute to Saul at the end. A Friday not too long after that she told her pre-K Montessori class that her dad was a hero. And that Saturday she woke up early; without fussing, without complaining about what shoes to wear and without arguing about her breakfast. Before Saul even finished brushing his teeth she stood by the door, fully dressed, including her coat, ready to watch the big race.

A simple 10K with no ties to the military what-so-ever, Saul ran in it because one of his younger troops asked him if he'd go with him to lead by example. At the halfway mark he found himself in the middle of over 2,000 joggers, but in the lead of a small pack a good 100 meters behind the next fastest group.

The sound "Yay Dadio!" cut through the clamor of the throngs gathered to support the runners, clear and distinct to his ears. He turned and smiled, and those two words spurred him on to run without concern for his body, to leap forward outside of his physical self, driving it forward while his consciousness stayed behind, back there, with that little girl and the pride she radiated for her father…

One tear escaped, then he forced the rest back and pulled himself to the present before leaning down to the car window.

"Tell me again how impossible it is to get this amulet."

CHAPTER 29

Aditi-Alhread spoke in a nonchalant tone without looking up from her hand.

"There's a well and a fountain in the center of the City of Shadows. Very pretty, very ancient, probably before the city was built. You get the idea. Anyway, the fountain pours water down into two streams that rejoin after a bit to flow into a well." She looked up to make a point. "Many of the ancient stories about rivers in hell stem from those two streams."

Saul nodded. "Keep going."

"Anyway, it never dawned on me until now that Nappy was responsible, but thousands of years ago someone dumped consecrated salt and iron nails into those stream beds."

"Sealing all the dead off from entering." Saul said.

"Yes." As she spoke, the sound of gravel underfoot alerted Saul as Aimee moved up behind him, then turned to lean with her back against the car, saying nothing as she did so.

"Most figured it was just another of the Netherworld's mysteries," Aditi-Alhread continued. "Some others, naturally, had to go and treat it as a holy place. They gather there to worship or declare their faith, thinking only the truly zealous or penitent will be able to step across."

When she turned back to her hand Saul prompted, "And once across…?"

"And once across, they believe they would be taken to their heaven or they would ascend or get some other cosmic reward."

"But someone still alive could walk across no problem, right?" Saul said. Aditi-Alhread dropped her hand, reviewing what he just said. Aimee's relaxed pose stiffened a bit. Silence. "I mean that's how Nappy put the amulet there in the first place, right?"

Aditi-Alhread turned back and looked him in the eye. "Saul, Nappy is immortal." When Saul's expression didn't change, she continued. "Angry spirits, jealous spirits… hungry, hungry spirits couldn't do him any harm."

"What about the offerings you talked about?" A tiny smirk crossed his face. Out of the corner of his eye he noticed Aimee standing with her arms crossed now.

Aditi-Alhread only took a second before responding. "Those would help you for a little while, but the instant you defiled their sacred shrine and stepped across the water…"

"I'd be protected by the consecrated salt, right?" The smirk returned, and again he forced it away.

"Yes, and you'd have the rest of your life to think about how you wouldn't be able to leave again." Aditi-Alhread's voice hinted at irritation.

"But if the amulet is there, and it is as powerful as you say…" He said.

"Saul…" Aimee interrupted.

"But if the amulet is there," he spoke with a deliberate tone and stood up straight, "and if it is as powerful as everyone says…"

Aditi-Alhread allowed herself a soft smile. "You know I couldn't protect you there."

"Do I have to be sleeping for you to take me there again?"

"I'm in." Aimee spoke so quietly Saul didn't register what she said at first.

"What?" He spun to face her.

"I'm in. I'm going with you." She spoke not out of excitement, but as a person with little else to lose.

"Look," Aditi-Alhread opened the car door and stepped out. "I had a hard time on a good day just pulling Saul through the Curtain. I'm not sure what it would take to take two people through."

"Do you want this or not?" Saul's temper rose a little as he spoke.

"There are places," Aditi-Alhread said, "I suppose, where the Curtain is weaker than normal."

"Perfect." Saul said.

"I've always wanted to do a graveyard concert." Aimee added.

Saul raised an eyebrow. "Really? Why?"

"Well think about it." Aimee's stance relaxed again and she moved over to slide up onto the hood of the car. "A place filled with lonely souls, freshly ripped from their families, and I could, you know, give them a few moments of song. Maybe cheer them up a bit."

"That's lovely." Saul said with a smirk.

"Oh and graveyards make me wicked randy." She added just to trump him.

Aditi-Alhread held her head in her hand for a moment and then looked up. "We won't be going to any graveyards."

"Why? I wasn't being serious." Aimee said.

"No," Aditi-Alhread replied, "that's not it. Graveyards don't inspire death. They inspire memories of life." She reached over and opened the driver's door and gestured for Saul to get in.

Without a word they loaded back up and headed off down the road. The nearest town sat behind them, but that meant crossing through a wall of ghost sentries or scouts or whatever they were all over again, so instead they continued back west.

An hour and a half later they hit a suburb of Sacramento called Rocklin, and Aditi-Alhread guided Saul off the highway and down some side streets. Her voice varied now, shifting between different people, or different accents, sometimes in the middle of sentences. Through the rearview mirror he caught a glimpse of her eyes and noticed that the black of her pupils had sent dark veins out into the whites.

By her instructions they went into a grocery store along the way, buying mostly food and the biggest kitchen knife they could find. They left, and a few side streets later Aditi-Alhread tapped Saul on the shoulder.

"There," she said at last, "that will do."

Saul studied his surroundings for the place she thought would make the best place to cross over into the Netherworld. A Starbucks, a Best Buy, a private doctor's office and a small dental clinic huddled together on one side of the road, while a large building labeled "Eternal Rest Senior Living" dominated the block across the street. Saul found himself stuck for a moment, as he was easily able to make convincing arguments on how any of those places could inspire death.

Instead he pulled over into a parking spot and waited.

"We're going there," Aditi-Alhread said, pointing at the Eternal Rest building. "Before we do that… Well, in many of my lives, at this point, before something this dangerous, someone would tell the troops that now was the time to make any final arrangements. Letters to loved ones, prayers, that sort of thing."

They sat without speaking or moving, and for a moment it seemed like they were just going to sit there, perhaps rethinking the whole idea, for the rest of the afternoon.

"Aimee," Saul said at last, "can I borrow your cell phone?"

"Sure," she dug it out of her pocket and handed it over. "But I thought we said no calls."

"If the cops are looking for us, then at best they will realize I'm out of state. Way out of state. If they wanted to coordinate any sort of cross country hunt for me – and by the way, really, why would they – by the time they arranged it all we'd be long gone." Saul took the phone and punched in a few numbers. "Honestly though, I don't think the police are really our problem anymore."

A twisting in Saul's stomach, probably shame, he figured, tried to talk him into making this call away from the other two, but at this point, he saw no point in hiding anything from them. If they thought lesser of him, it was probably no less than he deserved.

Lisa answered in the cautious voice of someone desperate for a specific call, but still wary of telemarketers. Saul relished the instant he told her who he was and the spike of her emotion that followed. Excitement and worry, plus a scream back to Rose to tell her who was on the phone. He relished it because he expected, quite correctly, for it to be short lived. As soon as he explained that he had decided to take an unplanned trip and lost his cell phone and was just checking in, anger and frustration seeped into Lisa's tone.

She explained how the police questioned their whole family once about him, and then again when they found his car and his cell phone abandoned in a hotel where he wasn't registered. While the cops wouldn't discuss the nature of their queries, they did include questions about whether Saul had a history of violence or anger management issues, and if he'd ever been involved with illicit drugs. By the time they left, Lisa resolved to not let anyone in the house watch the news or any *America's Most Wanted* knock offs until she had a chance to talk to Saul again.

He spent a few minutes explaining that the police didn't suspect him, but that he had inadvertently met up with some people they did think might have committed some bigger crimes. In the end, Lisa settled on suppressed irritation that escaped in little bursts about how worried she was and how even though she didn't say anything about it, this had taken a terrible toll on Rose as well.

Finally Lisa handed the phone off to Rose, and Saul explained the entire situation to her as well.

"So, you gonna be gone for a while?" she asked. Not when he'd be coming home, but how long could she count on him being gone. Still, something in her voice gave an impression, however small, of relief, or concern.

"Yeah, it'll probably be awhile."

"My friend Elizabeth says you found a new girlfriend and you've been in some skanky hotel this whole time."

In a rare moment of clarity, Saul heard a glimmer of hope in her voice. All this worry would be dismissed if the whole thing was just about him being a horn dog.

"Yeah, you totally caught me." He smiled. "Want to talk to her?" Aimee's eyebrows lifted a bit, although she continued to pretend not to overhear.

"Uh, sure, OK I guess."

Saul covered the phone and handed it to Aimee.

"Here." He said.

"What are you doing?" Aimee asked.

"Pretend you're my girlfriend."

"Why?"

"Because no one else needs to spend their nights wondering if I'm going to be dead the next morning."

"But you might be dead the next…"

"I know." Saul's voice softened. "Please."

Aimee took the phone.

"Hello?" she covered her other ear as she spoke, probably a habit she developed in bars. "Yes. Aimee. British, yes, very good."

She listed for a moment, nodding her head. "Yes. Right, in fact we'd just finished a proper shag right before he called." Aimee winked at Saul when she said it. "Oh sure. Every time, right. Oh you're going to have to ask your mum about that one." She flinched, remembering. "Eh, I mean your auntie, ask your auntie. Sorry for that awkward moment."

Aimee mouthed "sorry" to Saul and kept listening.

"Hey what music is on in the background?" Aimee said. "That your favorite band?"

She listened for several more minutes. In the quiet of the car, Saul could hear enough to recognize Rose's voice speaking in a fast excited tone, but not enough to make out any of the words. Again he found himself jealous that someone, apparently anyone could get her to speak so easily.

"I dunno I just don't think their new drummer is up to it." Aimee added at last. "Yes, much cuter. Yeah I gotta go too."

She hung up and tossed a friendly glare at Saul.

"There," she said, "we'll have spent quite literally our last moments on earth lying to a little girl. Aces."

Saul threw open the car door and the others got out with him. To make themselves a little less conspicuous, Aimee tied a long-sleeved shirt around her waist so it concealed the blood caked T-shirt tied around her leg. As they crossed the street, Aditi-Alhread moved slower than usual, and all her actions seemed very deliberate, simple, and forced.

Carrying their grocery bags, they walked up the sidewalk to the two-story wooden building. A shaded porch lined with multi-colored flowers encircled the entire ground floor as far as Saul could tell, and white wisps of light curtains danced inside most of the large windows on the second floor.

"I really owe you." Saul said to Aimee.

"Oh I haven't forgotten." She said.

Damn, Saul thought, hoping she had.

As they approached, the reality of 'senior living' crept in on the building's pretty external façade. Near the front door, a soft ball of an old woman sat curled up on a large wicker chair watching them without speaking. An IV drip hovered behind her and sent its single translucent vine down and into her arm. Saul realized then that the woman wasn't actually looking at them or anything else he would be able to see without that same IV drip.

"Somebody put me to bed!" Another voice, old, male, filled with the angst of a lost lifetime, echoed out of one of the open windows of the second floor. "I said somebody put me to bed!"

Saul, Aimee and Aditi-Alhread stopped just before the door.

"Wow, I really don't want to go in there." Saul said.

"You have to." Aimee replied.

"I'm not sure I do."

"It was your idea."

"Still."

"I'll show you my tramp stamp." Aimee kept looking forward and smirked a little when Saul's head spun towards hers. "I saw you looking at it. At the lake." Then she tilted her eyes up to his.

"Wait... wait," Saul said as she reached for the back of her shirt. Before she could do anything he added, "OK, let's just go in..."

"I thought so." She said as they moved forward as a group.

CHAPTER 30

Saul moved straight to the nurses' station in the main entryway, trying to take in as little as possible as he went. The woman behind the counter easily met the age requirements to be a patient, and held a visible air of distain for those who reminded her of a possible future. She sat under a big sign that read, "Those who say only sunshine brings happiness have never danced in the rain," which Saul translated into "Take pride in your sucky life." Talking to the woman, he learned that Eternal Rest divided itself into wings named after movie stars. They stood now in the Jerry Lewis area, while the hospice wing for the terminally ill shared its name with Marilyn Monroe.

The trio moved deeper into the building, past people with their minds in varying states of functionality, all in bodies pushing against their sell-buy dates. Saul forced himself not to dwell on his own mortality and a time when even simple bodily functions would betray him.

Aditi-Alhread moved ahead as they approached the Monroe wing, gaining strength as she moved. She took Saul and Aimee by the hand, led them past the individual hospice rooms and turned the corner. There a large man in scrubs stood at the end of a hallway isolated from the view of the nearest nurses' station. The man smiled and reached to open a door for them. Something triggered

Saul to tense up as he realized on some level that neither the man nor the door existed on this side of the Curtain. The hallway, too, deteriorated before his eyes, growing a layer of tattered torn wallpaper more dilapidated closest to the doorway. Extra sounds, distant and muffled, filtered in from all sides, while colors faded almost to the hue of a sepia picture.

"Aditi," the man in scrubs said with a friendly nod.

"Thank you," she replied and then turned back to Saul and Aimee, still holding their hands. Feeling no resistance from either of them, she stepped through what appeared as a doorway to them, a blank wall to the rest of the living.

The soft rose-violet glow from above engulfed them immediately, and Saul realized then that the sky never changed in the Netherworld. While he didn't recognize the specific cliff where they materialized, his confidence rose a bit when he gazed down onto the Valley of Souls and its crown city of jet black spires and towers.

"Is 'cool' the right word to use at this point?" Aimee whispered the question. "Also, am I allowed to take pictures with my cell phone?"

"No and no." Aditi-Alhread responded and took the grocery bags from the two of them. She seemed rejuvenated and powerful again. "Sorry. I meant you could try it, but technology won't work here."

Aimee didn't show any disappointment, and just watched as Aditi-Alhread dumped the contents of the bags onto the hard gray stone.

"OK," she said, "I'll carry everything that's still sealed. Aimee will offer the open stuff to anyone we pass nearby and I'll hand her new stuff as she runs out of whatever she is holding." She addressed Aimee directly. "Sprinkle it at them, toss it at them, think of it as a parade, or possibly a Catholic mass. Don't tease the crowd, but make it last. We don't want to run out."

Aditi-Alhread handed her a container of milk, and then offered Saul the extra-long kitchen knife.

"Seriously?" Saul asked.

"A gun wouldn't work. A sword would have been better." Aditi-Alhread replied. "Did you have a sword?"

"You're a much better hand-to-hand fighter than I am." Saul said, still not taking the knife.

"First," she said, standing, "I'm better with my hands and teeth, possibly a Baker Rifle. I have no idea how to wield a knife. Second, and this is important, it isn't the weapon that matters here, it is the hand that holds it."

"You lost me." Saul realized she'd already won the argument and grabbed the silver handle.

"If I were to cut someone here with that, they wouldn't even notice it." She knelt back down and repackaged the groceries in a particular order. "When you hold it though, your aura, your living energy, covers it as well. Makes the blade extremely painful, and as close to lethal as is possible in the Netherworld. But try not to cut anyone. Just hold it out, menacing but without specifically threatening anyone. Actually cut a person and three more will jump in to defend them."

"So, ration without teasing, menace without threatening." Saul said to Aimee. "We don't seem to have a lot of margin for error in this method."

"Is this the part where I remind you whose idea this was?" Aditi-Alhread stood up, packages in each hand. Saul smiled and gestured for her to lead the way.

She moved over to a pathway on the side of the cliff Saul doubted he ever would have found. Thin, but sturdy, it continued straight down to the valley floor without any turns or cutbacks. Saul turned to Aditi-Alhread as they walked.

"So, you never told me why me, I mean specifically."

She regarded him a moment as Aimee's facial expression seemed to validate the question, yes, why him?

"Three reasons," Aditi-Alhread replied, "You're a soldier, you felt the pain and loss of several people close to you, and 'stand to.'"

Saul thought a moment before responding. "OK the first two I get, but what does 'stand to' have to do with anything?"

"Not to mention what is it?" Aimee added. "I thought I just heard you wrong at first."

"So," Saul started, "in many of the old wars, for one reason or another, generals liked to attack at dawn. Ideally they'd catch the enemy still asleep and kill everybody before they could really get into fighting positions. Right about the time what was left of the enemy started fleeing or fighting, the sun would have risen and everyone could see again."

"Right." Aimee said.

"I'm not sure when it started, but 'stand to' is when everyone gets up about an hour or two before sunrise, and gets ready to fight in the dark, so if the enemy does show up, surprise! Everyone's in position and we kill them instead of them killing us. Although when you practice it in peacetime, you do it without the enemy obviously."

"Not seeing the link." Aimee replied.

Saul started to reply, then stopped and, finding he had no reply, turned to Aditi-Alhread for her to take it from there.

Aditi-Alhread stopped to talk. "I noticed, talking to soldiers, that lots of them had learned it, but for most it passed by unnoticed. For Saul it really resonated."

"Resonated how?" Aimee asked.

"You start in a sleeping bag," Aditi-Alhread continued, "warm, secure, and then someone rouses you out of it against your will. You fumble around in the dark, cold, awkward, longing for what you left behind, until finally you think you're ready to go. Then, nothing happens. Forever, nothing happens. You stand there, staring up at the void, lost in your own thoughts, shivering, waiting for the warmth and the light, wondering how long it will take, aching for it to happen, wondering if you did everything you were supposed to do or if you missed something in the dark."

She gestured down to the valley below.

"That's what we have to look forward to between lives?" Saul asked.

"You've both done it before." Aditi-Alhread turned and continued down the path without another word.

"Maybe," Aimee suggested to Saul on the side, "we should just stop asking her questions."

The howling of the vale became clearer as they approached, splitting into the discrete mumbles, wails, or just conversations of an open field filled with people. Or rather, wraiths. Shades of people. People missing limbs, people burning with a lightless fire, people wearing historical clothing, people pierced with railroad spikes, people in hospital gowns, people, Saul noticed with a pang, with black suicide veils covering their faces, all forms and all types somehow avoiding the main glow of light from above, keeping their features difficult to read at a distance.

They stepped down off the path and Aimee's hand moved to the top of the milk container. Aditi-Alhread reached over and stopped her.

"Not yet." Aditi-Alhread said without looking at Aimee. "Once you open that, half the valley will smell it."

They continued on, moving in a slow meandering path that ultimately led towards the City of Shadows. No one approached them at first, and only a few seemed to notice them at all, which just made Saul wonder if it would be a mad mob when the dead finally caught on.

As they moved Saul focused on the distance traveled and how far they still had to go. He kept the knife just barely out in front of him, and avoided eye contact but also didn't look down. He saw something to his side, however, which pulled him to a stop. What looked like two men, a woman, and a child-sized gargoyle-like creature sat in a circle around a sphere of bright light about the size of a basketball. Inside the sphere, even from this distance, Saul could make out smaller, colorful images dancing, twirling, and transforming. The audience of four stayed transfixed on the sphere. When a second row of curious onlookers got too close, the gargoyle spun and snarled at them like a starving dog protecting its first meal in days. The effect was the same, and the others kept their distance. Aditi-Alhread gently tugged Saul by the sleeve and they continued on.

They wove between misshapen spires for several more minutes, until Saul noticed a pair of boys followed behind them. Aditi-Alhread didn't turn, but went ahead and signaled to Aimee to start with the milk.

Tearing off the top of the container drew attention like a ring tone at a funeral. The instant Aimee splashed a little of it onto the rock, both boys dove forward and alternated lapping it up from their hands or directly off the ground. With just that one partial mouthful, both boys stayed down on the ground like cats in catnip, only with a fluorescent afterglow that radiated out from their torsos.

Saul looked up from the first two to find a cordon forming in their path. Hundreds of spirits moved to intercept, and the sound of the wailing quieted.

"Oh bugger." Aimee mumbled.

Aditi-Alhread touched them both on their arms for support, and then continued on as they'd planned, Saul in the front, Aditi-Alhread in the middle, and Aimee in the back. Saul found the mere presence of the knife gave him a wide berth, and for the most part, the crowd waited patiently for whatever Aimee threw down in their wake. Still, Saul felt the potential for sudden energy and violence, a charge of electrons gathering under a thundercloud on a hilltop, ready to release without warning.

They continued that way for over a mile. Aimee went through two gallons of milk, six bottles of wine, and had tossed out the better part of a large bag of flour when they reached the city gates. Two massive rectangular columns marked the opening to the city, with no sign of hinge or door. While originally carved with ruins and alphabets long forgotten, now deep claw marks and fingernail scratches obliterated everything within arms' reach of their bases.

One nearby temple appeared to have once been something ancient, possibly Chinese in architecture, but now swarmed with figures dismantling it and using the stones to build a more modern, sleek skyscraper-like building in almost the same spot.

"Could we… get a tour, maybe?" Saul said under his breath. The crowds just inside the entrance gathered twice as thick as anything they'd seen outside, and he felt the need to cover his own fear with an attempt to distract the others, or at least Aimee.

"You're going to want to go down the middle of the most obvious street," Aditi-Alhread said, "you'll know it when you get there."

"I wasn't kidding about the tour." A little tremor escaped his voice. The spirits pushed harder against the open space around him now, and from time to time one would brush against some part of him with frozen fingers.

"Right on." Aimee added, dumping out the last of the flour.

Aditi-Alhread handed her another bag of flour, discarded her final grocery bag, and followed Saul empty-handed.

"OK," she started, "that's the marketplace." She pointed to an open courtyard filled with stalls and booths made from the same black brick as the rest of the city. As they passed by, she pointed out a few of the specifics.

In the more shoddy booths, artists used long fingernails to carve patterns and shapes into the bodies of their customers, or in some cases, to warp their entire beings into macabre twisted forms. Saul felt certain that Escher, Giger and Hieronymus Bosch all working in tandem couldn't have created some of the monstrosities leaving those stalls.

They continued on, noting poets reciting from atop stacks of stones, interpretive modern dancers writhing around on the ground to drum beats or music only in their own ears, and scores of various types of leaders, teachers, gurus, and wise folk leading flocks around with sermons, parables, or simply a commanding voice.

In larger, more elaborate booths, dream peddlers hawked spheres of light like the one Saul saw earlier. It appeared to Saul that the dreams changed hands as tear-drop bottles with flakes of radiance bouncing around inside, which Aditi-Alhread explained would expand when opened. One of the vendors, he noticed with unease, kept an assistant or employee next to him who wore a modern suit, but with what appeared to be a flat-screen TV for a head, and apparently previewed images of their stolen fantasies for potential customers through his own face.

"Dreams are one of the two primary commodities of the Netherworld," she explained, although Saul could barely focus on anything she said. As welcome as the distraction had been, the hungry looks from the growing throng pushed the limits of his ability to appear calm. Either oblivious or indifferent, Aditi-Alhread continued, "The dead have huddled around the light and warmth of misty subconscious visions since man first stepped out of the jungles. You ever wake up knowing you just had an incredibly weird or intense dream and couldn't remember any of it? Harvested by one of these guys."

"Down to about half a bag here." Aimee said with a strained voice. Saul hadn't noticed until that point that this bag was the end of it.

"How close are we?" Saul asked, unable to see anything now but endless waves of morbid faces with some massive twisted towers in the background. In a different situation, he might have asked about what lived or worked inside of those too.

"Just there." Aditi-Alhread pointed.

Saul strained and finally made out the top of what must have been the fountain in the center of the city. He mistook it for one of the background buildings at first, as the fountain's height and jet black material blended right in. Too stressed to pay much attention to its aesthetic details, he registered little more than the sights and sounds of running water before pressing towards it.

Saul felt the resistance of the crowd grow as he moved, thickening with every step, daring him to brandish that blade near someone's face.

"Hey!" Aimee yelled. "Piss off!" Saul looked back and saw a cloud of flour in the air behind her. She clutched the bag close to her chest now, and Saul reasoned someone must have snatched at it enough to spill part of its precious contents.

"How much now?" He asked over his shoulder.

"Two or three handfuls. That's it!" Aimee yelled back.

A few steps later and the throng stopped parting. Saul recoiled back, like he'd almost walked into a wall. A new crowd stood before him, similar in dress and style enough to register as a group. All bore a mark carved deep into their foreheads, something that looked like a half-melted Christian cross. Saul looked for their limits, and found more random crowd to their left, and another group bearing a different symbol – this time a seven pointed Star of David – to their right. Figuring the more he saw religious types clustered together the closer he must be to the water, he shifted down the line of zealots.

"We're not getting through them." Aimee said, sprinkling her second to last handful of flour onto the ground. She turned and reached past Aditi-Alhread to grab Saul's shoulder.

"Make sure you get Watts, OK?" She said.

"What?"

"Same plan as before," she replied, "It worked for… oh I can't call him Nappy. It worked for Ut."

"The 'distract the bad guys by sending someone running screaming at the enemy' plan?" Saul said loudly.

"It did *not* work for Ut. He's captured and being tortured to death over and over. That is mission failure. We're not doing that."

"Saul, don't make me…" Aimee started, but Aditi-Alhread reached up and covered her mouth.

"Hold still." Aditi-Alhread spoke and then ripped the blood caked T-Shirt off Aimee's leg.

"Oh you divvy bitch!" Aimee danced with pain. "You tore off the scab!"

"Yes I know." Aditi-Alhread pressed the shirt back up against Aimee's leg until it dripped with new blood. She held it up and thousands of lifeless gray eyes watched it like a dog – a starved dog – watched a treat. Based on the looks on their faces, whatever food was to the dead, blood was a thousand times more so.

"Who wants it!?!" She yelled, and then turned and spoke softly to Saul and Aimee. "In a very critical minute, they'll realize that they can get a whole lot more of this from the original source. I'm going to toss this away from the fountain, when I do, throw the bag the other way. Then whatever you're going to do, do it fast."

Without waiting for a reply, Aditi-Alhread launched the shirt in a high wide arc over the crowd. Aimee and Saul didn't hesitate like they had with Ut-Napishtim. Aimee waved the bag of flour out at arm's length, giving them a dusty screen as they all three ran through the crowd. Figures behind them fell upon the white dust and drops of blood they left behind, snapping at the stone with no regard for their physical safety.

Some sort of animalistic rush overcame Saul as he ran, and he slashed at anyone in front of him along the way. At his hand, spirits screamed, went rigid, and some split into smaller pieces which hovered in the air as he raced past them. Then something slammed into his chest and his legs flew up in the air in that half-second before the inevitable crushing collapse of his torso hitting the stone.

Wincing, he looked up and into the eyes of a man dressed like an ancient Roman gladiator, complete with bronze spear, helmet, cloak, shin guards and breastplate. As Saul backed away and rose to a knee, he realized the man didn't wear a helmet, shin guards or breastplate, but rather his head, legs and chest had been molded and textured to look like the appropriate armor. Both Aimee and Aditi-Alhread stood behind the gladiator on the bank of the stream.

The large man lifted his foot, revealing the kitchen knife, which he then picked up and threw so far away it Saul lost track of it long before it hit the ground. Saul stayed still while the gladiator circled him, studied him, waited for him to make a move.

"Umbra Custodis," Aditi-Alhread yelled to the city guard, "we ask that you withhold sentencing or punishment until the magistrate arrives."

"Big request coming from the friend of the soul eaters." The gladiator's voice growled deep.

"Yes," Aditi-Alhread's voice carried a gentle tone. "Yes, it is a big request."

Good, Saul thought. If he read the situation right, at this point she took the role of defender of the fallen warrior, and he should act as fearless as possible. Possibly defiant. Really he had no idea.

"Three more today!" the gladiator yelled at Aditi-Alhread. "And six yesterday! Warriors from all times, all eras, sucked away! Their souls being devoured, even as we speak, and yet *you* somehow escaped."

"It has to stop!" yelled a nameless female voice in the crowd.

"The dead shouldn't be afraid," this came from someone Saul could see, one of the hooded men with the melted cross on their foreheads. "This is supposed to be our reward!"

"We're being picked off one by one Aditi," the gladiator growled. "If we find out you're working with them, helping them in any way, and somehow fooling us..."

"You know I fight on your side, Umbra Custodis," Aditi-Alhread said, again humble.

The gladiator bent down and grabbed a handful of the back of Saul's shirt in one hand while the other kept the point of the spear aimed towards Saul's face. With a sinister laugh, the man tossed Saul towards Aditi-Alhread. Saul skidded and slid more than flew, but still went further than he would have thought possible. It also ended with less pain than he expected.

"Well," the gladiator said with a grin, facing the pack of hungry spirits that only his presence kept at bay. "I will grant your request. I will leave and return with the magistrate, and until then I will do nothing to hinder you."

Saul's heart sank. The instant the city watchman took one step away from Saul and Aimee the horde would close the gap and rip the both of them, at least, to pieces. He wondered the point of even attempting to fight, or take up a fighting stance against the endless hungry dead.

"They think they have our backs against a wall." Aimee said.

"And for me," Aditi-Alhread said, "they're right."

Saul cursed himself as an idiot. One glance at Aimee told him she'd figured it out too, they were right where they needed to be.

Saul spoke to Aditi-Alhread, "What's going to happen to you when we..."

"Go NOW!" She yelled. He caught a glimpse of motion out of the corner of his eye, a wall of hunger and grasping hands that feared losing their prey, and somehow he knew he wouldn't even have to time turn his head their direction before they reached him.

He leapt out at the water, and in the slow-motion instant he hung in the air he noted Aimee's figure flying feet first over the stream. He broke the surface already paddling and kicking, and swam hard and ungraceful through the chilly water until his hand hit the other bank. He didn't pause to look back until he'd pulled himself up and completely out.

He stumbled back almost at once when the sound hit him, a roar of an angry crowd amplified far beyond normal distortion levels. Looking down he saw Aimee floating a few feet from his edge, pushing herself on with lazy, distracted kicks while her attention focused on the far shore. There a line of spirits poured up against an invisible barricade like ocean waves breaking against glass. They climbed over each other, on top of each other, with absolutely no concern for those below, until the vacillating mass of arms, legs and outraged faces reached thirty feet into the air. Each of their howls carried the frustration of several lifetimes and who knew how many animals, and the entire multitude released all that at once.

Saul watched without speaking, without moving, waiting for the unseen barrier to crack and fall and release all that madness to descend upon him, but after several minutes, the blockade still held. He allowed himself to breathe when Aimee touched his shoulders, and only then realized he couldn't see any sign of Aditi-Alhread.

"She'll be alright," Aimee said in a quiet voice without conviction.

As his breathing calmed, Saul studied his surroundings. The island between the two streams reached only about fifty feet wide at its center, where a small ziggurat sat reaching from almost shore to shore. The uneven terraced pyramid rose up three levels, assembled with asymmetrical gray stones instead of the black bricks of the rest of the city.

Without any discussion, they walked, dripping wet, towards the stairway cut into the center of the building. They followed it up to the second level and through the arched entrance to a shadow filled chamber.

Saul stopped a step into the room, hoping his eyes would adjust to the darkness. When they didn't, he concentrated on listening to the room, filtering out sounds one by one, searching for something that didn't belong. Again, nothing. He moved in, Aimee behind him, both careful to stay within the rectangle of light coming from the doorway. On either side of him, the utter absence of light implied an endless void in all directions. To dispel that image, he kicked a pebble to his side, but it made no sound once it entered the gloom.

"Hold on a sec," Saul whispered, simply because a place like this seemed to demand it. He knelt down and with a slow, purposeful motion, reached for the rock floor just outside of the illuminated path.

And felt nothing. His hand immediately disappeared, and he felt no floor of any sort.

He cursed and explained to Aimee that the shadows didn't just look absolute, they actually embraced oblivion. Saul wondered whether the light perfectly matched the solid ground, or defined it. His own shadow traveled gray in front of him, with soft edges and, Saul discovered with some relief, a hard ground beneath it.

He stood and they continued on, resisting the vertigo that called him to lean over either side of the pathway, to speculate how deep the abyss went, and to simply leap in and discover for himself. He prayed to anyone interested that Ut-Napishtim hadn't tossed the amulet off either side of the path. That seemed unlike him though, given his status as one of the original hoarders.

A few steps later a glint near the far wall caught Saul's eye, and he forced himself not to rush forward. Easing along his way, testing the floor and tapping it with his foot, they continued until reaching the dead end. There he saw it, simply lying on the floor, without padding, gem-encrusted case, ruin-covered jar, booby-trapped pedestal, ceremony, or protection. He leaned over and studied the amulet before taking it. Dark metal, probably iron, twisted into two long strands shaped into that of an ankh. Two curved points rose up from the loop like horns on a demons head, and what looked like a gray piece of amber filled the loop hole.

He reached down for it and froze, just short. Movement to his left. A sound, subtle, like cloth or feathers rustling, coming from only a few inches away. A spike of pain pinched in his chest as he tensed his entire body trying not to jump or scream. He eased his head the tiniest degree in that direction. Something breathed on him with a foul putrid scent and a guttural growl so deep Saul felt the sound vibrate in his arm.

"Shit!" Saul jumped up and back so fast he smashed into Aimee and nearly sent her flying into the void on their right. She let out a high-pitched yelp and then cursed along with him. Saul hadn't meant to move. Fear had him now, worse than anything he'd felt before, and his best efforts could only keep him from turning and running back the way he came. He held his arms up in a fighting stance, more because he'd tightened every muscle in his body than because he planned on hitting anything.

The growl repeated itself, and Saul saw the shadows bend slightly nearby. No, something protruded out of the darkness -- the tips of two folded wings covered in black oily feathers, massive enough to support something Saul's mass or bigger.

Two white spots appeared next, which Saul took as eyes glaring back without any pupils. Saul clinched his teeth. He had either woken something that lived here, or a guardian now toyed with him, and either way Saul didn't feel like waiting.

Finally a black talon eased out into the light and uncurled two long lanky fingers tipped in shiny claws like volcanic glass. The points of the nails settled on the ankh at the end of the corridor, and then slid it across the floor until it rested at Saul's feet.

"Seriously?" Aimee spoke and then covered her mouth. Neither she nor Saul reached moved towards the amulet.

The talon pulled back into the abyss, vanishing the instant it left the light. Saul still waited, afraid something would rip his luck out of his torso at the first hint of any wrong motion. The talon returned, so smooth and quiet Saul would have missed it completely if not for the swatch of bright green color that came with it. Saul didn't recognize the item until the horrid barbs released it to fall to the floor.

He knelt down to verify he understood the offering, and confirmed he looked upon a green tie, most of it missing, like it had been dipped repeatedly into a paper shredder. It belonged to Seamus' lackey, the first one, the one Aditi-Alhread pushed through the office window. Another quick snort and Saul caught a glimpse of teeth, two inches long, straight and thin, just barely reflecting a few shimmers of the light, and they took the form of a large, twisted smile.

At that point his fear faded. Saul scooped the amulet off the stone and finally exhaled.

CHAPTER 31

Sitting on top of the ziggurat Saul had a much better view of the City of Shadows. The distant towers reached up and into some sort of fog he hadn't noticed before, making them appear to fade into nothing, like the sun-bleached edge of a painting on gray-white canvas. Hovering near the top of one of the towers floated an all-black zeppelin with long birdlike wings and no sign of any propellers. It rested there, bobbing gently in the air, with no hint to its purpose or destination.

The fountain, Saul noticed now, consisted of a base of animals spewing up and out of one another, all reaching, biting, or clawing up, until at last ending in a mass of human arms and hands holding a giant tilted urn that poured a torrent of water down seven huge tablets. The tablets looked like the sort that held engraved words once, but over the centuries the water washed them all away. Around the marketplace, the city's shadowy population milled about now like people might in any small town, as if an angry mob hadn't tried to eat Saul and Aimee alive a few minutes earlier. Aditi-Alhread stood rigid, alone on the banks of the stream staring directly at him.

Saul felt he needed this moment of calm, dangling his legs off the edge of the pyramid's summit, although he still kept an eye on the main entrance of the structure, just in case that thing inside changed its mind and came out looking for him.

"What just happened in there?" Aimee asked. She stood behind him, not quite ready to relax.

"The enemy of my enemy is my friend." Saul replied. "I think we just made some sort of deal." He went on to explain the green tie and what he knew of the man who used to wear it.

"So what now?" Aimee continued, pointing at the amulet in Saul's hand. "Can we use that? Do we know what it does?"

Saul sat without speaking for a moment. "I don't know, I don't know, and no, we don't." The metal of the dark ankh felt cool in his hand, but also tingled against his hand like when he put his tongue on a 9-volt battery. "I guess we see if we can find Aditi-Alhread so we can give it to her and she can get us out of here."

Aimee pointed. "Isn't that her right there?"

"Yeah." Saul said with no energy.

"So what are you on about then?" Aimee knelt down beside him, sensing something in his voice.

"I wanted to try something first. I think. Maybe."

Aimee sighed, then sat with her legs over the edge as well.

Saul looked down at the amulet, tracing his fingers across the smooth dark metal. Conflicting emotions welled up inside him, but he didn't feel like sorting them out. He found his mouth starting to form words before he pulled them back in.

"I was wondering," he started to say, but didn't. He took another prepare-to-talk breath, and let it out without words. "Do you think it's a good idea…"

"Saul." Not Aimee's voice. Softer, and in fact it startled Aimee so much she nearly slid off the edge.

"Saul." Nicole's voice.

Saul eased himself around, unsure what he would find looking back at him. The body seemed familiar enough it could have been her, standing in the shadows that seemed to permeate every corner of the Netherworld. Loose-fitting pants, tank top, those also matched his memory, along with the length of hair hanging down her back, although a shade darker than he recalled it. His mind assembled everything he knew about her to check and double check what he saw, since the veil, the horrible black veil that looked like lace-patterned rigid plastic, covered every portion of her face.

"Hey," was all he could think to say as he stood. All the negatives of the situation simply didn't register to him at that moment. In some sort of instinctual response, his body reacted with a sudden vigor like the nervous energy of picking up a prom date.

"You can't see me here Saul, not like this. It isn't allowed." She stood with her hands crossed in front of her, not moving. The harshness of her voice added a pang to the energy, but he ignored it and forced it back until he couldn't feel it any more.

"I didn't mean to see you," he started, squeezing the amulet in his hand to punish it for obeying his wishes so literally. "I mean, I'm glad you're here."

In a moment of self-destructive folly, he waited for her to return the compliment, to reach out, embrace him, tell him how much she missed him.

She tilted her head down, just so. "Send me back please."

"What?" He looked around. Aimee stood now, backing away from the conversation, but eyes fixed on Saul. "I don't know how to send you anywhere."

"Then leave." Nicole replied without hesitating. "Either way, one of us has to go."

"You'll be trapped here," Saul said. "You won't be able to get past the…"

"It's still better."

As fast as it came, the strength waned from his limbs. He took a step back, turned, eased up to the edge, and then turned back to face her.

"When I said I would have gone on the deployment even if I didn't have to, I didn't mean what you wrote in the letter. I didn't pick the army over you." The edges of his vision clouded, leaving only Nicole's covered face in view. "I promise I didn't pick the army over you. I was just trying to describe a sense of duty. I thought it would help you understand better. Feel like we weren't so powerless, because feeling powerless to me is the worst…"

"Saul!" This time her voice quaked, an unperceivable amount to someone who didn't know her, someone who hadn't lived with her for years, or fathered a child with her. A single bead of ink-like liquid slid into view beneath the veil and formed a hanging droplet on her chin.

Turning his gaze away from her, he lowered himself down over the edge and down to the next level. He moved over to the stairs, careful not to let any part of his field of vision face her way, and didn't stop until reached the bottom. As if to taunt him, silently, or judge him, Aditi-Alhread still held her position looking him in the eye, waiting without a word.

He did nothing until the sound of shuffling feet told him of Aimee's approach.

"You ready?" He said in the most carefree tone he could manage.

"That's the tone people use when they don't want to talk about it." Aimee said, still behind him.

"Right." He tilted his head a little in her direction. "So you ready to go?"

"If you say so."

Saul walked out and over the water and plunged down into it, Aimee right behind him. This time when he came up, he treaded water and moved towards the occupied bank with slow even stokes. He gripped the amulet with the irrational fear that something in the water might try to take it away from him. No one approached as they reached the far bank, but they did turn to watch. A semi-circle of shades formed about twenty feet away, this time with the air of a curious, but respectful crowd. With all eyes watching the amulet, Saul had no trouble understanding why. Even Aditi-Alhread stayed a few steps back, allowing them to pull themselves out of the water.

"Thank you Saul," she said in a sincere tone.

He walked over and stood in front of her, cold this time from the wet clothing. He smiled a sad grin then, grateful for a chance to use the amulet once, but feeling glad to be rid of it if his first use set the tone for its future.

Before he handed it over though, the tingling of the amulet increased in Saul's hand, and Aditi-Alhread changed.

In front of him now, all in the same space, stood a handful of people, adults, children, men, women, even one newborn. He recognized the old attenuated woman named Aditi-Chic'Ya from the lake people and their mounds of crimson flowers, and he felt he knew the boy Aditi-Iyar, short lived bowman who dreamt of love and working in the king's library. The rest he skimmed over, interesting trivia only, until he caught a glimpse of a tall man with dark skin and dark hair, a self-titled 'doctor' named Aditi-Ioannes.

Within that man Saul saw a common link back to the other two of Aditi-Alhread's lives that he knew. All three carried a layer of intimacy for the soul named Kigal, who they all knew now as Seamus. Except Aditi-Alhread had hidden this one from the vision she'd given Saul and Aimee before.

Saul dove into this Aditi-Ioannes, demanding he reveal the secrets of a lifetime, knowing resistance was impossible. Childhood years flew by, unnoticed, insignificant, until the man reached adulthood and had a visit from a young woman begging him to help her suffering family.

Saul watched, felt, recoiled at the feelings that Aditi-Ioannes formed then; absolute self-centered lust for this desperate soul, the soul Aditi-Iyar had longed for, and Aditi-Chic'Ya loved unconditionally, and who now hunted them with an army of enslaved ghosts and hired gunmen. A wave of images flew into Saul next, moment after moment of every perversion and degradation Aditi-Ioannes put this poor mountain maiden through for his own whim, pleasure, or simple idle curiosity. The acts themselves weren't what knotted Saul's stomach, no, what affected him most were the looks of pain and shame on Kigal-Cliantha's face, the tears even, which went ignored, or sometimes even mocked, as Aditi-Ioannes pleasured himself with her in exchanged for bags of useless herbs.

Then the end of the vision came, the end Saul understood Aditi played over and over, the part where the armored Azabs pulled the young woman away screaming, leaving her children crying in that alley, and Aditi-Ioannes wouldn't even look at them. They bawled and tugged his pant legs and he didn't acknowledge them. He resolved instead not to take on any new 'problems' or complications to his life, especially this close to true wealth and status. Later that night, while they still huddled whimpering next to his doorway, a band of religious elders came and took the children away.

The image flashed to five years later when Aditi-Ioannes heard that his young lover from the mountains died in prison, and her children hadn't seen her since they day she entered. He forced himself to believe they ended up somewhere good, probably better, and deluded himself until that day he died and the truth of the travesty rushed over him and gripped him in the darkness of the Netherworld for the next eighty years.

"You hid this from us." Saul said, with tears welling up unnoticed. Shaking his head, squeezing shut his eyes, he forced the images and the souls to merge back into the form he knew as Aditi-Alhread.

"Yes." Aditi-Alhread crossed both hands behind her back.

"I see the guilt wafting off your soul," he continued, trembling.

"Yes."

"If Seamus dies today, that thing back there," Saul gestured to the ziggurat, "will rip him apart and paste him back together again for eternity… or worse."

"Maybe."

"But if you give Seamus this," Saul held up the amulet, "he'd be safe and protected and able to rest."

"Yes."

"You'd finally have atoned for everything you did to him… to her…" Saul spoke with anger, and Aditi-

Alhread wilted in front of him. "Tell me now you aren't doing this to make amends. Tell me you don't plan on giving this to Seamus." She remained silent. "Tell me!"

Aimee stepped around to their sides, straining not to interrupt but unable to withhold her questions for much longer.

Aditi-Alhread straightened herself up and looked him in the eye when she spoke. "When I think of Seamus, I do see Cliantha, and I ache for her." She took a half step closer. "I ache for what I did, I wonder if he knows who I am on some level or through some spell, and I've ached for the better part of the last three hundred years. But I wanted the amulet, I *need* the amulet to stabilize myself, perhaps even to reverse what's been done to me, eventually return to the natural order of things." Her tone took on a velvet edge. "To be born again."

Aditi-Alhread kept her eyes open, a gesture Saul now recognized as an invitation to examine her soul, to see if she lied or not. He decided not to bother.

"I'm going to keep it for now, and we are going to put Seamus down, got it?" He said. "I'll decide later if you need to be carrying this around or not." Aditi-Alhread's face contorted then, showing actual suppressed anger. For a moment Saul feared that she might try to fight him for it, but something told him that the amulet wouldn't let itself be simply grabbed and taken. No, the throng of spirits in the background had proven once before they weren't afraid to take what they wanted. Since they weren't trying now, there had to be a reason.

"What are you two on about?" Aimee stepped in to catch their attention.

Saul explained it to her, everything he'd seen, while Aditi-Alhread said nothing to argue or defend herself or her actions. Aimee's face revealed less disgust than Saul expected, which made him wonder both more about her background, but also a tiny part of him, very tiny, wondered if he'd been too quick to judge Aditi-Alhread. No, screw that.

"Lead the way back." Saul said at last, waving towards the city gates. Aditi-Alhread took a few steps in that direction and Aimee stopped them.

"Hold on," she said. She reached up behind her neck, slipped the red and black swirled guitar pick off of its leather strap and offered the strap to Saul. "Here. You'll get tired of carrying that after a while."

"Thanks." Saul ran the strap around the amulet and placed it around his neck. "Wasn't that important to you, or something?"

Aimee shrugged and tossed the pick onto the ground, watching it like she threw away more in that moment than a simple piece of colored plastic. "Eh, it belonged to an ex-boyfriend. He was sort of a poser anyway."

They moved much faster out of the city than they had on the way in. No spirits, of any sort, came within ten feet of them, and Saul saw no sign of his buddy the gladiator. A few spirits even tipped their heads or offered comments like, "No hard feelings! Just hungry" or "Most excitement we've had around here in five hundred years," all in thick unidentifiable accents.

Just before the city gates, Saul heard someone in the distance yell, "It's happening again!"

Anyone within earshot headed towards the voice, including Saul, Aimee and Aditi-Alhread. The curiosity of the crowd overrode their fear of the amulet, and Saul's protective circle shrank to a mere three feet to his sides.

When they broke through the crowd, they found a man dressed in a Union Civil War uniform and a woman in a Japanese modern skirted suit holding the arms of another woman, young, this one wearing a traditional Asian Indian dress. The Indian woman writhed about like an alien was about to burst from her chest.

The other woman yelled words in Japanese which Saul interpreted as "Hold her arms!" or something similar, and the man did his best to obey. The Indian woman rose up off the ground and thrashed the other two off of her like insubstantial annoyances.

"Another warrior!" Saul heard from a nearby boy – one of the twisted Escher/Giger/Bosch Collection with his entire torso torn apart and woven back together like strands of rope.

Saul touched his hand to the amulet and let his vision go blurry on the Indian woman. At once she split into several people all occupying the same space. He filtered through them as fast as he could, ignoring whole lifetimes as if they were TV shows he wasn't interested in watching, until he came across the one he knew the rope boy spoke of. At first glance, she appeared an old woman, in her late 50's, with nothing special about her. Looking deeper into her though, back into her youth, Saul found a female soldier, Russian, still holding a World War Two rifle and scope. He even found a name, Lyudmila Pavlichenko, the most celebrated female sniper in Soviet history.

"They've got her! They've got her!" Someone screamed, horrified.

And then the Indian woman flew up into the air, wailing in another language as she disappeared into the purple-red void. The Union soldier fell to his knees. The Japanese business woman put her face in her hands and stood there sobbing. Rope boy turned to Saul, realized what he saw, and then glared.

"Either destroy us all, or stop them," the boy said in a quiet tone, "but don't leave us like this, taken one at a time, living eternity in fear."

Saul's face twisted, combining shock and a complete lack of how to respond. He ended by simply nodding and turning back towards the gate. As he passed through, he realized Aimee and Aditi-Alhread followed.

They headed into the valley without speaking, each adrift in their own thoughts, looking back at what they left behind in the City of Shadows. Saul wondered what it meant, famous warriors cherry picked out of the Netherworld. Seamus creating an army... but that didn't answer how he planned to use them. Military dead and civilian dead standing around as alarm systems should work all the same, and they all had plenty of animal lives to fight with.

Saul sighed and kept walking. The soft moans and wails of the Valley of Souls took on a new context for Saul now. He imagined any of them to be the cries of warriors, screaming and ripped from this world and deposited into a flask held in Seamus' hands. Then he pictured souls by the thousands, perhaps millions, hiding behind rocks or the dreams of the living to escape the terror that they might be next.

They kept walking.

A few hundred meters shy of the cliffs, Aditi-Alhread fell to her knees. Saul thought it part of his recurring horrible daydream, and didn't react at first.

"Ah!" she grabbed her chest. "Saul, give me the amulet."

She seemed genuinely in pain, but Saul still said no.

"Nappy told him where we were." She strained to speak. "Give me the amulet!"

"No!" Saul fired back, and gripped the dark ankh just in case.

"Saul," Aditi-Alhread held out one hand. "I can resist summoning in the real world, but not from here. Please."

Saul realized Aimee studied him for what he would say next. "I can't," he said. Aditi-Alhread wreathed in sudden agony and screamed.

"Then at least stop the summoning!" Aimee gripped his arm.

"I don't know how!"

Black tendrils flew off Aditi-Alhread like she was a sand sculpture in a growing windstorm.

"Saul!" she screamed with closed eyes.

His mind raced. "Can we come with you?"

"What?" Aimee asked.

"I don't know," Aditi-Alhread's voice grew weak.

Saul pulled her up, wrapped his arm around her waist, then held another arm out to Aimee. After an instant's hesitation, she rushed towards him, and they all three stood together arm in arm.

"If this doesn't work," Aditi-Alhread said in a voice little louder than a whisper, "he'll trap me, and you'll be stuck here."

Saul didn't hear her. He held them both with a grip as strong as he could manage, stopping just shy of hurting Aimee's ribs. He didn't know if it would do anything, but he pictured the amulet, felt the warmth of it resting against his chest, and held onto that warmth. He called up an image in his mind of them all linked together, tied as one, moving as one...

And then they were.

CHAPTER 32

For a few moments, it felt as if someone pulled the earth down a few yards and off its normal set of gears, spun it beneath Saul's feet, and then pushed it back up again. He felt no sense of movement, no breeze, no internal momentum. And yet, he knew he – they – moved.

His body changed too, in ways he couldn't completely quantify, as it shifted from the Netherworld back to the land of the living. The only thing to signal the trip had ended consisted of the terrain no longer moving around them.

"Where are we?" Aimee asked. Someplace dark, outdoors, but with a regular hazy star-filled sky and a quarter moon.

"Just shy of where he wanted us." Aditi-Alhread said as she wiggled free of the group embrace.

"What happened?" Saul said.

"I'm not sure," Aditi-Alhread answered. "A summoning calls spirits, which, in effect, we were a minute ago. When spirits enter this world, they remain spirits. When we entered… well, I guess our solid forms stopped the spell early."

Saul studied their surroundings a little more carefully. Cool air, what appeared to be some sort of fir or pine tree silhouettes against the night sky, a few points of electric lights, but no major highways or residential areas nearby.

"How close are we?" Saul asked. "To wherever they wanted us, I mean."

"Hold on." Aditi-Alhread concentrated a moment and then inhaled a long, deep, breath. In the darkness Saul couldn't be sure, but he thought her nose might have contorted for a moment into something bigger, animalistic, primal even.

"There," she said, pointing at the nearest albeit dingy light source. Saul strained his eyes and realized that tungsten bulb hung above a doorway of a larger building, possibly a warehouse. Saul could almost make out a pair of figures beneath it.

"Two guards?"

"Plus another on the roof and a sharpshooter out in that field, facing this way. Probably fifteen or twenty scents total." Aditi-Alhread scanned the area. "Spirit guards too, roughly two for every human."

"So if we approach," Aimee started, "they'll tell Seamus we're here regardless of whether we managed to slip by the sentries or not."

"You got it." Aditi-Alhread replied.

"Suggestions?" Saul said it and barring his military unit loaning him an up-armored Humvee with a fifty-cal mounted on a turret, all he could think about was calling the police and hoping Seamus engaged in something illegal inside he could be arrested for.

"Well," Aditi-Alhread's voice sharper than Saul had ever heard it, "if *I* had the amulet, first I'd free all those spirits and send them on their way. Since I *don't* have the amulet, I'm just going to go in and kill a bunch of people."

"Killing's easy for you, isn't it?" Aimee asked.

When Aditi-Alhread turned, she bared her teeth and furled her brow for a quick instant before snapping back to normal. "When I look into the eyes of someone with mostly good lives under their belt, but the one they are in now sucks, I kill them, put them out of their misery, hurry them on to another chance." She turned to Saul. "I know what it's like, obviously, to have one bad life to dwell upon."

"So that's it then," Saul said, ignoring her last comment, "you'll just run in and kill anyone that moves?"

Aditi-Alhread turned and crouched down. "They don't have to move."

Saul nodded, frustrated, unable to affect her or the situation. Sarcasm took over, as it often did when he felt helpless. "Hey you know what would really capture the moment?"

"What?" Aimee asked.

"The Immigrant Song." Saul stopped before adding 'by Led Zeppelin' at the end, remembering just in time that they all knew the band, albeit through different perspectives.

"Saul, they have guns." Aimee replied.

"I know…"

"We have a piece of jewelry."

"Sorry," Saul said, "pre-combat banter." He turned back and down towards Aditi-Alhread. "If I was going to free these spirits, like you said, how would I do it?"

"You figure it out." The instant the words left her lips she darted off, in human form, but bounding on all fours in the general direction of the nearby field. Saul guessed a large sweeping arc to take out the sharpshooter before he could scream or fire.

"We don't have long." Saul said.

"I know." Aimee's tension came out in her voice.

"I can't even see them." In his mind he cursed Aditi-Alhread, knowing she could see the dead all around them, and probably knew how to release them.

"I might be able to," Aimee said, "maybe I could guide you?"

"How would you see them? Do you have music?"

She reached down and checked her iPhone.

"This thing isn't working." She said, holding down a button.

"Could you sing?"

She cast a sideways glance at him and narrowed her eyes. "I think I might be able to pull it off, yeah."

"Then how would you guide me? Clever hand gestures?" That might have been too harsh a tone for someone trying to help, he thought after the words escaped.

"Wanker," she said, and spun him around to face her. She peeled back the fingers on Saul's hand, the one Aditi-Alhread cut open earlier, and scratched open the wound. She did the same to the cut on her leg and then grasped Saul's blood-covered hand in hers. "I only remember the English parts."

"That's good, I guess, given that you are English." Saul gave out a half chuckle.

She grinned politely, then her face went stoic. She took in a few deep breaths and closed her eyes. Then she opened them again.

"You have to close your eyes too." She said.

Saul didn't remember that happening before, but took her word for it. The instant after he did as she asked, Aimee kissed him, soft and warm, and reached her free hand up behind his head to hold him there. After nearly two years of no physical contact, Saul flashed back to junior high, when kisses were sex, better than sex, and sent waves of energy throughout his whole body instead of one localized area.

Almost a full minute later, she pulled back.

"Why did you do that?" Saul asked.

"Because you didn't."

She watched him a moment, cradling the back of his head, and then let her hand fall back down to her side. Aimee shut her eyes again and took another deep breath.

"The bond of blood is the bond of life." Aimee said alone. She repeated it three more times, but Saul did not feel the urge to repeat it with her.

Saul's heart sank. She repeated it again and still nothing happened. He put a hand on the dark ankh, feeling foolish, but not wanting to miss any possible aid or lucky ritual, even from something he doubted was anywhere near as powerful as everyone thought. He'd never questioned or mocked any superstition when gunfire or explosives might be involved.

"The bond of blood is the bond of life." she said it again, still nothing. Saul lifted the amulet and placed it between their bloody hands.

"The bond of blood is the bond of life." this time her voice changed, and after the fact Saul realized his lips had mouthed it with her. Twice more she said it, and Saul found himself unable to resist repeating it. On the fifth time, they both said it aloud in unison.

She opened her eyes, pupils all black and dilated, then she changed the words.

"My eyes are your eyes, your eyes are my eyes, so mote it be." Saul mouthed this one with her right off. Again on try number five, they spoke together. Saul felt sleepy again, but didn't fight the weight of his eyelids.

"Did it work?" Aimee asked him. He opened his eyes to that same surreal sensation of staring at his own face.

"And immediately there fell from his eyes something like scales, he regained his sight, and he arose and was baptized." Saul whispered.

"What was that?"

"Vacation bible school." He took a moment to test his limbs. Everything worked right, just from a strange point of view. "OK, I'm going to try to face that warehouse." He said, and turned. Aimee stayed behind him, looking over his shoulder, so he could see roughly where his body pointed. Afraid to let go, he squeezed her hand and the amulet so their moments wouldn't accidentally jar their fingers loose.

"It doesn't look any different." Saul said in a quiet voice.

"I'm not singing." She replied.

Saul nodded and waited. Aimee closed her eyes again, cleared her throat, and started humming. He realized she needed the prelude to a song to ease her into it. The lyrics came out relatively soft, just the right volume for that close to his ears.

She sang in a clear voice, with even, almost ethereal tones, a love-song Saul knew better than to assume had anything to do with him. It carried gentle sadness into the night air, and being held there in her arms, Saul let himself fall deep enough into her melody that he forgot a world of twisted spirits or angry necromancers. Two verses later, she opened her eyes.

The night looked different enough at first that he didn't recognize it. The sky lighter, closer to purple, and someone standing nearby, a little translucent boy, glowing bright blue. The boy studied them a moment, then turned and sprinted for the warehouse. In the distance Saul saw five more glowing figures, varying shades of blues or greens, with their arms stretched out to their sides like an undead fence. Aimee kept singing, giving the scene an eerie soundtrack.

"Stop." Saul said, and the boy hesitated and skipped a step before continuing on. "STOP!" Saul growled, squeezing the amulet as he did so.

The boy's feet flew up into the air like he'd been grabbed by the collar.

Saul waved his free hand in a circle, and the boy turned to face him. Saul studied the boy until he noted a lighter blue shackle around the kid's ankle, with a chain that ran off and into the warehouse. The five other figures, two men and three woman, backed away in shock. Saul found more chains on their ankles, and lifted up his hand and opened it. Picturing what he wanted in his mind, the chains flew towards him and into his hands, still attached to their ankles.

On a different layer of his vision, at that moment Aditi-Alhread flew sideways into the two living guards, taking them both out of the tiny sphere of light cast by the bare bulb and into the shadows. One of them managed an agonizing scream so loud Aimee stopped her song for an instant, and during that moment all the figures faded like the afterimages of a photography flash.

When she started back up singing again, Saul found himself still holding the ends of six lengths of nether-chain, with six people watching him with wide terrified eyes.

"I want them all." He said, more to himself than anyone else. He strained to see more, and realized what appeared as tiny beams of light stretching out from the warehouse actually formed a web of chains that flew off in all directions long past the horizons.

Blam! Blam! The Guard on the roof put two rounds into the darkness below, followed by a black blur leaping up the wall and upon him. He thrashed like a man on fire and then fell backwards with Aditi-Alhread wrapped around his torso. So much for the element of surprise.

This time Aimee didn't pause, and Saul focused on a beam of light, drawing it to his hand until another chain snapped into place. Somewhere in the back of his mind he recognized that his heart raced and his body trembled, but he kept his concentration on his outstretched hand. Another chain snapped to his palm, then another.

Aditi-Alhread leapt down and kicked the door to the warehouse off its hinges. The inside erupted in gunfire.

Three more chains flew to Saul's hand, then something clicked, an understanding of the method, and a constant stream of insubstantial metal links hit his fingertips in rapid succession. Saul let out a low scream, and let it build and the chains kept coming. His voice rose as the links came in, both building until in one tremendous crescendo, the last one snapped into place with a resonating clank of metal on metal. Saul turned his body so he'd have the weight of his torso behind it, grasped a thousand ties to a thousand souls, and pulled.

Prehistoric predators, tiny carnivores with no appreciation of scale, and the instincts of every creature threatened with its own life bounced from target to target. The spirit named Aditi kept no identity then, letting the most savage and desperate beasts surface and fly free without any sense of control. She clawed, bit, gripped, slashed, spun and dove in a dizzying cross between Jackie Chan, a tornado, and a logging buzz saw. The screams, the blood, the ripping flesh, the bullets, all objects in the background, distant and unreal to the unholy energy she released into the world. Then, in a single sobering moment, something hit her, hard, across the jaw, and she crumpled.

Wheezing on all fours, Saul strained to regain his breath. He couldn't be sure of what he'd just done, flush with power he'd couldn't verify, terrified at any instant he'd realized he imagined it all, or someone would take it from him.

"By the way," he said between mouthfuls of air, "I liked that song. Did you write it?"

"No," Aimee still stood, showing no signs of physical exertion.

"Old English folk song?" Saul guessed.

"Cowboy Junkies." She said.

"Oh." Saul knew better than to admit he didn't recognize the band. He'd Google it later.

As Saul and Aimee walked quickly to the warehouse, they went over what to do next. They haggled over some options while Saul leaned down and examined the guards' weapons. MP5s Saul noted proudly, the same type that SWAT teams and Special Forces guys used.

"This one has an ipod." Aimee said, taking it and snapping it to her shirt. She popped the ear buds in and thumbed through the song list. "Eh, it will have to do."

Saul kept one of the submachine guns, gave Aimee a quick class on how to fire the other one, and then finalized their plan. He asked her to stand by the door as he eased towards it, concentrating on all the tactical building training he'd gone through, and then remembered the kiss from earlier. Wanting another one, but yielding to the severity of the moment, instead he turned to stare at Aimee's face, grinned a sad sincere grin, and edged around the doorway.

The lack of movement inside surprised him at first. Three lines of cargo racks, ten feet wide and thirty feet tall, dominated the right side of the building. Nearest the sickly track lighting, they caught the eye first, until Saul followed the image down to the warehouse floor, and the bodies. A few twitched, one coughed, most did nothing.

A few steps in, avoiding pools of blood and people with a tint to their skin tone he knew all too well, Saul moved around to the side and Saul saw a big open space once used for incoming shipments of paper or electronic parts or whatever this warehouse used to hold. He caught a glimpse of a shirtless barefoot man with something all up his arms bouncing around like a kick boxer at a match, and Aditi-Alhread curled up in a ball in front of him, her hands covering her head to shield her from more damage.

"Down! Down!"

"Drop the weapon!   Drop the weapon!" Two voices, one from each side, moving closer from out of the shadows. Saul risked a slight head turn towards one, but knew better than to let the gun even jerk in that direction. The bearded man, assault rifle up at his eye, came in from that side, and Saul figured someone similar moved in from his other blind spot. Saul turned back to the scene in front of him and considered his options in the two seconds he had before somebody might shoot him in the legs just to get his attention.

The man near Aditi-Alhread stopped bouncing, and Saul finally recognized him as Seamus. He wore black karate pants, but his hands and arms up to his elbows and his legs from the top of his feet to his knees darkened with a dark leather sleeve, bristling with what Saul figured must be iron nails.

"You'd have to aim to hit me from here Saul!" Seamus shouted in a fast tone, recognizing the volatility of the situation, "and you know those two will have you perforated at the first finger twitch."

Saul bent down, in a slow deliberate motion, and set the gun on the concrete. He noticed a line of salt and nails there a few yards in front of him, and when he rose, hands up in the air, he took a few steps towards it.

"Freeze!" The bearded man barked. One step later Saul obeyed.

"Hey Saul, lookit this!" Seamus spun around and shin-kicked Aditi-Alhread in the side, sending her sprawling backwards. Saul, of course, did nothing.

Instead he gathered more details about the room. He recognized one of the corpses, just inside the line of salt, lying on his side in a circle of dark red, clutching his stomach with mouth and eyes wide open. He allowed himself to glance at two other nearby bodies, just in case they concealed any information he could use, even though he knew he'd retain those images for the rest of his life. The first one just a man on his back, normal in all respects except the left half of his neck missing with the edges jagged and torn. The other Saul thought might be still alive for a moment, sitting up against a wooden crate, until Saul realized the man clutched the better part of his entrails in his arms.

A horrid coughing in the back of the room caught Saul's attention next, and when he strained, he noticed a hooded figure hanging by the neck in the corner. The person twitched and then went rigid... again. Yes, it had to be Nappy, dying, coming back, and then dying again, over and over in a torturous cyclic ritual no one even paid attention to any more.

Seamus strolled over to what looked like a large birdbath, picked up a can of spray adhesive and sprayed the leather from his fingertips to his elbows. Then he rested his arms in the large flat bowl, first with palms up, then over again, and walked like a doctor drying off sterilized hands. Saul noticed a fresh layer of white coated Seamus' leather gloves when he pulled them up.

"Actually Saul I'm glad you're here," he said as he moved, careful to keep as much salt on his arms as possible. "Otherwise I would have had to kidnap your daughter, hold her ransom, all very cliché." He shot up into the air and came down smashing his fist into the back of Aditi-Alhread's head. She flattened against the floor.

"I don't have the amulet." Saul said as the two men approached him. One moved him forward another step and gave him a quick pat down for weapons, while the bearded man took Saul's gun and tossed it to the side.

"Of course you don't." Seamus said. "Incidentally, Saul meet Alan and Jerry." He gestured to the man Saul didn't know and then to the one who attacked Nappy's home. Seamus leaned over and whispered into Aditi-Alhread's ear and then took a step towards Saul.

"You may have noticed Dennis didn't make it," Seamus pointed at the curled up figure Saul recognized before. "Or as you know him, dead lackey number four."

With a casual air, Seamus sprayed both his shins with the adhesive and sprinkled handfuls of salt on them as he continued. "I recently purchased a special mix of souls just for this moment. Alan, Jerry…" he looked around and pointed to another lifeless form on the floor, "…and Colin there – sadly he also didn't make it – they are the next generation of bodyguards slash hired muscle.

I gave them the memories of Vietnam Special Forces, masters of the original martial arts, mercenaries from the Middle East… the list goes on and on. But, as always, I saved the best for myself."

Aditi-Alhread rose to one knee behind Seamus. For an instant she looked like she might spring, but Seamus turned first, skipped over, and kicked her in the ribs. She winced in agony and grasped her side, but made no sound.

Saul pictured how the fight must have gone. Aditi-Alhread felt no pain, normally, but had to guard and recover her memories after each cut, slash, or shot that took a piece of her. Distracting to her maybe, but probably not something Seamus' guards were able to take advantage of. The ring of salt and nails grew thick, smooth, and deliberate against the walls, but the line in front of him seemed like a hurried job, thrown down by people – the only two people left – rushing to close the circle behind her after she'd gone after the primary target waiting as bait in the center of the trap.

Seamus hit Aditi-Alhread again with a basic right cross, and her head snapped around and spewed black droplets onto the ground. As she held out a hand to call them back to her, Saul feared Seamus would leap over, step on them with his bare feet and absorb them.

"Do you know why she isn't fighting back right now?" Saul said.

"Nope, don't care." Seamus turned, distracted, wanting to move towards her spilled memories. He missed this chance, but there would be others.

"If you had any idea the things she did to you in your last life." Saul took another step forward, felt the two men beside him raise their barrels, and stopped.

"Really?" Seamus regarded Aditi-Alhread a moment, "so you're saying I should stop playing around, chop her up into twenty ounce containers and get on with absorbing her then?"

Saul didn't know how to answer.

"And after I learn all her secrets," Seamus moved over to a machete lying on the floor and picked it up, "skip torturing you, go straight to the killing; then summon your spirit and take in your memories of where you put the amulet?"

"They're waiting for you!" Saul shouted. "They can't wait to see you, the 'seller of souls,' and if I'm not the one to send you…"

"I am *not* some petty drug dealer," Seamus growled back. "Dennis!" Seamus pointed, "Dennis was a petty drug dealer. He claimed if he didn't do it someone else would. Some of my other colleagues in the field say they're just providing a needed service. But I, I know better!" Seamus stepped towards Saul, who took another step to meet him.

"Really?" Saul said.

"For whatever reason, every life we gain experiences, we learn something new, from insect to animal to farmer to banker to who cares!" He took another step forward, Saul followed suit. They stood only fifteen feet apart now. "Hundreds of years pass between each life, but I've found a way to speed up all that. If I absorb another person, I cut centuries off the process, combining all our experiences together. The more I soak up, the faster it goes, for everyone. I…" he pointed to his chest, "…am an evolutionary!"

"It won't change things when you cross over." Saul took one final step forward. Jerry moved in and jabbed him with the rifle barrel, signifying he'd gone far enough. It didn't matter now. Aditi-Alhread crawled away from Seamus on all fours.

"But the amulet will change things Saul, and I know you have it or you wouldn't be here, couldn't, be here." Seamus glanced down at the machete and turned towards Aditi-Alhread. He moved towards her as he spoke. "I don't fear the dead! Screw them! Let them come! Line up every man woman and child who ever died and see if I care!" He reached down and grabbed her by the hair.

Saul turned to Jerry and looked him in the eyes. Hands still above his head, he moved one step towards him, as if daring him to shoot. Saul's face held the resolve of a convict on his way to death row. If he fell now, if he died here, in this room, he was OK with that. But as Saul moved, he purposefully slid his foot across the line of salt, creating a two foot gap.

And then Aimee gave the word.

For most of the world, a college girl wearing head-phones, a gun strapped to her back, and an interesting Egyptian necklace stepped through a doorway and yelled "Thundercats are go!"

From another point of view, a host of angry spirits flew into the warehouse and funneled through the gap in the salt like a swarm of bats leaving a tiny cave window at dusk. They fell upon Seamus and Jerry and Alan en masse, swarming, slashing, biting, screaming, years of captivity and lifetimes' worth of rage expended in a single instant. Each soul capable of delivering only a tiny scratch or bruise, they pushed the Curtain to its limits, ripping through it and into the three men with the death of a thousand cuts, flaying them alive. All the while Aimee advanced forward, driving the spirits in front of her by cursing Seamus with every profanity ever uttered, British or American.

Saul ducked and dove out of the way just before Jerry unloaded his carbine at the whirling invisible blades he imagined all around him. One bullet caught Alan in the stomach and chest, and after Jerry's legs gave way with loss of blood, he cursed loudly in a language Saul didn't know and shot himself in the head.

When the noise stopped, Saul took a 9mm pistol from another dead minion and crouched as he moved to where he could see the center of the circle again. There Seamus twitched on the ground, flat on his back, and all but for a few scraps of flesh here and there, completely skinned. Saul raised the pistol and moved forward, ready to spin on any movement.

Aditi-Alhread caught his attention, pulling herself across the ground to Seamus' side. Trembling, she whispered something in his ear. Seamus' eyes opened a little more, struggling to focus or turn towards her. She reached up and stroked his temples, and cradled him the way he'd held her in a different life, in a different era. And then, without warning, she raised her arm and brought it down upon his throat, crushing it.

Aimee shook her head and pulled out her ear buds.

"Aces." Something in the tone of her voice bothered Saul, a distinct lack of a feeling of victory. He chalked it up to the carnage, and moved over to help Aditi-Alhread to her feet.

She stumbled to move away from Seamus, and when Saul asked why, she pointed back at the body. No, a spot just beyond Seamus. A dark spot spreading across the floor that Saul felt but couldn't see. The temperature of the room dropped enough Saul saw his breath, Aditi-

Alhread's face contorted with horror, and Saul thought for a moment he heard the flapping of very large wings.

And then the air calmed again.

Without asking what just happened, Saul took the role of clean-up crew. He checked the room for survivors and found none. Any that lived when he entered hadn't survived the wrath of the ghost slave revolt.

Saul watched Aimee sit down, weary and distant, lost in her own thoughts. In an attempt to cheer her up, he pretended to think out loud, "Do you need organ donor cards if the organs are already out?"

No effect. Possibly exactly the opposite effect he had been going for. Not the right audience for military gallows humor. He didn't feel particularly triumphant either at that moment, and set himself down on the hard concrete beside her.

"Big Thundercats fan?" He asked in a dry voice.

"What?" She stayed lost in her own thoughts for a moment and then snapped out of it. "Oh, no, the movie Juno."

"Oh."

Aditi-Alhread recovered in a few minutes, and went back to cut Nappy down from his noose. Saul chuckled because he'd completely forgotten about the immortal and wondered how many times he'd died again in the time since Saul entered the warehouse.

Still chuckling, he turned to Aimee to share the joke with her, hoping one last time to lighten her mood. Instead he found her with lines of tears down her cheeks. That seemed extreme, especially considering how well she handled herself at Nappy's.

"Are you OK?" Saul asked, knowing she wasn't.

She shook her head and didn't speak.

"Anything you want to talk about?" He almost touched her shoulder, then drew back.

"Saul," she turned to face him. She choked back a few gasps of air and said, "Watts wasn't here."

CHAPTER 33

Saul stared into Aimee's eyes, not quite certain he grasped the significance of her words.

"We freed everyone Seamus ever bonded." Aimee said. "Sidney is here, Kami-ko is here, even Ginger Tim, he was here for a bit before shuffling off."

Saul started to suggest the alternative that his old army buddy just left for bigger and better things. It happened, or at least people moved on to the Netherworld. Then he remembered the night Aimee saw Watts ripped away.

"He's gone, Saul, absorbed by one of these sodding minions so they could get his great aim with a large caliber weapon or some shit like that." She clinched her teeth. "He's *gone*."

She seemed ready to hit someone – anyone – and at that moment he wouldn't have minded if she'd picked him as a target. In fact, if it made her feel better, he would have welcomed it. Saul didn't know what to say or how to fake that he did. His focus drifted from Aimee's face and off to some indeterminate spot in the distance.

"Do you think we could use this," she took the amulet off her neck and held it in her hand, "to bring Seamus back and then rip him apart again?" Her hands tensed around the dark ankh and wrenched it. "And again. And bloody again."

Years of dealing with soldiers trained him to listen without physical contact, but he finally reached over and rested his fingertips on her arm. "Hey." He spoke in a soft voice, and she looked up. "I think someone else has that covered. I think we're good."

Aimee nodded without conviction.

"Whoo-whee!" A male voice, it took Saul a second to recognize it as Nappy's. "This is better than the Battle of Greasy Grass Creek." Nappy strolled around surveying the massacre with a childlike lack of concern. The torn shirt covered in dried blood and the rope burns around his neck only added to the visual. Aditi-Alhread followed behind him as he walked. "Wow. Nice."

He stopped in front of Aimee and Saul. "So. How you two doing?" He said.

"Still breathing." One of those practiced neutral answers that relayed false hope. Saul even managed to put enough energy into it that it sounded almost upbeat.

"I wonder." Nappy said, arms crossed.

"About what?" Saul asked.

"Shut up! I'm wondering." Nappy moved his hands to his hips. "I think we can assume I wasn't born yesterday, so what's going on with you two?" Saul sighed and then explained the situation with Watts, starting with him being absorbed and then going all the way back to the patrol that got him killed.

"Well, tell you what I'm going to do for you," Nappy said, "Can't do anything about this Watts person, but if you give me your socials and leave your shoes at the door, I can certainly take some basic everyday life stress off your mind while you sort everything out."

"You want our shoes?" Aimee asked.

"It's that or your underwear," he said, expression stoic. When no one laughed, he moved on without apology. "So really, I'm going to have to call in every clean-up person I know to dispose of all this," he gestured at the nearest bodies, "and the last thing we want is one of you walking out of here with somebody else's blood on your boots."

Saul thought about that a second. Different to kill people illegally. He'd never had to worry about hiding what he'd done before. In fact, he'd gotten used to writing official statements with sentences like, "ordered the gunner open fire on the car, killed three insurgents," or "two civilians wounded in the crossfire. We called for medics and they managed to save one," and then going about his business or on to the next mission. "Killed three people today, what's for chow?" Probably not a bad sign when killing and death become hard and unpleasant things again.

"Oh yeah, and I'll need the keys to that thing you call a truck," he spoke to Aimee. "Since you left it in northern California somewhere, gotta get rid of it and report it stolen – I'll try to remember to read up on what ethnic group to blame it on this year. Anyway, I'll have someone drive you wherever you need to go next."

Aimee reached into her pocket, twisted a car key off the keychain with the dangling silver skull at the end, and handed it over. He took it and slipped it into his pocket.

"And lastly, I need your socials for tax purposes," Nappy continued. "I'll give you each a check… figure around fifty thousand each will be a good help without drawing too much attention from the feds. Put you down as 'contractors' or 'advisors' to my new book or something."

"You're going to make a book out of this?" Saul asked, stunned.

"Hell no!" Nappy laughed. "But the taxman won't know that. Just something to show I employed you, took out withholding, etc." Saul barely registered Nappy just offered to pay him a yearly salary (minus combat pay) for no real reason. Actually, Saul thought, cutting him down from the noose that perpetually killed him probably counted as a reason. But then again, they were the cause of him getting caught in the first place.

Breaking his chain of thought, Aditi-Alhread stepped around Nappy and knelt down. "Aimee," she said.

"No." Aimee said and pulled back. "You can't have it. Not yet."

Aditi-Alhread's eyes narrowed, but Aimee followed up with "please" before Aditi-Alhread had a chance to reply. Aimee glanced at Saul, and when she did, for an instant he thought he saw something akin to jealously cross Aditi-Alhread's face.

"Well whichever one of you ends up with that thing," Nappy glanced at the dark ankh, "send me a postcard so I can track it and don't have to hire someone to follow you around."

Aimee nodded to Nappy and then stared at him and Aditi-Alhread with no intention of saying anything more. Eventually they felt uncomfortable enough to tend to some other business in the warehouse.

Saul eased his fingertips away from Aimee's arm and she reached over and grabbed his hand. She didn't turn towards him though, so they sat there, holding hands and without saying anything while Nappy and Aditi-Alhread continued their tour and commentary of the battlefield. Saul looked away when he caught a glance of Nappy sitting up one of the bodies and putting its arm around another one. Arranging them in aesthetically pleasing poses seemed fun to Nappy, and while Aditi-Alhread stayed nearby him, she neither participated nor commented for or against it.

"Saul," Aimee said at last, "you need to go see her."

Aimee's words brought Saul back from the nearby macabre activity. He thought about Rose and what he might say the next time they were together. How he might straighten everything out. "Don't worry, I planned on hanging out with her before my leave is over."

Aimee closed her eyes tight enough wrinkle her forehead. "No Saul, not Rose."

Saul studied her face, confused. Aimee stood up and held on to his hand.

"Stand up," she said. He just stared. "Stand up, please."

A little reluctant, he pulled himself up to his feet, and then realized who Aimee meant.

"No," he said, eyes widening.

"You need to go see her," Aimee replied.

"No."

"Yes."

"Look…" Saul started.

"I'm calling in the bet." Aimee said, unraveling the amulet's leather strap as she did so.

"That's not…"

"Yes it is." She cut him off again. "I was going to save it for something really wicked, but this is more important… fortunately for you." She reached up and looped the strap of the dark ankh around his head, but held on to the actual amulet.

"Aimee, I can't just…"

"Belt up already!" She held the amulet up and off his chest. "If you do this for me, I'll feel a little better about never having a chance to do this with Watts. OK?"

She used that special tone women knew to melt his resolve in particular, and he found himself nodding almost without realizing it.

"Now do what I say," she said, "and go."

Aimee let go of the amulet and it fell – slower than gravity's normal firmness – until it bounced off his chest with a deep bass boom that shook his body and reverberated in the back of his skull.

The world flew off like a painting sucked into a small drain, and the ceiling opened into a cloudless sky of reddish purple. He recognized the howling of the wind first.

A few spirits stood beside him on the top of the cliffs, but this time they moved away as soon as they saw him, or the amulet, one of the two. Most avoided eye contact, and one even ran and leapt off the ledge's lip and down to the vale below. A few diehard snoopers hid behind rocks and walls and watched him from a distance.

"Maybe I should get an apartment here, possibly a timeshare," he said to himself. "No never mind." He looked out across the Netherworld not wide-eyed and overwhelmed, but now interested in the details, the organization, the… he started to say biosphere and then amended it in his mind to necrosphere. He watched until a few patterns emerged, a few groupings of like sorts of spirits, and then cursed himself for deliberately wasting time.

Saul wondered what to do next. He held the amulet out and pictured the mother of his child, but nothing happened. For fun, and partially because he felt he had to crack jokes whenever he got nervous, he shook the dark ankh next to his ear like a broken toy, watching for reactions from the crowd as he did so. One of them might have chuckled, maybe, but Saul doubted he could expect much more.

"Nicole." He said out loud. Still nothing. Anger replaced nervousness and he shouted her name across the Valley of Souls.

He felt her arrive before she spoke.

"I told you this isn't allowed," she said in a strong, quiet voice. It cut through noise just like Aditi-Alhread did when she talked.

"Not my idea," he said. The figure standing near him frustrated his memories, giving him every piece of the person he loved except for that part hidden behind a black censored square above her neck.

"That's what you said last time," perhaps self-conscious about the veil, she turned to look down into the valley. "Twice in one day seems hardly coincidental."

Had it only been one day? For sure less than twenty-four hours.

He didn't want a repeat of earlier, but didn't know what to do to make things different.

"Anything you want me to tell Rose?" Take the attention off the two of them, the blatant evidence that they failed together, that might work.

Nicole spun, and Saul felt like he struck a nerve.

"Are you actually going to spend some time with her?" Perhaps too strong a nerve. Saul took a step back from her, and then Nicole softened.

"Look, call me a bad dad all you want, she doesn't want to see me," he said. "I go or not, I stay or not, they don't care. And while I'm around I'm just an annoying guy in the corner asking questions about stuff he missed."

"Then stop missing stuff." Said softer, still painful.

"Easy for you to say," Saul thought, but some very wise part of him quelled those words right before they left his mouth. He understood. She bore the guilt for herself, but if he failed too, she'd carry the weight of destroying three lives. But as much as he wanted to help, nothing changed the way their daughter felt about him.

"Nicole," he said instead, "I just don't think Rose…"

"She keeps your dog tags in a box by her bed." Nicole said, taking a step closer.

Saul opened his mouth and said nothing.

"She never looks at them," Nicole continued, "but she looks at the box."

"OK, good, but…"

"Sometimes she dreams," Nicole stopped in front of him, "Sometimes she dreams about dancing… or learning the monkey bars… or when you used to read dinosaur books to her at night…"

Her voice cracked. For a moment she reached up to wipe her eyes and then stopped when she realized the veil prevented it.

"She misses you Saul," she said, and then the wave of sadness burst out of her so strong Saul almost saw it. "I miss you."

She rushed forward and wrapped her arms around him and pulled him against her, not in a sexual way, but to feel every part of him that she could all at once. He curled his arms up under her back and turned his cheek to press against her neck. He pulled away, startled, when he felt how cold she was, and then eased back to her, hoping she gained something from his warmth.

This hug, however strong, did not arouse him, it did not warm him, and it did not feel like a flashback to junior high. Instead, it felt… nostalgic. As he came to this realization, something similar must have crossed her mind, because they separated at the same time. Saul looked up, forgetting for a moment he couldn't see her eyes, and tensed when he saw the cursed veil again.

"Can't you take that damned thing off just for a minute?" he said.

"I can't take it off ever. It *is* a damned thing," mixed emotions filled her words, not the pure ones from earlier.

"I'm going to take it off." Saul said, reaching for it. She grabbed him by the wrist and stopped him. Somewhere behind him he felt the crowd of curious spirits thickening.

"Saul! Listen to me!" she pulled his hand down a little. "It can't come off. I have to suffer. I have to pay for the ones I hurt…"

"I'm the one you hurt." He said in a sharp tone.

Saul twisted his wrist out of her grip and grabbed the amulet with his other hand. The dark ankh grew warm in his touch, almost hot enough to burn. "And I say…" Saul reached up, slowly, and this time she didn't stop him, "…it comes off." He tried to grab the veil, but wherever his skin touched it simply evaporated. He waved his fingers lightly in front of her, wiping away the darkness, until her glowing smile poked through his fingertips. And her eyes, black now instead of green, but wonderful just the same. He thought he heard a murmur from the audience, but they kept their distance.

"Wow," she said, sniffing. Then with a laugh, "You're in trouble now."

"Yes," he pushed back a tuft of her hair from her temple, and then brushed her cheek. "I'm sure the dead police are going to come by any minute to give me a ticket."

She stepped back, now fighting the type of tears that came with soldiers coming home and couples learning they are going to be first time parents. "You know your way home?"

"No not at all." Saul said, and realized after he said it that wasn't a joke.

"OK, close your eyes and keep your hand on that swanky necklace." She moved back another step. "I'm not sure this will work the same as when ghosts do it, but it might. A few other things you do seem to work the same." Black liquid still pooled at the bottoms of her eyes, but none spilled out. She moved like a giddy kid.

Saul did what she asked. "Now what?"

"OK, now picture a field of daisies," she said, a hint of mischievousness in her tone.

"What?" Saul laughed when he asked, but kept his eyes closed.

"No, you're right, that won't work. Hurm." Clearly she was screwing with him, stirring recollections of the type of flirting that drew them together in the first place. He went along with it. "Well, try this then. Think of some place you've always wanted to go."

"OK."

"Like," she continued, "Germany, or Japan… oh wait, I know! How about England?"

As soon as she said the word he heard Aimee's voice in his head calling him a wanker, and then he saw her face and remembered her pulling him forward, pressing her lips against his… Saul suddenly felt like someone grabbed him by the collar and hauled him up and into the air.

"Gotcha." Nicole's voice. He opened his eyes and saw her waving goodbye in the distance as the Netherworld rushed off away from him. "Thought I didn't know, didn't ya?" That last part he heard in his head, a sweet voice cutting through untold distances, a lighthearted jab with a hint of approval, just before the walls of the warehouse reformed around him.

He stood there, a few feet behind Aimee and Aditi -Alhread – no sign of Nappy – clapped his hands and threw his head back laughing. When the women approached him, their expressions sobered him right away.

"Everything OK?" Aimee asked.

Saul regarded her before he answered and explained the short version of what just happened, leaving out the part about how Nicole tricked him into traveling back to the land of the living. Aimee responded with bittersweet feelings, happy he'd left Nicole on better terms, maybe also glad he'd put his feelings for his ex-girlfriend to rest, but behind all that, Aimee ached with the fact she'd never see Watts again… no one would ever see Watts again.

They made small talk for a few minutes and Aimee explained that Nappy had gone to get the clean-up crews. As instructed, they left their shoes at the door and waited in silence until a blue four-door car pulled up and honked at them. Aimee and Saul climbed into the back seat with only a grunt of greeting to the rather tall bald man at the wheel. Aditi-Alhread took the passenger seat. The man, "Slice," as he introduced himself, turned out to be far more cheery than any of his passengers could tolerate. He informed them that they were west of Portland, but had just chugged down three Mountain Dews and would be happy to drive them the two hours up "the five" and back to Tacoma. Then he not only gave them a guided tour of that section of Oregon but also tossed a pair of men's boots and a set of old tennis shoes back to Saul and

Aimee, apologizing that they were the best he could do on such short notice.

Aimee insisted on the boots.

Before they'd reached the edge of town, both Aimee and Saul let their last remaining vestiges of energy go free. They drifted off to sleep, not in a romantic or graceful way, but each more like a helium balloon partially deflates and leaves a half-filled husk behind.

Saul woke first, stirred by the lights of Tacoma cutting through the late night. His body cracked and stung him for bending it like a sadist and leaving it that way. He stretched, and judging by Slice's lack of enthusiasm and Aditi-Alhread's silence, Saul gathered the two hours had passed without much casual conversation. Aimee's head lay wedged between the seat in front of her and the window, drool all down the side of the car door.

"I feel like I know you better already," he said, although no one replied. Not sure exactly why, Saul pushed her a few times until she finally stirred awake. She wiped her mouth, gathering up her dignity as quickly as possible, and sat up straight.

Saul noticed then Aditi-Alhread watching him between the seats. Her expression said everything, her patience wearing thin as she waited for the amulet. Saul avoided her glare though, not quite ready to hand it over. For some reason he felt doing so ended something, which, obviously it would. His mood fell as he resigned he'd run out of reasons not to do it.

"If I give this to you," Saul spoke to Aditi-Alhread, "what happens next?"

"I stop fading in this world and running in the next," she replied. "And eventually I'll figure out a way to right what's been done to me."

Saul thought about that a moment. "What about what's been done to other people? Like, all the souls that have been carved up and consumed?"

"I know they're being taken somewhere." Aditi-Alhread said. "Rumors are that the people who absorbed them are being punished in horrible, dreadful ways with no limits beyond the imagination of the dead. But no one's actually *seen* any of them after they were taken away."

Saul looked at the amulet. "Any way I can use this to bind you to your word or anything?"

Aditi-Alhread smiled. "No Saul, but I don't need a promise to you to try to undo all this."

"Watts first though, OK?" Aimee said.

"Aimee you know I can't promise…" Aditi-Alhread started.

"Say Watts first. Say it, please." Anger almost snuck into Aimee's voice, but she smothered it.

Saul wondered how painful it must have been for Aimee, growing up ignored or mocked by the living, bonding with the dead. Moving from song to song in order to see them, to talk to them, to have her imaginary friends turn real if only for a few minutes. Traveling back and forth from the States to England again and again, ghosts loyal to her, protective of her, listening to her problems, helping to raise her in the vacuum of parental advice, then to leave her completely alone, to abandon her all at once…

"Holy shit." Saul said, then looked up from his thoughts to the other two. "I don't think Watts is gone."

CHAPTER 34

Saul regretted the words the instant they left his mouth. He hated the idea of potentially being That Guy who announced some 'ah-ha!' moment, getting everyone's hopes up, only to turn out completely wrong. The rest of the trip he downplayed it as best he could. No amount of "never mind," or "I'm probably wrong," or "sorry, it's nothing" consoled Aimee, however, and she watched him and prodded him all the way up into her parking lot.

"So?!?" Aimee said, her tolerance for his antics nearly at an end.

"I'd tell her if I were you chief," Slice chimed in, breaking out of the background scenery with an abrupt burst of energy.

"Still got your house key?" Saul said to Aimee. She glared at him, unmoving. "Just give me a couple of seconds to look around and I'll tell you what I was thinking. But don't get your hopes up."

She passed the key ring over, sans key she gave to Nappy, but her expression didn't change. He snatched it, hopped out of the car, and flew up and into her apartment. He sighed as soon as he entered, now less confident he would find anything, convinced he'd have to let Aimee down again. Just to make sure they wouldn't barge in and find him in some compromising position of failure, he locked the door bolt behind him.

Without any idea what he needed to find, he searched the place for anything out of the ordinary. Out of the ordinary for Aimee, which proved a lot harder than he'd hoped when he stuck his head into her bedroom. As he aimlessly tossed items aside, he imagined clocks ticking, counting off until Aimee and the others grew so angry in the car they got out and banged on the door.

Too much pressure, too little time. He'd make some harebrained theory up, announce that he failed, and then take his time studying her and her place in secret until some evidence appeared that he could use.

When he opened the door, Aimee, Aditi-Alhread and Slice all stood leaning against the car in the barely lit parking lot, both women with their arms folded, making Saul want to just back up and lock it again. Deciding against that option, he walked forward, in no rush, face down to the sidewalk and the surrounding yards rather than look anyone in the eye. Then his heart skipped and he all but shouted.

"Hey!" he calmed himself. "Everyone follow me for a second."

They stared, unimpressed and in no mood to move. Except Slice. Saul waved them forward in a pleading motion and they eased up the sidewalk.

"We're just going to take a quick walk around the complex for a second, OK?"

Aimee and Aditi-Alhread inched further to genuine anger, but waved him on. He turned and cut across the grass, sticking close to the buildings, and they all followed.

"Do we know where we're going?" Slice asked, whispering. No one answered.

Saul leapt ahead of the others. He wanted to turn in anticipation, but instead, just listened. He slowed and listened to the others behind him, fingertips trembling, waiting… waiting…

"Ow." Aditi-Alhread said.

Saul almost jumped and cheered. Instead he whirled and said, "What? What?!?"

She didn't have to answer. While the others continued forward, Aditi-Alhread stopped at one of the patches of dead grass.

"We're going in!" he said in a loud voice and ran up to Mrs. Crabtree's door. He flew up and kicked it with one crashing blow, only to have his foot bounce off the old solid oak, shooting a spasm of pain all the way up his thigh.

"Ow mother f-er!" Saul bounced away, holding his leg.

"Oh for the love of…" Aimee started.

"You need in there chief?" Slice asked and Saul nodded, still bent over in pain. Slice grabbed a nearby rock from the garden, shoved it through the window by the door, and reached it to unlock it. "There you go."

Saul recovered enough to leap up again, not quite as easily as before, and threw open the door. A few feet in the hall opened into a large living room, or what would have been a living room in a normal house. Here the wooden floor held candles instead of reclining chairs, incense burners where side tables should go, and detailed chalk runes in the circle that would have just held a central carpet. Saul passed through the wall of unusual scents and stopped just shy of Mrs. Crabtree, who sat cross-legged and naked in the center of the runes, eyes rolled back in her head, oblivious to his presence.

"Hey!" Saul yelled. Aimee and Slice filled in behind him. Aditi-Alhread stayed outside. "HEY!" this time he bent down near her face.

Her eyes flew open like a sleepwalker ripped from a dream. She struggled to make sense out of her sudden situation, arms flailing, pupils dilated and darting back and forth.

"Slice," Saul said.

"Yes captain!" he replied. Saul ignored his natural instinct to point out his actual rank.

"Can you go outside and dig around in those lines of dead grass out front? Carefully though, probably has salt and rusty nails buried there. Move enough of that and our other female friend should be able to join us."

Slice saluted the way people with no military experience salute, and rushed out the door.

Aimee knelt down in front of the still struggling Mrs. Crabtree. The old woman still didn't even realize she sat naked in front of other people. Aimee watched her for a few minutes, waiting in silence for any sign of recognition to cross the woman's face. After well beyond what Saul would have normally tolerated, the woman's wild-eyes narrowed and Mrs. Crabtree seemed to concentrate on Aimee.

"Hey there." Aimee said, soft and sweet. "Hey, remember me?" Before Mrs. Crabtree could really focus Aimee slapped her across the face so hard she flew back and smashed her head on the hard wooden floor. No blood, but anger seemed to have replaced some of Mrs. Crabtree's confusion.

"You unbelievable sodding twat." Aimee growled. "'Oh, I love musicians,' you said," Aimee stepped closer to the woman, "'You can stay in my complex at a special discount,' really? 'and I just so happen to have this one unit open, right next to my wall' and 'Oh, those parties don't bother me any Sweetie.'"

For a moment Saul feared Aimee would leap over and strangle the woman to death right there. Instead she leaned down and put her face just barely an inch in front of Mrs. Crabtree's. "Where... the fuck... is WATTS?"

"At this moment giggling like a school kid behind you." Aditi-Alhread stepped into the room just in front of Slice.

Aimee turned around, taken out of her own moment, and then sighed and smiled.

"Also, he's chained to the wall." Aditi-Alhread amended.

"I can fix that." Saul said, feeling the weight of the amulet.

"I could do it faster," Aditi-Alhread said, "and without any sort of..." she glanced at Aimee, "special preparations."

Saul still didn't want to hand it over, holding on to that same arrogance that kept fathers from letting their little daughters fix something because Dad could do it faster. Anything important, like Watts, well that needed to be handled personally. The potential for something to go wrong was too great. And so for precisely all those reasons, he lifted the dark ankh over his head and held it out to her.

Aditi-Alhread reached out her hand and Saul eased open his fingers until it rested in her palm. A swell of calm ran through him, the type that comes with a resolve to release a long tense hold on a fear or anxiety. Whatever happened next, happened. Insha'Allah.

"Thank you Saul." Aditi-Alhread lowered it over her head and in that instant the contrast of her body changed, giving more definition to the separation between clothing and flesh, brightening the red stripes on her uniform, and warming the tone of her skin. She focused her attention on some random spots around the room, twitched her hands a small amount, and then said, "There. All free."

Aimee stood up and smiled at Aditi-Alhread, no words necessary.

"What are you going to do…?" Mrs. Crabtree pushed herself up using the wall to help steady her feet. She made a futile effort to cover her aging body.

Saul laughed, "Well, we're probably going to have to…"

"Saul, if you don't mind?" Aditi-Alhread said, "If you don't mind, I've got this one."

This time, perhaps the light tone of her voice, perhaps because it sounded more like a question than an order, Saul didn't mind at all. He stepped back and gestured for Aditi-Alhread to continue.

She faced Mrs. Crabtree.

"I am going to kill you." She said in a flat voice. "Not today, because then the evidence would point to these three."

Mrs. Crabtree strained to argue, but found no words.

"But you've enslaved souls," Aditi-Alhread continued, "and you've sold souls to people like Seamus for consumption and experimentation. So, I will watch you, and someday, I will kill you."

Aditi-Alhread turned and headed back out the door and the others followed, leaving a naked woman behind to slide down the wall and curl up on the floor.

"Aces," Aimee said to Aditi-Alhread as they walked back out across the yard, "that seemed a lot harsher than I thought it would. I mean, do you have to…"

"No. I don't have to." Aditi-Alhread said without looking, leaving it hanging whether or not she would come back and kill again someday, or if she'd moved on at last.

EPILOGUE

Saul stood on the overgrown patch of weeds and wiped his forehead sweat onto his shirt, despite the coolness of the opening days of summer in Tacoma. The back of the open U-Haul laughed at him like an endless cornucopia spitting out things to lift and carry away.

He sat on a box labeled "kitchen utensils," which he knew contained no such thing, and took a few deep breaths. His leave ended on Monday, and he'd already let his chain of command know he wouldn't be reenlisting when his time ran out in August. The employment prospects weren't amazing, but Lisa and Richard agreed to help him with the job hunt.

Off in the distance his two favorite figures crossed the street, wobbling the way two people do when they are into a conversation, aren't exactly sure of their route, and don't want to bump into each other.

Aimee's shiny black hair, again in pigtails, dangled down bouncing off her worn "Two Headed Cat" rock tour T-shirt, which in turn left about an inch of bare belly showing above a long pair of cut-off tight jeans.

"…what anybody says," Aimee continued, approaching Saul's hearing range, "if you aren't careful, and you don't think it through, then before you can say, 'I'm not that kind of girl,' you will be."

"Wow," Saul said with a small nervous laugh, "that sounded incredibly age inappropriate."

Aimee held up her hands, "I didn't give any specifics. Promise."

"Dad," Rose said with a genuinely irritated tone.

"Dadio," he corrected.

She sighed. "*Dadio*, you can talk to me like an adult sometimes."

"You're eight." He replied.

"Nine this weekend," she corrected. Rose's hair ran back into a long sandy-brown pony tail. Seeing her stand next to Aimee, Saul wondered when his daughter would tire of the big baggy plain shirt and the normal fitting jeans look. Then he pondered what he could do to postpone that day.

"Right," he got off the box, literally and figuratively, "You going to help lug some stuff?"

"Nope." She said, not joking. It stung a bit, but he held back any initial comments, waiting for his emotions to catch up to the idea that he couldn't expect major changes overnight. Rose pointed at Aimee and said, "How'd you get her to help anyway?"

"Won it in a bet," Saul replied, mood rising a little.

"His first," Aimee said, casting him a sideways glance hinting at all the intimate wagers they'd made in the last few weeks.

"Good thing I know better," Rose said, looking around, "this is all Pete Tong."

Saul glared at Aimee who laughed and pretended she hadn't been inundating his daughter with British slang.

"Ro-ose!" Lisa's voice from down the street. Four houses or two hundred and seventeen steps to be exact, Saul thought, from Lisa's house to a crappy fixer-upper that cost fifty percent more than it should have. "Rose honey!"

Rose rolled her eyes the way all kids do when a parent calls, even a surrogate parent.

They waited for Lisa to catch up, carrying another box as she approached.

"Hey," Lisa said to everyone, making eye contact before turning to her niece and shifting her tone from social to stern. "I told you to bring this with you when you came over."

"I might need that stuff," Rose said, mood crashing fast. She'd cried for half an afternoon when they suggested she move some spare clothes to Saul's new place. Working with Lisa, Saul had arranged a compromise of just a few things for sleepovers and day trips, plus some toys and games. Even with that, Rose somehow forgot to sort the things, forgot to pack the things, and now forgot to bring them.

Baby steps, Saul thought, baby steps.

Lisa and Rose haggled a few minutes more until Rose agreed the box could stay. She pointedly did not agree to carry it inside.

After Lisa left back down the street, Rose perked back up a little. "Can we bring Aimee on Saturday?"

A month ago Saul would have agreed, welcomed the help, the company, someone to take the edge off the awkward separation between himself and his daughter, like covering something with a sheet instead of cleaning it up. Even after the strained conversations with Lisa and Richard to get them to agree to let him have her on her birthday after they'd already made plans, even after working for hours to warm Rose up to the idea of a day at the beach, he still wanted to give in for the relief of someone else there with them.

"I'm sure she'd love to come," Saul said, picking up Rose's box, "but this is strictly a father-daughter expedition."

One of Rose's feet lifted an inch of the ground and stomped the asphalt, and when Saul recognized the possibility for a breakdown, he added, "Tell you what, when you and I get back from the coast, maybe if she's free Aimee can come over and watch a movie with us. How's that?"

Rose tensed. "But I want her to come…"

"Rose." Saul brought out a hint of the military tone, again pretending he didn't want Aimee there at least as much as Rose did.

"OK," his daughter said and then turned to Aimee, "can you watch a movie with us?"

"If this place isn't still all Pete Tong I might," Aimee said and smirked as she did so. "But does that mean you'll come to my show?"

"Ew, the graveyard one? Uck."

"Oh what are you on about? It's a covered area," Aimee said, "for family reunions, which just happens to be surrounded on all four sides by a quaint little cemetery."

"And it will be at night so you'll hardly even notice them." Saul said, making his voice sound extra enthused as he lit up his face, a trick that, in the younger years, convinced Rose to do all sorts of chores and things she wouldn't have normally. That ploy, Saul figured, had two or three good uses left, tops.

"I'll try." Rose said. One of the mantras Nicole taught her early on. If you aren't sure, don't promise yes or no. Probably a lesson Saul could have used too. "OKgottagobye." All one word. She spun as she said it and walk-skipped back to the house she still called home.

When she left earshot, Aimee moved over and gave Saul a quick kiss. Not like the first one, but still strong enough to ease his tension.

Saul smiled, remembering the night he rested beside her, both of them sweating, and he asked if he'd passed the audition. That was after Aditi-Alhread helped Watts cross over and he stopped spying on them, of course. Neither Saul nor Aimee had seen either of them since, and afterwards Aimee promised not to bring any new invisible friends over to Saul's place.

Saul's nights had passed ghost free for the most part after that; ghosts of all sorts, from the physical one who throws people through windows, to the ones hovering felt but unseen in the corners of his perception, to the ones that exist as faces or memories of the bodies left behind in the sand or dust.

Seeing Saul watching Rose in the distance, Aimee turned to watch too, both vicariously drawing from the child's boundless energy.

"What time does your shift end tonight?" Saul said.

"Not 'til one."

"You coming over?" he turned to look at her and take in her presence like he vowed to do every day he could.

"Maybe," Aimee said, "have to check on my dad first though, he's had trouble sleeping."

"Sure, sure," Saul said, "I won't see you until three at the earliest." He reached up and put his hand on her neck, rubbing it with light fingers.

"Two, at the latest." She tilted her head down, the universal sign for push harder and make this into a back rub you rutting bastard. The rutting bastard part less universal and more between the two of them.

"Three."

"Two."

"Threeee."

She turned back and smiled at him, "Wanna bet?"

"At night when the streets of your cities and villages are silent and you think them deserted, they will throng with the returning hosts that once filled them and still love this beautiful land. The White Man will never be alone.

Let him be just and deal kindly with my people, for the dead are not powerless."

--Chief Seattle

.